CHASING EMBERS

James Bennett

www.orbitbooks.net

ORBIT

First published in Great Britain in 2016 by Orbit

1 3 5 7 9 10 8 6 4 2

A CIP catalogue record for this book
is available from the British Library.

ISBN 978-0-356-50664-7

Typeset in Plantin by Palimpsest Book Production Limited,
Falkirk, Stirlingshire
Printed and bound in Great Britain by Clays Ltd, St Ives plc.

Papers used by Orbit are from well-managed forests
and other responsible sources.

MIX
Paper from
responsible sources
FSC
www.fsc.org FSC® C104740

Orbit
An imprint of
Little, Brown Book Group
Carmelite House
50 Victoria Embankment
London EC4Y 0DZ

An Hachette UK Company
www.hachette.co.uk

www.orbitbooks.net

For my family,
who believed

PART ONE

Questing Beast

It is curious to note the old sea-margins of human thought! Each subsiding century reveals some new mystery; we build where monsters used to hide themselves.

Longfellow

ONE

Once upon a time, there was a happy-ever-after. Or at least a shot at one.

Red Ben Garston sat at the bar, cradling his JD and Coke and trying to ignore the whispers of the past. The whiskey, however, was fanning the flames. Rain wept against the window, pouring down the large square of dirty glass that looked out on the blurred and hurrying pedestrians, the tall grey buildings and sleek yellow taxicabs. The TV in the corner, balanced on a shelf over the bar's few damp customers, was only a muffled drone. Ben watched the evening news to a background of murmured chatter and soft rock music. Economic slump to the Eagles. War in Iran to the Boss. The jukebox wasn't nearly loud enough, and that was part of the problem. Ben could still hear himself think.

Once upon a time, once upon a time . . .

He took a swig and placed the tumbler on the bar before him, calling out for another. The bartender arrived, a young man in apron and glasses. The man arched an evaluating eyebrow, then sighed, poured and left the whole bottle. Ben could drink his weight in gold, but Legends had yet to see him fall down drunk, so the staff were generally tolerant. 7 East 7th Street was neither

5

as well appointed nor as popular as some of the bars in the neighbourhood, verging on the dive side of affairs, but it was quiet on weekdays around dusk, and Red Ben drank here for that very reason. He didn't like strangers. Didn't like attention. He just wanted somewhere to sit, drink and forget about the past.

Still Rose was on his mind, just as she always was.

The TV over the bar droned on. The drought in Africa limped across the screen, some report about worsening conditions and hijacked aid trucks. Strange storms that spat lightning but never any rain. What was up with the weather these days, anyway? Then the usual tableau of sand, flies and starving children, their bellies bloated by hunger, their eyes dulled by need. Technicolor pixelated death.

Immunised by the ceaseless barrage of doom-laden media, Ben looked away, scanning the customers who shared the place with him: a man slouched further along the bar, three sat in a gloomy booth, one umming and ahhing over the jukebox at the back of the room, all of them nondescript in damp raincoats and washed-out faces. Ghosts of New York, drowning their sorrows. Ben wanted to belong among them, but he knew he would always stand out, a broad-shouldered beast of a man, the tumbler almost a thimble in his hand. His leather jacket was beaten and frayed. Red stubble covered his jaw, rising via scruffy sideburns to an unkempt pyre on his head. He liked to think there was a pinch of Josh Homme about him – Josh Homme on steroids – maybe a dash of Cagney. Who was he kidding? These days, he suspected he looked more like the other customers than he'd care to admit, let alone a rock star. Drink and despair had diluted his looks. No wonder Rose didn't want to see him. And in the end his general appearance, a man in his early thirties, was only a clever lie. His true age travelled in his eyes, caves that glimmered green in their depths and held a thousand secrets . . .

That lie had always been the problem. Since his return to New York from a six-week assignment in Spain, his former lover wouldn't answer his calls or reply to his emails. When he called round her Brooklyn apartment, only silence answered the buzzer on the ground floor. Sure, he'd hardly been the mild-mannered Englishman, leaving her high and dry, dropping everything to run off on the De Luca job. And it wasn't as if he needed the money. He'd been around a long time. He got bored. He got restless. He *went into his cave*, as Rose would've put it. The jobs were a way of keeping in shape, and of course, his choice of clientele meant that no one was going to ask too many questions. Now he was paying the price for this diversion. A week back in the city and Rose was another ghost to him.

But once upon a time, once upon a time, when you didn't ask questions and I could pretend, we were madly in love.

Outside, the rain lashing the window, and inside, the rain lashing his heart. April in Insomniac City was a lonely place to be. Ben took another slug of Jack, swallowed another bittersweet memory.

A motorbike growled up outside the bar. The customers turned to look. Exhaust fumes mingled with the scent of liquor as the door swung wide and the rain blew in – with it, a man. The door creaked shut. The man was dressed completely in black, his riding leathers shiny and wet. His boots pounded on the floorboards, then silenced as he stopped and surveyed the bar. His helmet visor was down, obscuring his face. A plume of feathers bristled along the top of the fibreglass dome, trailing down between his bullish shoulders. The bizarre gear marked him out as a Hell's Angel or a member of some other freeway cult. The long, narrow object strapped to his back, its cross-end poking up at the cobwebbed fans, promised a pointed challenge.

As the other customers lost interest, turning back to their chatter, peanuts and music, Ben was putting down his tumbler of Jack, swivelling on his stool and groaning wearily under his breath.

The man in the helmet saw him, shooting out a leather-gloved finger.

"Ben Garston! This game of hide-and-seek is over. I have some unfinished business with you."

Ben felt the eyes in the place twist back to him, a soft, furtive pressure on his spine. He placed a hand on his chest, a faux-yielding gesture.

"What can I say, Fulk? You found me."

The newcomer removed his helmet and thumped it down on the end of the bar. It rested there like a charred turkey, loose feathers fluttering to the floor. The man called Fulk grinned, a self-satisfied leer breaking through his shaggy black beard. Coupled with the curls falling to his shoulders, his head resembled a small, savage dog, ready to pounce from a thick leather pedestal.

"London. Paris. LA." Fulk named the cities of his search, each one a wasp flying from his mouth. Like Ben, his accent was British, but where Ben's held the clipped tones of a Londoner, the man in black's was faintly Welsh, a gruff rural borderland burr. Ben would have recognised it anywhere. "Where've you been hiding, snake?"

Ben shrugged. "Seems I've been wherever you're not."

Fulk indicated the half-empty glass on the bar. "Surprised you're not drinking milk. I know you have a taste for it. Milk, maidens and malt, eh? And other people's property."

"Ah, the Fitzwarren family wit." Through the soft blur of alcohol, Ben looked up at the six-and-a-half-foot hulk before him, openly sizing him up. What Fulk lacked in brains, he made up for in brawn. Win or lose, this was going to hurt.

The whiskey softened his tongue as well. He made a half-hearted stab at diplomacy. "You shouldn't be here, you know. The Pact—"

"Fuck the Pact. What's it to me?"

"It's the Lore, Fulk. Kill me, and the Guild'll make sure you never see that pile of moss-bound rubble you and your family call home again."

But Ben wasn't so sure about that. Whittington Castle, the crumbling ruins of a keep near Oswestry in Shropshire, was in the ancestral care of a trust. The same trust set up back in 1201 by King John and later bestowed on the Guild of the Broken Lance for safe keeping. The deeds to the castle would only pass back to the Fitzwarren estate when a certain provision was met, that being the death of Red Ben Garston, the last of his troublesome kind. The last one *awake*, anyway. Of course, the Lore superseded that ancient clause. Technically, Ben was protected like all Remnants, but he knew that didn't matter to Fulk. The same way he knew that the man in front of him was far from the first to go by that name. Like the others before him, this latest Fulk would stop at nothing to get his hands on Whittington and reclaim the family honour, whether he risked the ire of the Guild or not. Vengeance ran in Fulk's bloodline, and his parents would have readied him for it since the day he was born.

"The Lore was made to be broken," Fulk Fitzwarren CDXII said. "Besides, don't you read the news? The Pact is null and void, Garston. You're not the only one any more."

"What the hell are you talking about?"

Before he could enquire further, the man in black unzipped his jacket, reached inside and retrieved a scrunched-up newspaper. He threw it on to the bar, next to Ben's elbow.

It was a copy of *The New York Times*. Today's evening edition. Warily lowering his eyes, Ben snatched it up and read the headline.

STAR OF EEBE STOLEN

Police baffled by exhibition theft

Last night person or persons unknown broke into the Nubian Footprints exhibition at the Javits Center, the noted exhibition hall on West 34th Street. The thieves made off with priceless diamond the Star of Eebe, currently on loan from the Museum of Antiquities, Cairo. Archaeologists claim that the fist-sized uncut gem came from a meteor that struck the African continent over 3,000 years ago. Legend has it that the Star fell into the possession of a sub-Saharan queen.

According to a source in the NYPD, the thieves were almost certainly a gang using high-tech equipment, improvised explosive devices and some kind of ultra-light airborne craft, a gyrocopter or delta plane. Around midnight last night, an explosion shook the Javits Center and the thieves managed to navigate the craft into Level 3, smashing through the famous 150-foot "crystal palace" lobby, alighting in the exhibition hall and evading several alarm systems to make off with the gem. The police believe the thieves took flight by way of another controlled explosion, fleeing through the Javits Center's western façade, out over 12th Avenue and the Hudson River, where police suspect they rendezvoused with a small ship headed out into the Bay, across to Weehawken or upriver to . . .

God knows where. Ben scanned the story, plucking the meat off printed bones. The details were sketchy at best. Between the lines, he summed them up. No fingerprints. No leads. No fucking clue.

The bar held its breath as he slapped the *Times* back down. No one spoke, no one chewed peanuts, no one selected songs on the jukebox. The rain drummed against the window. Four-wheeled fish swam past outside.

"Clever," Ben said. "But what does this have to do with me?"

"More than you'd like." Fulk grinned again, yellow dominoes lost in a rug. "You're reading your own death warrant."

"If this is a joke, I don't get it."

"No, you don't, do you?" The man in black shook his head. "I've travelled halfway around the world to face my nemesis, and all I find is a washed-up worm feeling sorry for himself in a bar. Is it because of your woman? Is that why you returned? She won't take you back, you know. Your kind and hers never mix well."

"You came here to advise me on my love life?"

Fulk laughed. "You're asleep, Red Ben. You've been asleep for *centuries*. The world holds no place for you now. You're a relic. You're trash. I only came here to sweep up the pieces."

"Yeah, your glorious quest." Ben rolled his eyes at their audience, the men sat in the booth, the guy with a palm full of peanuts frozen before his mouth, the one shuffling slowly away from the jukebox. "You need to get over it. Mordiford was a very long time ago."

A storm rumbled up over Fulk's brow, his deep-set eyes sinking even further into his head. Obviously it was the wrong thing to say. The ages-long river of bad blood that ran between Ben and House Fitzwarren was clearly as fresh to the man in black as it

11

had been to his predecessors, perhaps even to the original Fulk, way back in the Middle Ages.

Muscles tense, Ben sighed and stood up, his stool scraping the floorboards. Despite his height rivalling the slayer's, he still felt horribly slight in Fulk's shadow. The whiskey could make you feel small too.

He didn't need this. Not now. He wanted to get back to the Jack and his heartbreak.

"It was yesterday to us," Fulk said, the claim escaping through gaps in his teeth. "We want our castle back. And Pact or no Pact, when we have it, your head will hang on our dining room wall."

The bartender, cringing behind the bar, guarded by bottles and plastic cocktail sticks, chose this moment to pipe up.

"Look, fellers, nobody wants any trouble. I suggest you take your beef outside, or do I have to call the—"

The sword Fulk drew from the scabbard on his back was a guillotine on the barman's words. The youth scuttled backwards, bottles and cocktail sticks crashing to the floor, panic greasing his heels. He joined the customers in a scrambling knot as they squeezed their bellies out of the booth, tangling with the other guys pushing past the jukebox to the fire exit at the back of the bar. In a shower of peanuts and dropped glasses, they were gone, the fire exit clanking open, a drunken stampede out into the rain.

Ben watched them leave in peripheral envy. He grimaced and rubbed his neck, a habit of his that betrayed his nerves. Then his whole attention focused on Fulk. Fulk and the ancient sword in his face. There was nothing friendly about that sword. They had met before, many times. Ben was on intimate terms with all fifty-five inches of the old family claymore. Back in the Middle Ages, the Scots had favoured the two-handed weapon in their border clashes with the English, and while this one's saw-toothed edge revealed its tremendous age, the blade held an anomalous sheen, the subtle glow informing Ben that more than a whetstone had sharpened the steel.

"Who're you having lunch with these days? The CROWS? That witchy business has a nasty habit of coming back to bite you on the arse." Ben measured these words with a long step backwards, creating some distance between the end of his nose and the tip of the sword. "House Fitzwarren must be getting desperate."

"We are honour-bound to slay our Enemy."

"Yeah, yeah. You're delusional, Fulk – or Pete or Steve or whatever your real name is. Your family hasn't owned Whittington Castle since the time of the Fourth Crusade, but you dog my heels from Mayfair to Manhattan, hoping to win a big gold star where hundreds of others have only won gravestones. And as for this," Ben nodded at the gleaming blade, "tut tut. Whatever would the Guild say?"

"I told you, snake. The Lore is broken. The Guild is over. And now, so are you."

The sword swung towards him, signalling the end of the conversation. The step Ben had taken came in handy; he leaned back just in time to avoid an unplanned haircut. The blade snapped over the bar, licking up the tumbler and the bottle of Jack, whiskey and glass spraying the floorboards.

Fulk grunted, recovering his balance. The weight of the claymore showed in his face. His leathers creaked as he lunged forward for another blow, the blade biting into beer-stained wood. Only air occupied the space where Ben had stood moments before, his quick grace belying his size as he swept up his bar stool and broke it over the man in black's head.

Cracked wood made a brief halo around Fulk's shoulders. His strap-on boots did a little tango and then steadied as he regained his balance, his shaggy mane shaking off the splinters. He grimaced, his teeth clenched with dull yellow effort. The sword came up, came down, scoring a line through shadow and sawdust, the heavy blade lodging in the floorboards.

The stroke dodged, Ben rushed through his own dance steps and elbowed Fulk in the neck. As the man choked and went down on one knee, Ben leapt for the bar, grabbing the plumed helmet and swinging it around, aiming for that wheezing, brutish head.

Metal kissed fibreglass, the sword knocking the helmet from Ben's grip. Sweat ran into his eyes as Fulk came up, roaring, and smacked him with the flat of the blade. If this had been an ordinary duel, Fulk might as well have hit a bear with a tooth-pick. The Fitzwarrens' attempts to slay their Enemy had always remained unfairly balanced in Ben's favour, and over the years he had grown complacent, the attacks an annoyance rather than a threat. Now his complacency caught him off guard. This was no ordinary duel. Resistant to magic as he was, bewitched steel was bewitched steel, and the ground blurred under his feet moments before his spine met the jukebox. The air flew out of his lungs even as it flew into Jimi Hendrix's, a scratchy version of "Fire" stuttering into the gloomy space.

The song was one of Ben's favourites, but he found it hard to appreciate under the circumstances. He groaned, trying to pull himself up. Stilettos marched up and down his back. His buttocks ached under his jeans. He tasted blood in his mouth, along with a sour, sulphurous tang, a quiet belch that helped him to his feet, his eyes flaring.

Across the bar, Fulk's eyebrows were arcs of amusement.

"Finally waking up, are we? It's too late, Garston." The man in black stomped over to where Ben stood, swaying like a bulrush in a breeze. "Seems like my granny was wrong. She always said to let sleeping dogs lie."

Fulk shrugged, dismissing the matter. Then he brought the sword down on Ben's skull.

Or tried to. Ben raised an arm, shielding his head, and the blade sliced into his jacket, cutting through leather, flesh and down to the bone, where it stuck like a knife in frozen butter. Blood wove a pattern across the floorboards, speckling his jeans and Doc Martens. They weren't cheap, those shoes, and Ben wasn't happy about it.

When he exhaled, a long-suffering, pained snort, the air grew a little hot, a little smoky. He met Fulk's gaze, waiting for the first glimmers of doubt to douse the man's burgeoning triumph. As Fulk's beard parted in a question, Ben reached up with his free hand and gripped the blade protruding from his flesh. The rip in his jacket grew wider, the seams straining and popping, the muscle bulging underneath. The exposed flesh rippled around the wound, shining with the hint of some tougher substance, hard, crimson and sleek, plated neatly in heart-shaped rows, one over the over. The sight lasted only a second, long enough for Ben to wrench the claymore out of his forearm.

Hendrix climaxed in a roll of drums and a whine of feedback. The blood stopped dripping random patterns on the floor. The lips of Ben's wound resealed like a kiss and his arm was just an arm again, human, healed and held before his chest.

"Your antique can hurt me, but have you got all day?" Ben forced a smile, a humourless rictus. "That's what you'll need, because I'm charmed too, remember? And as for my head, I'm kind of attached to it."

Flummoxed, Fulk opened his mouth to speak. Ben's fist forced the words down his throat before he had the chance. The slayer's face crumpled, and then he was flying backwards, over the bloody floor, past the bar with its broken bottles, out through the dirty square window that guarded Legends from the daylight.

Silvery spears flashed through the rain. Teeth and glass tinkled on asphalt. Tyres screeched. Horns honked. East 7th Street slowed to a crawl as a man dressed head to toe in black leather landed in the road.

Somewhere in the distance, sirens wailed. Ben retrieved the newspaper from the bar, thinking now was perhaps a good time to leave. As he stepped through the shattered window, he could tell that the cops were heading this way, the bartender making good on his threat. Who could blame him? Thanks to this lump sprawled in the road, the month's takings would probably go on repairs.

Stuffing the *Times* into his jacket, the rain hissing off his cooling shoulders, Ben crunched over to where Fulk lay, a giant groaning on a bed of crystal. He bent down, rummaging in the dazed man's pockets. Then he clutched the slayer's beard and pulled his face towards his own.

"And by the way, it isn't sleeping dogs, Fulk," he told him. "It's *dragons*."

Then he took flight into the city.

TWO

The hour after nightfall found Ben on 12th Avenue, looking up at the western face of the Javits Center. It was cold for spring, the clouds torn into rain-wrung shreds, the stars too weak to penetrate the pervasive neon glow. Insomniac City buzzed on. 12th Avenue was a ceaseless, sluggish river of light. The traffic sloshed by, grumbling towards the Lincoln Tunnel or south along the West Side Highway – what the natives cheerily used to call Death Avenue – and deeper into the heart of Manhattan. Exhaust fumes washed over the Hudson, an urban, imbroglio scent, carrying the heady notes of fast food, dead fish and garbage.

Ben's heightened senses amplified each sound and smell, his impressions above and beyond the human, but such innate gifts had their downside. The stench of crack in DeWitt Clinton Park. The taste of smog in the back of his throat. A heated domestic on West 31st – all these things could be niggling distractions. Learning how to muffle them was something of an art, and tonight his attention was solely for the plate-glass fortress before him. Everything else was a background hum.

For all that, he didn't want to be here. After the De Luca job – effectively shutting down a rival gun-smuggling gang for his last well-heeled crook of a client – the breather in New York was a welcome relief, his boredom, for the meantime, alleviated. Even if it was steeped in whiskey and the absence of Rose, it was good not to break heads for a while. Take stock. Lick wounds. But if Fulk was right and Ben had been asleep, then the bar fight had served as an alarm clock, shaking him out of his torpor. Even if he had no clue what the slayer was on about, it was obviously important enough for Fulk to stage a direct attack in broad daylight – the first such attack in fifty-five years – and that was hard to ignore. Ben told himself that curiosity alone had sent him speeding to 12th Avenue on this chilly night, a need to see the crime scene for himself, but he wasn't so tanked that he couldn't hear the fear beating beneath it. A fear that owed its genesis to Fulk's claim.

The Pact is null and void, Garston. You're not the only one any more.

And that, of course, was impossible.

Wasn't it?

"Just what the hell is going on?"

The hole in the face of the Javits Center, lined top and bottom with jagged glass and fluttering with police tape, was a sixty-foot-wide gaping maw that couldn't answer him. His senses, however, retained their upside. He healed quickly, as Fulk had seen in the bar, and along with his ability to smell junkies in a park a mile away and hear a hissy fit three blocks over, Ben could also see the broken panes on the third floor as if he was using a telescope. It only took a little concentration to focus in on them; a blink of his inner, nictitating membrane to switch from everyday, human vision to the vision bestowed on him by birth.

If anyone in the passing cars noticed the dull golden sheen in his upturned gaze, they would surely put it down to the street lights, the headlamps of other vehicles or the sleepless neon dome sheltering the city. Manhattan was no place for secret manoeuvres. Too many people bustled on the streets for Ben to enter the centre and take an up-close look, inspect the Nubian Footprints exhibition for himself. Much as he wanted to, he had no choice but to chew over the *Times* and content himself with this outside view, extraordinary though it was. The wind off the Hudson stoked the embers of his hair as he scanned the shattered façade. The article proposed that the thieves had smashed through the centre's eastern side by way of a small controlled explosion and an ultra-light airborne craft, snatching the Star of Eebe and making off over the river. Scanning the hole, Ben wondered whether the article was simply the product of a baffled police department and an insatiable press, both of which had to offer *some* theory to the New York populace. In the long shadow of 9/11 and other, more recent, terrorist attacks, the NYPD would hasten to calm the public's fears about any explosion in the Big Apple, no matter how minor, how local it seemed. This probably explained the evening edition's colourful headline, the Chelsea precinct quick to present the baying media with the possible reason for the blasts.

"Except that there weren't any."

There was only the wind to hear him, the wind to confirm or deny it, but the shattered glass above him reflected the naked truth. He was long in the tooth and sharp enough to see that no explosion had caused the destruction before him. No smoke had stained the Javits Center. He saw no trace of melted glass. Shards glittered on the sidewalk and in the road, most of it swept behind a feeble-looking and unattended police barrier propped in the lee of the building. The debris supported the article's claim that the thieves had fled the exhibition this way, but the fact seemed as lonely as an abandoned lighthouse. Whoever – he suppressed the thought *whatever* – had broken in and out of the centre last night, they had done so with nothing more than balls, weight and velocity.

That raised all kinds of questions. Questions that Ben didn't like. He reached into his jacket and flipped out the *Times*, once again scanning the piece. Now it read more like a Hollywood film script than anything approaching the truth. Was this a case of smoke without fire? Was the latest Fulk just trying to scare him? Put him on the back foot with lies?

You're reading your own death warrant.

But that would only be true if . . . No, that was bullshit. He wasn't about to believe it.

Ben looked up at the dark, silent maw in the face of the Javits Center. Now it was grinning down at him, each plate-glass fang gleaming with secrets, hinting at events that were logically absurd. The wind blew. The river reeked. The endless traffic shuddered by. His sixth sense buzzed with *change* regardless. Change and danger. Change and threat.

His breath struggled from his throat, his lungs feeling tight and shrunken. He rubbed his neck without realising he was doing so. In all the confusion, the slayer's boasts and the fight in the bar, Ben realised he had overlooked a part of that threat, a grim implication in Fulk's mockery.

Is it because of your woman? Is that why you returned?

His breath escaped him in a single word.

"Rose."

The bike wove in and out of the traffic, a fly buzzing through a herd. Tail lights watched the Harley Davidson roar up behind them like devil eyes, an infernal blur winking out as the bike sped past. Low in the saddle, helmetless, Ben squinted into the wind. The steer skull hanging from the crossbar rattled and danced in the churned-up spray and billowing fumes. The squeal of brakes on either side – joined by a symphony of horns and profanities – promised police attention, and sooner rather than later, but Ben refused to slow down. The thought of Rose in danger outweighed all other concerns.

Stealing the bike had only been an afterthought. It was no great trick to rummage in the slayer's pockets and relieve him of his keys. He could've reached the Javits Center more quickly, of course, but the direct route, during rush hour on Friday night, would've seen Ben make his own headline, and across the front of the very rag that currently spurred him to action. He wasn't sold on the whole "discretion is the better part of valour" thing – sometimes risks were necessary – but he was mindful of the Lore and the limits it placed on him. All the same, as he choked the throttle, gunning the engine to greater speed, he knew that Rose would've heard him knocking on the door of her Brooklyn apartment *right this second* if he hadn't needed wheels to get him there.

Thundering south down West Street, Chelsea's tenement blur giving way to the West Village and then to glittering SoHo, Ben tried to collect his thoughts and calm his galloping heart. On his right, the velvet Hudson, scored by ferries and reflected skyscrapers, an inverted city under the sea. Even the water here was radiant.

Ben's kind liked the water, its cool boundaries a long-time favourite habitat. Coastal areas, river valleys, waterfalls and forest pools – even the occasional loch – all provided primal comfort, a place to drink and bathe. But right now, if someone poured the Atlantic over Ben's head, he didn't think it would soothe him. If Fulk had meant to put the cat among the pigeons, then his work here was done. Ben hoped he wasn't starting at shadows, or worse, that rushing to the rescue wasn't just an excuse to see her, to win through where unanswered calls and emails had failed. The cynic in him – an old friend greased by days of Jack – thought it likely that Rose would see his sudden reappearance in her life as a last-ditch effort to save their relationship. A relationship that screamed *over* like an umpire screams *out*. How could she trust him now?

The traffic ahead was slowing, cars, trucks and coaches backed up at the tollbooths feeding the Brooklyn–Battery Tunnel. Ben wanted Vinegar Hill across the East River, and the bridge would take him there quicker. Whizzing between the crawling cars, blind to the red lights and the fanfare of horns, the Harley left the freeway, veering past the park. The Statue of Liberty loomed from the water, and Ben imagined that great green goddess glancing down at her tablet of law and shaking her head as he accelerated.

Navigating traffic, he didn't notice the limo until he swerved on to Greenwich, plunging into the shadow of skyscrapers, a canyon of glass and light. The traffic flocked here, forcing him to slow down, the bike growling between cabs and executive cars, a sluggish mix of weekend partygoers and workers keen to get home. The limo pulling up beside him only stood out because of its make. It was an old model, a British classic, a Rolls-Royce Phantom IV, its sleek black body distorting the light from the nearby storefronts. Ben could recall when the cars had appeared on the London streets back in '52, delivering the young Queen Liz to her first royal engagement at Westminster Abbey. The Phantom was designed to be an exclusive vehicle, transporting aristos and heads of state, and as far as he knew, there were only a handful left in existence. Like most guys, he read the occasional car magazine. It didn't surprise him that in this day and age some big shot had sold a Phantom into private use – but still its appearance nagged at him, something familiar (and unwelcome) in the sight. The vehicle's smoked windows mirrored his face back at him, his anxious expression sliding over glass.

The limo was close. *Too* close.

He kicked the bike forward, frowning. You could shake this city and watch the freaks fall out. He wasn't about to let one of them slow him down. Reaching into his jacket, he flipped out his mobile phone, deciding to give Rose a heads-up. He prayed that it was her night off; she didn't usually work weekends. Yeah, he knew she'd ignore the call, but at least he was *trying*.

Turning right on to Vesey, one hand punching buttons, he didn't notice the Phantom growing in his rear-view mirror. The limo slipped silently forward, its bumper nudging his back wheel. The bike lurched and the phone skipped along his fingertips before falling to the blacktop and cracking into pieces. He heard the small crunch as wheels rolled over it. Ben shot a glare over his shoulder – and his curse died on his lips as he saw that the Phantom's windscreen was also a sheet of smoked black glass. The mascot on the bonnet was not the traditional silver figurehead, the famous Spirit of Ecstasy leaning forwards with arms spread, her dress billowing out behind her, resembling angel's wings. He'd read somewhere about other figures – a *Pegasus* and *Nike* – but he was damn sure he'd never read about a bare-breasted hag riding a broom.

Most alarming of all was the Phantom's number plate. It was personalised, mud-stained and Very Bad News.

CROWS

"Shit."

Again the Phantom drew up beside him, its engine impossibly soundless. When the rear passenger window rolled down, it did so like silk over oil, in one slow, deliberate movement. The darkness beyond watched him intently, without eyes, without judgement, simply with cold, unblinking awareness. Goose bumps rippled up and down his arms. The proximity of magic, black, malefic, and strictly forbidden under the Lore, drew bile into Ben's throat like thick shake up a straw. The rolled-down window, revealing that lightless, depthless void, spoke fear into him like no words could.

Still, words came, like snow gusting over a grave.

"*Draco* Benjurigan."

Twisting the throttle, Ben sped between a Winnebago and a crowded tour bus. Fingers pointed in gleeful alarm. A driver honked and shouted. Hair a flaming streak in the night, man and bike arrowed over Broadway, narrowly missing a collision with a Porsche. Smoke squealed from his rear wheel, the steer horns clacking as he swerved and zipped up Park Row, a crouched, streamlined figure heading for the Brooklyn Bridge.

The Phantom shot after him, a smooth black bullet. A glance into his rear-view mirror confirmed its relentless pursuit. And now the traffic was pulling over on either side of the road, as though for an ambulance or fire truck, making it clear that the Rolls was employing some *mumbo-jumbo* to influence the surrounding drivers. Ben wasn't sure what, but he'd bet that most of them experienced a pressing need to slow down and stop: an imagined flat tyre, a faulty fuel gauge, an important file left at the office . . . When he roared on past a police car, idling in traffic a lane over, the cop behind the wheel barely looked up. The Phantom was a missile locked on his tail and the creatures inside it wanted a clear shot at him.

The bike whined, screaming up the ramp to the bridge. The lanes grew wider here and the evening traffic edged along the freeway, crawling from Lower Manhattan and out over the river. As Ben zipped through the jam, diesel and sweat thick in his nostrils, he heard a series of crashes behind him, the Phantom's patience coming to an end. Trucks kissed bumpers with sedans. Buses crushed station wagon doors. Horns bawled. Tyres shrieked. Tail lights tinkled. The traffic parted like the Red Sea for Moses, pushed over to the hard shoulder by an arcane force and sardine-canning there in squealing, dented rows. The Phantom swept unchecked through the gap, black, deadly and silent.

Shadow thrown before him by its headlights, Ben took advantage of the miracle, growling along the bridge. He sped under one of the great Gothic arches, straight down the middle of the three-lane span. Suspension cables whipped by above him like rays from a steel moon. Below him, a tugboat chugged lonely through the night, its lights dim in the glare of the city. Ahead, Brooklyn, calling to him with faint hopes of safety and forgiveness.

He risked a look back, pleased to see the Phantom falling behind, empty road stretching between them. The Harley pulsed between his legs as he pushed the engine to the limit. He patted the bike's fuel tank like he would the neck of a faithful horse, confident that he'd made good his escape.

Damn CROWS. You'll need more speed than that to catch a—

A scaling scream rubbed out the thought. His head whipped around, back to the bridge ahead. Shock squeezed the air from his lungs. Slowly, inexorably, a car pulled out in front of him – pulled as if by a scrapyard magnet – the Buick screeching from

25

the pile-up on the shoulder and into the middle of the road. The way that the driver, a blonde in her early thirties, scrabbled at the wheel told Ben that her obstruction was far from intentional. In the back seat a couple of children watched him approach with bright, dime-shaped eyes.

Ben choked the brake. The bike popped a wheelie, wings of smoke enveloping his body. Speed wobbled under his wheels. Rubber painted the asphalt. The bike lurched, a bucking bronco with Ben clutching the reins. In a widening pool of headlights, the bike threw him from the saddle and tossed him, rolling, into the road. The blacktop bit at his arms and legs. Blood filled his field of vision. Free of its rider, the bike crashed over on its side. It spun across the empty lanes trailing sparks, exploding against the bridge railings. Flames spluttered. Steer horns flew. Smoke fouled the air. A girder screamed, busted outward. The city peered in through the breach, her distant lights jealous of the fireworks.

A hush washed over the bridge, a murmuring tide carrying prayers.

Ben groaned and swore – his annoyance aimed at the tears in his jacket rather than his wounds, which faded to scars even as he stood, a swaying figure in the road. He spared the woman in the Buick a brief, helpless shrug, and turned to where the Phantom sat idling twenty feet away. Fog wreathed its wheels, chugging from its silver exhaust. Its windows reflected the draping bridge lights, stars lost in a void.

The Phantom's rear door swung wide, revealing nothing but darkness. Cold, lifeless, watchful darkness. In the past, Ben had seen bats fly out of that dark, born from whatever spellbound depths comprised the inside of the vehicle. Each weird manifestation preceded the appearance of the passenger, and that passenger was always the same: the Three Who Are One. The Coven Royal of Witches Subdued functioned as a triumvirate, existing on the edges of the Guild's regime, an underground, breakaway cult reluctantly heeding the Lore.

Tonight they were deliberately flouting it.

The passenger emerged, climbing from the silent car and stabbing the air with her Cuban cigar.

"Good evening, Benjurigan."

Ben pulled a face, wiped blood off his lips.

"It was when it was me, my thoughts and a bottle of Jack."

Babe Cathy was a dwarf, her body hunched and shrunken. Up close, she would've barely come up to Ben's waist, and she must have procured the tux she wore, complete with bow tie and tails, from some specialist tailor or other. The snappy attire failed to soften the blow of her face, a face so lined he couldn't make out a clear patch of skin, her features like a mouldy prune under her purple perm. Rings glittered on her stubby fingers, emeralds and rubies catching the headlights. She took a long drag on the Cuban and shuffled a few steps towards him.

"Ignorance is bliss." Expensive smoke seethed through her smile. "How do you like our Black Knight?"

"I'd like him more on a leash," Ben said. "What's this about? What do you want? You and your brute are breaking the Lore."

"Are we?" Her Texan accent snickered and snapped. "Things change."

He found it hard to argue with this. Change was the theme of the night, and Babe Cathy wasn't untouched by it. With the drafting of the Pact and foundation of the Lore, the Guild had officially outlawed magic, and three of the most powerful witches had banded together in paradoxical union, a dark and deathless trinity. It had been the same way for eight hundred years. Rumour had always surrounded the CROWS. Some said that the *grande dame* of the Coven Royal liked to move among humans as one of them, seducing and manipulating those poor curious souls who were drawn to the blackest kind of witchcraft, never quite grasping that witches – these kind of witches – had never been anything close to human, despite their similar appearance. Witches, real witches, were what Ben tended to think of as ambitious elementals, evolving from the servile magic of their creation and climbing, green-fingered and black-nailed, into their own twisted, quarrelsome future, where they prolonged their lives with stolen spells. Perhaps that was why the CROWS so loved to draw ordinary men and women into their fold, naïve acolytes that they could poison and pervert in turn. Together, the Three had formed a clandestine cult. The Guild could never prove it, of course, and was notoriously reluctant to confront the witches outright, face one of their supernatural facets, the withered aspect of Babe Cathy the oldest and wisest of all. As long as the witches remained in the shadows, appearing to honour and heed the Lore, the Guild, typically, turned a blind eye. Ben believed it was around the Battle of the Somme that he'd heard about the CROWS' relocation to the States, the grapevine that snaked between his few remaining friends whispering with unease. The witches' current appellations were just a modern affectation, he thought, a reverent nod to Irish mythology and an age long gone.

That aside, babe was not a word he would use to describe her.

"We made the Pact to protect us all," Ben said. "Every Remnant from the Old Lands. Don't know what ditch you signed yours in, but I signed mine at Uffington in 1215. Until the Guild says otherwise, I reckon I'll abide by it."

"The Old Lands. Bleurgh!" Babe's contempt was ugly in her throat. "You mean the world gone the way of the dodo. And here we are: endangered species. Refugees. Fugitives from our own power, subjugated by the rules of men."

"It's how we survive. It's how we go on."

"Is it? When those steel-clad fools put down their swords and took up their quills, did they really think they could scribble their way out of reality? With what? Promises on parchment?" She spat between her shiny black shoes. "It's how they survive. Them and their machines. Them and their progress. We were in the way and so they had us removed."

Ben wanted to argue that the Pact had come without resistance, without compromise, but he couldn't. Only the Remnant leaders, cornered, coerced and, ultimately, conned, had agreed to the magically binding agreement. The rest of the Remnants had found themselves lured and lulled into the Long Sleep, mesmerised – anaesthetised – by a powerful enchantment.

He could only utter the reason. His reasons, sour as they sat in his mouth in these late times.

"The war had to end. We chose peace."

"And now they're just killing each other."

"But we endure. The Lore—"

"The Lore is an ass. A means to an end. A bard's song to bind the bestiary. It could never contain the likes of us."

Ben wanted to shake his head, but again he heard some truth in her remark. The words written down on that scroll all those years ago, had been translated many times, but were nevertheless imprinted on his soul.

John, by the grace of God, King of England, Lord of Ireland, Duke of Normandy and Aquitaine and Count of Anjou, doth decree and grant this day, by common counsel of our kingdom, this Pact devised by the Curia Occultus and witnessed by those guardians of our realm. Those Remnants of the Old Lands, which yet linger amongst us, shall forthwith succumb to the Long Sleep, their ancient liberties henceforth annulled throughout all counties, hundreds, wapentakes, trithings and demesne manors of England, Scotland and all lands beyond the sea. With the goodwill of his Majesty and all future monarchs, and to secure the peace, but one of each Remnant may endure, awake and unfettered under the Lore, governed, protected and guided by the Guild of the Broken Lance, hereby appointed wardship of this bond for all the time to come. And all the ill will, hatred and bitterness that has arisen between our people and Remnants, from the date of the quarrel to this of our truce, we have completely remitted and pardoned to all. Those few bodies learned of this treaty shall henceforth never hunt Remnants or otherwise seek to do them harm · · ·

For centuries, the latter stipulation had kept the Fitzwarren family at bay, although of course they had never stopped looking for loopholes and orchestrating all manner of "happy accidents", from unexplained explosions on cruise ships to untraceable poison in food. They wanted Whittington back and they wanted it bad. In the past, there had been several stand-offs, the old family claymore swinging at Ben's neck on more than one occasion, but without proof (and with a whole heap of human bias), the Guild had never summoned the Fitzwarrens to court to probe the matter further.

Ben made it a habit to survive these attacks. But this latest attempt on his life was different, taking place in public and assisted by forbidden witchcraft. He didn't need the wide round eyes behind the wheels of the stalled traffic to tell him this. Or the sirens of the approaching police cars, the officers waking from a spell. This latest attempt on his life was a bold and brazen breach of the Lore. In short, it was unheard of.

But he wasn't about to show Babe Cathy just how shaken he was.

"It's late, Babe. Maybe we should do this over sushi some time."

Babe Cathy actually cackled. "It is late. You've got that right. Too late for you."

Ben snorted. "Maniacal laughter. Footlights fade. Exit stage left."

"She's not going to stop at the *Star*, you know," the witch said. The wind wreathed cigar smoke through her purple hair. "This is just the beginning. She'll track down every last one of her gifts and kill anyone who gets in her way."

"Who? You're talking about the Javits heist, aren't you?"

"Star, Crook and Pschent. Star, Crook and Pschent." Babe Cathy started to sway, her chant sailing across the space between them, a lullaby on ill winds. "A new flame will scour the sky, heaven-sent and hell-bent. Hope called her forth, but revenge drives her on. We shall rely on the latter."

What was she babbling about? What the fuck was a pschent? Christ. Witches.

Ben moved in her direction, fist raised, demanding answers. Babe Cathy's lips were a fishbone, rattling out an incantation, and he stumbled to a halt, watching her. What he'd told Fulk in the bar was true: magic used directly against him could do him little harm. Folks like the CROWS drew their power from the *nether*, a seemingly endless gulf that surrounded the physical world. The *nether* wasn't space, nor the ambient cosmos, but a place that lay beyond, or between, as *inner* as it was *outer*. Perhaps it was the raw, empyreal stuff of Creation, for all Ben knew. Things lurked in that astral sea, creatures hungry for life, and all magic had its price. When a person drew on the *nether* – drew on it like a thread in a carpet – they risked unravelling the world entire. But that same magic was in Ben's blood, its warp and weft responsible for his very existence. The triangles, squares and arcane symbols tumbling from Babe Cathy's mouth, a riddle colouring the air, would only bounce off his charmed flesh like meteors burning up in the atmosphere. All the same, he knew that she could hurt him. Indirect spells still held clout if they affected another target, animate or otherwise. If the witch's weaving cigar bobbed over some mundane object – a sword say, investing it with power – then by God, she could hurt him.

In this case, her muttered symbols wrapped around the Phantom IV. The bodywork bubbled like boiling tar, the bonnet growing short even as the roof grew longer. The grille reared liquidly upwards and the car started forward, its increase in size not just due to its approach. The wheels deliquesced, branching out into thin strands, a host of scuttling legs. The windscreen split, amoeba-like, into several compound eyes, each pale orb reflecting Ben's alarm. Mandibles quivered and dripped where moments before headlights had shone. In no time at all, the vehicle resolved into a behemoth, a hybrid of darkness and warped dreams, its horns a razor-sharp curl of silver, its shoulders brushing the girders above.

Screams rose from the nearby cars. Engines revved as drivers tried to force their way out of the gridlock. Those who could opened their doors and tumbled into the road, fleeing for Manhattan or Brooklyn. Ben watched them go. At least they had earned a tale for their grandkids. The CROWS could magically influence the area, affecting matter and human minds, but it was a scattershot and temporary art. They couldn't drop a curtain over the bridge. Sooner or later, people would talk about what they'd seen: cars that moved of their own volition, a man who rose unscathed from a bike crash and a giant bug that appeared from nowhere. They'd hold up their camera phones to show others strange clips, smeared, shaky images that could've been anything, the audience gasping and shaking their heads. Some would call helplines, others seek counselling. Tomorrow, the *National Enquirer* would see a surge of new material. Hell, it might even trend on Twitter. And nothing at all would change. In a world immunised by Hollywood movies, miracles were often confused with madness. No one accepted the truth any more.

The bug was shaped from shadow and steel; an illusion spurred by the witch's spell and lent substance by dread. The sweat prickling on Ben's brow, his thudding heart and widening eyes, these were its ingredients, allowing the bug time and space in the real world. They told him that the bridge trembled under his feet as the creature came on. They told him that a stench filled his nostrils, blown from papery flanks. They told him he flapped like a matador's cape as he stood in the road. Red Ben Garston. Red, red, red . . .

Only the most skilled of conjurors could withstand and dispel such hostile impressions, having trained themselves to assert reality, or at least to retaliate with visions of their own. With few exceptions, most people were slaves to their instincts, perception comprising what they thought of as real, their reaction based on that acceptance. Facts had nothing to do with it. If you thought the beast was coming to get you, then you ran regardless.

Ben could still meet the bug on its own terms. He could leap forward and grab those horns, draw on his prodigious strength and try to rip the summoning to shreds. On the other hand, Babe Cathy could prove too potent, and he too spent, the bug sucking weight from his doubt and trampling him to death in the road.

He wasn't about to stay and find out.

Rose was in danger and he would be no good to her dead. Plus he had questions that needed answers. He couldn't pursue them as a corpse. Sometimes, discretion was the better part of valour.

As the bug's shadow fell across him, eclipsing the mangled traffic, Ben spun to the railings. His torn jacket flailed about him, new rips rippling up his sleeves as his forearms bulged, his sinews mercurial with rapidly swelling flesh. His outstretched hands blossomed into three-pronged claws, hubcap-sized on this occasion, reaching for the barricade. Babe Cathy howled as metal twisted under his grip. Pincers snatched at his neck but he dived forwards into the night, tumbling over the edge of the bridge.

For a moment, there was only a man, falling, falling, the night air screaming in his skull. The river stung his nostrils, clawing at his eyes, a tugboat down there rushing up to meet him. The water was a flat black sheet, as unforgiving as iron. Manhattan a psychedelic blur.

A sharp report echoed off the water, the snap of unfurled sails caught by the wind. The tugboat cringed on the tide, the surrounding waves washing outward and catching the sudden, pummelling downdraught.

A shadow swept eastward under the bridge, a vast red oddity spearing through the night.

Duul

Far to the north, on wings of darkness out over the greater ocean, an essence that had once been a girl curled against a thunderous heart and remembered. She remembered the girl as if she, within the darkness, was not herself. In a sense, she was no longer. She remembered how a girl had crossed the desert, hoping to wake a god.

The girl had set out from the African village she had always called home, leaving behind the filthy old tumbledown shack, a shambles of scavenged wood, crooked nails and spit. Frowning over the map her mother had given her, sketched in charcoal on a little ragged cloth, Khadra had clutched her bag – a shabby thing of stitched grey fur – and struck out into the sands.

Alone.

At first, she had followed the highway north, occasional cars charging past like warthogs through the rippling mirage. In her grimy T-shirt and football shorts, her hair precisely plaited in cornrows, she coughed in their billowing, fume-black wake. This skinny child with skinned knees sipped sparingly from a plastic one-litre Coke bottle and stuck out a trembling thumb.

A truck took her as far as Qardho, a city in the Nugaal Valley. There she begged for food and water. Later, an old woman took her in, calling to the girl as she wandered in a daze through the marketplace. The woman's toothless smile and offer of meat was enough to draw Khadra into her hovel, even if her drooping, deformed left ear made the girl hesitate and shudder. Inside, the animal skulls hung on the walls and the jars of eyeballs lining the shelves revealed that the old woman was in touch with *sixir*, the old magic. Khadra's mother had told her that magic was forbidden, had been since long ago, and that there were no witches left but one, far away across the western sea. Still Khadra took no comfort from the fact. The girl ate her stew and fell asleep by the fire.

She woke with a start past midnight, the stars peering through the single window. The old woman crouched beside her, her hand halfway through her inspection. Khadra's arm was a snake, striking out. In her grip, the hag's wrist felt like a twig. A twig she wanted to snap.

"Old woman, what are you doing?"

Shamefaced, the hag drew her fingers away from where they'd been busy pinching her thigh, in the same way a farmer might pinch a fatted pig.

"Your mother chose well, sending her daughter, the lone fruit of her womb. The Queen will be pleased. No point sending some *dhillo*, eh? No point sending some whore."

For a moment or two, both of them were just eyes in the dark, four watchful orbs.

Then, "Get away from me, hag! What do you know about my mother? What do you know about the Queen?"

A soft cackle troubled the gloom.

"Poor girl. Who do you think gave your mother that map? And do you think that the shard in your bag fell from the sky? Nothing falls from the sky these days."

The shock of this, the shared wisdom and strange acquaintance, did nothing to calm Khadra's heart. No wonder the hag had called to her in the marketplace. Wise women spoke to wise women, she supposed, but unlike her mother, the old woman's gaze was far from kindly.

"Your mother fears greatly and the Queen sleeps deep. Yes, sleeps the sleep of three thousand years." The hag sucked her gums, then grinned, a toothless, grey and slimy enticement. "Come, girl. The fire is low and the road lonely. Let us take comfort. We can still eat and leave you more or less intact . . ."

Khadra ran. She raced with the dawn into the city. Disgust drove her onwards, away from the desperate, grasping herd, the crowds that swarmed around the big green trucks in the market-place. To her, the bright red crosses on their canvas flanks looked like the markers on a grave. That the famine, the curse, should reach even here, blowing on evil winds from the south, from Mogadishu and Abudwak – the knowledge gripped her like clammy hands. Horror drove her north and east, in the back of a bus to the Port of Boosaaso and the mocking, roaring laughter of the Gulf.

The Gulf of Aden reflected a sky of polished steel, bolted to the edges of the world. Rolling waves broke the immensity, crashing against the bleached white shore. Other dangers lurked out there, she knew, though not necessarily for her. Somali pirates, stalking the surf for millionaires' yachts or tankers loaded with cargo. American warships, manoeuvring within operable range of the Middle East. Arabian storms. Sharks. The vast waters sang like scorn, a ceaseless, thundering taunt. On dry land, dust was the only tide, washing over the ancient ruins that littered the sands around Elaayo. March brought with it *jilal*, the harshest season of the year. Drought had withered the crops long ago, swallowed the last strips of green.

The girl, Khadra – a name that her mother told her meant

lucky – limped across the waste, clutching her little bag to her chest. She put one foot in front of the other, stumbled, but did not fall. Then another foot, heavy as lead and puffing up dust. She wore the heat like a second skin; bore the midday sun on her back. And Khadra was hungry. Hungrier than the scorching sands. Her ribs were like a marimba, her heart beating a hollow song.

According to her mother, Ayan, this ancient land had once belonged to the pharaohs – those proud, mysterious ghost kings of Egypt, a country many kilometres north. Copper, amulets, naphtha, ivory, animals, plants – all had sailed up the Red Sea in exchange for Nubian gold. So rich were the new-found southern resources that the pharaohs came to know Punt as Ta Netjer, words meaning *God's Land*. Soon temples rose from the sands, from the hard yellow rock. Men named new and terrible gods. Crowned shining kings and queens. Worshipped winged, fiery beasts.

It was hard to picture such riches now. The Horn of Africa was empty. Some said drunk dry. Worn stacks of stone were all that remained of the temples, broken pillars pointing at the sun. These unexplored ruins dotted the Sanaag. Political quarrels and civil war left little time for digging up relics. The same went for the drought. Deep in disputed territory, far removed from prying eyes, these ruins were crumbled theatres for the wind, offering nothing but secrets and silence.

Khadra drew no comfort from the past. The old gods were dead, the Queen was sleeping and her people starved. A hundred thousand this year alone, men, women and children. Corpses lined the streets of Dhuroob, the numbers rising, rising in her village. And as for the living . . . Khadra remembered their dull eyes, too weak to blink away flies. She remembered the mournful wailing on the wind and the helpless, staggering infants. The crows pecking at bleached bones. She remembered Death's ever-grinning skull. Saw it again in the landscape before her . . .

The past held no comfort, true, but it still held promise.

The sands shifted, swirling around her ankles. Acacia perfumed the breeze. Somewhere a jackal barked. She could not stay out here for long.

Smooth stone steps rose from the waste, climbing into imposing rubble.

This is it. Khadra could barely believe it. *The taalo. The tomb. How have I come so far?*

Destiny, the sands replied.

Necessity, her mother countered.

A pillar protruded from the ruins, slanting at the sky. Faded hieroglyphics ran around its base. Maybe it was just fatigue, but the scene was brightening a little, the hieroglyphs growing a touch sharper. Curious, Khadra moved towards them, her fingers outstretched. Sand trickled to the ground as she traced the outline of feather and wave, eye, cat and knife. Sand glittered in the light. The sun was slipping from the tyranny of noon but the ruins shone with an inner splendour, the shadows withdrawing from the wide stone steps, parting to form a golden carpet that snaked up into the rubble.

Too tired to question the mirage, Khadra clutched her bag and followed it.

Lizards skittered from her path as she climbed, quick slicks of green. The little map fluttered in her hand. She let it go to the wind, no longer having need of it. The ragged, charcoal-smeared cloth came to rest on some nearby blocks, a limp, exhausted moth. The steps ascended to a broad area of crooked slabs, the gaps between them lying in wait for a stray foot, a misstep in the rubble. Unsteady cylindrical stacks rose into the burnished blue, the roof caved in centuries ago, flint strewn across the temple floor. Khadra picked her way into the ruins, a thief in an ogre's lair.

Or the tomb of a god.

Was it just imagination, a vague, dehydrated impression cooked up by her mind, or did the atmosphere hold more than dust and heat? Her sore feet tingled on stone and she moved forwards as if through water, a subtle magnetism drawing her on, the sense of little teeth nipping at her budding breasts. Ants swarming in her guts. She stared in awe at the crumbled rocks in the middle of the chamber.

Had this been an altar once? The worn motifs around its flanks would suggest so.

Hands trembling, Khadra tugged open her grey fur bag. The polished stone was heavy in her grip, a cylindrical shard of black rock, ringed by arcane symbols. She tested it with her finger, feeling the keenly honed edge. In a way, the rock was the key to the altar, but she doubted that anyone would guess its use if they happened to find the thing once her task was done. The knowledge, like the sun on her back, did nothing to warm her.

She closed her eyes, whispered a prayer. To Eebe. To God. To any who could hear her. Then she climbed the steps to the altar.

She spoke the words her mother had taught her, a week and five hundred klicks ago, crouched around the fire in the little shack, one of several in dry, dwindling Dhuroob. Her mother, Ayan, dabbling with *sixir*, casting bones and chanting to the ancestral spirits, her eyes rolling back in her head like pearls sewn into flyblown hide.

Khadra weighed the shard in her hand. Her fingers closed

tightly around the object, holding it with point turned downwards above her other palm. Squeezing her eyes shut, she sucked in a breath and drew the honed edge across her flesh, blood welling up from the cut. She gasped at the sacrifice, at the sharp, stony intrusion. Still, she was satisfied. Her journey was complete. She had succeeded in all that her mother had asked of her. Despite the burning pain in her palm, she muttered a prayer in thanks.

Blood speckled the yellow stone. A measly river trickled off the edge of the altar, a crimson snake slithering to the ground. *Drip, drip, drip.* Scarlet beads sank into the dust, precious, powerful and pure.

Khadra felt the silence. Under her palms, the ruins hummed. The broken pillars and crooked slabs moved like reflections in wind-stirred pools, rippling into a blur. The temple was a vast stone wheel, with her sat bleeding at its hub, the scene spinning into nausea. An unmade world smeared before her eyes, a world of yellows, blues and trickling reds, needles of light that splintered apart, engulfed by a smothering darkness.

Khadra tumbled to the temple floor, spittle speckling her lips. A waste of water in this dry, dead place.

She did not know how long she lay there, the sun and the buzzards wheeling overhead, aeroplanes pissing vapour in the blue. When she opened her eyes, long shadows had slipped between the pillars, cool bars across her skin. Across her palm, a dull, nagging fire.

Once again, the temple was solid. Raising her head, she saw nothing different in the scene, one fallen block much like another. But the atmosphere vibrated and hummed, the magnetism pervasive, prickling in her hair, her mouth, behind her eyeballs. Static sparked off the nearby pillars, thin blue lines dancing on stone. In her mouth, the tang of sand, iron and salt. The slabs underneath her were cold. Too cold for the afternoon shade.

"Little girl, you should not have come here. This place is not for the weak."

Khadra struggled to sit up, but the strange pressure kept her down.

"Or perhaps it is, now," the air mused. "I look at these walls and see no palace . . ."

Squinting across the temple floor, tracing the sound of that sepulchral voice, Khadra thought she was looking at the base of a statue, so dark and still were the feet on the slabs.

"I am not . . . weak."

The feet moved, floating towards her.

"All flesh is weak. Still, you survived Dhegdheer. Not many children can say that."

The name of a childhood nightmare trapped the breath in Khadra's throat. She remembered her mother's tales around the fire, about old Long Ear, a fearsome demon who roamed the waste, sometimes in the shape of a hag, sometimes as a hooded vulture. The demon hunted out the young and the lost, sucking the marrow from tender bones . . . Khadra recalled the old woman in Qardho, the animal skulls that hung on her walls and the way she had sucked her pale grey gums. Her hurried pre-dawn inspection.

Shock forced her to sit up, exhaling dust.

"Yes, you are lucky, little girl. Now tell me, why have you come here? Why disturb my dreams?"

Khadra looked up at the Queen. The late-noon sun gilded the sands around Elaayo, slanting across the ruins, spears formed from swirling motes. The light shone through the woman too, her tall, striking, ghostly form, naked from head to toe. She was

43

like a vase in womanly shape, care given to her glass curves, her etched muscles and sharp cheeks. Someone had filled the vase with oil, pouring darkness into her breasts, the oval of her stomach, the slit of her neat, hairless *siil*. The motes danced inside her, glittering, alive.

The Queen stretched out an onyx hand, her palm sparkling and wet.

"Why have you given me . . . this?"

The blood!

Khadra found her tongue, licked away awe.

"My . . . my mother, Ayan, sent me. Our people . . . our people are dying . . ."

"I hear their cries on the wind," the Queen said. It was clear that she needed no explanation. "The land weeps, but no rivers flow. Gone is the glory of Punt. This land has been a wasteland before, blighted, stricken and lost. And before, this land has healed under the blessed rains. Now the ages have turned once again, from gold into rust. Do you know why I went to my grave, girl? Do you *know*?"

Khadra watched her. Trembling. Afraid. She quickly shook her head.

The Queen was no longer looking at her. She studied the walls, the static crackling there, a frown creasing her forehead.

"Long ago, this place welcomed a woman who was king. A pharaoh. Chosen of the gods. The land of Punt lay in ruins and her empire offered us aid. They came to me from Thebes. From Egypt's highest throne. Their gifts were many and rich. And yet I was betrayed, my treasures stolen. By a man, girl. A cruel, jealous man."

The Queen's eyes flashed, sapphires in the sun.

"And now you have awakened me."

Khadra swallowed.

"Can you . . . will you help us?"

The Queen regarded the girl for a moment, the same way she might regard a flea. Then she glided to the altar in the middle of the chamber, a shadow sweeping through shadows, and caressed the newly wet stone.

Fingers red, she dabbed her lips.

"I am Atiya, a serpent-born servant of Eebe. Yet I became something . . . *more*," she said. She seemed to think on it, as though the past was carried on the wind, ghost speaking to ghost. Then, her neck straightening, proud, "This land is mine. It always was. But I stand here between two worlds, the world of myth, and yours of flesh. If I am to rise, this will not do. I would wear my earthly shape. Take back the treasures he stole from me." She lowered her voice again, silk over sand. "I will need . . . *substance*."

"Take what you need. Anything."

"Blind *addoon*. To think I need permission to fly."

Light flickered. The Queen stood before Khadra. She spread her glassy, slender arms. Shadows fanned out, flooding the ruins. Darkness eclipsed the sun. Electricity sang, spinning silver between the pillars.

Then Khadra, skinned knees, cornrows and all, found herself in a depthless embrace. The Queen held her fast, drawing her down into the dark, drinking in her solid substance, joining with her flesh.

Absorbing her. When it was over, only a woman stood in the ruins, tall and proud, her skin as slick as obsidian, her eyes a static-blue fire.

Then the woman too was gone, and only a beast remained. The beast roared and lashed her tail, stirring the grit of three thousand years. A whirlwind swept across the ruins, out into the empty Sanaag, out over the laughing Gulf. Lightning zigzagged up from the ground, trailing dust, rubble and sparks. Wings of night unfolded, obscuring the steel sky.

And the sands whispered *duul*, fly.

The sands whispered *noqo*, return.

A storm swept north over the desert.

THREE

The city was a golden web. Canyons of light, banked by temples of commerce and greed, bled a flux of cars like iridescent veins. The Bay reflected the dim stars and the surrounding buildings, which loomed with sheer, tapering heights into the metropolitan night. Aircraft warnings blinked and spun, strobing from the upper reaches where pigeons perched, puff-chested and grey. Above the satellite dishes, water tanks, girders, gargoyles and lightning rods, the moon shone through the city glow.

There was a place where the shimmer faded, thinning out like surf on a beach, the city lights growing diffuse. Neon gave way to night. True night. Planes traversed the darkness, sketching smoke on the emptiness. Smog drifted, spewing from the Eastern Seaboard's ceaseless industry, chemicals and oil scenting the air. It was cold. Ice cold. In this vast ephemeral pasture, this last primitive frontier, another winged shape swept through the night, veiled by the dirty sheen that lay between the city and the sky.

With the benefit of a telescope and luck, the people in the houses below might look up and recognise this shape. They would know it from storybooks, from paintings and films, images made by artist on artist, rendered in flag and statue and tasteful tattoo. They would know it from symbols in stone, on brown parchment, or printed in digital font. Words that fell from parent's lip to child's ear down the spiralling ages. Despite shock, despite disbelief, every human would *know* this shape on a deep level, the same level that made men and women cower from the beast, from the wolf at the door, the snake in the grass. The shape was a silhouette on the stellar curtain, a metres-long reptilian shadow. Great pinions, leathery and veined, beat a steady rhythm from the wind. Metacarpals the size of a yacht's mainmast pushed against the air, propelling the seven-ton scaly bulk, a red titan, through the sky. The colossal beast was graceful and sleek, his arrow-tipped tail rippling behind him, a rudder navigating stars. Claws hung under his belly like spiny copper fruit. Embers smouldered in his cat-like eyes, peering down a narrow, horned snout, his cavernous nostrils trailing steam.

Yes, this shape would be only too familiar, if the people below happened to see it. And under all the fine clothes, the designer dresses and sharp suits, their flesh would instinctively know and shiver, hear a vestigial echo of a roar. Fear would make them children again, huddling around the fire in the hut. Or, these days, around the flat-screen TV. Unlike Ben's metamorphic hide, the human reaction never changed. It didn't matter that his kind were as varied in their temperaments and tastes as their hominid neighbours. Sure, you had your carnivores, like Mauntgraul the Terror, the White Dog, thankfully slumbering in rock on distant shores. Then you had what idiots like Fulk liked to call *milk drinkers*, those few of Ben's kind who wouldn't eat humans or, in his case, abstained from meat altogether. The term arose from a medieval myth about the supposed origin of dragons. Some said that maidens in the Old Lands had suckled baby snakes, turning the humble everyday viper into something much more singular and dangerous. It was absurd, of course, an old wives' tale, and a choice insult. Ben was no more related to snakes than he was to dinosaurs. Fulk probably thought it was funny.

All things considered, such cock-and-bull stories spoke volumes about superstition, how fear rendered people blind to the truth. To most human beings, it just didn't matter. Regardless of villainy or virtue, if the people below happened to look up and see him, they would scream, run and raise the alarm. After that, it always tended to go the same way . . .

Up here, where the eyes of the world couldn't reach him, Ben let the air rush into his lungs, the night surging into a visceral cave. In, out, his lungs throbbed, pushing against two tubular chambers lower down his tusk-like ribs, secret respiratory organs lined with hundreds of alveoli, little sacs containing a super-ordinary gas. Among other things, this inner buoyancy helped his bulk stay aloft, assisting his unfurling wings as they caught the buffeting airstreams. Now, his wings carried him away from danger. Or so he hoped.

Anxiety gnawed at his diving-bell heart. He was a ball in a pinball machine, flipped into flight by circumstance, bouncing off the bumpers of chance. He had the *what* but not the *why*. Anger and fear conspired with resentment – Fulk and the CROWS had tried to kill him! No news there, but their alliance didn't only go against the Lore, it also went against logic. Colluding with witches was far from wise. Ben wondered what the CROWS had demanded and what the Fitzwarrens, an ancient but human dynasty, were willing to pay. In his experience, the price was usually greater than the buyer had banked on. Why, after all this time, had House Fitzwarren chosen this precise moment to strike? Obviously, Fulk's attack wasn't just due to a Shropshire castle and the bloodthirsty provision of a deed. Whittington was a crumbling husk, a medieval blot on the landscape, a place over-looked by the National Trust and managed, at least on the surface, by its local community. Ben found it hard to believe that anyone would risk their neck for it, ancient vendetta or no. House Fitzwarren's inactivity for fifty-five years almost said as much.

No. The jagged grin across the third floor of the Javits Center implied different, darker motivations. The theft of the Star was clearly involved, and besides, he didn't think the CROWS would help the Fitzwarrens with their petty feud. It was too basic. Too *human*. It just wasn't their style. Babe Cathy had practically confessed that on the bridge, her short figure trembling with pride, her lips trembling with rebellion.

This is just the beginning. She'll track down every last one of her gifts and kill anyone who gets in her way.

All of which begged the question: *who?* The jagged mouth grew wider now. What was it about that maw that he couldn't see? No explosions. No melted glass. No fucking clue. Eclipsing this was his niggling shame at his exit from the bridge. It wasn't in his nature to run, but if escape meant that he got to warn Rose and live to pursue the mystery further, then he'd push his pride to one side. And of course, he would get to see her again, even if it was for the last time . . .

These hopes followed Ben down into Brooklyn.

Vinegar Hill. Six blocks of Federal architecture huddled along the East River, a district wedged between the Brooklyn Navy Yard and the Manhattan Bridge. By day, a latticework shadow bled across the district, and by night, a necklace of bulbs in the sky. Factories, vacant lots and warehouses dotted the antique charm, flaking graffiti and dented road signs, mixing the neighbourhood's small-town feel with a declining modernity. A power plant thrust derelict smokestacks above the cobblestoned streets, rust-ringed fingers supporting the dark. Neon blazed from liquor stores and boutique windows. Music lilted drunkenly from bars, joined by the blare of Hudson foghorns and the round-the-clock growl of traffic. Litter jigged past fire hydrants and along sidewalks, where restaurants shone in intimate gold, roast chicken and charred vegetables mingling with the river's brackish tang, garbage, oil and fish.

Trees brushed against the brick façade of the familiar Gold Street warehouse, the building converted into apartments. The five-storey structure looked east over Wallabout Bay and yet another bridge, the scattered shores of New York stitched together by steel and ingenuity. The Towers apartment block was like all the others in the area, offering the boon of rent control and a short commute to the island. The only thing that made it different was the woman who lived here.

Rose McBriar, the daughter of a fourth-generation Irish immigrant, worked part-time as a waitress downtown, surviving in the city on a scholarship and tips. Last summer, Ben's generosity had secured the place on Gold Street, a fair-sized penthouse that was way beyond her means. Before they met, Rose, a grad-school English student, had been living on the cramped campus of Long Island University, but as their relationship had grown more serious, Ben had wanted to support her, provide them with a space of their own. Deaf to her protests, he'd dipped into his ample funds and bought the apartment. In the end, she'd only accepted the place on Gold Street because her digs over on Rockwell Place had been a goldfish bowl and Ben was no fan of strangers. For a year, Gold Street had been his home too, a beautiful blink in the long gaze of history. It hurt to come back here, but the thought of Rose in danger hurt more.

The roof garden was handy, if small. Plant pots leapt and ornaments dived as Ben clumsily alighted. His hind legs, each the size and thickness of a tree trunk, made short work of the flower beds, roses and tulips spewing petals in the air. His forearms, the muscles like rope around a ship's capstan, ended in three splayed claws that scraped across the wooden decking, the planks splintering under his weight. A spade crumpled as if it was tin foil. A trellis crashed over, shrubs flooding the garden table, sending a half-finished bottle of wine into a terminal somersault. Fairy lights flickered through the dust. The surrounding balcony shuddered and shook, an invisible train rattling past, a section of railing twisting. A clothes line snapped, damp lingerie, bedclothes and towels trailing in the scattered soil. Under a billowing sheet, Ben's body bubbled and warped, lessening the load on the building. Great wings beat at the air, and then rustled inward like collapsing tents. Pink skin flooded in, covering his ruddy scales, moulding his quivering mass back into human form. His arrow-tipped tail whipped back and forth, smashing panes in the little greenhouse even as the long appendage thinned and shrank, coiling up into his spine. His horned snout crumpled, melting back into anthropoid guise. Josh Homme on steroids. Right. The embers in his eyes winked out, extinguished by the transformation, replaced by anxious glimmers of green.

In this fanfare of destruction, blasting petals, crushed pots and whirling dust, Ben stepped, completely naked – clothes could not survive the change – from the large sheet pooled around his feet. He did this just as the door to the roof flew open and Rose McBriar, a shocked blonde blur, came stumbling out into the wreckage.

"What the—"

She froze when she saw him, confusion elbowing shock out the way. In one hand she clutched a bottle – clearly the noise had interrupted her drinking, and he didn't register the fact at first, the oddness of the booze, this dent in her usual sobriety. At the sight of him, she held the bottle up like a club, red wine dribbling down her arm. Rioja wasn't much of a threat. Her gaze skipped over his newly formed muscles, pointedly avoiding the one at his groin. Her eyes caught and mirrored his scars; even healed wounds left their mark, and his memory of himself, this costume he wore, carried his past as a matter of course. Rose shook the bottle, the threat already growing feeble. Her other hand gripped the hem of her dress, bunching the washed-out floral pattern. Her ponytail was a pendulum, swinging back and forth. Too many late nights had darkened the skin around her eyes, visibly twanging her nerves. She blinked hard, her wintry gaze, like pale blue stones, returning to his face. Slowly, she lowered the bottle, her slightly pointed, elfin features trying to master her confusion.

"Ben?"

"Hello, Rose."

"What are you . . . How did you get up here?"

He pointed feebly. "The fire escape."

"So you thought you'd come up here and trash the place?"

"Not exactly. It was an accident."

"But . . . you're naked."

He looked down at himself. "You never did miss much."

This reference to her past suspicions was absolutely the wrong thing to say. His sarcasm worked like an acid, dissolving her shock, and a frown crawled over her forehead, impatience pursing her lips. All the same, he thought she was pleased to see him. You didn't get to eight hundred and sixty years old without knowing a thing or two.

"I'm going to call the cops," she said.

OK, maybe you did.

"Don't. I didn't come down here to give you grief. I mean, the garden . . ." He flapped a hand vaguely about him. "It's . . . it's a Central Park thing . . ."

She raised an eyebrow at that.

"There's something I should have told you."

The eyebrow came down, felled by annoyance. "No shit."

At least she seemed prepared to listen, for however brief a time. The ghost of the obelisk in Central Park still haunted her eyes, a memory of a snowy day two months ago, a day that wasn't Valentine's Day and wasn't their first anniversary, but had been pretty close to both. He guessed his admission kept her from running for the phone, anyway. That and maybe something else. Call it curiosity. Call it lingering affection. He didn't dare to hope. Christ, it was good to see her again. Ignored calls, unanswered door, wrecked garden aside, it was definitely good. The centuries had held a fair share of lovers – some chained to posts, others not – but Rose was surely his favourite damsel. Why? The poetic version: she was a gem, her clear facets reflecting his soul. The truth: she was a gem he couldn't quite own . . . Emotion fanned the coals of his heart, sparking memories and warmth. He couldn't let their flames distract him. Right now, her suspicions stood like a knight before her, guarding the bridge to the chance of forgiveness. Ben reached out to grab her doubts by the gorget.

"That night, before I left. I never really explained."

"No. You didn't." She looked so tired. So thin. "Do you remember what you said to me? In the bar. Do you remember what you said?"

He did remember. He didn't want to, but he did.

"Rose, look—"

"Ben, you better start talking."

Where to start? There seemed so much to tell her, none of

which she would like. He'd always laughed them off in the past, these little mundane incidents betraying the mythical truth. Like the morning he'd been cooking her breakfast and the frying pan had flared up in the kitchen, a fiery pillar engulfing his arms. When Rose came rushing to his aid, she peeled back his charred shirtsleeves to find his flesh untouched by burns. *It happened so quickly,* he told her. *Somebody up there must like me.* Or when he had picked her up for a date and she'd waved down to him from her bedroom window. He'd informed her over the lobby intercom how much he liked the smell of Chanel. Rose buzzed him in, pale and mystified. *How could you tell what I was wearing from five floors down?* A nervous cough, a gallant grin. *A classy girl like you? Lucky guess . . .*

The Central Park thing wasn't so easily explained. How could two months feel so long ago? *Once upon a time.*

"Well? Do I call the cops or not?"

But he still didn't have the balls to tell her. He didn't think now was the time.

He grimaced and rubbed his neck. "Dial 911. Order a pizza. One is just as good as the other. I came because you're in danger, Rose."

For a moment she just stared at him. Then, "You come up here drunk and butt naked after six weeks away – God knows where – trash my garden and scare me half to death, and now you tell me you're here to help. *My hero.*"

"Like you haven't been drinking? What's with that, anyway? Your father—"

"Oh fuck right off."

"OK, OK, sorry." He steered the conversation back on to safer ground. "I know how this looks. Just . . . you have to trust me, OK?"

"You Brits. You're crazy. I don't *have* to do anything. The only thing I have to do is kick your sorry ass out of here."

What could he tell her? That the four hundredth and twelfth descendant of an outlawed noble English family had burst in on him tonight in an East Side bar and tried to kill him with a bewitched broadsword? Or that the cigar-smoking *grande dame* of an underground coven had chased him halfway across Manhattan in a classic Rolls-Royce, resulting in him diving head-long off the Brooklyn Bridge? And that somehow it had something to do with an African diamond stolen from an exhibit at the Javits Center, and that this in turn had something to do with *him* because, you see, he hadn't been entirely honest, and when it came right down to it, he wasn't even human . . .

No. Now definitely wasn't the time.

"Rose . . ." He reached for her. "You're mine, remember?"

She slapped his hand away. "Yours? Like a trinket, right? Or a doll."

"I didn't mean it like that."

"Yes. You did. I don't know what the fuck is wrong with you. You're not right. You're not *normal*." Ben opened his mouth to protest, but the wheels of her anger rolled right over him, her arms jerking in a mime of grievance. "*I bought us a place*, he says. *A place where we can be together*. And a few months later, Central Park happens. Central Park and that damn obelisk, and will he answer my questions? No. And then the drinking starts, and where the hell is his money coming from anyway? Is it really his inheritance? What does he actually *do*? More importantly, what did he do before he met me? So I ask and I ask and then, that night in the bar, he tells me. *Dumb dangerous jobs for dumb dangerous crooks*, he says, and then—"

"Rose!"

"Then he ups and leaves." She spoke softly, her storm blowing itself out. "He takes me away from my friends, away from my *life*, and he locks me up here in my ivory tower. Like a fucking . . . doll. Then he just runs away and he doesn't say goodbye."

Silence settled over the garden, the shadows clinging to the debris. Fairy lights sparkled in her hair and glimmered off her skin. The moon shone down, cold and unmoved. There was no way to ignore her tears.

"I'm sorry. I wish I could kiss you and make you forget."

"Yeah? Well you can't. I remember everything. Even the weird stuff. The stuff you're never going to explain."

"It's not that simple. You and me . . . we're *different*, Rose."

"Yeah, you said." Resentment tugged at her upper lip. "And you should've known better. Better than to get involved. Better than to make me . . ." She caught her breath, jettisoned the words. "You know what your problem is?"

"Like the back of my hand."

She let that pass, continuing regardless. "You saw me as treasure, a jewel you had to protect. That's why you bought this apartment, so you could keep an eye on me. But I'm not your *possession*, Ben. I'm not part of your stash. And when I wanted the truth, you couldn't handle it, could you? You turned tail and ran."

Ben didn't know what to say to this. Over the years, several women had almost torn out their hair trying to tell him, and he was forever trying to learn. He naturally treasured their company; they were all princesses, all damsels to him. He'd hate to admit it, but if it had been down to him, he'd have locked them *all* up in an ivory tower. Possessiveness was part of his nature. Jealousy coiled in his heart. Over the years, it had caused him no end of trouble, from barroom brawls to bitter rows. With

Rose McBriar, he liked to think he was getting better, that he was mellowing with age, but the sad understanding trickling from her eyes laughed in the face of that one.

He coughed away guilt, focusing on the matter at hand.

"Rose, listen. I've run into a little trouble and I don't want to see you get dragged into it. It could be nothing. I could be paranoid. But until I figure out what's happening, I need you to go to your sister's in Vermont. You can catch a train up there tonight. Just pack a bag for a week or two. I can wire you all the money you need."

"Vermont? Ben, I have my exams on Monday." The bottle of Rioja shook in his face, a testament to heartbreak. "Haven't you heard a damn word I've said?"

"Yes, and we'll talk about it. Honest. But if you stay here, exams will be the least of your worries."

"What are you saying?"

"Some fuckers tried to kill me tonight. *Twice*. And one of them mentioned you."

Her face paled to rival the moon. The bottle in her hand returned to her side, the dregs sloshing. He hadn't wanted to scare her, but they could stand out here all night raking over the coals of the past. And all the while, Fulk and the CROWS could be creeping closer, eager to stuff the meat of tragedy into a hollow threat. Sure, Fulk had wanted to put him on the back foot, but it wasn't a risk he was willing to take.

"Rose. Please . . ."

He reached for her then, the walls falling down. Shock, sorrow and trepidation screamed like a whirlwind around her, but she slapped his hands away, unforgiving. He leant in to kiss her, smelling bergamot and wine, but she turned her head, her neck stiffening. When his arms closed around her, she sagged a little and he realised he was right: she *was* pleased to see him, despite her angry words. Some of the coals rolled aside, uncovering the rekindling embers, flames that hadn't died. Then she grew rigid again, her words tight as she tried to push him away.

"I miss you," she said, quiet and fierce. "I hate you."

Defeated, Ben rested his head on her shoulder, smoothing down the flowers on her dress. He let her anger hit him like a wave, tasting her muted fury at her love for him. Since he'd first crawled out of his egg, it had always been this way. Some women went for the knight. Others wanted the beast. Neither stood a chance of a happy ending. Until Rose. Rose who only wanted the real him, a secret he could not share. There among the scattered tulips, in a cold and silent embrace, the two of them said welcome home.

Rose made him sleep on the couch. In the early hours, with the moonlight slanting through the apartment windows and Ben snoring like a king under his blankets, she crept out from her bedroom in her nightshirt and stood looking down at him.

Why him? she wondered, a fretful finger tugging at her lips. *With all his secrets and lies? All the trouble that seems to follow him* . . .

But she knew why. Even in sleep, his ruffled hair and strong bones rendered him handsome; his almost sensuous lips, the lines and depressions that lent his eyes a permanent sorrowful cast tugged at places in her she fought to suppress. She had found an appealing strength in him, true, a strength that was unlike her father's, whose heavy hands had left their marks, rendered invisible with time, perhaps, but inside her nevertheless. Ben's strength lay under gentleness, a need to do good, even when it went against the grain of him, whoever he really was, and in that sense she felt he was lost, wandering – what was she but a lighthouse, calling him home?

Maybe once upon a time. It was too late for her to believe that this could have a happy-ever-after. It was time to wake up.

She sat down beside him, perching gently on the edge of the couch. She stroked his face, a soft, sad soothing. More than anything, she wanted him to see the real her, the woman she was who didn't need protecting, but in all these months, she knew she had only caught a fleeting glimpse of him.

"Oh Ben," she whispered. "You still think I'm the one who needs saving."

Then, with her golden hair shrouding her tears, she tiptoed across the apartment, closed her door and climbed back into her big cold bed.

In the morning, Rose woke him up by tossing an old pair of jeans, a faded Led Zeppelin T-shirt and a patched-up bomber jacket on top of him. Breakfast was civil, but terse. Before leaving the Gold Street apartment, Ben dug around in the bedroom closet and unearthed a pair of trainers, lurking in the gloom like stuffed rats. All these clothes he had left behind with Rose, six lonely weeks ago. Once he was dressed, she told him he looked like a tramp, but Ben guessed that was better than a streaker. He couldn't afford a run-in with the law. Besides, his destination was far, far away. The clothes wouldn't last long anyway.

His transformation on the Brooklyn Bridge had left him at somewhat of a disadvantage. His wallet, cash and credit cards inside it, was somewhere on the bottom of the East River. Ditto his keys. His other belongings – a couple of shirts, slacks and smalls, fake passport and battered copy of poems by Lorca – were back in the Village, stuffed in a bag at his cheap, under-the-radar hotel. He didn't think it wise to return there. So he and Rose caught a cab to Cadman Plaza and hurried down into the subway. It was only a five-minute walk from the apartment, but Ben didn't want to risk the streets, especially this close to the bridge. If Fulk could find him in an East Side bar, then he could find him in Vinegar Hill. His fear was a subtle disease, infecting everything around him. The way that Rose sat close in the back seat, her hands wrapped tightly in his, told him all he needed to know about her state of mind. Here in the Five Boroughs, dark alleyways ran everywhere, frequented by drunks and gangs. Also by witches and black knights.

Too soon, they stood on the platform, islands in the ceaseless pedestrian stream. Trains came and went, rumbling to a halt with doors bumping wide, disgorging passengers or swallowing them whole. Kids slouched by, high-fiving and giggling. Families scuttled past in brisk, watchful huddles. In the percolating air, diesel fumes blended with deodorant. Sweat with subway soot. Rats nibbled on dropped burgers and loose wiring. On the curving walls, last year's shows competed for attention like old whores in peeling paper dresses. In Insomniac City, nothing stayed new for very long.

Rose shouldered her bag. She said something, but a discordant xylophone announcing an approaching train swallowed her words. He could see that she was fighting back tears, and she tried again, without looking at him.

"You're not coming back," she said. "You can say what you like, but you're not coming back. Why can't I go with you?"

"I told you. It isn't safe. I won't put you in—"

"That's your line? For real?"

He wasn't going to lie again. He had told enough lies. Only danger had brought him back to her; it was the only reason the two of them were here. She might not like it, but he knew she believed him when he'd said that New York was no longer safe. Now danger was taking him away again, and she could only bruise the moment with scorn.

"Go to your sister's. Take my advice. Please."

"Take me with you, you arsehole. You *arsehole*."

He stepped forward and planted a kiss on her forehead, letting her hands beat weakly at his chest.

"I want you to know something," he told her. "That last night. That night in the bar, Rose, before I left."

"Yes." It wasn't a question.

"It was the worst lie I've ever told. I do love you."

She grabbed his face then, sealing his lips with her own. Riddles and secrets gyred around them, but as the train drew into the station, at least she had answered one of his questions. Maybe one day she would believe it.

She released him gently. Studied his face.

"Why won't you tell me what's going on?"

"I . . ." He really wanted to. "I can't."

Rose looked ready to pursue the matter, her eyebrows knitting together. Then she threw up her hands, beyond long-suffering, knowing he wouldn't answer.

"So where are you running off to this time, Ben?"

He didn't have to think about this one. His troubles this weekend had begun with a breach, a brazen flouting of the Lore. The Pact was a burden all Remnants must bear. It was often uncomfortable, often a grind, but he had always upheld his side. What good was the Guild if it wouldn't uphold its own? For all Fulk's gloating, all the CROWS' threats, their actions last night amounted to a crime. Ben was heading east to report it, to alert the Guild to their violation. Maybe, just maybe, they could help.

It was a whole heap of maybes, waiting for a train.

"Home, Rose. I'm going home."

He reached for her again, his damsel in distress. But his hands came up short as he looked at her face, saw her regard of weary disbelief. Had he ever really thought that she could belong to him? She had always been her own person, no possession, no trinket of his. And she made that clear as she turned and walked away.

FOUR

The flight back to London seemed to take forever. It was no use heading directly over the Atlantic, not unless he wanted to play chicken with one of the world's busiest airline routes. Plus give several hundred passengers enough unexplained sightings to keep *Fortean Times* in business into the next millennium. Strictly speaking, he was breaking the Lore as much as the CROWS with all these red-backed manifestations, but with no money, no passport and no time to arrange funds via his bank, there was no alternative. He hadn't been able to bring himself to ask Rose to lend him the cash; his pride wouldn't allow it. JFK to Heathrow in a first-class seat with à la carte dining, private lounge and champagne on tap was infinitely preferable to such a basic and lengthy migration, but getting home the old-fashioned way was the only option left to him.

So, this stepping-stone jaunt. His stamina was great, his reserves of energy a deep well. Under his wings, discreet gills – lined with filaments of tissue and hair – sucked at the rushing air, cycling in time with cavernous lungs. The taut anatomical grille augmented and smoothed his great speed. Coupled with his mill-vane wings, he could cross hundreds of miles in a matter of hours. Whether in his original skin or *in forma humana*, it took a lot to tire him out, though long distances and aerial boredom would eventually take their toll. Monstrous muscles, keen sight and an aerodynamic frame were all great biological gifts. The magic responsible for his birth, liquid starlight running through his veins, translated these gifts into his morphology. A punch thrown by a fourteen-stone man could carry a seven-ton weight behind it. A fall from a building usually only left him with bruises. Conversely, a fast-food bucket meal could satisfy a Moby Dick stomach, when shrunk to anthropoid size. How to control these strange abilities had been the first lessons of his youth, lessons that proved key to discretion as much as to survival. But control and discretion did not always work. Four-hundred-odd Fulks would attest to that. So would Mordiford, a tiny village on the Welsh border, if only it remembered its troubled past as anything more than legend . . .

Wings stirring the midnight smog, Ben soared into the northern skies, leaving New York and heartache behind. When it came to distance and speed, not even an albatross could rival him. The Arctic tern ate his dust. He swept upwards at a sharp incline, a corneous shadow across the moon, piercing the clouds and startling birds. Far below, the Eastern Seaboard glittered like diamanté on widow's weeds. Twinkling ships scrawled their journeys across the polished slate of the sea. Up and up he soared, mainmast pinions spurning gravity. His underbelly of tough white flesh shone in the moonlight. The thermosphere dwindled in his wake, until the cities and the towns sank under the clouds, the roads vanishing like threads in a rug, and his snout streamed with vaporised crystal. Bladed spine skimming the heavens, inner gases keeping him warm, Red Ben Garston crossed the dreaming world.

He touched down for a drink at a lake in Newfoundland, then arched with the dawn towards Greenland. On Tunu's snow-draped shores he spent an hour catching his breath and then plunged over the Denmark Strait, carried by the winds of day across the southern rim of the Arctic Circle. He raced the shadows of whales into the dusk, their depthless dirge leading him on. The sun found him again in Iceland, Vatnajökull rumbling far below, a bubbling red eye, smoke wreathing his aching wings. He rested for a while on the mountainside, the restless volcano dwarfing his heat. Then on and on across the waters, the waves licking the dying sun, bronze upon the Scottish coast, the fanged boundaries of Britain. The stepping stones passed in miles and hours, in ragged breaths and twitching muscles. After a nap in a hinterland glen, Ben arose as dawn kissed the hills and began the final leg of his journey.

Monday afternoon saw him reach his destination. April fog wreathed the Thames, Tower Bridge afloat, castles in the air. The grey skies shrouded his descent as he landed wearily in Regent's Park. Unable to see the pentagram of paths, he alighted in some hawthorn bushes next to an empty bench, whipping up a tornado of twigs, leaves and broken branches. As the noise died down, he reached out his five-fingered pink-skinned hands just in time to catch a football flying at his head. Too exhausted to hide, he staggered out across the open green, in the direction of Barrow Hill Road.

"Afternoon, lads."

Emerging from the fog, he handed the ball back to the gaggle of teenage boys, trying to ignore their gaping mouths, and then their laughter at his naked behind. He walked as quickly as he could into St John's Wood, keeping to wheelie bins, parked cars and alleyways, and only prompting one or two screams.

The spare key was where he'd always kept it, under the stone gryphon at the top of the steps to his Victorian town house. The classical pillars and tall façade of number 9 Barrow Hill Road might fit the architectural style of the area, but to Ben the house was also a trespasser, an encroacher here as much the newsagent's on the corner and the double yellow lines painted on the road. Once, the Great Forest of Middlesex had covered all of this space, dense trees concealing all kinds of wild animals, stags, boars, wolves and bulls. The forest was old when the Romans came, older still when the Saxons followed them. And before both the Romans and Saxons, when the Old Lands had still lapped against these shores, a slowly ebbing tide, there had been other beasts besides, among them pale, glittering beings who called the forest by different names depending on their moods. Even though the Fay had been centuries gone by the time Ben was born, the place still held a magic for him. He had found his way here many years ago, after fleeing a certain borderland village . . .

The forest was gone. Long gone. The gnarled stumps buried under tarmac, train tunnels and pipes, and under them a millennium of muck. Street lights formed the new canopy, gutters and eaves the new boughs. Parking meters lined the kerb like fossilised grey plants. To most of the residents of St John's Wood – of London, Britain and the world – the Old Lands didn't even amount to a memory. These days, they were only a quaint, subconscious echo, glimpsed in flashy genre movies, Romantic art and children's books.

Ben slipped through his front door and leant against it in relief. He waded through bills, charity bags and pizza pamphlets, the impersonal bumf of his solitary life, past the stairway and into the lounge. It was a sparsely furnished, neglected space, the huge bay windows shaded by blinds, the floorboards covered in dust. The walls were all but bare. A Queens of the Stone Age poster hung by the door and a large framed print of William Blake's *The Great Red Dragon and the Woman Clothed in Sun* hung over the fireplace. The latter disturbed him more than impressed him; the painting so closely resembled his own fabled state. There was no computer and no phone. Potential clients found him via word of mouth or happened upon him in bars. An ad on the web would be as good as sending up a flare. The Guild forbade any trace of his existence, his presence in society, as anything other than a man, a rich one perhaps, but otherwise reclusive and ordinary. That was a crucial condition of the Pact. Of course, the crooks who hired him did so because he was anything *but*, his feats of strength and endurance turning him into another kind of myth, a whispered story over cards in a back room and a secret weapon of the underworld. It was another example of Remnant survival, the Lore bending, but never to the point where it actually broke. Naturally, Ben never revealed his true self to his clients. He did their dirty work, took their money, then, muscles stretched, boredom alleviated, faded back into the shadows . . .

Tins filled the kitchen cupboards to last through the next Ice Age. Fruit and vegetables rarely graced the racks. Ben didn't kid himself by tending plants, and he was absent much too often for pets, flying away on shady missions for generally shady men. Not that cats or dogs would come near him anyway. Only a lizard or a fish wouldn't think he had bought them for lunch, and neither gave a shit about companionship. Ben rarely ventured upstairs, but he knew that the sparseness continued up there, a maze of cobwebs and blank white walls. All the furniture was modern and stylish. Beds stood in bare rooms with carefully aligned, pristine pillows, just as he'd left them months before, clean and collecting dust. The bathrooms lacked the usual items of personal care, no towels, toothpaste or soap. The inside of the house was a tasteful tomb. Loneliness by IKEA.

A shadow to his naked flesh, number 9 Barrow Hill Road was a mask.

Christ, Rose. I wish you were here.

But that was a fire hope couldn't quench, so he went to the fridge and quenched it the only way he knew how. Jack in hand, he left footprints across the dusty floor as he padded to the couch and sank into its plush black leather.

He flicked on the TV and half watched the news, the various reports flickering across the screen. More on allied manoeuvres in Iran. Anti-capitalist riots in the City. North Sea oil rigs running dry. Massive cracks in the Arctic. Unprecedented drought across the Horn of Africa . . .

"Plague and pestilence. Famine and war. Same as it ever was."

Except it wasn't, not really. The world was changing, and not for the better. The disasters of the past, from the Black Death to the world wars, had all left their scars, but now it seemed like the earth itself was in revolt, straining under pollution and industrial advance, threatening to destroy the swelling population. And perhaps the waves surging on the surface swayed the vestigial weeds in the depths, the Remnants growing restless, sensing the turn of the tide . . .

The broadcast ended on the usual sunny note, the newsreader perking up to mention an eclipse in Egypt, best viewed from Cairo the following Sunday. A darkening sun blazed on the screen – some recent stock footage – a shimmering crown of shadow and gold, nature flaunting her mystery.

Ben was too tired to feel awed by it. He switched over to an afternoon game show, let cheesy one-liners and canned laughter wash away the taste of social decline. He sipped Jack, his old friend, and slipped snoring into sleep.

If he dreamt, he didn't remember. He awoke with a start. Orange slashes through the blinds told him that night had fallen. It was half past anytime. Some midnight limbo. The TV was a blizzard of static and it took him a moment to register the oddity. Show schedules didn't end these days, certainly not on the mainstream channels. Soap operas and documentaries partied until dawn. This fact made him fully open his eyes, and he blinked in confusion at the screen. A power cut, surely. The draught on his neck turned his head, sucking his forehead into a frown. As far as he could see, the windows were closed. Why was the room so bloody cold? His draconic senses snapped around, ears straining for a squeaky floorboard, a creaking door, quickly confirming that the house was empty – so why didn't it feel that way?

That smell. What was that smell? It reminded him of a blown fuse, although a lot more pungent. The fuse box was down in the cellar, so maybe a plug in the lounge had overheated . . . His rational mind suggested these things at the same time that his instincts dismissed them. The TV static was prickling on his skin, some residual charge crackling in the space, a subtle, needling pressure. No fuse or plug was capable of that. Even a split SCART lead wouldn't infuse its immediate surroundings. And the scent held more than electricity, more than escaping volts. There was *life* to it. Organic energy. If a thunderstorm could sweat . . . His nostrils flared with the impression.

He surveyed the room again, nictitating membranes working overtime, increasing the available light through his pupils. His human eyes vanished. Reptilian slits became golden moons. A realisation wrenched him to his feet, where he stood like a naked statue in the gloom. Footprints wove through the dust across the floor, and some of them weren't his.

No fucking way.

He dropped into a crouch, instantly defensive. Scales wavered across his back, muscles bulging, battle-ready. A small array of blade-like plates rattled up from his shoulders and down his spine, a quick, tense undulation. Transformation was merely a thought, an extension or retraction of will, and he could slide with ease between its varying stages, fluid and chameleon-like. He was rhino-sized and steadily swelling, but when no enemy presented itself, the lounge remaining dark and silent, his shape gradually dwindled to a red, bristling figure that was not quite beast and not quite man.

Ben-between-states sniffed the interloper's footprints. His shortening tail thumped the floor.

Who was it? Who the fuck broke into my lair?

He didn't think it was Fulk. If House Fitzwarren knew of his whereabouts, an assassin would have tried their luck long ago, tossing a hand grenade through the window or posting an anthrax letter through the door. That was their style. The CROWS would've hidden in the trees on the street, waiting for him to step outside and into some vile spell, indirect and complex, of course, but no less murderous. Witches heeded a plethora of codes – their magic wouldn't work otherwise – and even a novice understood the repercussions of breaching certain, secret thresholds, particularly one belonging to *his* kind. You didn't just waltz in, whistling and hoping for the best, not unless you wanted your beldam buddies to sweep up your ashes with a broom . . .

And then there was the matter of the Lore.

Babe Cathy cackled in his head.

Things change . . .

Ben studied the footprints. They were smaller, narrower than his, easy to make out. They danced among his prints like mockery, a confident, shameless taunt. *I can walk here and you can't stop me.* They danced up to the edge of the couch and then stopped dead. Fanned dust betrayed the place where the interloper had stood, dallying there, looking down at him. Watching him while he slept. *Watching him . . .*

He pulled a face, one clammy palm squeezing the back of his neck. Then, hunched over and breathing hard, he followed the tracks. The footprints danced back the way they had come, then diverged from his. As he headed into the hallway, another realisation struck him, a pail of ice poured down his back. Bare feet had left these prints, the toe marks and curve of the soles apparent in the dust. Clenching his jaw, he saw a bold, slender twin to his own tread and the taunt became a slap. Whoever had dared to enter his house had done so without wearing shoes.

The footprints ran out six feet or so from the front door. Vanished like smoke. The door was open, the source of the draught. Ben loped over to it, inspecting the lock and finding it undamaged. *Someone just walked the hell in here?* The automatic bolt dispelled any doubts about vigilance. So did years of caution. He would have locked the door. Hadn't he leant against it when he came in? *Yes.* He poked his head out, peering up and down the road. A fox crossed the street through sodium pools, on its way to the park. Nothing else moved.

He tried to tell himself he wasn't spooked, even as he went to close the door. Then he noticed the mark etched upon it, gouged deeply in the bright red paint with patience and a blade.

It was a rune. One of the old ones. Not Norse, not Futhark. Runes from the Lands that were now long gone. The runes that only a few remembered. The runes that they used to call *wyrm tongue*.

The one on his door – rough, large and boldly graven – obviously symbolised an *A*.

Ben swore. The letter meant nothing to him. It wasn't a glyph of House Fitzwarren or a sigil of the CROWS, that he did know. The symbol wasn't magically charged; it wasn't some binding spell. It was a calling card, pure and simple, a stark, knowing signature. It was all the threat that anyone would need.

I have been here. I know where you live.

He shivered in the cold night air. Instinct told him that a fight was coming. In the Legends bar, he'd seen it shine like heraldry in the Black Knight's eyes.

Rampant combatant.

He had urgent business, but first he needed rest.

The lounge no longer offered any comfort. It was a chill and violated space. He glared at the stranger's footprints, then angrily downed a quart of Jack. Confusion gripped him, along with shame. He had been caught naked and snoring, completely exposed to some faceless other as he lay on the couch. He couldn't work out what pissed him off most: that someone had managed to sneak in here, or that they hadn't attacked him. He wasn't home often enough to tell if anything had been stolen, but he didn't think so. The visit amounted to a message, surely, whether he grasped its meaning or not.

Still, the house, this empty sham of bricks and mortar, no longer felt safe. He headed through the kitchen and down into the cellar, where he lightly pressed a section of wall. It slid back, revealing steps leading further into darkness. Thick cobwebs and stale air assured him that these secret depths remained undisturbed. The knowledge calmed him with every step as he made his way down.

Long before the house was built, before the Romans and Saxons, Ben's ancestors had lived here. *Dwelt* here. Unlike their more aggressive kin, who favoured mountains and windy heaths, the Great Forest had been their stamping ground and they'd lived in peace with their human neighbours, serving the masters who gave them life. Those were golden times. The long summer of the Old Lands. The long summer of Albion. Two worlds that overlapped as one, where stunned squires pulled swords from stones, and betrayal and war were vague omens scattered by Druids in bird bones and blood . . .

Then came the fall of Arthur, that legendary king in whose blood ran the very union of magic and Man, who symbolised in flesh and steel the binding of the worlds, earthly and other. In his folly, the King had sown seeds of darkness, mortal and malevolent. His son, Mordred, incest-born and warped by demonic spells, rose up from the ranks of the Round Table to tear apart any hope of a golden age. Mordred's treachery brought about a great battle on Camlann Field, men against men, with Remnants caught between them, the various divisions of witches, wizards and fabulous beasts forced to choose a side. Some fought

74

for the usurper. Some fought for the King. Battle between dragon and dragon, giant and giant, dwarf and dwarf. Between men and women who would claim Albion's throne as their own, between reason and dreams. As the green lawns of Albion ran red with blood and crows pecked gleefully at eyeballs, the King lay dying on a nearby lake shore, his marshal knight by his side. Arthur's last breath signalled a crack in history, a final surrender of magic and myth, an end to its reign on these shores. If the Fay had devised this paragon, this Golden Example, in the hope of abiding peace, then they had failed. Where history and legend had intertwined, fate now wrenched them apart. Human lust and treachery had proved, at least to some, that the two worlds could never be one. The Fay had turned their backs in disgust and strode off into the endless nether, the outer dark that surrounded Creation, taking their golden age with them. An era of beauty and glory was done, and things would never be the same.

For those few of the Old Lands left behind, the going was bitter and hard. As city walls grew and roads advanced, Ben's kind gradually withdrew. The Matter of Britain no longer mattered. The Fay had left this brave new world to it, their art and their wisdom forgotten and crushed under the wheels of progress. The Romans came, and on their heels the Vikings and Saxons. Those tribes, pagan as they were, were tolerant enough of Remnants, and many survivors from the war scratched out a living in deep, dank caves and lonely woods, blasted fells and misty moors. The Middle Ages was when the real trouble started, around the time of Red Ben's birth . . .

Ben knew his history all right. The *true* history of Britain. He thought most of it read like a fantasy novel.

As he wound deeper under the house, into the belly of an

old forest hill, he caught the first glimmers of the trinkets down there, collected long ago by the Fay, the vanished race of masters. Between fat, rune-carved pillars, under a vast vaulted roof, lay heaps and heaps of burnished gold, glittering mounds of age-old coins, shields, helmets and swords. Crystal veins that ran through the granite shone sorcerously down on the trove, glowing in the depths of rubies, sapphires and diamonds, some of the jewels fatter than a fist. Buried in the endless slopes were statuettes and gilded mirrors, pearl necklaces and silver crowns, gem-studded tomes and knot-work goblets. Around the shadowed edges of the hoard, set carefully against the worn tapestries that lined the grey stone walls, one might find other, more recent treasures, amassed by Ben through his age-spanning life. Tudor seals made of gold. Relics looted by Cromwell and Napoleon. Victorian clocks. Fabergé eggs. Ming vases. Ivory triptychs and lost Masters, depicting sea serpents, saints and queens.

He reached the bottom step and sighed. The last time he had visited this place, air-raid sirens had wailed and whooped through the streets above, the Blitz raging through London. He could feel the gold reflected on his face, a sun of wealth, easing his fears. To reach out here, to let emeralds spill through his claws, was to touch a vanished world, feel the heritage to which he belonged. The hoard was both history and legacy.

It was also a bed. In full natural shape, sprawled across yards of untold riches, Red Ben Garston folded his wings and gathered his strength in restless dreams.

FIVE

Paladin's Court was only three miles from Regent's Park, where Ben rose from the bushes this Tuesday night, wings spread to meet the sky. Below him, the lights of London, tangling down the serpentine streets, the sight as familiar as an old map. Over the years, these buildings and alleyways, cemeteries and stations, had spread under his private supervision. The wanton urbanisation was like a deluge on the world he once knew. London City shouted in the dark. Traffic, construction and the roar of stadiums merged into a dissonant blare, echoing into the void.

He climbed directly upwards, the golden river of the A41 snaking far below, a makeshift compass. Soon the orange pools of Belsize Park gave way to the sweep of Hampstead Heath. And beyond the woods, Paladin's Court. The sixteenth-century mansion, a glut of gable, chimney and turret, stood at the end of a winding driveway on the north side of the Heath. Its location was hardly a secret. Why would it be? A creature like Ben was crazy to come here, and that was the Court's best defence.

Yes, there were ways to ask questions. And ways for the Guild to avoid giving answers. The Guild's regime reached far beyond Britain. Agents and spies operated around the globe, overseeing and, on occasion, enforcing the Lore. These agents provided contact points for all querent Remnants, always keeping the Court at some remove. In short, you didn't come to the Guild.

The Guild came to you. If Ben had tried to make an appointment, to visit the Court in person, his request would have met with stony silence, followed by a letter of rejection reminding him to use the proper channels. Just because the Guild and the Remnants had managed to reach political accord, it didn't make them friends.

Paladin's Court had been in the care of the Bardolfe family for nine generations. Over the years, the role of chairman had passed between several aristocratic houses, but never left the chosen circle, those rare few humans wise to the Pact. Now it was Maurice Bardolfe's turn. Maurice Bardolfe. Philanthropist. Explorer. All-round good egg. The faces changed but the titles never did. Maurice Bardolfe. Lord of the Guild of the Broken Lance.

Sir Maurice Bardolfe. *Knight.*

The resentment summoned up by that word lent Ben the strength to make his own appointment. Three thousand feet above Hampstead Heath, he folded his wings in close, pointed his snout earthward and dropped like a bomb. The wind screamed and seethed through his gills as his bulk descended. The Court's brick façade grew larger, the expertly tended lawns, the chimneypots and mullioned windows rushing into view. Mossy statues ignored his approach, the gardens an expanse of shadow and fog. A fox yelped and ran for cover. Soft light glowed behind the huge round window above the crenellated entrance hall, picking out St George and the Dragon in exquisite stained glass. St George, the official patron of the Guild, and indeed all England, sat astride his great white charger in his Templar tabard, his shield raised, his lance spearing the typically green and flaming dragon under his horse's hooves. Symbols surrounded the image, this famous figurative submission, a cheerful border of crossed swords, apple trees and crucifixes. War, sin and death.

Ben knew the truth behind the image. The slaughter had taken place many miles from here, in a place called Silene, now known as Libya. In the early eleventh century, soldiers from the First Crusade had brought the tale home with them, shoehorning George – a Byzantine general – into Britain's hagiography. The tale was pretty much the same now as it had been back then: venomous dragon menaces city, people chosen by lots to appease it, the draw falling on the King's daughter. King promises gold and half his realm if his subjects spare said daughter. His subjects refuse, daughter gets sent in bridal gown to the dragon's lair (because one should always look one's best when one is about to get eaten). George rides by, sees chained-up damsel, battle ensues and one bloody, grievous wound later, the dragon dies and everyone is happy.

Good story, and it *was* a story. The way that Ben had heard it from his kind, there had been no damsel, and good old George was drunk that day, blind drunk and looking for someone to take it out on, having lost at dice to his military pals. On his way to visit a whore in an outlying village, he had come across a hillside cave and stopped for a while to smash up some eggs, kicking green and blue yolk all over the walls. Then, seeing a way to earn back his gold, he had taken an old giant skull from the back of the cave and galloped into Lasia, the nearest city, to declare himself a hero and saviour.

It was, of course, a very famous murder. All those eggs, the leavings of a poor dead beast, slain before they could hatch. Ben took pleasure in his descent, muttering as he drew near the ground.

"Come not between the dragon and his wrath . . ."

His rapidly transforming form, rhino-sized, horned and scaled, crashed through the middle of the stained-glass window.

Coloured chips and strips of lead showered the entrance hall, tinkling off the threadbare rug and panelled walls in a cacophonous rainbow. Echoes raced like imps into the mansion, slapping the corridor walls and sprinting up the grand staircase. As he landed in the hall, wings spread to slow his fall, the chandelier jangled over his head with a shrill, crystalline din. A painting fell, the frame cracking open, some lacquered earl scowling at his sudden demotion. A shield-skinned hulk in the moonlight, half returned to human shape, Ben straightened, cricked his neck and waited for attention.

It arrived in the form of two Dobermanns, racing around a pilastered corner and into the hallway, their clipped paws scuttling on wood. Their low growls never blossomed into barks. One look at the scaly man-beast in the hall and they whined and turned stubby tail, trotting back into the dark. Ben would have laughed if not for the arrival of Maurice Bardolfe at the top of the stairs. His hair was a blizzard atop his skull, his pyjamas disarrayed. A World War II revolver trembled in his hand.

Ben's protest, rough and short, flew off his lizardine tongue.

"Now wait just a min—"

The old man didn't wait. Shots rang out, biting into wood and stone. Cordite spiced the musty space. Ben threw his arms in front of his face as Bardolfe tottered down the staircase, a gaunt grey bird peering from the landing.

"Demon! Fiend! Get out of my house!"

More shots, fired at random into the gloom. Bullets sparked off Ben's forearms and bounced on to the floor. Still, they *hurt*. He heard Bardolfe gasp and the trigger click, the cylinder empty. Ben came lunging out of the shadows and leapt up the stairs, confronting the man as he shrank against the banister. Bardolfe's querulous gaze travelled over Ben's shoulder. Breath wheezed out of his lungs as he took in the shattered window.

"You . . . you *vandal*! You *brute*! Do you have any idea of the cost?" He looked about ready to cry.

"It's only glass, knight. Tell me what I want to know and I'll gladly pay for repairs."

"The *historical* cost, you oaf! You think I need your money?"

Ben shrugged. "Then it's still only glass." He gave the old man a meaningful stare. "Glass and lead. Flesh and bones . . ."

Bardolfe forgot all about the window. His body shook. His lips trembled. It was as if he was seeing Ben for the first time. Ben, dwindling from his half-beast state and into his full human form, a six-foot, scruff-haired man standing naked in the hall. The moonlight must have made his muscular frame and angry green eyes all the more apparent.

"It's you. The Sola Ignis. The milk drinker. You're in breach of the Lore by coming here, you know. Uffington, 1215, remember? My ancestors—"

"Don't lecture me, old man. I was there. I know what I signed."

Bardolfe raised the gun, a futile gesture, the heirloom or whatever it was feeble in his grasp. Ben took it from him. To make a point, he squeezed it in his hand. The grip curved in to meet the muzzle, crushing the empty barrel between them. He tossed the crumpled gun over his shoulder, heard it go thumping down the steps.

Bardolfe watched it go, his wrinkled gizzard rising and falling.

"Well, what in blazes do you want?"

And so Ben made his appointment. "We need to talk, you and I."

He gave Bardolfe a minute to recover. The old man went to

a cupboard under the stairs, rummaged around for a minute and flung a moth-eaten raincoat over his shoulder at Ben. *So you won't catch your death*, he muttered, as if he genuinely cared. Ben, vaguely embarrassed by his nakedness, shuffled into the coat and followed his host into the study.

Antiques packed the room, Persian rugs, Chippendale chairs and Tiffany lamps making an elegant medley of the space. A bust looked down from a shelf above the door. Janus, Ben thought, some fancy fellow like that. Bardolfe, another fancy fellow, went doddering over to his felt-topped desk and the baroque cabinet set behind it, pouring himself a generous Scotch from a crystal decanter. He raised a wiry eyebrow at Ben, who shook his head in brusque but reluctant refusal. He hadn't come here to socialise.

Bardolfe took a long, quivering sip, licked his lips and regarded Ben with a look that he probably thought courageous.

"Now then, what's this all about?"

Ben tilted his head. "Seriously? As if you didn't know. How many pies does the Guild have fingers in these days anyway?"

"I'm afraid I—"

"Corporate cartels. Religious sects. Embassies. You've built yourselves a right little empire. All on the bones of the Old Lands."

"Now listen here—"

"No, you listen. Your Pact means shit. Friday night in New York, Fulk Fitzwarren tried to kill me. He walked right up in an East Side bar and tried to chop off my head." *Tried and failed.* "The attack took place in broad daylight."

Bardolfe digested this for a moment and then gave an indifferent grunt.

"Well . . . you and that family have never exactly traded Christmas cards. Not since the Mordiford incident eight hundred years ago, if we credit our history." Bardolfe took another sip of Scotch and tipped his glass at Ben. "You know we keep the deeds to Whittington Castle. The family often make petitions, calls to amend the Royal Clause, to rescind the seal of King John. I'll wager that their present interest has more to do with the principle than the actual place. Whittington is a heap of rubble." The old man sighed. "This is all so much water under the bridge."

"Easy for you to say. You don't have leather-clad thugs trying to turn you into mincemeat."

"Fulk Fitzwarren – whichever one of them currently goes by that name – is nothing to us. The Guild, as ever, remains neutral. We're impartial, like Switzerland. We simply can't afford to get involved in petty disputes between our various wards."

"No?" Ben glowered. "That's helpful."

"Look, I'll accept that such an attack is illegal. All Remnants, all humans privy to your existence, must obey the Lore or what good is it? I don't see why you had to smash my window and wake me up in the middle of the night to tell me this. If you want to lodge a formal complaint, then—"

"Then what? You'll summon the Fitzwarrens to court? Hold a fair hearing? Right. Maybe when Hell freezes over."

Bardolfe's eyes were chips of ice. "No one is above the Lore."

"According to the CROWS, there *is* no Lore. They were there too, Bardolfe. In Manhattan. Turns out they were backing Fulk. Babe Cathy almost ran me down on the Brooklyn Bridge – with a little help from magic, of course." He enjoyed watching the old man squirm. "Yeah, seems to have something to do with some fancy rock – the Star of Eebe – stolen from an exhibition at the Javits Center. Babe was all hocus-pocus about it, you know how that lot are, babbling on about crooks and killers and new flames scouring the sky . . . But the Guild wouldn't know anything about that, right?"

Bardolfe set his glass down on the desk. He smoothed the front of his dressing gown.

"Come on, Maurice, your little Rotary Club must know *something*."

But Ben could see that the old man was shaken. His hands fluttered at his sides like restless pigeons. Bardolfe might be rich and the Guild powerful, in its covert, venerable way, but the man before him was only human, and staring down the barrel of a thankless grave after years serving as chair. Ben almost felt sympathetic.

"The Star of Eebe, you say?" The old man cleared his throat. "I don't know about this breach in the Lore, but I do know a thing or two about antiques. I'm practically one myself." He attempted a laugh, abandoning it as he glanced at Ben's face. "The name rings a bell, anyway. The Star of Eebe. An African gem, I think. Or whatever was there before Africa. Come with me."

Bardolfe shuffled out the door and down an adjacent corridor. They wove deeper into the mansion, fraying rugs and thick walls muffling their footsteps, the only sound in the still. Ben found the peace surprising. He realised that no alarms had sounded when he'd crashed into the hall. No guards had come running from the gatehouse. Bardolfe could surely afford such measures. Only the dogs had challenged him, and what good were they? The knight must have felt so safe in his little castle, so sure that no Remnant would ever dare to come here, that security at the Court had grown a little lax. He bet Bardolfe regretted that now.

The old man tottered down some steps and under an archway,

a mahogany mouth of carved roses, emerging at one end of a long gallery. Moonlight glowed behind a tall row of windows, an Edwardian addition to the house. *Objets d'art* and dusty antiques lined the panelled walls. Bardolfe flicked a switch, gentle lamps winking on, and walked over to a nearby painting. He stood regarding it with obvious reverence.

It was another dragon, this one blue and loop-tailed, falling under the sword of a mounted knight. The battle was taking place in a village meadow, the crude medieval rendering giving no thought to scale or size. Blade and fangs were impossibly long. Blood and fire garishly red. The peasants in one corner of the painting were taller than their cramped thatched hovels.

Under the painting, embossed on a small brass plaque, Ben leant forward and read:

Ther reigned at a toune called Wormesgay a dragon in a field that venomed men and bestes with his aire; Sir Hugh on a weddings day did fight with thys dragon and slew him, and toke his heade, and beare it to the kynge and gave it hym, and the kynge for slaying of the dragon put to his name this word dolfe, and did call him afterwards Bardolfe.

Ben rolled his eyes, and not at the grammar.

"Much has changed since the old days, eh?" Bardolfe the umpteenth descendant said. "Since *the gaunt wolf and winged serpent held dominion o'er the vale*. Men knew how to settle scores back then."

"You think so? Thousands died. I'd hardly call those times idyllic."

The old man pursed his lips, his expression suggesting that the matter was debatable. Then he shook himself from his reverie and proceeded up the gallery, passing other portraits, flags and shields, Ben a looming presence at his side.

"The Old Lands faded from Britain like a dream." Bardolfe spoke as if to himself, lost in the forest of his thoughts. "It was like the Rapture, I suppose. An apocalypse in fairyland. Of course, they left you lot behind. The Fay are notoriously fickle."

"Some might say cruel." Ben conceded the point grudgingly; he didn't want to give the knight anything.

"The Fay created you. All of you . . . *creatures*." Ben sensed that this wasn't the word Bardolfe would've chosen in different company, but the old man moved swiftly on. "Why? Their reasons, as ever, remain inscrutable." He flapped a hand, frustrated by the mystery. "Pets? Servants? A hierarchy of fabulous beasts, whole dynasties of spell-born magic users, and spirits tangled with wood and stone . . ." His eyes slipped sideways at Ben. He knew he was pushing it. "Then your masters upped and abandoned you. You Remnants . . . remained."

"Yeah, well, I hear Camlann was kind of messy. No wonder the Fay flew the coop."

Betrayal. Incest. Murder. War. Ben had read the legends of Arthur and his fall, the stories of his draconic lineage that fifteen hundred years later were fairy tales even to him.

Fairy tales. They sprang up wherever the Fay set foot, like forest vines trailing in their wake, surrounding them in mystery. Some said that the ancient spirits had been gods once, the First-Born lords at the dawn of Creation. Others that the Fay were mere children of gods, running wild in the playground of the world. Either way, what most tales agreed on was that some kind of cataclysm had taken place, some grievous shift in the cosmic order, way back where the reach of history ran out and all was fog and speculation. The gods, some said, had perished. Or rather, lost all sanity and self-control, become a potent soup of chaotic force summoned and shaped by human belief, each god simply a facet of the whole, wearing a face to mirror the needs of the faithful. And in the chaos, the First-Born had fallen, become the Fay, choosing an enchanted form of flesh and mortality rather than embrace cosmic madness, forever bound to the fractured planes of existence, wandering the gulfs of the nether from dreaming world to world . . .

The reasons why the Fay had decamped from this world were well documented – in the right circles, at least. After centuries of counselling and guiding humans (and some of them befuddling and leading folk astray), the Fay gave up in disgust and returned to the nether whence they came. Most Remnants lived in hope of their return. When the Fay returned, the Long Sleep would end. Ben guessed that it was something to live for, a hope on which to hang. Although he often scorned himself for it, begrudging his own naïvety, wasn't that why he clung to the Pact where so many others had grown bitter? Well, that and his private affection for humans, a species that played into his natural desire to protect . . . Peace, the cynical part of him told him, was a lot to hope for, a nigh-on impossible dream. The battle of Camlann had severed two worlds. One had withered like a dead branch on a tree and become myth, become laughable, childish stories. As the centuries stretched on, desperation had set in. He was well aware that among the Remnant leaders, the ones still walking the earth, he was perhaps the least jaded – but his faith was wearing thin. No Remnant was living the life they had envisioned under the sheltering Lore. Had the Fay really left them to die?

Messy? No, messy didn't quite cover it. Ben rubbed his hands. The admission felt weak. An excuse he made for his makers that he didn't really believe.

"Might've helped if people had left us alone." Did he sound surly? He wished he could come across as less childish. "Humans. Do you realise how *noisy* you are? Back then, it was feasts and battles, chiselled stone and chopped trees. These days, it's planes, trains and automobiles. You never, ever shut up."

"Progress, my friend. It's called progress."

Ben came to a halt, arrested by a suit of armour in an alcove on his left. It stood there guarding the gloom, a steel scarecrow with pointed helmet, curved pauldrons, dented breastplate and scarred greaves. And spikes. Lots and lots of spikes. Spikes protruded from every available space, sticking out of hinged elbows, collar and cuisse. The helmet was an evil star in the lamplight, the sieve-like visor bristling with blades. Someone had recently polished the suit, and as Ben paused to inspect it, trying to ignore the ghost of hatred haunting its hollow, vulturine beak, he saw his horror reflected back at him.

"Where the hell did you get this junk? Should've been scrapped long ago."

"Oh, it arrived a couple of weeks back." Bardolfe seemed happy to explain. "One of our wards sent it as a gift. A collector of occult memorabilia and military souvenirs. Would you believe they had the thing in their cellar? The Guild were happy to take it off their hands."

"I'll bet." Ben scowled.

"Come now. Lambton was a very long time ago." Bardolfe sniffed, moving on from the grim suit of armour. "I believe there were casualties on both sides. Far too many to start laying blame."

"Oh yeah?" And now his cynicism was breaking through. "There are – what? – twenty of us left on British shores. A few scattered in other lands. You lot are *everywhere*, breeding like it's going out of fashion. Just what sacrifice did you make? What did you give up for the Lore?"

Bardolfe looked at him. For a moment, the old man's stare was disbelieving, then it softened into something approaching sympathy.

"Why, magic, of course."

Ben found that he couldn't argue with this. There were countless tales of humans using magic before the Pact and few of them had ended happily. He dropped his gaze, glaring at the suit. He recalled the story behind it. A northern squire, Lord John, had gone out fishing on the Sabbath and a witch had dropped down from a tree to warn the young sir that no good could come of it, to get himself to church. Typically, John ignored the witch and, rod over shoulder, continued on his way. Later, having caught no fish, he went hunting along the banks of the River Wear, and there he found a strange nest, a tangled mess of stones, twigs and shells. He plucked out a bright green snake-like creature. In disgust, he threw the thing into a nearby well and went whistling back to hearth and hall.

Seven years later, John returned home from the crusades to find a giant wyrm wrapped around Penshaw Hill on his father's estate.

The story didn't exactly have a happy ending either. Not for the wyrm, at any rate. But Ben knew that such folk tales were mostly down to bravado. He called it the St George Syndrome. Men destroyed what they didn't understand and then liked to call themselves heroes. Looking at the suit, the Iron Maiden also came to mind. He might have reminded Bardolfe that for all human growth and advancement, sometimes they turned the spikes inward too . . .

These thoughts made him notice just how many weapons

lined the walls. Battleaxes and morning stars. Scimitars, halberds, pikes and clubs. Chain mail hung above a row of Norman helmets like warlike washing on a clothes line, and as Ben traipsed after the knight, leaving those chilling spikes behind, modern weapons crept into the mix: Jacobite grenades, flintlock pistols and Napoleonic muskets. Hell, there was even a Gatling gun. When it came down to hurting each other, there seemed no end to human ingenuity. All the same, he conceded Bardolfe's point. Remnants had been at fault just as much as humans. There were many aggressors among his own kind, those who had fought the expanse of the cities tooth and claw, and thwarted scientific advance with countless confusing enchantments. Some, like Mauntgraul, the White Dog, had even taken pleasure in resistance, razing towns and demanding virgins, giving the rest of them a bad name.

"King John and the barons had to do *something*," Bardolfe said, appearing to reach some inner conclusion. "Things couldn't carry on as they were. Surely you have to accept that the Pact saved the Remnants from extinction? There were so few of you left . . ."

Yes. Something had to be done about it. The King had summoned his advisers. By royal decree, John had founded the Curia Occultus, the Hidden Court. The high council was comprised of three divisions, military, ecclesiastical and – temporarily – magical. The administration of the Lore had fallen to the Guild, of course. The military arm. The knights. The descendant of whom, Sir Maurice Bardolfe, had just stopped before another painting.

This one was larger, grander, than the ancestral dragon slaying. The painting looked out on a midsummer's night – Uffington, 1215. The moon picked out a spindly horse etched in chalk atop a hillside – except it wasn't a horse, was it? Merely a crude but clever sketch of a winged beast that used to haunt those parts, long ago . . . Ben looked at the long table set up in the Manger, the lush dell that stretched below White Horse Hill. He looked at the scroll unfurled there, the quill in the knight's hand as he leant over it. Some of the gathered men wore tunic and hose, their casual attire signs of their faith. Others wore armour, the mistrust of fools . . .

One of the men had red hair. He stood among the others, a snake among apes, and whatever his qualms at the time, the artist's brush had swept them from his face, replacing them with a confident smile. The quill in his hand dripped with ink. The picture screamed *accord* and not *reluctance*.

The St George Syndrome again. It was so familiar, Ben almost laughed.

"The Magna Carta was not the only contract the King sealed that year." The pride was back on Bardolfe's face, a fire in wrinkled folds. "At least he put his seal to this one willingly. As agents of the King, my ancestors were right there at the heart of things, deliberating with the Remnant leaders. You argued for months, calling for all manner of amendments. In some cases, Remnants mounted a resistance and battles took place. Eventually, all of the leaders signed, including you. Lackland might not have complied with the Carta, but at least the Remnants have with the Pact."

"What choice did we have?" The shadows deepened on Ben's brow. "You said it yourself. In the end, we chose to survive."

Where they could, the Remnant leaders had commanded, cajoled and pleaded with the other members of their magical tribes to heed the wisdom of the proposal, to make peace and obey the Pact. And, weary of war and wanting to believe in the greater good, many had done just that. Witches put away their brooms. Wizards handed in their wands. Trolls stopped skulking under bridges. The Remnant leaders had stayed among humans, one representative from each tribe, sheltered by the Lore as long as the Fay's forsaken children pledged to keep the peace and live out their days in secrecy. Those who could agreed to exist in human form. Those who couldn't went into the wilderness, the Himalayas, the Rockies – even a Scottish loch. The rest had gone into the Long Sleep.

Ben was practically glaring now. "Hundreds of others were lulled. Sedated. *Banished*. Robbed of their place in history till such as a time as Remnants and humans could live in peace. Isn't that what the Pact states?" Bardolfe didn't answer, leaving Ben to snort. "The impossible future. Meanwhile, the Guild made busy turning us into myths. Don't make it sound so bloody heroic."

"Oh but it was." The old man shot a glance at Ben. "What is it you think we *do* here? Type up newsletters? Sit around playing bridge? With the Pact signed, it became our duty to uphold it, and that meant the monumental task of erasing you from history. In the Middle Ages, we spread tales and songs, the more unlikely the better. Throughout the Enlightenment, we cast doubt on your existence, put it all down to superstition, ignorant reactions to storms, comets, the aurora borealis. We flooded the markets with Jenny Hanivers, stitching frog heads, snake tails and bat wings together and pickling them in jars, which merchants claimed were proof of dragons. We gave them narwhal horns as proof of unicorns. Skate fins as proof of mermaids. No matter how cunningly made, whenever people exposed them as fakes – as they invariably did – the doubt would deepen and spread." Flecks of spit at the corner of his mouth revealed Bardolfe's passion. He shook his head, catching his breath. "Our work at the Court is *tireless*, but still incidents occur. Why, only this morning I read a report about mass hysteria in New York. A hundred-odd people swore blind that they saw a monster on the Brooklyn Bridge . . ." Reaching the end of the gallery, Bardolfe halted in the shadow of a bookcase and turned to Ben with a pointed look. "This devil is not as black as you paint him. The Guild is hardly House Fitzwarren. We, at least, tolerate your existence."

Ben shrugged that off, homing in on mention of the report. "So you *have* heard something."

Bardolfe smiled. "Fingers and pies, Mr Garston. Fingers and pies."

Ben was thinking of the jagged mouth in the face of the Javits Center, that sixty-foot-wide shattered grin that had worn police tape like lipstick. A mouth that kissed the Hudson dark, blowing no smoke, breathing no fire . . .

"Do you know why the CROWS tried to kill me?" He moved closer to the bookcase, crowding the old man against it. "Do you even care? You know, it would've been nice of you to ask."

"Well now, I'm sure you're going to tell me."

"Fulk said that the Pact was broken." *The Pact is null and void, Garston. You're not the only one any more.* "Babe Cathy agreed with him. And we both know there's only one way that could happen . . ."

He let this sink in, watching puzzlement weave across Bardolfe's face. Then the old man laughed, husky echoes bouncing off the books.

"Preposterous. You think that the Guild wouldn't have known? A disturbance in the Long Sleep? The Lore so dramatically breached?" The echoes fell to the floor like leaves. "Fulk Fitzwarren is wrong, old boy. His lust for vengeance has made him desperate. The CROWS, I imagine, are just trying to scare you."

"Hmm." Ben was not convinced. "And the Star of Eebe? The heist? I came here hoping for information."

"Ah yes, your African gem. Well, if it's information you're after, then information you shall have."

The bookcase was a rosewood giant soaring up to the cobwebbed heights, a narrow ladder propped against it. As Ben looked on, the elderly knight climbed a few rungs, wheezing and scuffing dust to the floor. His mottled hands caressed the shelves, brushing copies of the *Historia Regum*, the Gutenberg Bible, a gilded edition of *Le Morte d'Arthur*. The rows resembled a different kind of grin, a bared rictus of knowledge.

"I'm sure we kept a copy of *The Lost Jewels of Alkebulan*." Bardolfe gave a tut, his fingers straying over a missing tooth. "It was a first edition, one of a hundred printed on hand-made paper. Now where in buggery has that got to?"

"Do I look like a librarian?"

Bardolfe ignored him, his crabby expression descending from the gloom.

"Well, I'm afraid that's all we have on old African artefacts," he said. "It looks like we're fumbling in the dark."

"So you're saying you can't help me?"

The knight met Ben's gaze, tapping his lips for a moment. Then a light came on behind his eyes and he clicked his clothes-peg fingers.

"As it happens, you're in luck. Tomorrow night, Professor Winlock, the noted archaeologist, is giving a talk at the British Museum. It's all very hush-hush, of course. An exclusive event for the Society. He's putting his private collection on display and was kind enough to invite me. I'm afraid I can't make it, but I'm sure with a phone call I could send you instead." Bardolfe nodded, as if trying to convince himself. "If you want to know about long-lost treasures, Winlock is your man. But . . . are you sure you want to go to all that trouble? I mean, what you've just told me, Fulk's claim – it honestly is absurd."

Ben might have turned away then, chalked Fulk's attack up to desperation, Babe's threat to bluster and ravings. He might have let the house and the coven keep their gem, if they were the ones who had stolen it, and flown back to America, tried to patch things up with Rose. Like cards in a deck, he might have packed all these players away – witches, slayers and knights – and gone back to his everyday life, drinking, growing bored and waiting for calls from prospecting criminals . . .

He heard Fulk Fitzwarren in his skull, a hoarse, boastful challenge.

You're asleep, Red Ben. You've been asleep for centuries.

He remembered the symbol etched on his door, a stark, knowing calling card.

And he saw something in Bardolfe's eyes, a flicker of insincerity. Something that had at first escaped him.

Doubt.

"I'll go," he said. "But what if I have more questions?"

"Then you'll have to take them up with my secretary." Bardolfe was all business again. "I have a flight to Cairo in the morning. I'm going to watch the syzygy."

Another strange word. "The scissor *what*?"

"The Egyptian eclipse. I'm attending a bash with some astronomer friends of mine. Even old knights need holidays, you know." He reached up to pat Ben's shoulder. "Go and see Winlock at the museum. I'll let him know you're coming. One conversation with him and I'm sure your little quest will reach its end."

Ben stared at the knight for a moment, then sighed and nodded. If this was the only thread on offer, he guessed he would have to take it.

"And you can send me a cheque for the window."

SIX

In dreams, Ben saw Rose. Before obelisks. Before doubt. The day they met.

In hindsight, he should have heeded the north-east wind blowing against him as he made his way back from Gowanus over to Atlantic Avenue. The February cold whipped off the Bay like a giant hand pushing him back, slapping his cheeks and pinching his ears. He wasn't in the best of moods. He was only in Brooklyn on a clean-up mission, and one that had left a sour taste in his mouth. Remnants tended to live long lives and sometimes, alone and isolated, the odd one or two would go a little cuckoo, as in the case of Gard Jordsønn. Gard had come from a long line of flesh eaters, tracing back to the cave-dwelling trolls of Norway, who had since all gone into the Sleep, leaving their nocturnal descendant to make his lonely way in the world. He had sailed across the sea and found employment in a Brooklyn scrapyard. He'd generally kept himself out of trouble until, as was often the case, the modern world came creeping in, the isolation becoming too much. Eventually he had caved in to hunger and started dining on the local residents, something the Guild just wouldn't stand for, and so they had charged Ben with the task. Ben found the troll weeping and wringing his big grey hands in a filthy hole near the Carroll Street Bridge, and after a brief debate about the Old Lands, he had performed an ad hoc cremation and left the neighbour-hoods of Gowanus, Prospect Heights and Red Hook to sleep easier in their beds.

Dispatching fellow Remnants, whatever their proclivities, didn't tend to put a spring in his step. Nevertheless, these necessary evils were part and parcel of the Pact, a drawback of upholding the Lore. Without them, all hell would break loose. He was thinking these thoughts, the wind resisting his stride along Atlantic Avenue, when he had come across the bookstall. A laden trestle table rested on the sidewalk at the bottom of the steps to an old and obviously ailing library, the sunken brownstone cake of a building sandwiched between used-furniture stores and chintzy-looking boutiques. The stacks were high and teetering, and some of the books shared their stories with the sky, their covers flip-ping back and forth in the intermittent gusts. His hand was already up, a *no thank you* on his lips, when the woman stepped forward to shake her bucket at him.

"Hey, mister, come on." And before he knew it, she was standing in his way. "Surely you can spare a couple of bucks for the Crown Heights orphanage? The cutbacks could be shutting us down soon and, well, these kids gotta eat."

He would like to think that he stopped due to a sense of charity. Charity that reached out like a gracious spirit and pressed lightly, ever so lightly against his lips, pursing the profanity there. Maybe it was down to the stray curl of gold that dangled from under the woman's woolly hat, or the way she planted her pumps on the pavement, a guard forbidding entrance. Maybe it was her winter-cloud eyes looking up and assessing him, her lips closing, her smile becoming a disappointed line, finding him wanting.

"I'm sorry, I'm . . ."

Maybe it had nothing to do with looks at all.

"Busy, sure." And she was pissed. He could see that. "Don't let me interrupt your life or anything. What's a few homeless brats, right? Have a nice day."

She was turning away, bucket, gold, grey and all, when he reached out and touched her gently on the shoulder.

"Hey, that's not fair," he said. "Can't a guy just walk down the street any more?"

She didn't apologise. She didn't even look at him. For the woman called Rose, a name he would come to learn like a song, Ben no longer existed. Or if he did, it was just as someone to shrug at, to quickly dismiss. Some kind of urban troll . . .

"Some folks have it harder, is all. It doesn't take much to . . ."

Bergamot drifted on the air; her perfume, he guessed, spiced by annoyance. Common sense said it was wrong. He knew it was wrong. Drawbacks to the Lore forgotten, he said it anyway.

"Tell you what, I'll make you a deal. OK?"

She glanced at him, cool and wary, and spoke to the passing traffic in the road.

"A deal? What kind of deal?"

"Shelter from this goddamned wind for starters. A five-minute coffee across the street."

"Mister, are you serious? Can't you see I'm—"

"And I'll make a donation. I promise."

"You will, huh?" She shook her head, smiling. Then the winter clouds returned. "My time is worth a couple of bucks. Is that what you think?"

He stood there, basking in her Brooklynite sass and her open suspicion. He hadn't failed to notice the way she glanced at the other collectors working by the stall. The flip-flapping books. Obviously considering.

"No, I don't think that at all. I'll buy every last one of these books."

"*All* of them? Are you nuts?"

"No," he said, and he told his first lie. "I'm just your average, ordinary guy."

Later – with the taste of mocha still on her lips and a niggling attraction tugging at her mind, or so she had once told him – Rose had looked in her plastic bucket and found the million-dollar cheque. He'd imagined she'd have a hundred questions and maybe even feel laughed at, so he had written his number on the back.

Wednesday morning. Rain swept a curtain over the city. Drizzle hushed against the window, a persistent visitor, rousing Ben from whiskey-tinged sleep. He woke up on the couch in the lounge with centuries of history spinning around his head, narrated by Sir Maurice Bardolfe. That and the vague memory of bergamot drifting on a February wind. Surprise surprise, he was naked again, his borrowed raincoat lying in tatters somewhere on Hampstead Heath. At least the streets had been dark when he'd come home, but all these transformations were going to cost him. One of these days, he was going to get caught. He stretched, yawned, scratched his balls and flicked on the TV. The news-reader delivered Armageddon with a smile. Three minutes of breakfast news and he flicked the TV off again. Who needed a morning dose of depression? He felt low enough as it was.

Barrow Hill Road no longer felt safe. He knew he would have to get over that. There was no easy way to relocate the hoard. Anyway, discretion versus valour aside, he wasn't about to run and hide. Let his midnight visitor enter his lair. Let whoever it was find out what that meant when he woke up and caught them . . . He went into the bathroom and took a leak. Then he went to brush his teeth but found no toothbrush or paste. There wasn't even soap for a shower, and he rubbed his copper stubble in annoyance. Life wanted him dirty, unable to wash away his fears. Entering his supposed bedroom for the first time in a year, he pulled on some jeans and a hoodie, found a cap and some brand-new trainers, forgotten in a box. In the kitchen, his ablutions consisted of a cold flannel over his face and a healthy slug of Jack.

As the liquor warmed him, Ben closed his eyes and remembered Bardolfe's invitation, the card trembling in the old man's hand before he'd departed Paladin's Court, leaving gouges in the lawn. With no way to carry such a delicate item without travelling home half naked by taxi, Ben had committed the card to memory. If he could recall eight hundred and sixty years, what were a few embossed lines? He was familiar with the British Museum, of course. He had only needed the time and the floor. Bardolfe might think there was nothing to fear. Ben wasn't so sure. In the Legends bar, Fulk had meant business. On the Brooklyn Bridge, so had the CROWS. The slayer and the witch at least *believed* that some event had broken the Pact, and obviously it had something to do with the stolen Star. Fulk had boasted that Ben wasn't alone any more. Babe Cathy had mentioned another, some mysterious *she. Revenge drives her on* . . . Apparently the Lore held no weight for either of them; they had attacked him without hesitation. Then there was the doubt on Bardolfe's face. Ben reckoned that the Guild were out of touch, shut away in their ivory tower in NW3, as far removed from current events as the Lambton armour from public display. No matter how Bardolfe dismissed Fulk's claim, Ben wasn't prepared to risk it. Maybe this Professor Winlock could shed some light on things, pluck him from his growing confusion and put him on the path to the truth.

In the meantime, Ben did what any self-respecting myth would do under the circumstances. He went shopping.

Making use of an old travel card found in a kitchen drawer, he caught the tube to Belgravia, where his private bank, the Blain Trust, kept their humble headquarters. Dealing with high-street banks only led to complications, the regular drafting of fake wills creating a paper chain to his existence. It was bad enough securing identities across the ages, let alone having to attend his own funerals, pretending he was some long-lost cousin or foreign nephew, the sole beneficiary of a grand and ancient fortune. The Blain Trust understood his situation. In many ways, the company shared it. A dwarf chieftain ran the small Chapel Street office, dwarves being one of the few Remnant groups that could fit into modern society completely undetected. Beards counted for a lot. Tight lips counted for more. Ben trusted the bank implicitly. Dwarves were natural-born financiers, and Delvin Blain, CEO, had helped Ben out of more than one scrape in the past. Blain filtered Ben's wealth into several offshore accounts and forged the necessary documents to support his life in the modern world. It was hard to call the treasurer a friend – he was much too gruff for that – but given a choice, Ben would have chosen the Remnant's trust over any institution in the City, which gambled freely with people's cash and never picked up the bill.

He spent half an hour in Blain's cramped office, explaining his recent cash-flow problem to a man who looked more like a walnut and his leggy human assistant. The dwarf tended to favour tall blondes. A password was merely a formality, but Ben gave it anyway and emerged back on to Belgrave Square with a freshly printed plastic card and a six-figure credit limit. Buoyed up, he braved the drizzle and walked the twenty minutes to Knightsbridge, where he took a detour into the library and delved into the reference section, sniffing out a decent dictionary.

First, he looked up *syzygy*, trying several spellings until he hit the right one:

Syzygy/sizziji/ n. 1. *Astron*. Conjunction or opposition, esp. of the moon with the sun. 2. A pair of connected or correlated things.

Then he went looking for *skent*, and this time his search took him straight to the counter, where, after some contemplation, the woman who sat there told him the correct spelling of the word.

Pschent/skent/ n. The double crown worn by Ancient Egyptian kings, symbolic of dominion over Upper and Lower Egypt, previously known as two separate kingdoms.

The Egyptian connection wasn't lost on him. What was the New York exhibition called? Nubian Footprints. Nubia as in northeast Africa. And then there was Bardolfe, trotting off to watch the eclipse – the syzygy – in Cairo. Ben mulled over the coincidence in the crowds milling through Beauchamp Place, shoppers, tourists and beggars jostling like Trafalgar Square pigeons over scattered seed. He came up with nothing but more anxiety, but at least now he knew what Babe Cathy had been on about on the Brooklyn Bridge. He made sure to bear it in mind.

These whispers from the past made everything around him seem about as enduring as smoke. It only seemed an eye-blink ago that the buildings around him had been a woodland hamlet, home to one of Longshanks' mansions and a rickety "knight's bridge" that crossed the River Westbourne. Later, grandeur had come strutting into the suburb, snapping its glamorous fingers at the place and demanding grand oriental exhibitions and white stucco-fronted houses. Through it all, people had come and gone, in girdle, tunic and tux, rising and falling as quickly as flowers in a sped-up film, each one taking their turn while Ben watched them all blossom and fade, blossom and fade . . .

In this day and age, the River Westbourne ran underground and the robbers who had once haunted the bridge ran the local shops. London was playing a new allegro, a jumbled medley of the ages. Ben learnt the steps of the dance, trudging along the chewing-gum- and litter-strewn pavement. In amongst the Tudor relics, the decrepit survivors of the Great Fire, Christopher Wren's classic dome competed with the thrust of Gherkin and Shard. The streets he walked were a living museum, one he often found hard to look at, the memories crowding his mind as he strolled into Knightsbridge, Georgian houses filling the spaces where trees, meadows and maidens once rolled. To the north, the Hyde Park Barracks reared its ugly, crate-like head, the final nail in the coffin of *scenic*.

For all the changes around him, Ben took a strange kind of comfort in them. He lingered on a street corner to breathe it all in, the fumes and the noise, reminding himself . . . London remained a dragon's city. A dragon hadn't graced the Royal Arms of England since the reign of Good Queen Bess, but dragons still clutched the shield of London and guarded the City gates, the most elaborate statue rendered in bronze atop a memorial in Temple Bar. George still fought his dragon at St John's Church, and several dragons stood sentry on the Holborn

Viaduct, their red and silver flanks adorning the bridge. A dragon still carried a cannon on its back in Horse Guards Parade, and a dragon still hung in the National Gallery, the old painting by Uccello showing England's greatest patron about his usual business, beast slaying and damsel rescue. Dragons still danced on the Chinatown gates, spitting fire at evil spirits. Across the city – the *dragon* city – the beasts played out their time-worn roles of menace and mascot, peril and protector, resplendent in stone, metal and paint. Ben shook his head, striding out into the traffic with a sense of greater confidence (and without feeling overly concerned whether a cyclist smashed into him or not). The Thames Valley had suited his kind long before anyone had called it that, and the Great Fire aside, there were reasons why some folks called London the Smoke . . .

London roared and honked in his ears. Shops promised everything from dream holidays to endless beauty and Ben didn't believe a word of it. He made his way along Brompton Road, brushed by businessmen and avoiding the glances of gum-chewing girls. For a brief time he could pretend that he was one of them, some red-stubbled hunk strutting down the road, his lips set wryly in his strong jaw, his hair casually mussed, his everyday clothes hiding more than muscle.

In Gieves & Hawkes, he ignored the assistant's sceptical stare and selected a single-breasted gabardine suit. The dark, tightly woven fabric whispered *class* under his hands. The shoes he picked out were Italian. The cufflinks gold. He drew a line at a bow tie and chose a straight one instead, green silk to match his eyes. After this minor dent in his credit card, and equipped for the evening ahead, he stopped to eat a vegetarian wrap and fling some toiletries into a basket along with a fresh bottle of Jack, before heading back home.

For a while, these mundane chores stopped him from thinking about his predicament. But not for long enough. Whatever he would like to believe, or however Bardolfe had dismissed the notion, Ben sensed that his life was in danger.

The symbol etched on his stout red door wouldn't let him forget it.

SEVEN

Wednesday night. Ben arrived late at the museum. He hurried through the gates and up the steps, passing under the famous Greek pediment, the sculptures above him depicting *The Progress of Civilisation*. On the left side of the pediment, Man emerged from primal rock as a barbaric, ignorant being. After meeting an angel, a spirit holding the Lamp of Knowledge, Man spanned the carved tableau through a series of acquired skills – painting and science, geometry and drama, music and poetry – until he arrived on the right side of the pediment as Educated Man, learned enough to dominate the world. Someone had explained the scene to Ben years ago and he still had mixed feelings about it. Progress for some, it seemed, always meant decline for others.

He gave his name to an usher in the entrance hall, relieved to find that Sir Maurice Bardolfe had made good on his phone call. The usher led him through the Great Court, their footsteps echoing across acres of polished white tiles. A hundred feet over their head stretched the largest covered roof in Europe. The old reading room, a round white hub edged by broad, curving steps, threw out a tessellated web, a triangulate marvel of steel and glass that made a prison of the dusk. The lights were low, the museum closed to the general public, and Ben passed obelisks and totem poles, relics looming from the settling gloom. The Great Court was a juxtaposition of old and new, the courtyard walls lined with the façades of ancient temples. Despite his qualms about progress, it remained an impressive sight.

He bypassed Enlightenment and headed toward Living and Dying. The usher left these exhibits behind, hurrying downstairs into the education centre. Here, the caterers fussed over long tables laden with ice buckets, pyramids of glasses and trays of canapés for the after-show bash. Ben guessed he would have to corner Winlock with his questions. The usher directed him into the lecture theatre, and after finding a half-empty row in the darkened auditorium (and apologising to a hissing couple for half crushing their toes), he settled down to watch the professor.

"It was strange to return to Egypt after all those years," Winlock was saying, his bald head shining under the stage lights, a tanned, erudite egg. "But how could I forget Kamenwati's tomb? We stumbled across it in the mid-sixties, during the construction of the Aswan Dam. Of course, the Dam left many ruins underwater, and several important sites, including Abu Simbel, were dismantled block-by-block and shifted to higher ground. No mean feat, as you can imagine. The largely man-made Lake Nasser, while ending Egypt's dependence on the flooding of the Nile, drowned more than its fair share of tombs. Only a few survived, and when the Royal Society agreed to fund my return last year, I hardly expected Kamenwati's to be waiting for me, let alone with door intact."

The audience was rapt. Sitting like a schoolboy in his gabardine suit, backside shifting in the fold-down seat, Ben's discomfort felt like a flare blazing over his head. No one around him was munching popcorn. No one was necking in the back row. He didn't belong here, adrift in this sea of gold-rimmed spectacles and twinkling jewellery. Expensive cologne and choice perfume spiced the scholarly air. He could almost hear the surrounding brain cells bubbling. Wealth, of course, didn't auto-matically mean refinement – and in Ben's case, his acumen stemmed from experience rather than study. He knew his history because he had lived through a fair portion of it, but he was far from what anyone would call academic. London was a hot-ticket town, but for all tonight's exclusivity Ben wouldn't have paid to see Winlock speak, so it surprised him that in no time at all the little man on stage had absorbed him so completely.

"Baba Kamenwati was a priest in the New Kingdom, near the beginning of the Eighteenth Dynasty. He served under his master, the First Prophet of Amun, during the reign of Hatshepsut, the longest-reigning female pharaoh, over three and a half thousand years ago." Professor Winlock let this sink in, smiling in appreciation of his subject. "Was there ever a more famous queen? One more beloved of her people?"

Ben wondered. He could think of several, from Eleanor of Aquitaine to Victoria, both of whom he'd had the pleasure of meeting on different occasions, distant adventures many years ago. Hatshepsut was aeons before his time and he'd never heard of her before. All around him, expensive hairstyles and finely combed beards were nodding along and he was tempted to join in, make out he wasn't the dunce he felt he was.

"After the death of her husband," Winlock said, "Hatshepsut was made regent to rule for her stepson, Thutmose III, until the young man came of age. Nevertheless, this was not enough for her and she soon took the unprecedented step of declaring herself pharaoh, taking up the title of king. Fearless and proud, she insisted she was as fit to rule as any man."

Dunce or no, Ben couldn't fail to be impressed.

"And she proved it. Despite the expected uproar that usually meets usurpers, Hatshepsut's reign was a golden one, a time of peace and prosperity, filled with magnificent art and a host of ambitious building projects, the greatest of which was Deir el-Bahari, her mortuary temple near the Valley of the Kings." Winlock, a pristine figure in his white tuxedo, twitched his blonde horseshoe moustache and tapped the screen behind him with a stick. The projected image showed the entrance to a tomb. Thick yellow pillars stood on either side of the egress, half submerged in muddy water. The bank around the shadowed mouth bore the scars of recent excavation. "Baba Kamenwati was a favourite of this illustrious ruler, at least to begin with. The hieroglyphs outside his tomb tell us as much."

Ben squinted to see them, the outline of owl and lion, bowl and flame, hand and . . . whatever that was – the flaking symbols of a long-forgotten language. Some of the symbols had been scratched out.

Winlock's face grew serious, his tone darkening.

"Now, the Ancient Egyptians strongly believed in life after death. It was a complex system and I won't bore you with the details. In a nutshell, they preserved dead bodies so that the departed soul – the *ba* – could make use of them again in the afterlife, the supernatural worlds beyond our own. Once in the Duat, the Egyptian underworld, the jackal-headed god Anubis weighed the hearts of the deceased against *ma'at*, the feather of truth. If the heart didn't tip the scales, Anubis deemed the *ba* pure and the soul walked into the Fields of Yalu, there to live out eternity in peace. But if the heart was heavy with sin and the scales tipped, Anubis summoned Ammit, Devourer of Souls – a half-dog, half-crocodile demon – who consumed the corrupted soul, condemning it to endless suffering." The professor cleared his throat, betraying what he thought of these primitive beliefs. "For all his apparent devotion, Baba Kamenwati was secretly subversive, and later on, he came to be seen as a dangerous heretic. Behind closed doors, he worshipped Anubis, and not just as the Lord of the Underworld and the Judge of the Dead, but as the lord of *all* gods, superior to Ra himself."

This didn't surprise Ben. He'd lived long enough to know that where gods were concerned, some folks liked to play mix-and-match with entire pantheons, favouring the ones that served their needs best.

"All Egypt revered death in those days," Winlock went on. "Kamenwati took the notion one step further and established the underground 'jackal cult', a cabal of priests dabbling in the black arts, in sex magick and necromancy. The cult made sacrifices in the temple, sending countless infants to the flames, cutting out hearts on altars of stone. At the height of his power, Kamenwati was the most feared man in Egypt. He wanted to conquer death and live forever in this world, defying Ra and escaping the afterlife. Hatshepsut, once she came to learn of this ambition, could not allow such evil to continue. She sent guards to the Karnak temple and Kamenwati to the god he loved most.

"Of course, we only learnt all this once we had broken into the tomb. The hieroglyphics inside left us in little doubt that we had opened a lost chapter in history . . ."

The image on the screen changed, a window on to another land. The scene showed Winlock and his team knee-deep in muddy water, spades held high before the shattered tomb door. *Open Sesame.* Ben imagined the heat beating down on the desert sands and glittering off the lake, which lapped against the tomb as though to quench the thirst of the dead.

"Picture it." Winlock puffed out his chest, a trim white bird. "I felt like Howard Carter must have felt in 1922 at the entrance to King Tut's tomb. Was I worried about curses? Execration texts and poison boxes? No, not really. It was 2015 and I was much too excited. We stood there on the threshold of time, about to plunder the treasures of the past. And, by George, what treasures we found."

A spotlight blinked on, illuminating a thin pedestal on the left side of the stage. A silver burial mask shone upon it. The audience *oohed*, a wave of awe. The mask resembled a hollow-cheeked face, no piety in its expression. It was a simple but beautiful ornament, cleansed of the muck of ages – and surely unfit for a priest who had gone to his death in disgrace . . .

Winlock appeared to read Ben's mind.

"The tomb itself shows the esteem with which the Pharaoh regarded Kamenwati. Or more precisely, the *fear*." Winlock took a sip of water from a table beside him, pausing for effect. "Egypt was always a land of superstition. Considering Kamenwati's obsession with death, it's hardly surprising that Hatshepsut feared some kind of posthumous revenge. She might even have feared Anubis himself. After all, she *had* killed his foremost earthly ambassador. And so, despite Kamenwati's sacrilege, Hatshepsut interred the priest with all the trappings befitting his station. The tomb boasts beautifully painted scenes, depicting life in the Karnak temple. We discovered cartouches with the Pharaoh's name, revealing that the *sem* priests embalmed Kamenwati with Hatshepsut's blessing, and there are only two or three pictograms describing his crimes. Of course, his downfall would have been an embarrassment to both the temple and the royal family. It only makes sense that they would try to hush it up."

The image on the screen changed again, revealing the interior of the tomb. It didn't look like much to Ben, just a narrow chamber letting in diffuse sunlight, shining on dull and crumbling walls. Brown water pooled everywhere. Columns leant from the swamp like guards caught napping on the job. Faded frescos lined the walls – there an eye, a scarab or cat – and rows of illegible prayers, winged gods, worn renderings of Nile life. Fascinated by the history, he was disappointed by the actual tomb. He found it hard to imagine anyone plucking riches from it. He looked at the impassive silver mask on the pedestal again, and then another spotlight was blinking on.

"Mostly what we found was rot, the usual offerings for the dead. Wooden carvings, canopic jars and fossilised food. All decayed beyond restoration. I think you'll agree that our team did a great job on the mask." This prompted murmured assent. "Nevertheless, these magic bricks you see before you were an even greater find. Not only do they support the theory of the Pharaoh's fear, they are quite unlike any other find to date."

The spotlight shone on another pedestal, this one in the middle of the stage. Four statuettes, their bases rough and rectangular, rested upon it. Winlock clicked a button on his stick and the screen zoomed in for a close-up.

"The ancients placed these bricks in tombs to protect the dead from their enemies. They usually depict the sons of Horus, the god of protection. Positioned at the chamber's cardinal points – north, east, south and west – each brick bore a spell from the *Book of the Dead*, binding the deceased to Anubis, guiding the *ba* into the underworld." Winlock frowned, recalling some former puzzlement. "But these bricks are different. They don't depict gods, but *demons*. Here we see Ammit, Devourer of Souls. Apep, the Lizard. Shezmu, the Executioner. And Set, the Oppressor. Now you must understand, no archaeologist had ever seen such a thing. We discussed the matter long into the night and could only reach the vague conclusion that the *sem* priests had placed these bricks in the tomb to prevent the *ba* from *leaving*, to block its path into the afterlife. Many things in Kamenwati's tomb turned our former knowledge on its head."

Ben studied the figures on the screen, these fierce spiritual guardians. In their chipped, crumbling forms, he saw crocodile jaws and bird claws, forked tongues and cobra hoods, leonine manes and simian fangs. Set the Oppressor, the tallest of them, had a long curved snout like an aardvark, which crowned his muscular human body. The clay chimeras were primal nightmares, obviously designed to terrify, but seeing the human mixed with the bestial Ben shifted a little in his seat, reluctant to accept his sense of empathy. And his reflex disdain.

How human beings love their monsters.

"After three thousand years, and twice as many floods?" Ben heard Winlock say, responding to a question from the audience. "No, there was no mummy. All we found was mud, I'm afraid. Mud in the bottom of a cracked sarcophagus."

Another latecomer roused Ben from his thoughts. The auditorium doors swung wide and a slender silhouette entered through the brief rhombus of light. The doors swung closed again – *now you see me, now you don't* – and people craned their necks back to the stage, all ears for the impromptu Q&A session breaking out on the front row, flustering the little professor. The row Ben sat in vibrated gently as the latecomer found her way to the end seat, eight or nine spaces over from his. Glancing to his left, he saw a shapely shadow standing in the gloom, a shadow among shadows. Keen eyesight zeroing in, he could tell that she was African, the light from the screen reflecting off her skin. His gaze rolled over her tall frame, her hair plaited in threadlike rows. The style suited her sharply boned face and long neck, both turned regally to watch the stage. The dress she wore was dark and close-fitting, perfectly moulded to her breasts and bum, and a lump jumped into Ben's throat as the woman sat down in one fluid motion, oiled silk in the gloom.

Sensing his stare, she shot him a look. Proud. Dismissive. Cold. She folded her hands and sat forward, her lithe form oddly tense, head raised as she listened to Winlock.

"Ladies and gentlemen, please." The professor held up his hands, his moustache twitching. "I'll gladly answer all of your questions at the end of my presentation. In the meantime, allow me to show you the last of our finds. A relic that leaps from the pages of myth . . ."

A spotlight winked on in the middle of the stage. Raised at an angle on a velvet tray, a thin white object rested on yet another pedestal. Its cylindrical shape glowed in the radiance, lending it a mystical sheen. Gold glittered around the object, an inlaid filigree twist. Carved hieroglyphics edged the gilding, its polished length culminating in an arch, an almost-but-not-quite circle, like the handle of a walking stick, a needle's eye or . . .

A shepherd's crook.

A tongue of ice licked Ben's spine.

Star, Crook and Pschent. Star, Crook and Pschent. Wasn't that what the witch had chanted on the Brooklyn Bridge? Star, Crook and Pschent. And hadn't he, familiar with the common use of the word, assumed that Babe Cathy had been on about criminals? Perhaps the thief who smashed into the Javits Center?

Yes. He had. But here was another connection, tenuous and teasing. Just how many pieces made up this puzzle?

". . . which we were only sure of once our zoologists dated the ivory to the fifteenth century BC." Winlock was speaking again, nudging Ben from his thoughts. "The ivory is African, of course, originating in lands around the Horn. In olden days, southern Egypt and the Sudan comprised a vast kingdom known

115

as Nubia. South of Nubia lay the legendary Land of Punt, an unmapped, savage realm ruled by tribal kings and queens. The powers that some texts attribute to them amount to the wildest folklore – the ability to turn tides, crush mountains, control the weather and so on – typical primitive poppycock. It's likely that these kings and queens encouraged such notions themselves, striking fear into their neighbours, Egypt, Kush and Ophir.

"These days, we know Punt as Somalia and its reputation is tragic rather than grand. Still, the hieroglyphs carved on the *heqa* – the crook-staff, shaped to form a symbol meaning *ruler, prince, chief*, et cetera – relate a time of healing, of restoration and great prosperity. The hieroglyphs also claim that the crook can command the most powerful magic. No one is sure how Kamenwati came by it or why we should find it in his tomb. Considering his extracurricular activities, our team dubbed it the Jackal's Crook . . ."

Polite laughter rippled through the throng. No doubt the Society had heard such stories before, chalking them up to superstition or dewy-eyed romance. Ben thought it must feel great to be so sure of the world and its limits, to laugh off angels as cloud formations and ghosts as tricks of the light. While he envied the crowd's peace of mind, he did not envy their ignorance. Their self-assurance was a double-edged sword, one that granted comfort and security but blinded them to the truth.

The gulf between Ben's world and theirs was an abyss that could easily swallow him, if he let it. Here he was, a myth sat among ordinary mortals as they scoffed at the notion of magic, talents that stretched beyond the mundane. But any wizard or witch drawing on the astral substance of the nether would have scoffed at the crowd's arrogance. Ben found it somewhat disorienting.

He didn't have time to dwell on the matter. The row he sat in was shaking, vibrating with unseen force. Rivets creaked, straining against the floor, a persistent hum filling his ears. *A tremor? In London?* The spotlights stuttered and blinked, beaming through the dust motes. Up on stage, Professor Winlock took a step forward and steadied the pedestal bearing the Crook, the pull-down screen flapping behind him. A growing babble rose from the audience, panicked birds about to take flight.

Glancing around him, Ben caught sight of the woman at the end of the row. He had got it wrong. The dress she wore wasn't tight at all. She wasn't *wearing* a dress. Naked, she sat stiff and straight-backed, her fists clenched and her body trembling. Even in the gloom, he could see rage and pain battling across her pantherine features.

"*Tuug.*" The guttural word stabbed the air and she spat its meaning immediately after. "*Thief.*"

Like shadow, like smoke, she rose and stepped into the aisle.

The tremors increased, juddering under Ben's feet as he stood up, the fold-down seat snapping back. A familiar smell hit his nostrils, a blown fuse, an overheated plug, mixed with a raw, carnal undertone, an ionic, sentient storm. The stench had filled his lounge the other night, coupled with a mockery of footprints, laughter sketched in the dust. *I can walk freely in your lair.* He remembered the rune etched on his door, a forgotten wyrm-tongue glyph, and he looked in horror at the woman.

This was no earthquake, but the reverberation of magical force, feedback whining from the nether. Experience told him as much. And the woman was clearly its focal point. Static poured from her, tugging his hair and nipping his flesh, engulfing him like a swarm of mosquitoes. The prickling air enveloped her, *galvanised* her, and she slid forward, her feet floating inches off the ground. Sapphires danced in her eyes. Sparks cascaded from her outstretched arms, sizzling on the aisle carpet.

Was she a witch? Some kind of ghost? Ben was too stunned to guess.

The audience erupted. He fought his way through the stampede. The great and the good of the Royal Society surged toward the exit, bottlenecked into a jostling stew. Gold-rimmed spectacles crunched underfoot. Necklaces snapped, spilling jewels. Perfume and cologne curdled into a cloying morass. The auditorium shook with the thunder of feet, the soundproofed walls absorbing shouts and screams for help. People scrambled over the seats, some gasping and falling between the rows, sinking under the human tide. Others climbed over them, clawing at arms and legs for leverage, hands and high heels pressing on flesh. The crowd choked in the open double doors, the light from the foyer beyond casting a shadow play across the screen onstage, before which Winlock quailed, clutching the Jackal's Crook to his chest.

The woman, borne aloft on crackling tongues, was heading straight for him.

"*Ey!*" Her alien cry split the air. "*Jiir!*"

The words meant nothing to Ben. All the same, her fury was plain. Struggling past the press of bodies and into the aisle, he watched her rise, sailing upwards on ropes of lightning, the bright blue zigzagging strands bearing her slender weight. Sparks played in her braided hair, circling her breasts, trickling between her thighs. Rushing after her, Ben came up against a wall of pressure, ethereal, magnetic, slowing his pursuit. His tie flailed over his shoulder, his jacket flapping open. Alkaline force stung his nose and throat, the taste as sour, as organic as blood. Gritting his teeth, he forced himself on, reaching out for the woman's feet as she hovered over the stage.

Winlock, his lecture forgotten, was a china doll awaiting her judgement. He waved the Crook feebly before him, too frightened to run.

When the woman spoke next, Ben understood. The word was English, cold, and brooked no denial.

"*Mine*."

She moved forwards just as his hand closed, her ankle slipping beyond his grasp.

"I am Atiya, Queen of Punt." Her voice crackled, a detuned radio dropped down a well. "The *heqa-siin* is mine."

Professor Winlock sank to his knees, static dancing all around him. Sweat glistened in his moustache. The Crook was an ivory blur as he held it out to the airborne woman. An offering. Amends. A surrender.

The woman who called herself queen frowned and clicked her tongue.

"No, *nacas*. You do not give. I *take*."

She reached out and snatched the relic. With her other hand she grabbed the lapel of Winlock's tux and wrenched him into the air with no more effort than if he were a book or a bag. Veins stood out on her arms, her muscles taut. Winlock went limp in her grasp, his capacity for awe capsizing his senses, and the woman flung him like so much trash into the auditorium. He landed in the fourth row. Bones cracked, a distinct sound that cut through the shouting in the theatre. Ben took a step in that direction and heard the little man groan. A weak sound, but at least he was alive.

Gall turned Ben back to the stage.

"Was that entirely necessa—"

The Queen wasn't listening. Eyes closed, she held the Crook in both hands, pressing the relic against her navel. Ben's breath caught in his throat as her torso grew transparent, the flesh swirling into thick black smoke, breaking apart vaporously. In the hollow of her navel, something glimmered, a fist-sized glassy object much like an uncut diamond.

The Star of Eebe?

The woman, Atiya, placed the Crook in her open gut. The smoke wove lacily back together, shadow stitching to shadow, and her navel was whole again, flat, sealed and bare. A sheen rippled over her breasts and into her face, and Ben observed a brief transparency – the Queen's face rounder and younger than before, as though she had dropped a gossamer veil. A childlike visage gazed out at him, precise cornrows on a bony skull, a wasted, desperate stare shining from a rich, dark face, a shared ethnicity with the blazing woman.

Then it was gone, replaced by spite. Atiya was looking down at him, her eyes an azure fire.

"What the hell are you doing?"

She didn't care for the question. A descending storm, she was on him in a second, swooping down from the stage. The surprise more than the impact threw him on to his back, the coruscating woman astride him. He tried to get up, but she gripped his wrists, pressing his arms against the ground. His spine arched, electricity jolting through him. The surrounding carpet crisped and charred. Ozone filled his nostrils, and the sweet stench of burning flesh. Clinging to consciousness, he focused on transformation, summoning a layer of protective scales, red rippling over pink flesh. The pain receded, but cerulean tongues licked all around him, promising incineration.

"Get . . . the fuck . . . off me . . ."

"Weak *mas*." Atiya spoke casually, as if they were nibbling canapés in the foyer outside rather than joined together in a scintillating death lock. "When I found your hiding place, I expected a challenge worthy of a queen. *Ha!*"

Ben grunted, thrashing under her.

"What do you want? How . . . did you find me?"

"I am serpent. I am huntress. I breathed in the air of your city. I caught a distant fire, a scent of embers. And I followed it like smoke in the desert."

Sparks flickered, dripping from her to him, a sputtering web enfolding them both. Caught in the strands, vague impressions passed between them, a chill, invasive transmission. Ben realised she was searching his mind, probing his innermost secrets. In return, he caught his own mental shreds, thoughts overflowing her cerebral brim. *Desert ruins half swallowed by sand. A young black girl in grimy football shorts. New York under the stars.* The images meant nothing to him, his pain the logic threading them together.

Atiya pressed against him, her eyes boring into his skull, sharp sapphire blades. Even in his torment, he could sense something sexual in their clinch, an animal friction hissing between them. Her thighs gripped him like a vice. Despite the pain, Ben felt himself growing hard. The Queen leant in closer, unmoved by his excitement.

"You are nothing." She hissed in his ear, a soft furnace between her lips. "You hide in your lair like a beaten dog, drunk and alone, shackled by the laws of men. You bring shame on all serpentkind."

Then she was off him and standing in the aisle.

"You are not even worth killing."

He looked up as she brought her fists together. She may as well have crossed live wires. A blinding bolt spluttered upwards, striking the theatre ceiling. With a tooth-jarring crunch, bricks and plaster showered down, peppering the vacant seats. Ben shielded his head, debris thumping down all around him. Through locked arms, he watched the Queen leap upward, thrust by lightning into the breach.

He was on his feet at once. The last of the crowd squeezed through the doors, falling over each other as the bottleneck broke, spilling people into the foyer. He heard tables crash over, pyramids of glasses fall and shatter, the screaming guests heading for the stairs. The ozone lingered, a bitter pall. Shaking himself from his stupor, Ben looked up at the ragged hole. Beyond the breach, a resounding clamour, charging through the museum above him. He grimaced. His thighs swelled into haunches, ripping through his trousers, half-formed reptilian legs bulging with mythical brawn. Claws, each one the size of a breeze block, made short work of his shoes. Between two states, bestial and human, he crouched, muscles flexing, and leapt up into the hole.

Past pipes and girders, snapped wires and ruptured marble, he came crashing into the light. His natural armour absorbed the worst of it. Chunks of concrete dribbled from his shoulders, clattering on the rubble-strewn floor. He was in the Great Court, the steel and glass roof a hundred feet above, triangulating the sky. From the stairs on his right, shouts and screams echoed to his ears, the birds of panic flurrying toward him. He wasn't concerned about them. His eyes were only for the great glass roof and the giant shadow swooping under it, scudding from one wall to another, its bulk turning in the yawning space like a whale trapped in a bay. Or a pterodactyl caught in a net.

Ben staggered backwards. He almost fell into the hole behind him and only saved himself by dropping to his knees. Speechless, he watched the Queen rush by over his head, circling the central reading room.

Against the surrounding marble, Atiya was an ink spill on pristine paper. Her sleek scales overlapped tightly, forming a hide so dark he could barely make out the separate sections. Her fore and rear legs hung under her belly, terminating in razor-sharp claws – one of which, he now realised, had no doubt left the glyph on his door. Tail lashing, she struck out at the sheer white walls, gouging powdery scars. Blades lined her body from snout to tip, a barbed, shimmering spine. As she made another turn, Ben stared into her eyes, each one ablaze with frustration. A tiara of twisting black horns, similar to those of a ram, edged her narrow, scabrous head. Immediately, this rack was bearing down on him.

Lightning crackled, scorching marble. Ben ducked, shielding his head, as Fulk Fitzwarren gloated in his mind.

The Pact is null and void, Garston. You're not the only one any more.

He looked up as the Queen, before him in bestial guise, navigated a final turn in the Court. Then she spread her wings, a sixty-foot span of leather casting the cavernous space in gloom. She beat them once, twice, propelling her bulk up into the tessellate web. Countless frames screeched and twisted. Glass rained down, smashing like hail on the ground. A section of the roof lifted, splitting upwards and apart, the burst skin of some metal fruit. Then she was through, her wings melting into the night.

Ben climbed to his feet, a shocked figure shaking his head.

You think that the Guild wouldn't have known? A disturbance in the Long Sleep? The Lore so dramatically breached?

Sir Maurice's words came back to haunt him. Here was the proof that put the lie to them, undeniable in scaled flesh. Here were the wings that had crashed into the Javits Center, leaving no trace of explosion or fire. Here was the reason for Fulk's attack and the CROWS' exultation. Here, in sharp claws and blazing eyes, Ben read his own death warrant.

There was another dragon in London.

EIGHT

Ben stood in his tattered suit at the top of the museum steps. Faux-Greek columns loomed on either side, supporting *The Progress of Civilisation*. Squeezing his neck like a wringer, his face taut with unease, he scanned the orange-tinged sky. Midweek traffic on Bloomsbury Street drowned out the fading beat of wings. Marble dust mixed with the lingering stench, an acrid, carbonised pall. Having claimed what she had come for, absorbing it into her flesh, Queen Atiya was gone. The night skies were empty.

This is just the beginning. She'll track down every last one of her gifts and kill anyone who gets in her way.

Like Fulk, Babe Cathy took a ride in his head these days. But the witch was out of luck in terms of her threat. He was still alive, wasn't he?

The Queen's presence answered a question, but she had left a dozen more in her wake. In his mind, the sixty-foot-wide jagged maw in the face of the Javits Center laughed even harder. So he could pick the thief out of a line-up; that didn't mean he understood her motive. *Mine*, she'd said. *The* heqa-siin *is mine*. And there was more to this, wasn't there? Because in all his years in this dirty old world, Ben had never seen the likes of her before. She was a dragon all right, but she wasn't quite . . . *typical*, her breed unknown to him. Just how far did the Lore extend? How deep did the Long Sleep go? And who the fuck had roused the Queen from slumber?

Only the Guild could give him these answers.

He looked over his shoulder, jogged from his thoughts as Winlock's guests burst from the museum. Hair in disarray, jewellery forgotten, they must have picked their way through the Great Court, avoiding the debris and choking on dust. One or two of them gawped at him, this ragged man who was at least a *man* again and not some flame-eyed freak from a late-night creature feature. He turned from them, arms dangling at his sides, his clenched fists making wires of his veins. Dust powdered his hair, dousing the spiky red mess, but even dust couldn't hide his dismay, his wide green eyes searching the sky, his jaw hanging open. The guests' shock rendered them immune to his presence, and they flitted past him and down the steps without a backward glance. Survival, the great mitigator. He watched the last of them vanish through the gates, staggering out into Great Russell Street. Tomorrow, the tabloids would scream bombs and fanatics. The *Daily Mail* would see a surge in new material.

Ben chewed his lip. What should he do? Take to the sky and follow the Queen? With Atiya's sudden appearance, this was a fight-to-the-death situation. Only one member of each Remnant group could officially function in the world. That was the Lore. Those were the rules. That was what had granted Fulk the right to attack him, publicly and without fear of censure. And soon enough, others would come, not just agents of the Guild, but the Whispering Chapter too, and who knew how many more previously restricted enemies? The Pact was a magically binding agreement, sealed by scroll, prayer and harp song eight hundred years ago. Broken by the Queen's awakening, how long would it take till the Chapter learnt of it? How long before that austere and pious arm of the Curia Occultus came baying for his blood?

So what then? Hunt the Queen down and demand answers? He might not be the Brain of Britain, but Ben knew better than that. As if she would suffer him. Engage her in single combat? When was the last time he'd fought one of his kind? Yen-King, China. Way back in the Middle Ages. Some beasts had resisted the Pact more violently than others, thrust kicking and screaming into the Long Sleep. The scars that Ben bore to this day wouldn't let him forget Mauntgraul in a hurry . . . But that had been centuries ago. He was out of practice, growing soft. To go up against someone his own size? Someone apparently stronger? Well, it didn't seem wise.

On a deeper, primal level, something ached in him besides bruises. He didn't want to admit it to himself, this niggling underlying feeling, one he could only define as *yearning*. Firm thighs pressed against his heat. Hot lips at his ear. *Animal attraction*. Despite his close shave in the lecture theatre, the coming of the Queen meant that he was no longer alone.

The thought made him feel weak. No. He wasn't ready to face her . . .

That left the treasure hunt. The quest. Find out more about these stolen relics and get a better idea of who, or what, he was dealing with. He recalled the witch's chant on the Brooklyn Bridge. It wasn't hard to guess where the Queen was heading. She'd be after the Pschent next, wherever it was. The *why* of things would have to wait. For now, he was living on borrowed time. He had never been keen on detective work. Perhaps it was time to visit a friend, if he could call the envoy extraordinary that. With Queen Atiya winging over London, it was clear that he was out of his depth.

He turned back to the museum, intending to check on Winlock and call an ambulance – maybe follow the professor to the hospital and wait to pump him for information – when a movement by the gates snagged his attention. One glance and he slowly turned to face the street again, drawn by a magnet of shock. The air rippled, gauze over water, a glimmer working across the space. Energy. Magical energy. Through the haze, he made out a figure between the gates, her blonde hair tied back in a ponytail. Her eyes blue and confused.

"Rose . . .?" At the sound of his voice, she turned towards him. The aqueous barrier rippled with the motion, a liquid mirage. *What trick is this?* The image was surely an illusion. Rose couldn't be here. Could she? Either way, he found himself running down the steps and across the flagstones, tie flapping and fists bunched. He made it halfway across the courtyard before the gates clanged shut ahead of him. *Close Sesame.* There was no one around to shut them. No one he could see, anyway. Rose, or the illusion of Rose, drifted into fog. Vanished. He looked up at the surrounding buildings, seeing only empty windows. The mirage ballooned to envelop him, the museum and the buildings sinking underwater, some latter-day urban Atlantis. The air felt thick and close, and growing colder than a witch's—

The thought slammed into him. He wasn't running any more because he couldn't move.

Fuck.

Ben looked down. He was standing in a circle, a broad hexagram sketched in chalk on the flagstones. Familiar symbols bordered the ring, scrawled white glyphs. Udjats and inverted crosses. Sun wheels and dead man's runes. All-seeing eyes and swastikas. An alphabet of adversity. The symbols flashed, stirring into life, activated by his presence. They revolved slowly, a sluggish zodiac fencing him in. When he tried to edge forward, it was like trying to walk through stone. Somewhere nearby, a woman was chanting. A man laughed, gloating and gruff. Bile rose in Ben's throat. Vertigo clawed at his guts. The symbols spun faster, an occult merry-go-round. The world became a blank white blur.

Ben slipped into the nothing.

Interlude: A Shadow at the Door

Hospitals, the shadow thought, *only delay the inevitable*.

In one room, a newborn gave her first cry. In the next, a cancerous grandfather spluttered out his last. A weeping woman entered A&E. A man left reception whistling. Somewhere in the spectrum, the revolving door of accident, healing, disease and decline, there lay a central truth: humans are fragile and all humans die.

Death laughed in places like these. Laughed at all the bleeping machines, the bottles filled with unpronounceable pills. Laughed at the children lying in bed. Laughed at the doctors rushing back and forth, the nurses in their starched blue skirts. The pale, fidgeting visitors clutching flowers and cards. In the end, Death took them all. The game of life was stacked in its favour. So Death laughed. Laughed at human beings and their weakness.

But Death did not laugh at the shadow.

Not any more. No.

Guy's Hospital, Southwark, was much like any other. Every room was more or less the same. The same tired linoleum, worn by countless feet. The same drab wallpaper and TV on the wall. The door with the porthole, looking out on an empty, featureless corridor. The usual drip, fat with saline. A heart monitor pulsing with beats, a visual countdown to the inescapable . . .

There was the bed, of course, and its latest occupant.

The room smelled of medicine and soap. The window was slightly ajar, the Thames wafting brackishness in. The night wheezed through the enervated curtains. None of these scents disguised the one under them. Sweat, sickness and grief.

The shadow stepped out of the corner, the place where the moonlight shone weakest. He regarded the room and the man in the bed, the bedside table empty apart from a jug of water and a small plastic cup. No cards. No flowers. Big Ben had just chimed the hour of midnight, so it was much too late for well-wishers.

Another smell filled the room now, one that hadn't been there a moment before. The smell was dry and faintly sweet: herbs, wine and salt, a trace of arid mud. It mingled with the room's pervasive reek, joining it like a lover.

The shadow stood at the end of the bed and waited for the man to wake up.

Perhaps it was the smell that roused him. Perhaps the shadow's presence alone. The man's eyes flickered open and a hand fluttered to his face, tracing the length of tube taped to his nose. Then his gaze fell on the shadow, the outline of a man standing there. He tried to sit up, but bandages and braces held him fast, the traction apparatus rattling. He lay trapped in plaster and borrowed pyjamas.

"Please," the shadow said. "Don't get up."

The man frowned. His blonde horseshoe moustache twitched. Familiarity, vague, uncertain, rose to the surface of his face from an abyss of drugs.

"Good Lord . . . Is that you?"

The shadow shook his head. "No."

"Then . . ." The old man squinted in the gloom, uncertain. Along with several broken bones, Winlock had taken quite a blow to the head, and the drugs in his veins would only add to his confusion. "Who are you? How did you get in here?" He went to rub his hairless head, but thick white plaster made it impossible. "Come to think of it, how did I?"

"I'm afraid you had an accident, Professor." The shadow placed a hand on his breast. "We both have, it seems. I am . . . disappointed. Still, things change, don't they say? We are both old enough to understand that. Nothing is certain. Nowhere is safe. Nobody gets their own way all of the time." The smile on the shadow's face could have frozen Medusa in her tracks. "As to how I got in here, well . . . sometimes the dark is a doorway. There are many paths open to one such as me."

"What the devil are you on about? Something happened at the museum? I . . . remember . . ."

Winlock's bleary eyes told the shadow that he didn't remember much.

"Good job I've had time to prepare," the shadow went on. "Time to foresee this eventuality. My associates will clean up the mess. After all, they made it! Disastrous as it was, I should've known better. Birds of a feather and all that. Or in this case, dragons."

"I don't follow you."

The heart monitor bleeped a little faster.

"A shame," the shadow said, "how quickly you people like to forget. You made the acquaintance of a queen tonight. I'm sorry that she took your speech so personally."

"Ghosts . . ." Winlock fumbled towards memory. "*Ghosts from the Sands . . .*"

"Quite."

The shadow moved to the window, the large doctor's bag he carried bumping against one leg. He stood looking out in silence for a moment, down at the car park where police cars surrounded

132

a gaggle of press vans, presumably barring the journalists from the hospital after the evening's shocking events. The coffee machine down in reception must be rattling like a one-armed bandit. Both the police and the press would have to wait until morning to grill the professor, not that he could tell them anything useful. The shadow wrinkled his nose.

"Christ," he said. "I hate this city. So much noise. So much *stink*. Who do they think they are? Worms wriggling in the bottom of a bucket that like to think themselves gods. Someone ought to remind them." He turned back to Winlock, noticed his eyes resting on the bag clutched in his spotless white gloves. He held it up. "This, Theo? Just some of your . . . personal effects. I hope you don't mind. I took the liberty of retrieving them from the museum, once the fuss had died down. You see, I require them for a certain equation. Protection, if you will. I wish I had more time to explain. Besides, one could argue that they're not really yours, couldn't one?"

"What? My relics? I don't understand . . ."

"No? Never mind. I suppose it's all part of the pattern."

"P . . . pattern?"

"Indeed, my good fellow. Them out there with their cranes and drills, building up and tearing down, one civilisation replacing the last. Us in here, discussing ghosts and doorways. Doorways, I might add, that some intended never to open. When they do," the shadow clicked his fingers, "things change."

Winlock blustered. "I'm going to call the nurse!"

"Please tell me you haven't shat yourself, Theo. That would be unseemly, even for a grave robber." The shadow waved a hand. "By all means, go ahead. I believe there's a girl asleep at her station just at the end of this wing. She'll get here in five minutes or so."

The shadow watched the professor wrestle with the traction apparatus. Cables snickered. The bed squeaked. The jug on the table sloshed on the floor. Winlock winced. Age, pain and plaster prevented further movement. He lay back on the pillows, his moustache shaking.

"Well, what the hell do you want?"

Through his stupor, his anaesthetised haze, a sharper awareness gleamed. Was he taking in his visitor's clothes? The tuxedo, gloves and black bow tie would look out of place in the sanitised surroundings. As the shadow approached, Winlock's eyes lingered on the patch of fur at his shoulder, and awareness curdled into fear.

"I am merely fulfilling my destiny. That, I'm afraid, requires special tools. Your *magic bricks*," he made a jest from the words, "are now in my possession, ready for a new-found use. The rest is . . . shall we say, tradition? Doorways and all that. I'm sure you'd do the same, were you in my place."

At the edge of the bed, the shadow dropped the bag. Winlock cried out at the sudden pressure, the weight of its contents punching his guts.

"Please," he said, spittle spraying his chin. He tried to disappear into the bedclothes, hide from this thing leaning over him. "Please. Don't—"

Spotless white gloves cut off his words, fingers closing around his throat.

"Come now, Theo. Let's pay our respects. After all, one opened tomb deserves another. And what is death but a door?"

The gloves tensed, squeezing tighter.

"Ghk!" said Winlock. His hands scrabbled at the vice around his neck, but they might as well have been paper bags flapping at steel bars.

The shadow hadn't stopped smiling. He watched the network of fine red lines appear in Winlock's eyes, a map of asphyxiation. The old man's tongue popped from his mouth, a fat blue toad. Gristle crackled, the professor's larynx caving in. His Adam's apple bobbed to a standstill. His eyeballs bulged. Then he stiffened, a joyless climax, before falling back limp on the bed.

The shadow wiped his hands on his jacket and picked up his leather bag.

"Terribly sorry, old boy," he said. "Perhaps you should have given more thought to curses."

The shadow walked back to the dark in the corner of the room. He spoke a single word under his breath – more of a symbol, really, floating in the air – and left the hospital and the corpse to the night.

Somewhere, Death was laughing.

NINE

In dreams, Ben saw her. That golden night. The first time he knew.

Naked, they lay on the bed in her cramped room on the LIU campus, over on Rockwell Place. *The goldfish bowl.* The sheets were a crumpled tapestry, describing a secret history. Bergamot and sweat coiled under the ceiling like invisible smoke, the sweet and sour of recent arousal. Outside, the summer night hushed in the trees of downtown Brooklyn and even the traffic on Flatbush Avenue sounded like a lullaby. Distantly, through the walls, Ben heard the murmur of chat, other students talking. Probably about Rose and her silver-spoon boyfriend. He could also hear the thump of dance music, echoing his heartbeat.

Catching her breath, she moved towards him, pulling herself up on his chest like a mermaid on a rocky shore. Her skin, flawless, a land of cream, pressed warmly against his side. Up close, he could see the tiny scar on her forehead, half hidden by her tousled fringe. He wanted to ask her about it, but didn't, sensing the sleepy weight of her gaze.

"I wonder where this story is headed," she said. "I've never felt this way before."

Ben smiled. Murmured to express his pleasure.

A gentle slap. "Tell me you've never felt this way before!"

He squirmed a little. "Every time is different."

"So there was . . . someone?"

"Rose . . ."

"Tell me."

"Yeah, there was someone. Ages ago now. Centuries."

She sighed. "Sure feels like that sometimes."

He said nothing. Then, to change the subject, "This story ends with a happy-ever-after." He kissed her forehead. "Here, I got you something."

He reached under the bed, his fingers searching for the little black box he'd placed there a couple of hours back. Finding it, he shuffled his bulk up on the pillows and Rose sat back as he presented it to her. When she opened the box, the light from the bedside lamp sparkled on diamonds, playing across her breasts. Moonlight on forbidden fruit.

"Ben . . ." For a moment, she was silent. Then, slowly, "I . . . Thank you. I don't know where all this is coming from, but the restaurants, the flowers, the—"

"I told you," he said. "It's just my inheritance."

She gave him a look. Then nodded, non-committal. He thought he knew why. Since that day outside the library on Atlantic Avenue, and after she had called him on the phone, breathlessly demanding an explanation that he'd somehow turned into dinner and drinks, her discomfort over his wealth was obvious. It didn't surprise him. She worked part time as a waitress downtown. She survived in the city on a scholarship and tips. And as she often reminded him, her father, a marine engineer, had raised her in Queens single-handedly (and Ben had reason to believe that those hands had sometimes been rough), on no more than nickels and dimes. She'd be damned if she'd dishonour his memory by letting Ben turn her into a kept woman. For the most part, this went unspoken. For the most part.

"Look," she said, "I'm not looking for some knight in shining armour . . ."

He snorted. "You haven't found one."

But she pushed the necklace back at him – how could she know that the gems had once belonged to Marie Antoinette? – and closed his hand around it.

"You don't need all this," she said. "I'll be with you whatever."

The months they'd been together had proceeded on awe. Perhaps a little shock at her luck. Now she was rejecting it. She wanted the real him. Or what she thought was the real him. A little uneasy, he fumbled to save the moment.

"We should have a drink to celebrate."

He couldn't ignore the subtle frown that crossed her face. Almost a wince. A memory of a scar.

"You go ahead. You know I don't. My dad . . ."

He did know. It was why he was drinking orange juice these days. Drinking juice and not minding one bit. He was drunk on her. Intoxicated. High. It didn't matter if they didn't talk about the scar. They didn't talk about his, either, though she liked to trace them with her fingers.

She was looking away, out the window at the stars hanging in the trees. He sat up and tipped her chin towards his. They kissed for a very long time.

"OK," he said, a whisper in her ear, and he dropped the diamonds over the side of the bed. "But one thing you're gonna have to accept. I bought us a place. An apartment over in Vinegar Hill. A place where we can be . . ." *Normal.* "Together."

"Ben . . ."

"Is it wrong I want to look after my treasure?"

"Oh? Is that what I am now?" But she was laughing. This was before obelisks. Before doubt.

"As long as we're together," he said, and he told his second lie, "nothing and no one can hurt us."

Pain nibbled at Ben's wrists, rousing him from unconsciousness. His skull ached, feeling too small for its addled contents. Groaning, he struggled to get his bearings, his mind wheeling like a North Pole compass. How long had he been out of it? The blurred surroundings suggested hours. What had happened? Arcane symbols taunted his memory, swirling in slow, nonsensical patterns. Where the fuck was he? It felt like a cold-storage room in Hell . . .

Wherever he was, it was dim and dank, the air clammy, the light weak. He heard a soft ripping noise and moisture dripping somewhere nearby. *Scrape. Clink. Splash.* Someone digging? A burst pipe? The echoes were an ode to confusion. The place stank of concrete and oil, his nose questing for info. Far off, an engine growled and faded. Craning his neck, he made out a flat grey smear overhead. He blinked, his vision growing clearer, and the low ceiling filled in the blanks.

A car park. An underground car park.

He tried to move, a jolt of pain down his right side making him wince. His bare feet danced across stone, his toes barely touching the ground. His trousers, reduced to a pair of ragged shorts, flapped wetly with the motion. Damp prickled across his skin. He was bare-chested, exposed to the cold. Chains rattled an ominous song, the Ballad of the Awakening Prisoner. He looked up, muscles burning, and saw the golden manacles around his wrists, his arms stretched to the ceiling, the chains strung on a metal hook.

This was not good.

Scrape. Clink. Splash.

What were those symbols etched on his bonds? Hieroglyphs?

Yes, he thought so. A hand. A lizard. An illegible scrawl. The ancient characters belonged to a land he was starting to hate. The glyphs shone in the hung-over light, emitting some inner potency. This was magic. Old magic. *Magick*. No, even older than that. This kind of magic pre-dated the Middle Ages, Ben's original era. It pre-dated the Romans and Saxons. It was stronger than anything he'd previously encountered, whisking him away from the British Museum and binding him here like a choice side of beef. Binding him as if he was just an ordinary man, unable to shift into true form, beat his wings and roar . . .

He closed his eyes, but his will met a blank white wall, confirming his restraint. Like it or not, he was trapped here. Josh Homme in chains.

This was definitely not good.

Scrape. Clink. Splash.

Events juddered back to him. Professor Winlock talking on stage. The storm in the lecture theatre. The Dark Queen rising. Shadows in the sky . . .

"Rose . . ."

He groaned again. Sardonic laughter echoed in reply.

"You think this is a date? Your girlfriend isn't here." A gruff, faintly Welsh burr, horribly familiar. "Now what did I say about your kind and hers?"

Chains jangled. Rage shuddered through Ben's dangling body. The blur at his side, tall and broad-shouldered, touched him with the blade in its hand – fifty-five inches of Scottish steel rekindling the pain in Ben's side, a hot, wet fire.

"Fulk." He struggled for breath, seething through his gritted teeth. "If you touch so much as a hair on her head . . . I'll ram that sword so far up your arse you'll see the hilt in front of your nose."

"Shucks. Stop flirting with me. If you'd had the good sense to die, you wouldn't be in this mess now. Not that I'm complaining. Like I told you in New York, we have unfinished business." The blur moved closer, leaning into the blade. "No Lore stands between us now, snake." He cupped a mocking hand to his ear. "What's that you say? Beg to differ?"

"Go . . . fuck yourself."

Fulk twisted the blade. Nerve endings shrieked from hip to armpit and Ben bit down hard on his tongue, grunting through his agony. Sweat and snot dribbled over his lips. The sword withdrew, Ben feeling it tug at his side. Again he heard that ripping sound, a soft squelch, too close to home.

Scrape. Clink. Splash.

Pain sharpened his senses. He was in an underground car park like any other underground car park, a cold concrete hole stinking of countless exhausts. He made out a ramp leading upwards. Thick grey pillars. A sign for the lifts. Worn yellow arrows ran around the walls, street directions in blotched paint. They were hard to decipher from a distance, but he reckoned they looked English enough. He was probably still in London, bundled away under the Smoke. Not that it made much difference. He was going to die regardless.

Movement nearby distracted him from the thought. A neon strip provided the only light, but it wasn't strong enough to throw shadows like the ones on the walls. The dark, spiny shapes fluttered like moths trapped in a lampshade. Somehow they moved *under* the concrete, shifting beneath a grey stone sea. The shadows, Ben realised, were creatures from the nether.

Some believed that the creatures were half-formed nightmares, the phantom leavings of Creation. Raw, embryonic forms that never quite made the cut for the real world and roamed the wastes between reality and dream, the gulf that bordered the earthly plane like a spectral void. The great ghost-beasts lurked and hunted, sniffing out those who dared to bridge the divide, whose incantations, rituals and charms siphoned the eldritch fuel of the nether, invoking power to alter reality. Magic, as most people called it, did not come easy or cheap. The greater the usage, the greater the attention of the Lurkers, who had been known to pierce the skein of the world and pluck a conjuring soul out of existence . . .

Witches and wizards were rare for a reason. Both had been rare even before the Lore had restricted them to a single officially functioning Remnant. Magic was dangerous. The most dangerous force in the universe. Only the strongest of minds, the strongest of wills – human or otherwise – could handle it with skill. It was like a drug, corrupting and addictive. The more one used it, the more one *wanted* to, until it began to change the wielder, creeping insidiously into their soul.

The Lurkers, the Walkers between the Worlds, were necessary watchdogs. The threat of their presence ensured that nobody got too greedy. No one could say where they had come from or who had set them in place. Were they fallen angels? Demons pressed into service? Or merely amoebae, unformed life, a phantom inverse mirror to Creation? The magic responsible for Ben's origin was inherent, seeded and less active; the existence of the spell-born Remnants was either innately protected or immune to the Lurkers' attentions, which led some to suppose that the Fay had created the Lurkers too, back in the earliest days of the world. Who could say? Ben would be the last to know, but he did know a bit about magic. Magic was neither good nor evil, only a wild, fathomless force, but its long-term effects were rarely healthy. In essence – as a matter of survival – all witches and wizards, whatever their moral inclination, only used magic in three ways: carefully, sparingly and with one beady eye on the nether.

The shadows moving in the car park walls were here because they sensed powerful spells at work. Like hungry wolves circling a campfire, the Lurkers caught the scent of magic and scuttled mesmerised towards its source. The car park must be dripping with scrawled wards and clever decoys, all designed to stabilise reality, hold the barrier walls in place and keep the Lurkers at bay. And keep Ben trapped like a wasp in jam. Considering the manacles around his wrists, it seemed that this level of the car park was one big spell invoked for his benefit. All one orchestrated sorcerous cage.

Someone had gone to a lot of trouble. He almost felt flattered. Lord knows he'd spent a good deal of time getting up other people's noses, most of all House Fitzwarren's. But this dank hole would probably be the last thing he ever saw. He'd never see Rose again. Never sip another glass of Jack. It shrivelled his sense of pride.

He pushed the thought away, focusing groggily on Fulk.

"All this bloody *abracadabra*. It sure as hell isn't your doing." Ben coughed and spat out blood. "So the CROWS helped you find me. Did they gut a bird? Stare into a bowl? They souped up your sword and probably said you could kill me with it." It was a guess, but he thought a good one. "In return for what? There is always a price to pay for this shit . . ."

"So you said. And maybe I've already paid that price. Maybe it was worth it too. Maybe nobody *needs* you any more."

"The Dark Queen."

"Bingo. Move straight to GO. Collect two hundred pounds." Fulk chuckled. "She's dragon enough for what we have in mind."

"What . . . what do you have in mind?"

Fulk grinned, his beard parting. Even with sweat in his eyes, Ben could see the gaps in his teeth, the missing ivory lying somewhere in an East Side gutter. The sight gave him some small satisfaction.

"What am I? A storybook villain? What you don't know can't hurt you." Fulk moved closer, raising the claymore. Ben could smell his motorbike leathers, the black material stained by oil, and the sword shed heat on his skin, the old weapon steeped in witchcraft. "I, on the other hand, can."

"So what is this, Fulk? Death by a thousand cuts?"

"Nope. Only a few more." Fulk shrugged and his grin grew wider. "I'm gonna make myself one hell of a jacket."

The sword angled downward, slicing into Ben's waist. Notched steel tried to navigate his hipbone. Blood flowed, hot down his leg, dripping off his toes. His scream bounced back to him from the walls, the spidery shadows unmoved. With a butcher's grace, Fulk carved muscle and flesh, and Ben forced himself to look down, blanching at his wounds.

The sword had left ruin in its wake. His skin hung loose from shoulder to hip, red raw and slick with blood. His ribcage gleamed through the mess, pale edges of bone. As he watched, the mauled tissue bubbled and stretched, sinew stitching to sinew, throwing up a thin epidermis. His flesh grew hard, deepening in shade, pink to crimson. The brief crust thickened to scales, a shield clothing his flank.

Fulk grunted, his sword lodged in Ben's side. With both hands on the hilt, he levered the blade and again there came that soft ripping sound as he peeled a scale from Ben's body. *Scrape*. Once it was loose, he flung the saucer-sized item on to a little pile nearby. *Clink*.

Blood dripped. *Splash*.

144

Ben howled. His chains joined him in chorus. Then the magic kicked in, the glyphs on his manacles twinkling. Whatever the nature of the symbols, they clearly trumped his natural immunity, his inbuilt resistance to magic. Or did they merely work on the air around him, gripping and compacting it, containing the space required to transform? Either way, the spell was potent, more potent than any he had previously encountered, and it surprised him that the CROWS were capable of this, even as he wondered where they had found the strength. He felt the spell working on him, a subtle, nauseating pressure. His newly formed scales wavered and faded, withdrawing into visceral shreds, human skin covering his side, the circuit of pain coming full circle.

Fulk hefted the sword again, ready to repeat the process. The car park was a blur. Ben's head lolled on his chest.

"Oh no you don't." Fulk clutched Ben's jaw, thrusting his head back. "I don't want you to miss a thing." He sheathed his sword over his shoulder, a fluid, practised motion. Fumbling in his jacket, he tugged out a small white object and popped the cap under Ben's nose. Ben jerked, his eyelids fluttering open. Ammonia stung his nostrils. Tears mingled with sweat on his cheeks.

Fulk slapped him twice, hard, and blood dribbled over Ben's chin. "There. That's better. Now, where were we?"

The car park swam back into focus, sharper than before. The shadows on the walls retreated, the real world growing solid and painful. A few yards behind Fulk, Ben made out a parked motor-cycle, a dark beast with golden rims. A revamped model. A Triumph. The Black Knight liked his fancy rides.

"You were . . . talking shit, as usual."

Fulk snorted, shrugging off the insult.

"Look at you. All tucked in and ready for bed. I reckon it's

145

time to read you a story." He strode over to the bike and pulled out an object strapped to the luggage carrier. Then he turned, all shaggy-haired smugness, and held up the book in his hands. It was a large, square leather-bound volume, frayed yellow pages sticking out between the covers. "Are you sitting comfortably? It's one of your favourites."

Fulk walked back over to where Ben hung. Cruelty and madness danced in his eyes. Like a parent with a curious child, he stood beside Ben to let him see the pictures. The book opened with a creak of centuries-old hate.

Ben groaned. "Don't . . ."

"*Whisht! lads.*" Fulk chuckled, relishing the quote. "*Haad yor gobs, an' aa'll tell ye 'boot the a'fall worm . . .*"

The True & Tragic Tale of the Mordiford Dragon

Once upon a time, when King John sat upon the throne in England and the Great Forest swathed the land, a young girl by the name of Maud stumbled across an egg in the woods. This was no ordinary egg, being somewhat large and red as an apple, and delighted with her curious find, Maud carried it back to the village of Mordiford, which rested beside an ancient ford over the River Lugg.

Afraid that her father would take the egg from her, Maud kept it hidden under her bed in the old cottage. Then, one morning, she found pieces of broken shell scattered on the floorboards. To her surprise, she saw a tiny red thing in a corner of her room, its leathery wings flapping awkwardly, its little forked tongue flicking in and out. Maud had always dreamed of a pet, so she picked the thing up and gently stroked its snout and tail, the scaly beast purring in her arms.

As she would a stray cat, Maud fed the beast on saucers of milk. The messy way in which it drank made up her mind that it was a boy. His fangs suggested he might prefer meat, but the girl tried not to think about that.

The little beast, which the girl called Red, grew at an alarming rate. Soon enough her bedroom was too small for him and she had no choice but to hide him in a derelict barn up on Old Farmer Bryn's land. Every day she brought him pails of milk filched from the farmer's dairy and remarked upon his tremendous size. Staring up at Red's teeth, Maud could no longer see him as a cat. She began to suspect he was something much worse, something her father had warned her about, but she could not bring herself to say the word.

Then, one day at dawn, Farmer Bryn stumbled across the beast in the barn. The farmer had no trouble with the word in question and cried it loudly down the road and into Mordiford, rousing the sleeping villagers.

"Dragon!" he cried to Fishwife and Miller.

"Dragon!" he cried to Blacksmith and Priest.

"Dragon!" cried Fishwife to Miller, and "Dragon!" cried Blacksmith to Priest.

As one, the villagers grabbed their pitchforks and torches and made their way up the hill to the farm.

Meanwhile, a panicked Maud raced ahead of the mob and urged Red to flee into the woods, which he did, hiding himself in a deep, dark cave. The mob searched and searched, but their efforts were in vain. Come dusk, they returned to the village, grumbling about snakes and worms and horrible deaths. Many of them had heard what had happened up in Lambton, and they did not fancy the same trouble here.

In the following months, some folks claimed that the dragon's kin came to visit him in the woods and taught him their long and loathsome legends, along with the magical tricks that play a part in the rest of our tale. The priests thereabouts said that the dragon was the Devil himself, come to tempt a damsel into damnation, but all tales change in the telling and you can't always trust what priests say.

A few months turned into years. Hard years, all told, the long winters the least of it. Crops failed and poultry went missing. Farmers found sheep strewn up in the trees. Then cows in the surrounding fields began to vanish overnight, only one or two at first, then three, then four, then five. When Maud carried milk to the cave in the woods, she found the trough outside thick and sour, with fresh bones littering the ground. It seemed that Red's appetites were changing. Huddled in their cold hall, the villagers grumbled and griped. They said it was only a matter of time before the dragon took a fancy to human flesh.

When Maud tried to convince them otherwise, the fishwives muttered, "Witchcraft."

Fearful of a widespread panic, the Village Elder travelled to London to beseech King John. The King, already vexed by the war with France and a certain outlaw in the north, was most upset to hear the news from the Marches. In typical fashion (for he was not a nice king), he ordered his guards to flog the Elder and send him on his way. Dragons, though rare, were a constant thorn in the kingdom's side, and John lay awake at night wondering how best to deal with them. Nevertheless, when his chancellor advised him that an entire eaten village would mean less tax, John sent an urgent message to Shropshire summoning his greatest slayer to court.

From Whittington Castle, the glorious and handsome Fulk Fitzwarren saddled his horse and rode out. Fresh from slaying a wyrm in Carthage and another menace in Taunton, the noble Fulk knelt before the King and heard his peevish command.

"Rid Mordiford of the dragon. Slash it, gash it, dash it on the rocks." And the King – who was ever a man of threats rather than rewards – said, "Do this by Whitsun morn or surrender your keep and lands to the Crown."

His horse's hooves throwing up dust, Fulk Fitzwarren thundered back to the Marches.

Once there, he spoke with the Village Elder in the church. Fulk noticed a damsel praying at the altar, and between the Elder's sobs and curses, he learnt that the damsel's name was Maud. That night, he found Maud working behind the bar in the Moon on Two Rivers, and he sought to woo her with tales of his derring-do. Maud, who spent much of her time walking in the woods, turned her pretty face away and described a certain cold day in Hell. Much vexed, for no girl in the land dared refuse a knight, Fulk went to see her father. In secret, Maud's father promised his daughter's hand in marriage should the knight vanquish the dragon.

With a threat and a promise heavy on his heart, Fulk set out to do just that.

For the next three moons, he rode in and out of the woods, a proud figure in black armour (soon to become one with thorns in his hair and tears in his cloak). He leapt hedgerows and forest pools. He climbed hills and mighty oaks. He crept along cliffs and down gullies. He questioned hags in moonlit glades. He strung deer on low branches. He looked under rocks and in gnarled hollows. He built bonfires and clanged shields. He hired hounds and set them sniffing through the briar. Nothing led him to the secret cave and he never laid eyes on the dragon.

And all the while, cows and sheep still went missing from the nearby farms.

Before long, Mordiford was muttering again. Who, they said, was this fool that the King had sent them? The only things flying from the woods were birds! Fulk could hear them as he drank his ale in the Moon at night, muddy and moody in a corner of the inn. His scowl was enough to daunt company and his bold talk stuck like bones in his throat. His heart became as bitter as vetch, and when he rode up into the woods at dawn, he ground his teeth and tugged his beard, his weary horse stumbling on stones. A dragon was an unnatural beast, the earthly spawn of Satan. It was only fair that God should guide a knight's hand to its destruction, just as He had done before.

Fulk laid many traps in the woods. He spent all day digging pits and filling them with stakes. He hoisted nets into the trees and kicked leaves over iron snares. He poured tar into the ruts of forest roads, keeping tinder and flint hidden under bushes nearby. He rolled rocks to the tops of ridges and lodged them there with logs. He hid himself in barrels at night, their sides bristling with blades and spikes, while watching a well in a woodland clearing where some said the dragon came to drink. Finally, after many restless, impatient nights, he bought a potion from the local hag and poured it into the well, thereby poisoning the water. But nothing led him to the secret cave and he never laid eyes on the dragon.

And all the while, cows and sheep still went missing from the nearby farms.

As the days swept towards Whitsun, the villagers stopped muttering and started to grumble outright. The woods, they said, now presented more danger than the dragon! Those who dared the thickets had stumbled on bears impaled in pits and pheasants caught in nets in the trees. They found foxes and badgers crushed under rocks, burnt boar left lying in the road and wolves trapped in iron snares. And one afternoon, Ned the Tanner found a dead hag curled up like a spider by an old clearing well. If nothing changed, the villagers said, Sir Fulk would have slain the woods by Whitsun.

Might as well burn them to the ground, they said.

Poor, handsome, brave Fulk! In the blink of an eye, it was Whitsun Eve and all the knight had to show for his trouble was misery and scorn. Seeing his chance for glory slipping between his fingers, his reputation forever tarnished, he hurried on foot from the inn at dusk, snarling a desperate vow. If his castle was to fall into King John's hands, then he would heed the villagers' advice and leave no tree between himself and the dragon!

He was building a great bonfire in the woods when, by chance, he overheard muffled voices. It was a strange hour for travel even for gypsies, and considering the deadly repute of those parts, he thought it stranger still. Fearing robbers or worse, Fulk climbed into a tree and spied two figures enter the clearing. Imagine his surprise when he recognised Maud! The damsel appeared in some distress, scowling and pointing at the bonfire. It was clear that her companion vexed her, but Fulk, straining to make out their words, did not recognise the churl, a tall youth, strong of jaw, with a shock of red hair. The churl was trying to calm Maud, and when he put his arms around her, Fulk realised that the two of them were lovers. He gripped the branches around him until his palms bled. Maud's father had promised him his daughter's hand in marriage, and he would not see another steal his prize. In greenest envy, he watched the girl push the stranger away and flee along the woodland path, heading back to the village.

The red-haired youth did not give chase. Instead, he cursed under his breath.

"Damsels!" Then, bizarrely, he muttered, "Why are my tastes any business of hers?"

The churl stormed off into the trees, and Sir Fulk, vengeful and grim, dropped down from his perch and slipped quickly after him. For an hour and more he stalked the youth, mindful to keep to the shadows and tread softly through the brush. Again he was surprised. The path his quarry took led him to Farmer Bryn's land and the fields behind the derelict barn.

Fulk peered through the hedgerow and gasped, for there he laid eyes on a terrible sight – a man-beast sitting in the field, gnawing on a freshly killed cow! Scaly it was, red and fanged, its mouth dripping with blood. Its eyes resembled platters of gold, shining cat-like under the stars. Here, Fulk knew, he had found his dragon, a creature that could ape the form of a man and walk among other folk unseen. The churl was a monster. A beast of prey. A devil come to tempt damsels.

Brave and true, the slayer wasted not another second. He leapt from the hedgerow, sword unsheathed, and descended with a cry on his feasting foe. The man-beast roared and dropped the cow, but shrank away from a duel. On all fours, it galloped back into the woods, casting hot glances behind it.

Fulk cursed his lack of a horse. Armour clanking, he raced in pursuit.

He did not have to run far. In a gloomy copse, he found the churl strung between the trees, caught up in one of the great rope nets. The youth's struggles failed to free him, and Fulk watched his scaly hide fade, slowly returning to human guise. When the churl was simply a churl again, Fulk saw his knightly glory restored.

"Beelzebub!" he cried, and struck the churl on the head with the hilt of his sword. "Lucifer! Archfiend! Dragon!"

Then he dragged his insensible catch back with him to Mordiford.

*   *   *

At dawn on Whitsun Eve, Fulk Fitzwarren rang the church bells.

The sleepy villagers gathered in the square. Maud was in the crowd but the girl said nothing, perhaps knowing more about the sight before them than her yawning neighbours.

"Here!" cried Fulk. "Here is the one who ate your livestock! Here is the one who lurks in your woods! Here, behold your dragon!"

The villagers stared at the figure in the net.

Fishwife looked at Miller and Miller at Fishwife. Blacksmith looked at Priest and Priest at Blacksmith. Tanner looked at Alchemist and Alchemist at Tanner.

The Village Elder snorted.

Then all of them started to mutter.

Finally the Elder spoke. "Have you lost your wits, sir? Or perchance drank too much ale?" He strolled over to the net in the square. "Why, this is a boy, not a dragon. Have your nights in the woods driven you mad?"

Fulk raised his hands to protest, but the Elder poked the boy with his staff.

"You, boy, what is your name?"

"Ben Garston," the boy replied. "Red Ben to my friends."

"And what have you got to say for yourself, Master Garston?"

"That as God is my witness, I am no dragon," the boy said. "Simply a peasant and a thief. The knight caught me rustling cows up on Old Bryn's farm."

The Elder and the villagers gasped, for this was quite a confession. In those days, food was scarce and hard to come by, and winter in the Marches long. Coupled with the threat of the dragon, tempers in the village ran high, and no one stopped to hear Fulk's claims as they cried out for a lynching.

"The boy is the dragon, I swear it! As a knight of the realm, he is mine!"

Nevertheless, the crowd grabbed the boy and carried him high to the edge of the village.

Now, as it happened, there was an oak tree there that the villagers liked to use as a gallows. Frayed rope hung from the branches like deathly pussy willow. No one had met their end here for many a year, not since a travelling monk had made off with the tithe, but the tree remained stout and fit for purpose.

Fulk spat and swore and tried to smite the boy with his sword, his desperation great. Why would these fools not listen to him? The Blacksmith, having heard enough, tied the slayer to a nearby tree and put him to sleep with his fist. Lynching was a tricky business and entertainment in those parts was scarce. No one wanted an interruption, least of all from a babbling knight.

The rope slipped around Ben Garston's neck. The branches

155

above whispered grimly. The rope gradually drew tight.

"Wait! Wait!" the boy cried. "Will you not hear my last request?"

Fishwife looked at Miller and Miller at Fishwife. Blacksmith looked at Priest and Priest at Blacksmith. Tanner looked at Alchemist and Alchemist at Tanner.

The Village Elder shrugged.

"Very well. What is it?"

"Release me," the boy said, and everyone laughed. "Release me and I swear I'll slay your dragon. I'll bring the proof to the church by sundown in return for my freedom."

The villagers muttered.

"What makes you think that a churl like you can win out where a knight has failed?" the Village Elder eventually asked.

"I am young and strong and cunning as a fox, weighed down by neither ale nor armour."

"But what is to stop you from running away?"

"My honour," the boy said, and then he pointed at Maud in the crowd. "A maiden under heaven sees the truth. Let her judge me. Let the damsel judge the faith in my heart."

The crowd turned as one to face Maud. Fishwife looked at Miller and Miller at Fishwife. Blacksmith looked at Priest and Priest at Blacksmith. Tanner looked at Alchemist and Alchemist at Tanner. Maud made her way forward to the edge of the square.

And the damsel said, "Release him."

"God's bones, you think you can do this?" The Elder was privately hopeful, but he did not fancy another flogging. "What if you are wrong?"

"Then may the Devil dance on my grave."

The gathered villagers grumbled and nodded. In those days, such oaths held darksome weight.

"Very well," the Elder said.

The Blacksmith took the noose from around Ben's neck and put Fulk's sword in his hand. With a pat on the back, he sent the youth stumbling into the woods. Then the villagers went as one to the church, there to wait and pray.

In their folly, they left Fulk tied to the tree. They agreed he would only get in the way.

That was the longest day in Mordiford. Whitsun unfolded quietly, the festivities doused by expectation. The Priest lit candles in the nave, one for each apostle, but no one sang hymns or rolled any cheese. The Fishwife chewed the ends of her hair. The Blacksmith studied his dirty nails. The Tanner belched and dozed in the pews.

The sun crawled over the Marches sky.

By noon, folk began to mutter. They said that Garston had tricked them and would not return. Even when Maud stood at the altar and promised them otherwise, heads shook and lips curled.

Noon wore on. Soon the westering sun kissed the horizon, sinking into the hills.

"We are betrayed!" the villagers cried.

Then, when only a rosy line ran between the land and the sky, the villagers heard a shout outside. Led by the Priest, everyone hurried out of the church through the stout oak doors. There on the steps stood Ben Garston with sword in hand, the blade dripping with blood. Beside him on the steps lay a large red object, several feet long and much like a slug. Blood dripped from the object too, and a river of the stuff wound across the square and up the street, leading back into the woods.

"Behold!" the boy cried. "I have slain the dragon. I caught the beast sleeping on the banks of the Lugg, fat from gorging on cows and sheep. Through briar and fen I crept, and hacked the beast into a thousand pieces. Behold, before you, its tongue!"

Fishwife looked at Miller and Miller at Fishwife. Blacksmith looked at Priest and Priest at Blacksmith. Tanner looked at Alchemist and Alchemist at Tanner.

The Village Elder took a step backwards.

"How?" he asked in an awe-filled voice.

Maud, however, was already clapping, whirling around and around in the square.

"Oh joyous day! Our saviour has come! Mordiford is free of the dragon!"

And the villagers, caught up in the moment and very much relieved, joined her in her victory dance.

"Saved! Saved!" they chanted. And "Free! Free!"

The churl who was the boy called Ben (and something other besides) bowed low to the Village Elder, and the Elder, as promised, gave him his freedom. The old man was smiling for the first time that year. The muttering would stop now, at least for a while, and he might get a decent night's sleep.

As the songs began in earnest and the cheesemaker went to find something to roll, Ben Garston took Maud's hand and led her quietly into the woods, there to laugh and to kiss, and later to discuss the pressing matter of a necessary change of tastes. The threat had passed. The village slept easy. Surely this must mean that the cows and sheep should sleep easy too, if the dragon and the damsel hoped to have a happy-ever-after . . .

In those days, as in these, damsels often had the right of things.

Alas, fate is strange and often cruel, and there is one in our tale tied to a tree who knew the truth of the matter. As Whitsun waned and the villagers snored in mead-drenched dreams, Fulk struggled free of his bonds. When he staggered to the square and saw the great red tongue lying on the steps, he did not find it hard to fathom events. The devil and his whore had tricked the whole village and made a fool out of him in the process. Him, Fulk Fitzwarren, champion, slayer and knight of the realm! Or at least folk had called him that until this night. When King John came to learn that a simple churl had slain the dragon – and he would, for there was a lot of muttering in those days – he would stand by his royal threat, for he was not a very nice king. He would seize Fulk's castle and lands, and strip his title from him like bark from a tree.

Mad with rage, the fallen knight saddled his horse and returned to the clearing where he had built his bonfire the night before. With a curse, he set his torch to the pyre, watching the flames lick the lowest branches of the trees. Then his spurs bit into his horse's flanks and he galloped north for the place he had once called home.

Thus taking his revenge, the fearsome knight, Fulk Fitzwarren, rode out of our story.

All night the fire raged. Branches crackled and leaves set sail on the sky, a fleet of embers in the dark. Sparks showered down, igniting the tar on forest roads, fuelling the inferno. Soon enough, all the woods were ablaze. Animals darted this way and that, abandoning burrow, nest and den. Birds fluttered past the moon with wildly flaming wings, a bright omen of doom.

In Mordiford, the bells rang, and villagers hurried to the woods with pails in hand, desperately trying to quench the fire.

And deep in the heart of the woods, curled up in his secret cave, Ben was woken by Maud choking beside him, the girl overcome with the smoke. With no time to spare, he sheltered her with his wings. His scales shielded him from the heat, but Maud was not so lucky. Slowly her face was turning red and blisters bubbled up on her limbs.

Ben rushed from the cave intending to fly, but the boughs above barred his way. The canopy was a burning cage and he dared not risk Maud in the blaze. In a panic, he crashed through the brush to the old clearing well and frantically scooped up water in his claws, carrying it back to his lair.

Kneeling beside his lady love, he poured the water between her lips.

Oh sorrowful, grievous day! He could only look on in horror as Maud turned as pale as milk and clutched harder at her throat.

"Oh my egg!" she spluttered. "My love! What in God's name have you done?"

For the water was rank and deadly, poisoned days ago by the slayer. The rising flames had devoured the hag who lay dead in the clearing, leaving Ben with no warning when he had gone to draw from the well.

In despair, he carried Maud to the banks of the Lugg and rested her on the ashen ground. There his lips touched hers for the last time. Judged by God and damned by Heaven, he bade his lady love farewell.

This brings us to the end of our tale. And just as every tale changes in the telling, each one also leaves a shadow. The shadow of this one is years of bad blood.

In the days that followed, Red Ben Garston left those parts, unable to face the shame and the memories. Some said he walked into the sea, choosing to drown his sorrows for ever. Some said he flew up to the sun and joined his lover in furious flame. Others held that he travelled to London, meaning to drink and sleep and forget.

All he left behind him were tales, which grew and spread just as the trees in the forest once again grew and spread. The day that he fled the Marches, a curious painting appeared on the western wall of the church, depicting a dragon resplendent in flame. Down through the years, the painting remained. Sometimes the dragon was red and sometimes green, sometimes with a tail and sometimes without, but it was always a token of Maud and her end.

Until one day the painting faded and folk no longer knew truth from fairy tale.

One mystery lingers still. From that day to this, no one in Mordiford could say whence Ben Garston came. His name did not appear in the village scroll of births, and no family came forward to claim him as kin.

Like the shadow of his own tale, Red Ben faded into legend and time.

The End

TEN

Fulk closed the book with an echoing snap.

Just like that, Mordiford was miles – centuries – away again, having spat out an ember that mourned and cooled and changed across years. That learnt how to forget Maud's smell, Maud's laugh, the way she had kissed compassion into him. But Ben never forgot the way he had lost her, how his appetites had brought about her doom. Since leaving the Marches, he had honoured Maud's memory with caution and abstinence. He had never hunted again. His predator days were over. He became a milk drinker, harmless to livestock, to wild beasts and, of course, humans. At least the ones who didn't mess with him. Wasn't that why the Guild of the Broken Lance had chosen him for the Pact? Where some like Mauntgraul, the White Dog, found themselves lulled into the Long Sleep, their reign of terror brought to an end, Ben alone was allowed to endure, with only his scars for company. Scars and the memory of a young girl who had once stroked his snout and tail . . .

Here and now, strung up in the underground car park, he was painfully aware that the Black Knight was opening more than just physical wounds.

"You never had much luck with women, did you?"

Fulk tossed the book over his shoulder. The antique tome – which Ben guessed was a volume knocked together by some hired scribe or other and shoehorned into the Fitzwarren family library – smacked on concrete, several pages scattering. He unsheathed his sword, letting its length renew the distance between them, and stood swinging the blade like a golf club – this hulk of a man who was little more than a cheap hand-me-down copy of somebody else from long ago, an ancestor knight who'd first rolled the dice on an eight-hundred-year long losing streak. As soon as this latest version had wriggled from his mother's womb, his teachers would have been there waiting, ready to infect his mind with the bitterness of ages. In schools hidden deep in the country, a string of instructors would have taught the chosen one a host of combative arts – swordplay, boxing, judo, wrestling, shooting, archery and more. Over the years, the aggressive attentions of House Fitzwarren had made Ben's learning curve that much steeper, forcing him to adapt. The family trained each new Fulk in a deadly array of skills, from racing car driving to bull riding to high-altitude climbing. The patriarchs never let them forget that they were dealing with a dragon, the most dangerous creature known to man.

One slip, sonny, and you're toast.

"You were always a coward, running away."

Alongside the training, the trenchant education, the inherent, instilled injustice, the patriarchs talked about honour too, about glory and glory lost. They talked at length about *seisin*, the old law of lands and titles. They talked about a house betrayed, cheated of its heritage and cast down from its rightful place. King John, they said, was dead and gone, and Whittington Castle a ruin, but the principle still stood and honour could never be ignored.

Spei est Vindicta. That was the motto of House Fitzwarren. *Hope is Vengeance.*

Its coat of arms bore the hawk of perseverance on a field of gules.

The deeds to Whittington rested in the Guild's hands now, King John's clause unchanged. Until Ben Garston was dead, House Fitzwarren would remain outlawed, unable to take its official place in Britain's noble ranks. And when Ben came to sign the Pact at Uffington in 1215, the Guild had denied the family's vendetta with a dry and contradictory writ.

Those few bodies learned of this treaty shall henceforth never hunt Remnants or otherwise seek to do them harm . . .

This contradiction, a legislative knot that effectively cemented House Fitzwarren's fallen status, had only served to fan the flames of enmity. Of course, the House obeyed the Lore on the surface. In truth, their agents simply went underground. Across the ages, the hatred of Fitzwarren sons had matured like the rarest wine. They would never forget the Mordiford shame. Chained, raw and bleeding in the car park, Ben knew that the man before him could never, ever forgive. By the time Fulk rode out on the hunt, his motorbike wheels churning up dust, he had become a living weapon, a poison arrow of revenge.

There was no point trying to bargain for his life. But it wasn't only his funeral.

"I . . . like your take on the old tale." Ben twisted his face into a grin, hiding a mouthful of pain. "It's a little on the biased side, mind. The original Fulk was a drunkard well before he reached the borders. I wouldn't call him *fearsome*, either."

"You were scared enough to cut out your own tongue."

"It grew back." Ben tried to shrug, difficult with his arms stretched above him. "We were only protecting ourselves. Your *champion* did far more damage than I ever did."

"Trees grow back too. Honour doesn't."

165

"Neither do loved ones. This is like in the story, don't you see that?"

"If you think you'll convince me to let you go . . ."

Ben gave a snort, blood bubbling from his nose.

"I wouldn't waste my breath. I know your duty. I know you have to kill me."

"So what then? You want to debate the charter myths?"

"Let the girl go." Ben spoke with cool intent, devoid of emotion, matter-of-fact. "Rose has done nothing to earn your enmity. House Fitzwarren . . . you have no right. You can have your jacket." He nodded at the pile of scales near Fulk's feet, the takings of the *scrape*, *clink*, *splash* game. "Hell, you can drain my blood and eat my heart, live a few decades longer. I'm a coward who has no luck with women. A worm and a snake, fine. But let Rose go. She has no part in this."

Fulk rubbed a meaty hand through his beard. He squinted at Ben under the strip light, a spider inspecting a fly. Who knew what bitter seeds rolled around in his head, planted there by murderous tradition? The burst pipe dripped. Spiny shadows flowed across the walls, measuring out the slayer's contemplation.

Then Fulk laughed. A resounding guffaw.

"Fuck me, when did you get so noble?" He spat on the ground, wiped snot from his lips. "When did you get so *vain*? You think this is all about you, don't you? And isn't it always? Always *I'll tell you about the worm*, right? Never *I'll tell you about the knight*. Those charter myths have got a lot to answer for. They've gone to your fucking head."

"Then what—"

"Let's just say we need your girlfriend for a little game of smoke and mirrors. She's a damsel, right, and she's done the nasty with a dragon? There's power in that, according to the

CROWS. Think of her as a fish on a line. Think of her as *bait*."

"Let her go or I'll—"

"What, snake? What will you do?"

"I have friends!" Ben was shouting now, abandoning his cool. "If you hurt Rose, you'll answer to them!"

He didn't know if this was true or not.

"How touching. Beauty and the Beast." Fulk levelled the sword at Ben's face. "But just like Mordiford, this story won't have a happy ending."

Ben's head sank on to his chest. He reflected on the sequence of events that had brought him to this pass. It struck him now that he'd followed a trailing thread in the dust, from the Javits Center to Paladin's Court and on to the British Museum, chasing a mystery that was much bigger than it had at first seemed. The thread in the dust turned out to be a wire, a sparkling fuse that had led him down a twisting tunnel to a truckload of dynamite . . .

Once again in his long life, Ben was staring death in the face.

Death grinned back like he always did, a pale, long-suffering friend.

Ben looked up, took his last shot.

"Fulk, listen. Listen to me, you prick. The CROWS are obviously using you. Whatever you gave them in return for my head, trust me, it'll never be enough." He caught his breath, tasting oil and concrete. "This isn't what your family had in mind. This isn't what they meant by *honour*. I've fought enough of you over the years to know that's the truth. This isn't vengeance. It's a cakewalk. Where is the honour in killing a helpless captive?"

Fulk frowned, the claymore drooping.

"Shut the fuck up."

"Unchain me, Fulk. Fight me fair and square."

"Shut up, I said."

"Fight me like the first Fulk would have fought me."

Fulk licked his lips. He swung the sword, weighing the pros and cons. The thought was obviously tempting.

But not *that* tempting.

"Nice try, snake. You think I'm gonna go up against a seven-ton freak?"

"Then leave these cuffs on." Ben shook his bonds, the restrictive glyphs flashing in gold. "I'll face you *mano a mano*. In human guise. No scales. No tricks. What do you say?" He softened his voice, took a wild guess. "Imagine your father's pride . . ."

A smile twitched at the corners of Fulk's mouth, informing Ben he'd hit the mark.

"You swear?"

What a moron. "On Maud's name. I swear."

Fulk hesitated, a child about to open the cookie jar. Then he stepped forward and reached up, grabbing a length of chain. Whether he meant to slip it off the hook, and what the outcome might have been if he had, Ben would never find out. White light washed over the walls, the vaporous ghosts scuttling backwards, the dank surface regaining solidity.

A car was coming down the ramp into the car park. A Rolls-Royce Phantom IV. The sleek vehicle looked out of place in the dingy surroundings. The smoked-glass windows reflected nothing, blank squares leading into void. The long bonnet distorted the strip light, the two men warping across the fenders as the car rolled silently down the ramp. The silver figurehead, a bare-breasted hag on a broom, drew to a halt, hovered twinkling in the gloom.

Fulk looked at Ben and then at the Rolls. His hand fell limply

168

to his side and he tipped his broadsword over one shoulder, his stance conspicuously casual.

The Phantom faced them side-on across the cold grey space. Then the back door opened and wolves loped out. Ben counted six of the creatures, spilling out of the dense dark comprising the depths of the cab. Muzzles trailing steam, the scrawny, black-furred beasts padded across the concrete floor. The Phantom's headlights shone like coins in their hungry eyes. Claws clacked softly on the ground as the pack formed a loose corral around Ben, snarls rumbling in their throats. The wolves had caught his animal scent, the blood dripping from him, soured by sweat. They had smelled his otherness, too, and bared their fangs at the threat.

Ben swallowed and looked beyond his savage audience. The wolves were the least of his worries. They were merely familiars, spellbound pets. Their owner worried him more.

A stockinged leg emerged from the cab, a spider testing the strand of a web. Then the *grande dame* of the Coven Royal stepped out into the car park.

It was Miss Macha, a sovereign sister of the triumvirate. The Three Who Are One.

The cold didn't seem to bother her. She was only wearing a leather bikini, shiny black patches drawn so tight that they looked painted on over her curves. Silver studs covered the material. Her stilettos went up to the moon and her sunglasses threw Ben's anguish back at him, a prisoner in fisheye depths. A penta-gram adorned her upper left arm, the tattoo faded with time. A wild flood fell about her shoulders and she wore a hat as black as her hair, tall, conical and pointed, a cynical nod to her calling. Ben judged the witch to be in her mid to late twenties. It was hard to tell under all her make-up. The lipstick smeared across one cheek. The tears of mascara that dripped to her chin. Under the mess, her skin was as pale as a glacier.

Miss Macha was a fading star. A walking cabaret. The cabaret of death.

One of her breasts was bare. A wolf cub suckled at her nipple, a furry ball that she cradled in one arm. Milk stained pink with blood dribbled down her stomach and leg, but she showed no pain at this mockery of motherhood. Like Babe Cathy, the crone, the CROWS got a kick from these kinds of jokes. The witch took a drag on her Cuban cigar and smoke coiled up to the ceiling. Ben bet that it was from the same box as the one Babe had puffed on the Brooklyn Bridge. In essence, this was the *same* woman, and she greeted him as such.

"Well if it ain't the *Sola Ignis*." She rolled her Latin in a Texan drawl, tasting the obsolete echoes. "We simply must stop meeting like this."

"If we just stop meeting . . . that's fine by me."

"Oh Ben. You're such a drag." She took a deep one on the cigar. "Always pissing on our parade."

"And always a pleasure, ma'am."

Her hips slinked towards him. The car park didn't make much of a catwalk. The air leapt out of the way of her heels as she moved through the circle of wolves, patting one of them on the head. Its tongue lolled, lapping up her presence. The cub at her breast wriggled and whined.

Fulk didn't look so casual now. The slayer cleared his throat. "The spell worked, as you can see. Everything is going according to plan."

The witch removed her sunglasses, hooking them into her bra, a deft one-handed motion. Her eyes glinted, stoat-like, as she took in the pile of scales and the discarded storybook, its tattered leaves spread across the ground. Then she looked up at Fulk.

"Seems like we arrived just in time. We thought you said you wanted his head."

"I . . . I do, my lady. I was . . ."

"We know what you were doing. We've seen golems with more brains than you. How long were you going to stand there gloating, giving him time to escape?"

"With those hieroglyphs?" Fulk glared at Ben's manacles, colour rising in his cheeks. "I don't think he's going anywhere."

"Oh, is that so? Fulk, you're a goddamned delivery boy. Leave the thinking to us."

Fulk looked at his feet, silenced.

Miss Macha pursed her lips. Then she turned back to Ben in smoke-wreathed appraisal.

"I'm afraid this ain't a social call. We were hoping to find a corpse."

"You know, you say the nicest things."

"Time and tide, Ben. Time and tide. We girls have a schedule to keep."

"And I'm just getting in the way."

This earned him a flash of teeth. "Brains as well as brawn."

"Care to tell me why?"

Miss Macha raised an eyebrow. "We already did. Things change, we said." She moved in close and slipped an arm around his neck, swinging with him in a slow waltz, the wolf cub warbling between them. She smelled like roses and shit. "You shouldn't have run out on us before. This would all be over with by now."

"Excuse me for taking a rain check. There was something I needed to know."

"Ah yes, the Dark Queen. This town ain't big enough for the both of you, Ben."

"So I noticed. She's collecting those relics, isn't she? Your Star, Crook and Pschent. Why? What does she want?"

"The same thing we all want. Power. Glory. Revenge."

"Speak for yourself. I just want a glass of Jack."

Miss Macha barked laughter. "You never did have ambition. You're a milk drinker, for fuck's sake. An embarrassment to your kind."

"And you're a cold-hearted bitch. A perfect example of yours."

The witch didn't take this well. She stopped swinging, the waltz at an end. Her smile melted into a thin red line.

Then she plunged her cigar into Ben's eye.

Ben's scream hit the car park walls. The car park walls screamed back. A hot poker wound through his brain, chargrilling his thoughts. *Serpente arrosto*. Molten tears dripped down his cheek, the magma of flesh and blood. Scales burgeoned, thinned and faded. Hieroglyphs gleamed in gold.

The wolves yapped, roused by the smell. The witch hooked a leg around Ben's hip, pressing her body against him.

"You dreamt you were a dragon, flying across the sky. Now you wake up and wonder: are you a man who dreamt you were a dragon or a dragon dreaming that you are a man?" Her breath was an ill wind, frosting his cheek. "You've sleepwalked through this world too long, Benjurigan. Its limits have dulled you, made you grey. You signed the Pact just like we all did, but you actually *respect* it. You uphold and defend it. Bow to human rule. Doesn't the compromise stick in your craw?"

Ben's eye was already cooling, vitreous humour bubbling anew. Lens and retina reforming. Lashes curling out.

The pain lingered, making him sharp.

"The Pact was . . . the only choice left." And he thought this was true. The push and pull of the war between Remnants and humans had resulted in the Anarchy, a stalemate that saw chaos, fire and plague spread across the land. Villages were robbed and burned. Crops failed and the people starved. Law and order had broken down into sharp and bloody fragments. While king and pretender wrestled over the crown, most Remnants – abandoned, turning feral, unmindful of their leaders – had revelled in the confusion, feasting on nobles cast out in the muck, stealing castles and keeps, enchanting the clergy into profane acts and generally stirring England's troubled cauldron to boiling point. As progress faltered, mired in the mud, the Remnants themselves were dwindling, felled by sword and lance in ever greater numbers . . . Eventually, when Henry II ascended the throne, commencing the Plantagenet reign and restoring peace to the land, the scars and the echoes of the war lingered. Ben exhaled, remembering the destruction. The fires. The screams. Giants hurling boulders at ships in the Wash. Goblins riddling the nurseries, pulling children's hair until they were forced to flee into the street. Ghouls gnawing on the sainted bones in the crypt of Old St Paul's. And then, in 1212, an old and cantankerous dragon had taken to the skies over the city and burnt London Bridge to the ground . . .

It fell to Henry's son and heir, the notorious King John, to draw a line under the matter. Pressure from Rome aside, his disagreements with the barons had already threatened to bring about civil war, and once again the kingdom teetered on the brink of anarchy. Bowing to the will of the Church and the people, King John spoke to the Remnants' fear of extinction and offered them his truce.

"It wasn't perfect. What is?" Ben could only speak the truth as he saw it. "At least this way we get to live in hope, that the Fay will one day return. That we can make a lasting peace with humans, have some kind of future. Otherwise, neither of us would be standing here bitching about it. It was compromise or die."

"Yes. The Pact was enough for you, wasn't it? The Pact was precisely where you gave up. You shrugged on this form like an ill-fitting suit and joined the shuffling ranks of the tamed. You became like an unloved pet, mewling outside the doors of the world. Your fire fading to embers."

"The Lore protects us." And it had, for a while. Before the modern age came crashing in, promises turned out to be lies and the Fay had never returned. *"Protected* us. The Lore was—"

"Tyranny," Miss Macha said. "It was always tyranny. Who are they to herd us like sheep, make us graze on the scraps of human tolerance? We are the primal children of the earth, the foundations on which all else rests. Were we born to crawl in the shadow of industry, servile to an impotent God? No. And no more. The Pact is null and void. The Lore broken. Neither should have ever existed. Too long have we been subdued, shackled by our inferiors. Now we will rise and fulfil our destiny. Now we will rise and rule!"

Ben had heard this song before, up on the Brooklyn Bridge. It had sounded overblown then and it sounded overblown now.

"Drums roll. Lightning flashes. Stage blacks out . . ."

His bravado rang false. Her words had chilled him to the core.

"Why now?" he asked. "For eight hundred years you've suffered the Lore. Yeah, I know that the CROWS have hardly been saints, but outright rebellion? Why *now*? What's rattled your cage?"

"Cage is right," she snapped, but then she sighed and loosened her grip on him. A look that was almost beatific stole over the mess of her face. "We heard a voice calling in the dark. Calling, calling for a way back. Calling us to arms . . ." She glared at him, the malice returned. "And the CROWS answered."

"You want to cause a war?" He had no idea what she was on about.

"Not a war. A conquest."

"Someone will stop you. Someone always does."

"Then they'd better hurry." The witch released him, tottering away on her high heels. "Three days from now, everything changes. The chains of our oppression will break and the usurpers will pay for their crimes. Anarchy. Bloodshed. *Revolution.* These are the true cogs of progress, Ben. These are our guns and our bombs. With them we will reclaim the world."

"You're insane, you know that? You've always been fucking insane."

Miss Macha twirled a hand. "Sweet nothings, sweet nothings." Like a deathly ballerina in a concrete jewellery box, she spun on her heel to face Fulk, who stood sullen and brooding among the wolves. "Kill this fool," she said. "Cut off his head. Let's see how quickly it grows back."

Fulk, keen to prove his worth after her previous rebuke, hefted his sword from over his shoulder and shifted towards Ben. The witch drew back and the wolves moved with her, a furry skirt swirling around her legs. Face a portrait of spite, she cupped the cub firmly to her breast, almost smothering the thing. Studs glittered under the strip light. Blood and milk speckled the ground.

A touch theatrically, Fulk adopted a headsman's stance. He slipped the blade over Ben's shoulder, into the gap between arm and neck. The notched edge bit into Ben's skin, its charmed length vibrating against his jugular vein, which twitched like a frog in a net, his heart pumping with dread. Fulk's grin could have filled the car park. His heavy breaths, stinking of beer and cigarettes, betrayed his mounting excitement. Without doubt, the Black Knight was getting off on the thought of sawing the Enemy's head off.

Fulk's beard parted wider. Perhaps he wanted to give a farewell speech, a grand address rehearsed since birth in some ramshackle Shropshire mansion.

"Make it quick." Witchy echoes snapped around the car park, dashing any hope of ceremony. "The boss expects us in Cairo tonight."

Fulk obeyed. The old family claymore, this jagged, familiar foe, began slicing back and forth, iron teeth chewing into flesh. Ben screamed. Blood washed over his chest, a crimson robe spilling to the floor. His scream hit the walls and intensified in pitch, an eldritch thrum resounding in his skull. The humming grew louder and the vibrations stronger, a pneumatic drill skewering the air, the chains rattling over his head.

"What in Hecate's name—"

Fulk withdrew the blade and wheeled toward the source of the disturbance. Ben sucked in another scream, stale fumes filling his lungs. Even as his blood clotted and his skin started to mend itself, the car park was trembling around him, dust trickling from cracks in the roof. The strip light stuttered. Insectile shadows wove across the walls, a silhouette theatre racing through concrete. The wolves whimpered and yapped, their agitated mass carrying Miss Macha back towards the Rolls, where she clung to the open passenger door, her eyes darting over the walls. A blast of air rushed through the car park. Her hat fell off, lost to the pack. She cried out, her mouth a blotchy circle of shock.

The ground lurched, hurling Fulk on to his hands and knees, his sword clanging away from him. Scales scattered. The storybook pages flipped and flapped. The Triumph crashed to the ground, oil oozing from the motorbike's tank and forming a pool around the fallen knight.

Ben hung in chains. He looked at the walls, watching the way they throbbed and bulged, a thin skein filling with smoke. The pressure was building, stirring the Lurkers into a frenzy. But where was the pressure coming from? *There.* A larger shadow on the far wall, swelling like a cloud as it drew closer, thundering from the depths of the nether . . . And then there *were* no walls, the boundaries dissolving between the worlds, dispelled by the conjured quake. The barriers fell, the zoo set loose. Greasy tentacles reached out, drawn towards the heat and substance of reality.

Here they were, witch, slayer and dragon, thrown into the shark pool at feeding time . . .

A cry scaled through the chaos. Ben squinted into the writhing mass and made out a horse and rider charging towards him. The odd perspective clawed at his guts, as if he gazed into the back of a spoon. The stallion, its white mane flowing in the wind, came galloping forth regardless. The rider sat proud, a thin and determined form, red silk sweeping from limbs untouched by sun. A mask covered his face, a grinning Punchinello, long nose levelled like a lance at the people in the car park. As the two worlds joined, nether to real, the car park shuddered. Space curved. The pillars leant impossibly outward, supporting a bevelled roof. The place became a grey glass prism.

The rider yelled and raised a hand. Fluorescent spears sprang from his palm, spraying colour across the car park, a refracting mess of colliding planes. The spears hit the jostling facets and exploded, red, orange, violet and green, a blinding rainbow of attack.

The car park ballooned and shrank, and then reasserted itself, the prism breaking, the skein reforming, a wobbling meniscus dividing the worlds. The Lurkers drew back, hissing and flailing, into their nowhere realm. The white stallion whinnied and reared, the Punch in the saddle grinning down at Ben. Another rainbow flash. The golden manacles burst apart, the binding spell undone. Ben fell to his knees, the severed chains spooling around him.

Miss Macha swore. Despite the violent intent on her face, the witch knew when to take flight. Her bikini-clad form slipped into the back of the Rolls and the wolves leapt after her, vanishing into the stygian depths. The passenger door swung shut even as the wheels started to turn. The Phantom's headlights whitewashed the scene, the vehicle making a swift, silent turn in the car park before speeding away up the ramp. *Ding dong the witch has fled.*

The stupid thought brought Ben to his senses. He took in the rider, who hung back, the horse trotting back and forth in some kind of chromatic bubble, a gaudy toy in a snow globe. The mask grinned back at him, silent and watchful.

Knowing.

Ben glared at Fulk. The slayer was struggling to rise in the spilt pool of oil. His boots slipped and he dropped to one knee, his sword and the motorbike out of reach. He froze, sensing Ben's eyes on the back of his neck. Slowly, Fulk turned to face him.

"Wait!" he said, and the echoes laughed. "I was only fulfilling my quest!"

But Ben was already growing. Growing and deepening in shade, his flesh hardening, a sheen of scales. Muscles rippled. Haunches bulged. The last of the gabardine tore, expensive shreds

178

fluttering to the ground. Like a plant watered on rage, his tail snaked out, thumping into the car park wall. A ridge of horns pressed into the ceiling, dust and grit showering down. Newly formed claws gouged grooves in the ground. Wings folded out into the space, bunching like badly pitched tents against the support pillars. His snout stretched toward Fulk, golden eyes beaming down. Fangs gleamed in the strip light.

Fulk thrust out his hands and shrieked.

"You can't! You can't! You—"

The dragon roared. Deep in his lungs, hundreds of alveoli pulsed and opened, releasing a superordinary gas. The gas filled Ben's maw, and then his back teeth were scraping together, causing a tiny spark. Fire cascaded into the car park. The motorbike exploded, spraying parts. The antique tome went up in smoke.

Fulk shrieked to shatter crystal. Then the flames engulfed him too. Doused in oil, he went up like a human candle. His blackened form twisted in the blast, his beard and skin crisping, the meat instantly charred. Scream cut short, the blazing slayer stumbled and fell, lay twitching on the ground. As Ben inhaled, the flames dispersing, the Black Knight was ready to serve.

Ben felt his strength drain from him. He collapsed heavily, throwing up dust. A pillar toppled, broken blocks crashing on concrete. Then he was dwindling, dwindling, pulling himself in, wings and claws shrinking towards the pain at his core.

A naked man curled up on the ground, shivering despite the lingering heat.

Hooves clopped next to his ears. Ben made out a blur of red silk, pale hands reaching down.

Someone said, "Well, I think you made your point."

Then all the lights went out.

PART TWO

Occult Bodies

Because we focused on the snake, we missed the scorpion.

Egyptian proverb

The road, such as it w... her bare toes long and b... skirts swished through the ... ... cover the world, dust on dust on du... ... on bones. Dust like ghosts haunting the a... ... against the horizon, a hot steel bell, the un... ...pper of the sun ringing through the hollow blue. Sc... ... around her head, leaning on a staff carved from a *galool* tree, old Dhegdheer walked from the place where the mirage met the real and into the village of Dhuroob.

The hag sniffed. Death was everywhere. Huur, the Reaper, the Old Marabou, stalked the village ruffling his feathers, pecking at whatever scraps he could find. Death whispered in the cornfields, the stalks rustling like hair on a corpse. Death sang in the flies around children's mouths, their shrivelled forms huddled around the dry village well. The Red Cross had rumbled on to the cities, abandoning the sticks. Dhegdheer could smell as much. Death was far from new to her. On a different day, with better luck, the hag might have feasted here herself, but *jilal*, the harshest season of the year, had stolen all the sweet young things and the *gu* rains would not come, leaving her with nothing. No bones

185

en steered clear
ately slim. And the one
was following a trail of crumbs
left behind. Destiny had scratched
d. Necessity rendered her safe. Now she
of the gods.

, Dhegdheer pondered wryly, *do the gods serve?* The
since she'd met Khadra in Qardho had not been kind to
ese lands. A war somewhere drew foreign aid away, and despair
rained where the skies would not. Millions starved, and it was
down to Dhegdheer to do something about it. Dhegdheer, and
the one human left in these parts who still meddled with *sixir*,
spoke with the old spirits. Casting bones and staring into her
fire, Ayan had come to learn of the Pact and the Lore, forbidden
magic and sleeping gods . . . That was why, when searching for
a suitable pawn, Dhegdheer had chosen Ayan to summon the
Queen. Or at least to enable her summoning. Ayan might have
an ear for the mysteries, but she was long past the age when
her blood was of use, her innocence a memory. The woman had
made the ultimate sacrifice, choosing her only daughter instead.
She had taken the map and the shard that Dhegdheer had given
her, shoved them into Khadra's hand and sent the girl out into
the desert.

And now the Queen had woken. Now the dawn was near.

Dhegdheer walked into the village, between the thatched huts
that looked like so much debris blown here by the latest storm.
She trudged past a dead tree, so sun-bleached and crooked it
was hard to believe it had ever borne leaves. She trudged past
the village well and those who slumped there, half alive among
the piled corpses, clinging on to a desiccated hope. The dying
watched her without passion. Passion here was over and done,

and what was one more hallucination? One more famished dream? This hag who tottered by on her staff, plump, toothless, droop-eared and hunched, could not possibly be real. Her strange claws said as much.

Dhegdheer moved on, forgotten as soon as her shadow passed them.

Forgotten, she thought, as bitter as a brat's bladder. *Forgotten like all the* hambo *from the Old Lands . . .*

Forgotten, but not done.

Not quite. Not yet.

In the sandy circle in the middle of Dhuroob, where long ago effigies had burned and tribesmen danced, the old woman paused to take her bearings. Her left ear, the fearful appendage of many folk tales, detecting lost children in the waste, quivered and twitched. But this time she strained to hear magic not youth. A faint humming that she could not place fixed her attention to the ring of huts. She turned, a short, portly compass seeking the right doorway. She made out chanting, a muttered curse, a croaked prayer.

Ah, there *you are, storm stoker . . .*

She shambled up to the door and struck the corrugated surface with her staff.

"Woman! *Naag!*" Her voice clanged along with the noise. "No use skulking in there like a rat. Come out here and face me!"

The only answer was silence. The wind came up, stirring the dust. A bush rolled by, on its way to nowhere. Faint groans travelled on the breeze.

Dhegdheer raised her staff again. Her years had not made her patient. Before wood struck iron, the door creaked open. A corpse stood there, bare-breasted and bent, wrinkled like a sheet fallen from a line. Her skull grinned without grinning, her cheekbones sucking in the light. Her braided hair shook in denial. Bones and beads clacked around her neck.

She clutched her breast at the sight of Dhegdheer.

"*Demon!* Why have you come again? What more do you want?"

Dhegdheer grabbed the woman's wrist, pushing her back into the hut.

"Milk and peace, sister. May I come in?"

"*Demon!* Dead thing!" The woman pushed back. She was strong for one in the Reaper's shadow. "I did as you asked. I gave up my daughter. You will never set foot in this house!"

Dhegdheer shuffled backwards, her long toenails scraping in grit. She stood there a minute, hunched and panting, her eyes two cherry stones set in bark. Then she slipped her scarf off her head and wiped her greasy forehead.

"You fool, Ayan. Have you no faith? The Queen has risen. The matter is done."

Ayan regarded the hag, this creature from folklore stood on her step. Her eyes caught a spark of sunlight. She snatched a mouthful of passing dust.

"I thought . . . I dreamed . . ." She blinked away flies. "My daughter was successful?"

"Yes. The girl is a beating heart for a ghost. Substance for shadow. Flesh for a dream. Your seed has sprouted wings and lightning."

The grin widened, a death mask attempting a look of satisfaction.

"Then I am pleased. We are saved."

"You *are* dreaming." Dhegdheer straightened up as much as she was able, flapping her scarf at Ayan. "Your flesh and blood sustains a goddess, but we are not saved yet. And salvation will not come the way you imagine."

"What do you mean? Look around you, hag." Ayan thrust out her arm, a bony sweep that took in the shacks, the empty streets, the withered corn on the rise. "Look at all this dust and death. Once, long ago, this land was green. According to the tales, the rain fell when the Queen wished it. The sun shone at her command. If not for salvation, why would we wake her? You said that the Queen would bring the rains. You said that she would come and—"

"No. That is not what I said." A smile crept over the hag's face. There was cruelty in it, and relief. She no longer had to pretend. "I gave you the map and the shard. I told you where to find the tomb. It was only your hope that said all the rest."

Ayan considered this. Despite her undernourished state, her sunken flesh and bony limbs, a spark still gleamed in her. Charms had sustained her where scraps of food could not, and no one had ever thought her unwise.

Ayan considered. But she was not ready to hear the truth.

"No. I have seen it in the flames. The Queen has risen, and soon the sky will grow black. Atiya will bring *barwaaqo* to us. God's rain." In such a dry land, it was small wonder the tribes had a word to describe – no, contain, catch like a vessel – the sacred importance of water. The holiness of rain. Ayan trembled and stretched out her neck, daring the hag to challenge her. "I have seen it. A serpent in the sky . . ."

Dhegdheer was shaking her head.

"No," she said. "You are wrong. All tales have their ending, Ayan. All ages pass. Already the Lore is broken. The Pact has been undone. A new age is dawning. And it has no place for you."

Ayan's grin shrivelled up like the nearby trees.

"You have tricked me."

"I have *guided* you. For a higher purpose. Like in the old days, earthly tools for earthly ends. Human flesh," Dhegdheer licked her lips, "to moor the divine."

Ayan spoke as though in a trance, the hag's admission sinking through her shock.

"The Queen will not come."

"The Queen will not come. She flew off into the world to claim her treasures. To *awaken* them, as we knew she would. Atiya is simply another tool. A door that some would open. Some would even defy the gods."

"Who would *dare*?"

"Look into your fire again, Ayan. Tell me what some would not dare. Tell me where they draw the line on power. Tell me what quenches their thirst for control."

"No," Ayan said. Her twig-like fingers trembled around her throat. "Khadra. My daughter. This cannot be."

"You will never see your daughter again. Not in this world, woman."

And even in this arid place, a little water flowed. The hag looked away from Ayan's tears, her grizzled lips uncomfortably twisted.

"You should have sought counsel when you had the chance. Instead, you placed your faith in monsters."

"Since when did the elders listen to a woman? A woman prattling about old fireside tales?" If Ayan could have mustered spit, she would have speckled the ground. "Besides, the elders are gone. Gone or dead. You caught me between the lion and the cobra, blinded by despair. Now you tell me my choice was for nothing, when you promised us a storm."

"Oh, a storm is coming. But it is not the one that *you* brewed."

Wind gusted in from the waste. It carried a strange mechan-

190

ical drone, a hum in the air growing louder. Dhegdheer paid it no mind. She watched the woman, savouring her pain. Ayan put her head in her hands, mourning the loss of her child, the trap into which she had fallen. The beads around her neck shook with her sobs.

"What is done is done." For the first time in years, Dhegdheer tasted triumph. "The bones cast. The fire lit. Soon I might feast again, as I once did."

"Eater of children!" Ayan looked up, rage burning through her sorrow. "Liar! Bitch!"

"Shout all you like. Three days from now, the sun grows dark and casts a shadow across the land. A shadow in which we all stand."

"Why have you come here, hag? Did you come all this way just to crow?"

"No," Dhegdheer said, and then her knife was in her hand. It was an old blade, and a trusty one, the edge black with dried blood. "Tongues mean tales and secrets stay secret in silence. Other eyes watch, woman. Other eyes *see*. No one must live to tell of the tomb. No one must learn of our plan. All tales have their ending, and your part in this one is done."

Dhegdheer raised the knife. Leaning on her staff, she lurched toward Ayan. The woman stumbled backwards, her hands raised, her throat too dry to vent a scream.

The wind gusted, stronger than before. The droning sound filled the air. The corn shook like a sack of shells, and rags over windows set to flapping, pots and pans rattling like bells. Straw flew from thatched rooftops, whirling a yellow dance. Bricks tumbled from the pocked village wall, with its bullet holes like poems of war. All those battles had won was dust, and the same dust rose up now – a phantom army bombarding the village.

191

Both women, human and otherwise, scuttled in retreat. The sun rolled in frantic clouds. Swords chopped at the flailing sky. Ayan yelled and Dhegdheer looked up, scowling at the intrusion. *And Huur descends upon us!* Even as the hag thought it, she realised she was wrong. This was no giant beak come pecking, no sudden deathly attack. The ruckus above came from the engines of man-made machines.

Dhegdheer dropped her staff and knife and crouched down beside a wall, joining seamlessly with the shade. Then Long Ear wasn't there at all. A hooded vulture perched on a window ledge, watching the helicopter land.

As soon as the craft alighted, soldiers clambered out, bent low under the whirring blades. The craft was black and oddly marked, crossed swords over blank shields. The traditional motif had nothing to do with the UN, the Red Cross, the national army or any of the various factions currently fighting over the country. The soldiers' uniforms looked unfamiliar, but in the vulture's eyes they were instantly placed. The soldiers formed a *koox*, a local division upholding the much-hated Pact. They served the Guild, or the national arm of it. News of the breach in the Lore was spreading, and the hag guessed that the evidence pointed to Ayan. Pointed to her like a loaded gun.

Dhegdheer was too late.

The six men circled the doorway, AK-47s held high. Helmets shadowed their faces, their goggles reflecting Ayan's alarm. She stood there like a charred tree, arms branched out to placate them. Her rags whipped around her like a cloud of bats, her braids thrashing in the wind. Horror and grief slipped from her face, replaced by grudging defeat.

Oh storm stoker. Dhegdheer sheltered her head with her wings. *Curse your human luck!*

One of the soldiers stepped forward, a captain by the look of him. He threw something at Ayan's feet, a small ragged object. A little bag of grey fur. When the bag struck the sand, a shiny object fell out of it, a cylindrical shard of black rock, ringed by arcane symbols.

The captain did not question her identity. The beads and the bones around Ayan's neck betrayed her magical dabbling, and the fact that she was standing here, alive in a village that was mostly a grave, clearly seemed proof enough.

"*Mimsaab*," said the captain, his voice muffled by the steady *whoop whoop* of the helicopter blades. "You are under arrest. You must come with us at once."

"On whose authority? I answer to Eebe alone."

"Don't make this difficult. The Lore reaches even here. You have meddled with the Pact and roused one from the Sleep. You have pried into private matters and are therefore subject to our judgement."

"What matters?" But Ayan knew full well. "I acted purely in the interests of—"

"Destiny," the man said simply. "Yes. We know."

"Necessity," Ayan countered, and in that flyblown, barren place, she crossed her arms and glared to rival the sun. "Do you see a choice lying around here somewhere?"

The man ignored her. He raised an arm over his head and made a rotor out of his hand. In one fluid, practised manoeuvre, the soldiers grabbed Ayan and dragged her between the huts, bundling her into the waiting craft. Like a snub-nosed bird, the helicopter took once more to the skies, shitting smoke and dust.

Dhegdheer watched the craft dwindle overhead. Then she screeched in dismay. *The woman escapes.* She looked around her,

193

smelling rot and ruin, and was surprised to find she had lost her appetite.

The vulture flapped into the air, following the helicopter north.

And the sands whispered *mugdi*, darkness.

The sands whispered *kaw*.

Death.

ELEVEN

The dreams of dragons are deep and dark, filled with the sound and fury of ages. Unlike human dreams, which stem from daily life, fragments culled from conversations, strangers glimpsed in smoky bars, car crashes, radios and headlines. Humans shape fear and desire into myriad chimera, brief and flickering in the mind's eye. They dream quick. They dream bright. As quick and bright as their fleeting lives.

Dragon dreams are deep and dark. A dragon's dream is like a cave, yawning into damp silence where the jewels of memory wink and glimmer. Echoes haunt the curving walls, the strata of wars and famous matings, wounded bellows and fiery mirth. Eggs crack and blacksmiths hammer. Wyrmlings mewl and knights scream. Damsels whisper, chained to stakes, their breasts heaving with fear and lust.

Dragon dreams are deep and dark. As dark as the gulfs of space. As deep as time itself.

In Ben's dream, lightning flashed.

Silver raced through his mind's eye, jagging between the towering clouds. Silver sparkled deep in the billows, illuminating veins of darkness, backlighting skulls, pyramids and burnt-out woods . . . Unmoored from awareness, Ben sailed through surging memories, a leaf in a gale, tossed by warring winds. But with the inner knowledge of dreams, he understood that the storm

195

was not his, these passions foreign, due to another. He was lost in somebody else's rage.

In the storm, voices muttered, snatched away by the jealous wind.

You've been asleep for centuries . . .

Fulk was a fool, but he was right about that.

You are not even worth killing . . .

The Queen laughed, lashing the skies with electric scorn.

And this was *her* storm, wasn't it? His dreaming self grasped the fact in the shapes he couldn't remember, the sights he could not name. This was her storm, and when she had probed his mind in the museum, it seemed she had shared her essence too – a doubtless inadvertent exchange – their consciousness fusing with the contact and tainting each other with strange, alien fragments of thought.

A skinny girl in football shorts. A ring of shacks huddled in a dust storm. An African woman without teeth, grinning and pointing a bird-like claw . . .

Ben didn't want to see these things. He wanted to drift, unchained from his protean form, above his rekindling pain. Somewhere, ghosts howled impossibly in concrete, wolves loped into limousine doors and a man in black screamed and screamed. Each memory was an after-image of the sun, a negative in black and gold, making no real sense to him. All he could see were the clouds ahead, boiling into a sea of hands, every finger reaching towards him. Then the hands became a wall of mouths, lips stretched wide to swallow him. He could hear them moaning too: a susurration from parched throats, a song of hunger, loss and need . . .

Yes, it *was* a song. Or perhaps a prayer. A prayer for rain.

Into their gaping mouths he fell, the clouds closing over his

head. Motes swirled in the dark like flies. Or maybe dust. Dust
on dust on dust . . .
    Lightning flashed.
    Lightning laughed.
    Lighting sizzled and screamed . . .

Ben awoke with a jolt. The coruscation continued, however, an
intermittent neon pulse from behind a pair of long white curtains,
ballooning and twirling in the breeze. The glass doors behind
them stood open to the night, his only anchor in an otherwise
dark and empty room. Even as the dream left him, fading into
sparkling scraps, his extraordinary vision was kicking in, golden
lamps piercing the gloom. Sitting up in sweat-soaked sheets,
naked – naked again, of course – he rubbed his jaw and surveyed
his surroundings. Where had his adventures brought him this
time? Sanctuary, prison or tomb?
    Blink, blink, went the neon. *We're not telling . . .*
    He sensed no threat in the bedside table and the overstuffed
chair next to it, a cotton bathrobe thrown over one arm. The
wardrobe and the rug seemed unfazed by his presence. Legs
swinging over the side of the bed, his bare feet landed on
wood. When he stood, muscles groaning, it felt as though
someone had scrubbed his body with sandpaper while he slept,
sparing no nook or cranny. Ditto his tongue. Some medicinal
liquid coated his throat, the slightly syrupy turn of his thoughts
betraying the presence of drugs in his veins. Thoughts of healing
prompted memories of pain, and Ben's hand trembled to his
side. The flesh there felt tender and raw, but gradually on the
mend. Red marks circled his wrists, fading in the winking
light. His head ached like a broken tooth, and when he pressed
a finger to his eye, a knife travelled back into his skull, his

nerve endings stitching together, but still sulking over their wounds.

Fulk. The CROWS. They had chained him. Mocked him. *Tortured* him.

The balcony doors blinked red, black, red, alternating between the neon flashing somewhere beyond the discomforting darkness. As black as the hilt of Fulk's sword. As red as the end of Miss Macha's cigar. Black. Blink. Red. Hungry for air and a glimpse of his whereabouts, Ben shrugged on the bathrobe and walked into the light anyway, trying to recall the scenes in the car park. It wasn't easy. His brain yelped like a kicked dog, shying away from the memory. Already a grim suspicion was forming, making him feel like a fool . . .

Then he remembered Rose. After all his precautions, he had failed her. His hands closed, curling into fists. He went out on to the balcony, glaring down at four floors of thick white stone, some faux-rococo building with his room at the top. He was too far up for anyone to see him, this naked statue leaning on the railings, his taut skin criss-crossed by scars, flesh so pale his head seemed aflame in the neon. To his left, a network of rooftops crowned an angular sprawl of streets. A fizzy-drink sign blinked on a wall across the way, the insistent source of the neon. To his right, a raised railway bridge with dimly lit trains crawling along it. Traffic dotted the road below, a sluggish, coughing tide. Damp hung in the air, but it wasn't from the Thames. He would've known its brackish smell anywhere. Trees hushed beside arching street lights. Benches, mopeds and fast-food joints, the usual urban paraphernalia, slid under his questing gaze. The smell of bird shit laced his nostrils. So did the smell of grilled meat, and his stomach growled. When was the last time he'd eaten anyway? Before the Third Crusade?

The hunger in him was deeper, he knew, aroused by his clash with the Queen. It was the hunger of ages, a chasm of years spiralling without end . . . At that moment, his longing for Rose was a thorn in his chest. But that was not all. He sensed that another wound had opened, this one fresher and deeper still, awash with a yearning that Rose could not fulfil. Her humanity forbade it, her mortality a gulf between them. No matter how much they felt for each other, Rose would soon grow old and die. Like the flower after which she was named, the invisible worm would find her in the night, in the howling storm, and drag her down into the soil. Love could not change that. Rose would never know the solitude of ages, never need to hide in the shadows, forever unique, forever alone. Never know the memories that gave no warmth and the dreams that slipped out of reach. She would only ever know what it was to be human. Quick. Bright. Fleeting as dust.

And in his heart, this dark mirror. The Queen breathing his name.

Benjurigan . . .

Ben pushed the thought away, hating the stirring in his loins. How could he think of Atiya now? Rose was in danger. He couldn't protect her. He could only hope that wherever she was, her captors were not hurting her. If he believed Fulk's comment in the car park, that somehow Rose's coupling with him had invested her with power, some useful residual force, then he guessed he could hope that. Perhaps he still had time to save her, make up for his mistake.

Three days from now, everything changes . . .

Whatever Miss Macha had meant by those words, three days didn't feel like a lot. Scales rippled briefly over his skin like a split-flap display at an airport. His fists bunched tighter, newly formed claws digging into his palms.

Tenements rose across the road, some with balconies like the one he stood upon, bordering windows dark and lit. A plane roaring across the sky and faint laughter below offered no clues to his whereabouts. These days, one place was much like another. Cities grew more and more uniform, a collection of shops and office blocks with antique survivors hemmed in between them, cathedrals and castles gasping for air. All the same, there was something familiar about the view. When he closed his eyes, straining, his extraordinary hearing picked out words, guttural and clipped, rich with tones of feeling and intelligence. Over the din of a nearby stadium and the thump of dubstep a mile away, he discerned a European dialect. Gothic. Teutonic. Mentally riffling through his experience, he could only come up with one connection, and that connection was rather fond of this city. *Fond?* He would probably claim the city as his own, if not boasting that he'd laid the foundations, then at least taking credit for her survival. He recalled the Punchinello mask, the white horse, the flamboyant, prismatic display, the scattered impressions falling into place.

Berlin. He was in Berlin.

And if he was in Berlin, that could only mean one thing.

"Son of a bitch," he said, and stormed out of the room.

TWELVE

Four floors down a spiral flight of stairs and Ben found his unwanted saviour.

"*Abend, Liebling!*" Von Hart said as Ben strode through the purple swing door with the mirrored pentagram window. "I won't ask you if your dreams were pleasant. I imagine they were darker than a rat's *Arschloch.*"

Von Hart swivelled in his seat next to the catwalk, his sunglasses reflecting the bulbs that lined the velveteen walls. The catwalk itself was empty, a narrow black pier that jutted out into the equally empty club. Luminous paint shone on the walls, old symbols running around the seedy space, pink Seals of Solomon and blue mandalas competing with orange oms and yellow yin-yangs, a gaudy occult lexicon. The sight of them made Ben feel queasy, reminding him of his recent entrapment. He looked away, finding no relief in the gloom, where leather booths hunkered like bull-shouldered and shady patrons. Like *Lurkers.* Alcohol, dry ice and sweat, none of it quite stale, laced the dingy atmosphere. No doubt as planned, Von Hart was the centre of attention, the lecherous light picking out his hair, short, blonde and strictly parted. A too-generous section of thigh slipped out of his red silk kimono as Ben approached him through the vacant tables.

"You. Of course, you." Ben threw up his hands. "I thought

you agreed to mind your own business." He crossed a small dance floor, no hint of disco in his movements, and came to a halt under the spotlight.

The man by the catwalk looked undaunted. Smiled, even.

"Yes. Chicago, 1931. Has it really been that long?"

"You promised. Swore on Titania's tits. You said—"

"Oh come off it, Ben. When will you learn? Never trust the Fay."

"Trust you? Is that a joke?"

"The only joke is your attitude. Is this how you thank me? It appears that your *business*," maddeningly, Von Hart raised a hand and sketched quotation marks around the word with his fingers, "was about to get you killed."

He resumed interest in the half-finished glass of bubbly at his elbow. A bottle rested on the table beside him, Dom Pérignon on ice. Next to the bucket lay a stack of euros and a deck of cards, the cash more than likely the takings from one of his high-stakes gambling games. In those games, the cards tended to favour Von Hart (and not always through chance), as Ben's wallet had learnt to his regret in the past. You rarely played this man and won. His cheekbones were fine china, his skin as pale as sifted chalk. He had a natural, inscrutable poker face. Like most of his kind, Blaise Von Hart wore many guises, but in modern times, he favoured an aspect of aloofness and refinement. The stars printed on his kimono were only a feeble nod to tradition. A fairy living in the twenty-first century, he preferred to dwell in neon-lit realms, a young man who haunted bars and the edges of dance floors, where he claimed that magic could go unnoticed.

Like Ben, Von Hart had lived through centuries, a constant in the transient eras. The envoy extraordinary was older than him, much older. In comparison, eight hundred and sixty years would probably feel like a tea break. When the walls of Camelot rose, white and shining under the sun, they said that Von Hart was standing in their shadow. And when those same walls fell, when his fair and fickle race had left this world and strode off into the nether, he had remained behind, a reminder, an ambassador, a link between elsewhere and here. In a sense, Von Hart's role mirrored that of the Guild; he served as a counsel, a confidant, a sympathetic ear for Remnants on their side of the fence. As such, the Fay representative was only a Remnant by appointment, by simple virtue of remaining behind when his people had left the earth. In truth, he was Fay through and through. All the same, like the rest of the ditched and the abandoned, he still had to live under the Lore. Once, long ago, he had told Ben that the Fay hoped to return one day. Lord knew enough of the Remnants had cleaved to that idea: that the Fay would come back after their nigh-on fifteen centuries' long abandonment to restore balance and peace, announce that the dark days were finished, the great sacrifice was over . . . In fact that was the very reason so many of the Remnant leaders had agreed to the Pact in the first place. If it wasn't exactly its selling point, the promise, the hope, had kept more than one fabulous beast grimly compliant for hundreds of years . . .

Had.

If Ben had heard some inference in Von Hart's claim, some duty placed on the thin man's shoulders, the envoy neglected to clarify, and even if Ben had pressed the matter, he knew he wouldn't get a straight answer. Every now and then, every hundred years or so, fate or chance brought the two of them together. They were not exactly enemies and not exactly friends. In the same way one didn't wake sleeping dragons, only a fool would trust the Fay. The magical creators of all Remnants, the masters of the "bound bestiary", they were creatures of glamour, who only *appeared* human, after a fashion, but who remained inherently alien and other. If Ben credited myth – and why shouldn't he? – the Fay had once been known as the First-Born, gods or something like gods, dancing in the void at the dawn of creation. As time went on, and the gods relied more and more on mortal belief, some vague cataclysm had come about, according to the myths. The Fay had lost much of their power, becoming half mortal, wanderers of the infinite worlds spinning through the universe. The tales were as colourful as the details were vague, but the Fay had certainly entwined their race with this world, creating the fabulous creatures and magical minions that had populated the hills, lakes and forests of the Old Lands. Since their departure, Von Hart – or whatever his real name was – had set up home in the land he liked best and slowly but surely taken on a Germanic mien, in a way that Ben couldn't decide was affectation or admiration. These days, the Fay, or fairies, were the stuff of children's storybooks the world over. No one could know that only one member of the ancient and netherspanning race remained upon earth. Or just how *interfering* he could be . . . Who could say where the seemingly deathless race had really come from or how long they had guided, meddled with and, yes, on occasion, corrupted humans? Capriciousness was in their nature. So was a kind of thoughtless cruelty. When you added the role of envoy to the mix – a role appointed by the Fay high council shortly before their departure from earth – trusting Von Hart would be tantamount to madness.

Which was why Ben rankled at his rescue. Like it or not, he was in the envoy's debt, and being in debt to one of *his* kind was not something that one took lightly. Unease bit at his wounded pride.

"I had everything under control."

"Oh really?" Von Hart's accent was crisp and Germanic, with a strange, sing-song undertone shared by nobody else on earth. And it conveyed knowing humour. "It didn't look that way, *Liebling*."

"You've been spying on me."

"I kept an eye out for you." The envoy took a sip of champagne and started to shuffle the cards, spades, hearts, diamonds and clubs slipping through his delicate hands with all the smoothness of poured milk.

"Spying."

Von Hart pursed his lips, making it a moot point. "Since Thursday morning, the London papers have been screaming about a terrorist attack at the British Museum, hallucinatory gas, mass hysteria, you name it. People have yet to ask what point the terrorists hoped to make by traumatising a bunch of historians." He cut the cards, blended them together. "Same as it ever was, *ja*?"

"I'm not in the mood for chit-chat."

"Shame. I was going to tell you that there was also a murder. Sensational, to say the least. Later on, at the hospital. Your professor made like a human and . . . died."

This broke through Ben's umbrage. His eyebrows went up and his jaw hung slack, a discarded ventriloquist's dummy. He fumbled for his own levers and springs, replying in a splutter.

"Winlock's dead? He was alive when I left the museum, despite his nosedive off the stage." The sound of cracked bones fired a popgun in his ears. "I knew he was hurt, but . . ." He stared at the envoy. "The Queen. She killed him."

But that wasn't right. Didn't *feel* right. For one thing, where was her motive? She had already grabbed the Crook, smashed her way through the Great Court. *Revenge drives her on* . . . But was she so cruel that she'd take revenge on a feeble old man for the relic's recent unearthing? Ben didn't think so. After all, she had spared *him*.

Von Hart confirmed his line of thinking.

"No. Not the Queen." The envoy was clearly aware of recent events. No surprise there. "Unless throttling noted scholars in their beds strikes you as her modus operandi."

Ben winced at this casual description. He hadn't known Winlock personally, never got the chance to speak with him, but no one would find such an end pleasant.

"Then who?" Pointless rebuking Von Hart for his flippancy, of course. "The CROWS? What would they have against Winlock?"

"Do the Three need a reason? Murder to them is a day at the races. Still, I think they were busy with you at the time."

"Amazingly, something you don't know."

"Even I have my flaws."

"And I suppose you found all this out through your spells and mystical scrying?"

Von Hart shrugged at the sarcasm. "Some. Mostly from BBC News." He took a sip of champagne and feigned a glance at his wrist, watchless and alabaster smooth. "Tonight Club Zauber is closed to the public. All the same, I'm a busy man. And you were going to come here anyway. Right?"

Ben crossed his arms, the bathrobe straining at his shoulders. He wanted to deny it, but he *had* thought of Von Hart, hadn't he? Standing on the steps of the British Museum, wondering whether to get some help, pay the envoy extraordinary a visit. Von Hart's intervention had made the decision for him. He was here now, regardless. Here and beholden.

Christ, he needed a drink.

"You got anything in here that doesn't taste like piss? Near-death experiences give me a thirst."

Von Hart rolled his eyes and nodded at the bar on the far side of the dance floor. Ben walked over and slunk behind it, searching the crowded shelves. Jack was there, smiling down at him. He grabbed the bottle, popped the lid and took a long swig. *Better.* Wiping his lips on his sleeve, he returned to loom over the envoy at the table.

"So what's it to be?" he said, tipping the bottle at the ceiling, at an imagined sky. "A flight up there for a cup of starlight? Three hundred years of servitude? My firstborn child?"

Von Hart tutted, but at least it wiped the smile off his face. *Damn faeries.*

"Be like that. Next time I'll stay at home."

"Fairy, don't test me. The CROWS kidnapped Rose."

It was hard to confess this without a tremble in his voice. The fear was with him now, a constant murmur in his heart and mind, spiking into cold dissonance whenever he thought of her capture. But if he had expected sympathy, he was disappointed.

"Well, you will form these *attachments* to humans. Like trying to catch the wind. You should do what I do and keep a practical distance from them."

Ben snorted. "Your dalliances are not to my taste."

Von Hart waved the deck of cards. "Men, women. What difference does it make? They are all dust in the end. The *Sturm und Drang* of their little lives is seldom of any consequence."

Ben was glowering now. "Said with your usual compassion." He jabbed a thumb at his chest. "Rose is of consequence to *me*."

"And why is that, do you think? You've always been looking

for someone to save. All those women, all those loves . . . All beautiful, brittle and brief. You know, what happened in Mordiford wasn't your fault."

This reference to the past jarred Ben despite himself. The envoy had seen much more than he liked. Ever since Ben had fled the Marches and found his way to the Great Forest, Von Hart had been there, scrying his secrets. Or perhaps he'd just read his charter myths. Ben remembered the scene in the woodland cave, sheltering Maud with his wings as her skin and the trees blazed hellfire red . . .

"Careful, fairy . . ."

Von Hart shrugged and let the matter drop.

"I'm afraid that your current squeeze is of some consequence. And to more than just you. For some reason, she matters to the Coven Royal. Your relations with her taint her with power. *Smoke and mirrors*, wasn't it? *Bait*."

"Just how long were you watching them torture me?"

"I was trying to find out what the CROWS were up to. The Lore is broken. I felt it buckle like the Tay Bridge, and now another is among us. None of you are safe. So I looked in on you, and good job I did." Von Hart snapped the cards down on the table. "Is there anywhere you *haven't* blundered?"

Ben rubbed his wrists. The sting of sorcery still marked his flesh. Golden glyphs swam in his memory, twinkling primordial fish. Fish with very sharp teeth. Under the shoal, he saw ram-like horns and dark-scaled flanks, a beast from another time, a circling, fathomless sphinx. And he had been struggling in the depths, floundering from New York to London, following a path of stolen relics and chasing her arrowhead tail . . . Once again, he felt like a pinball, shunted around by unplanned events.

"I guess blundered is the word." If pride had made him forget his manners, the envoy reminded him of them. He gave a grudging sigh. "What you did in the car park. You shouldn't have risked it."

"Shouldn't I?" Von Hart removed his sunglasses, fixing Ben with sharp violet eyes. "Believe it or not, I have a certain responsibility. You may have forgotten, but back in the day people used to call the Fay *masters*. And a decent master looks after their pets."

Ben let this pass. The fact was the envoy spoke the truth. Von Hart was referring to Ben's origins. Back in the Old Lands, long before the Once and Future King was an envious itch in Uther's breeches, the Fay masters had gathered at Stonehenge to discuss how best to protect their treasures, treasures that included Arawn's Cauldron, the Harp of Avalon and the Twin Swords, along with mountains of gold and jewels. Even then, they could sense the coming darkness, a war that would sever the worlds. The details were sketchy at best, a myth within a myth, but some texts claimed that the Fay lords had turned to a more than ancient wisdom, the few shreds of knowledge salvaged from the First-Born, the gods that some said they had once been. *Dragons*, the lords whispered. *At the dawn of time, dragons flew, protecting the walls of paradise* . . . Dragons, of course, had long been extinct by that point, legends to even those deemed legendary. And the Fay, in their wisdom, in their folly, elected to give these creatures rebirth.

The masters had recreated Ben's kind, splicing the long-extinct and fabled salamander with the everyday human physique by way of lost science and spells. Of course, it made sense. The innate transformative nature of the beast was clearly conducive to secrecy and travel, as was the creature's power of flight. Leading a seven-ton monster around would have raised all kinds of awkward questions and likely have caused a kingdom-wide panic. Comprised of flesh, magic and fire, the reborn creature – the *dragon* – had mated, bred and guarded the Fay in their towers and caves. At least it had for a while. Unfortunately, the masters saw fit to grant the beasts awareness and brains that equalled theirs. In time, some of the dragons had grown greedy. Greedy, resentful and very hungry . . .

You might have birthed us as slaves, some said, *but watch as we claim our freedom.*

This was the spark to all the trouble, the font from which all the myths sprang. Myths that had created a thousand fires, a thousand damsels chained to stakes and a thousand lances snapped against scales. The rest, as they say, was history.

"You crossed the nether for me, Von Hart. I didn't think that was possible."

The envoy cocked an eyebrow and fanned the cards out on the table. "Spells can only stretch so far," he admitted. "When my people abandoned this world, disgusted by Camlann and human weakness, I wasn't the only thing they left behind." He shifted in his seat. Sharing the history of the Fay always made him visibly uncomfortable. "The Silver Leys cut through the nether. Roads, if you will, branching out from the earthly plane. Roads that the Lurkers won't come near, not if they can help it. The protective wards would mean the end of them."

"So where do these roads go?"

"Who knows? Avalon. Tír na nÓg. Hell. I've never followed them to their source. I try to avoid them if at all possible." The envoy looked pained. "The Leys want to . . . *pull* me. They speak to my blood. In turn, I get to pull and manipulate them, make the roads go where I want, within certain terrestrial limits. It isn't easy, as you might guess."

Ben recalled the seething shadows in the car park walls, spectral sharks stirred into a frenzy. He pictured a secret highway running through that infinite space, the unexplored gulf that edged the world. Narrow paths like water on oil, intersections and crossroads, their spooling threads knitted together by Von Hart's spells. The idea came as a surprise to him. How long had he known the envoy? Learn something new every day . . .

"That explains a lot. You do tend to turn up like a bad penny."

Von Hart sniffed. "The horse, of course, was only for show." He smiled again, flashing his teeth, his inherent mischief winning through. Still, the memory of his ride haunted his eyes, and Ben knew him well enough to see it.

"We're in deep shit, Von Hart. Without the Lore, we're sitting ducks. God only knows what the CROWS are planning. I went to see the Guild, but the chairman wasn't much help."

"I'm surprised that lot are still in business. And why would he help you anyway? The Guild merely tolerates your existence. It doesn't exactly support it." The envoy looked thoughtful. "And lately I wonder if the old guard might prefer us all dead."

Ben took a slug of Jack. He ran a hand over his jaw, stubble sparking his suspicions. The envoy spoke directly to them, stirring the doubts that festered in his mind. Doubts that were ever growing, having been planted in him at the museum and now sprouting razor-sharp leaves.

"Are you saying what I think you're saying? Bardolfe sent me to see Winlock, claiming he could give me the skinny on the Star and these other relics the Queen is after . . ." He paused, thinking. He saw the old knight in the gallery at Paladin's Court, patting his shoulder in the shadow of the bookcase. *One conversation with him and I'm sure your little quest will reach its end.* Then there was the Cairo connection. The syzygy. The Crook and the

Pschent. *Ghosts from the Sands.* The hieroglyphs on his bonds in the car park . . . Bardolfe had gone to Egypt on holiday and Miss Macha had said she was heading there too. He didn't need to look at the envoy to see that he was right. "I'm an idiot. Bardolfe must have known all along that the Queen was going to steal the Crook. He expected her to kill me. He sent me to the museum to die."

"What was it I said about blundering?"

Ben barely heard him. Now that his doubts had come to fruition, the implications staggered him. The thought of the Guild in cahoots with the CROWS, knights conspiring with Remnants, who in turn conspired with House Fitzwarren, forming a treacherous triad . . . The hate required to weave such a plot made his mouth feel dry. The Lore was broken and it seemed that the Guild had taken advantage of the breach, an unthinkable, unprecedented move. One that betrayed their whole purpose. Why? What did Bardolfe want?

Anarchy. Bloodshed. Revolution.

Ben shuddered. The dim confines of Club Zauber didn't seem big enough to hold all his questions, his scaling fear and confusion. He was in the dark. Floundering. He'd been floundering ever since Fulk had walked into the Legends bar, swinging a sword and the *New York Times*. He stumbled over to a nearby booth and sat down heavily, his head a flame-red ball in his hands.

"I could really do without this shit."

"*Liebling*, if I could wave a wand . . ."

Ben started muttering, trying to trace the course of the puzzle. "The Lore is broken because there is more than one active dragon. Something or someone breached the Long Sleep. You'd think that the Guild would try to restore it, not join forces with an underground coven who've resented the Pact from day one. It doesn't make any sense."

"Oh I'm sure it does," Von Hart said. "We just don't know how yet."

Ben threw the envoy a look, but Von Hart continued on his own route through the mystery. "If the Guild plays traitor, then perhaps only Paladin's Court is involved. Perhaps only Bardolfe and his inner circle, a conspiracy at high level. Perhaps your professor was somehow mixed up in it and Bardolfe sent someone to silence him. If the breach in the Lore isn't common knowledge, it might also explain why the Whispering Chapter hasn't come baying for your blood."

Mention of the saint cult frosted Ben's skin. It was another enemy, yet to pounce from the wings. The Chapter's grievance bore slightly more weight than the old Fitzwarren grudge, which the cult looked down on as petty and trifling. The Chapter had no interest in personal gain, in vengeance symbolised by bricks and mortar. No *Spei est Vindicta* there. Instead, they favoured pious judgement. Their absence from current events was odd, Ben agreed – agreed with goose bumps and a shiver up his spine.

"Right now, I've got enough worries. This has to start and end with the Queen. Atiya. She is the source of all this. According to Bardolfe, the Guild didn't even know she had risen. He actually laughed at the possibility."

You think that the Guild wouldn't have known? A disturbance in the Long Sleep? The Lore so dramatically breached?

"I'm sure he did. He must have seen you coming."

Ben swore. Bardolfe had been answering his questions after all, albeit slyly. That thin smile on his wizened face. *How could I have been so stupid?* Thinking about the Queen, her dusky wings thrashing around the museum courtyard, he stood and faced Von Hart.

"Who . . . what is she? What exactly am I up against?"

"I'm not sure," Von Hart said and gathered up the cards. With that simple motion, the pressure in the place was building, the air thickening like glue. Paradoxically, a wind came up, a private gale surrounding the pale figure by the catwalk, who rose to his feet, the consummate showman, red silk fluttering as he spread his arms. "But I was tutor to Merlin when the old lech went lusting after Nimue in the wood. I watched as she trapped him in the oak that is sometimes a tower of glass and sometimes walls of impenetrable mist. I shared books with the Rabbi Loew in his little black house on Siroka Street, Prague, and taught his pupils to steal a shroud from the dancing corpse of a plague-felled child, with the greatest success. And in his castle at Wewelsburg, I gleaned the wisdom of Herr Magier Himmler and used it against the Black Sun Priests to bring the Third Reich crashing to its knees." Von Hart grinned through his spiel. "I'm reasonably sure I can find out."

With that, he threw the cards in the air.

THIRTEEN

"The thing with myths is they never really die." Von Hart's sing-song tones pushed against the viscous surrounds, seeming to echo down an endless corridor. "Even when the memory of them fades, a seed always remains, spinning in the cosmic void. The Long Sleep was there long before the Guild called it that, imposing their makeshift medieval Lore on the fabled and numinous. The Long Sleep is simply a human term for a universal fact. All myths have their season, and in their time, pass. Dreams, monsters, ghosts, gods . . ."

The deck of cards fluttered from his hands and bloomed around him like airborne pollen. "And where, you might ask, do they go?" Each card hung suspended, forming a sphere in the middle of the club. The floor sucked at Ben's feet as the envoy conjured, compressing the surrounding atoms into a dense and invisible mass. Magic surged around Ben's body, the symbols tumbling from Von Hart's mouth diverted by his natural immunity. His ears popped. His skin prickled. Caught in the tide, he stood like a rock in a river. He pushed back, but it was like pushing against a wall of foot-thick cellophane. He stopped struggling and came to a halt, exhausted and peeved, at the edge of the dance floor.

"That's right," Von Hart said. "Don't fight it. Open your mind to the incantation. I want you to think about the Queen. I want you to draw on your memories."

Curiosity overrode Ben's discomfort. The dark shape swimming in his mind came up for air on the surface. The spotlight above Von Hart flickered, remembered heat, remembered lightning – and images went storming through Ben's head. A shapely shadow entering the lecture theatre, her sharp-boned face and long neck. Her cold, regal glance. How quickly her mask had tumbled to the floor, revealing the creature beneath, a burning beauty propelling herself up on to the stage and hurling the professor aside as if he was a scrunched-up ball of paper. That electrical, organic stench, like he'd smelled that night in his living room. Her smoky flesh absorbing the Crook. *I am Atiya . . . Queen of Punt.* Ben had looked *into* her, into her fluid substance, and in exchange for the vision, she'd swooped down on him, pushing him down, overpowering him. The memory stung as much as it aroused him.

"She . . . she looked into me, too." The Queen's eyes filled his skull, sparks dancing from her brow to his. "A desert, a girl, New York City. For a moment, we were one. One heart. One mind. I felt her rage, her lust for revenge. Then she changed again. Took on . . ." Took on the shape of the dragon. Or shrugged off the human lie. "She . . . she isn't the same as me, is she?"

"Yes and no." Von Hart circled his arm and the cards followed, a pictorial tide clattering around him. "Your Queen was originally serpent-born, true. One of the old breed, created by the First-Born, the ancestor gods of the Fay, who some view as our elevated forebears. This was back in the early days, the dawn of the Old Lands. But in time, Atiya became so much more, a dragon become a god . . . Now she is merely a ghost from limbo, rising from the gulfs of the lost and the forgotten that men, in their pride, came to call the Sleep. Once summoned, the Queen anchored herself in human flesh, but she isn't quite . . . corporeal."

216

"Yeah, I noticed. But what does it mean?"

The cards gathered before Von Hart at the end of the catwalk, flipping over to reveal their faces, diamonds, clubs, hearts and spades. The symbols were growing, Ben saw, the printed ink spreading out to fill the white on every card until they were bright, mottled rectangles, swirling with thaumaturgic light. The cards multiplied, crowding the space before the envoy, shuffling around him despite gravity, forming an airborne mosaic, some larger composite image. An elongated skull seen side-on. A severed heart. Or a continent.

Africa.

"With science and machines," Von Hart said, "Man has chased magic out of the world. Having toppled the forests and tainted the seas, humans quake in the shadow of destruction, a cataclysm of their own making. Yes, everything has its season – even humanity – but myths never die, they merely sleep. And some myths long to return to the here and now with an equal level of greed."

"Said like your average misanthropic Fay."

The envoy paid him no mind. "Some have waited for millennia. Spirits in the ether. Some of these spirits became gods, growing strong on faith. Throughout the ages, all have found themselves summoned and banished, summoned and banished, sometimes riding in human flesh. One by one the gods grew dormant, starved of followers and slipping into dreams, waiting for faith to rouse them once more."

The "magic bricks" that Ben had seen in the British Museum fleeted through his mind – Ammit, Apep, Shezmu and Set – the statues portraying a liminal union, the earthly with the divine, the empyrean with the carnate, demons from a younger, more credulous age.

"Why does this sound so familiar?" he asked. "These gods fell asleep like we do. Like Remnants."

"Not quite the same. Your kind were *lulled*." The envoy lifted his head, remembering, and then uttered some lines from a very old song.

> The king's harp shattered in three
> reforged then unmade a silver key
> a severed song the watcher's keep
> locking the door of endless sleep.

"Yeah, yeah," Ben said. "I know that old lullaby ad nauseam."

Von Hart sighed. "The gods were the first Remnants, in a sense, their season inevitably fading. You'll probably know them better as the First-Born, elemental beings of light and power, ultimately shaped by mortal belief. And eventually starved of it. But, as I said, something remains."

"The Fay ancestors." Ben's gentle disdain lingered.

"In all likelihood." And so did Hart's ambiguity. "People get lost, so people fear. They reach out in the darkness. They reach out with prayers and promises. Blood vows and libations. And now and again, that *something* will hear them. Trouble usually follows."

"Trouble like Queen Atiya."

"*Ja.* Your Queen is one such echo. A goddess summoned from the dark." Von Hart's hands fluttered like doves, his bleached features intent on the cards, reading symbols and signs. He was drawing on Ben's reflections, on the wisdom hidden in them. This was scrying. The world held everything, every thought, every feeling, every breath. It was all connected, all carried in time and the wind like fragments, echoes, leaves. Some had the eyes to see. "The history is scattered and vague," the envoy continued. "I see an African queen from the fifteenth century BC. Or some figment, unearthly and older, that simply adopted Atiya as an aspect, a way to secure its essence in time."

"Hold on a minute. Are you saying that she isn't even *real*?"

Von Hart spared him a look of cold violet patience. "*Mein Gott, Liebling.* Why do you think we call them myths?" He clicked his tongue. "This particular one began in Africa. South of Egypt, to be precise. In a land called Punt."

The name rang a bell. Hadn't Winlock said that the ivory *heqa*, the Crook stolen by the Queen, held some connection with Punt? Yes . . .

The cards shifted and turned, clattering. Ink flowed smoothly across them, red and black dribbling into jagged coastlines and forgotten borders. The Dark Continent dissolved, reforming into a close-up map of the northern region, from the Horn of Africa up to the Mediterranean, the long eye of the Red Sea bordered by the Arabian peninsula.

Apparently Ben was in for a history lesson.

"We know very little about Punt. It seems to exist outside time, like Atlantis, Lyonesse or Mu." Von Hart peered at the floating image. Obelisks and arches rose before him, the ephemera of lost cities and tribes, falling into ruin as he spoke. "Yes, I see it now. An account on crumbling papyrus, written during the reign of the Pharaoh Hatshepsut. An expedition sailed across the Red Sea, searching for materials for the Karnak temple."

Hatshepsut. Another familiar name. Ben placed it from two nights ago, Winlock speaking onstage in the lecture theatre. Today was – what? – Friday? Thursday was lost to the murky confines of the underground car park. So much had happened since he'd entered the museum that his mind struggled to keep up. And

219

academia wasn't his bag. This reminder of his lack of erudition, his scholarship of hard knocks, scratched at him like a stray pin in a waistcoat pocket.

Better wise up. Rose is counting on you.

The cards moved, rolling like waves. A breeze slipped through the heavy air, carrying a salty tang and the strident cry of gulls. Club Zauber rocked slightly, swaying on unseen tides. Before the envoy, patterns eddied and broke into new configurations, floating free of the cards. Ben caught blurred impressions, golden shores and sun-kissed skin, shaven heads and blunt beards. White bifurcating kilts. Tall sails reared above him, ghostly in the imagined dust. The story, it seemed, was coming to life.

"Several days into the voyage," Von Hart said, in the same chiming, hollow voice, "a sudden storm struck the vessel as it came within sight of land. The sky erupted with blue fire. The heaving waves resembled pyramids. Relentless and black, the storm smashed the ship into pieces, killing the hundred-strong crew . . . except for one man. Shipwrecked, this lone sailor washed up on a wasted shore, black as ash, where he was lucky to find a trickle of fresh water. For three days he rested under the blasted palm trees. He built a fire and prayed to his gods.

"Then the sailor writes, *I heard the voice of the storm.*" Ben noticed the sweat on Von Hart's forehead, the scrying taking its toll. "Trees toppled. The earth shook. A raging wind approaching fast and . . . and *alighting* before him. When the sailor dropped his hands from his face, a great serpent darkened the shore."

Ben was standing bolt upright. The envoy had his full attention.

"'Who brought you to this land? This sacred land of Punt?' the serpent demanded, his scales the colour of lapis lazuli, his golden eyes ablaze. "'If you will not tell me, you will become as ash, as one who never was.' And the sailor, flat on his belly in the great beast's presence, shivered and gasped, for the name Punt was known to him. He had heard whispers of a faraway land of lost gods and untold riches. At once, he told the serpent about the expedition, how his crew had come sailing south. 'A hundred of Egypt's finest sailors perished in that storm,' the man said. 'And all of their hearts the hearts of lions.'

"The serpent grew thoughtful and sad. He told the sailor to have no fear. 'Behold, for the gods have brought you to the land of the blessed.' He looked even sadder. 'What was once the land of the blessed . . . Soon, a ship will come and you will see your homeland again. You will hold your children and kiss your wife. Happy is he who lives to tell of the passing storm.'

"This caused joy in the sailor's heart, but the serpent still looked sad. 'The falling star boiled the waves and killed your crew, but know you are not alone in your grief. Before the storm, this land numbered seventy-five powerful serpents. When the star fell, all of them burned apart from my daughter and me. Now we rule as King and Queen of Punt.'"

Ben sucked in a breath, sensing the name at the heart of the mystery. *Atiya, Queen of Punt.* Von Hart studied the cards, his fingers trembling over the images, the shadow play hissing into new shapes.

"'Oh great serpent,' the sailor said, rising from his knees. 'I will relate your tale to my Pharaoh. She will come to learn of your mercy. I will praise you as a god to the priests in my city! I will slaughter bulls in your honour! I will send you ships loaded with goods from every town in Egypt, as befits one who spares a stranded sailor!' At this, the serpent laughed, for perhaps what the man said was foolishness to him. 'Go home and grow wise,' he told the man. 'That shall be reward enough.' And in time, a ship came as the King predicted and carried the sailor home, and some say that the sailor bore with him the myrrh that was native to that land, and on returning to Egypt, he planted the first tree of that kind outside the Pharaoh Hatshepsut's temple."

The cards churned, receding, reorganising. Von Hart stumbled backwards, released by the flux of the tale. Beads of sweat dripped from his brow. He leant against the catwalk, his breath sounding like a broken bellows. Somewhere, shadows moved, and Ben tensed, sensing company. In the corner of his eye he spied hunched, insectile shapes . . .

"Are you OK? You look paler than usual."

The envoy managed a weak smile. "I can't sustain the spell for long. And as you may have noticed, others sniff us out."

Lurkers. Lurkers in the walls.

Von Hart barked a laugh, addressing the look on Ben's face. "We have a little time. The wards will protect us a few minutes more."

Ben observed the symbols on the walls. Apparently they weren't just for show. Those DayGlo pentacles and solar squares were obviously in place to keep the envoy from becoming an astral hors d'oeuvre.

"A few minutes?"

Von Hart wasted no time offering comfort. He pulled himself to his full skinny height, brushed down his kimono and turned once more to the levitating cards.

"Like all myths, the Tale of the Shipwrecked Sailor holds a grain of truth. From these reliefs at Deir el-Bahari, we can see that the sailor's story must have reached the Pharaoh's ears. In the ninth year of her reign, Hatshepsut undertook a similar voyage – the furthest of its kind in three hundred years – sailing many leagues south on a mission of mercy." The cards replicated

222

worn temple walls, engraved ships borne on zigzag tides. The rustle of flax filled the club. Long oars splashed through water. "After weeks at sea, the ships alighted on strange new shores, and there the Pharaoh met Parahu and Atiya, the King and Queen of Punt. Rendered on limestone, both look human enough, this supposed tribal king and his daughter, though you'll note Atiya's strange physique, her large head, muscular arms and haunch-like legs. Compared to the slender forms of her people, it's almost as if she suffered from some disease . . ."

"Or was undergoing a transformation."

"Quite."

Serpente in forma humana.

"The Pharaoh brought a retinue of priests, soldiers and slaves, and according to these glyphs, many, many gifts. She listened to all the tales, how Punt had once been a land of plenty, where none who walked her shores were untouched by her splendour. Moved by the kindness the King had shown to a lone sailor, Hatshepsut told her royal hosts that she had come to repay kindness to Punt. She offered a thousand rich and shining tributes, not just food and water, but gold, oil and all kinds of precious stones. Tusks of ivory. Staves of ebony. Leopard skins and ostrich feathers. She swore to heal this once great land, restore Punt to her former glory and thereby make a lasting alliance."

With an envious twitch, Ben thought about the trove under his house, then quickly forgot it as the envoy threw a glance at the walls. Shadows swelled there, spiny, tentacular.

They had run out of time.

"For a while . . . all went well . . ." Von Hart forced the words through his teeth, the pressure building, ready to blow. "The two great nations were in accord. But clouds . . . gathered. Treachery . . . stirred. And something went wrong . . ."

James Bennett

An umbral claw reached out into Club Zauber. The symbols on the walls flashed. Von Hart cried out – Ben couldn't make out the word – and the floating cards swirled into frenzy, clattering into a new ragged shape.

Midnight wings. Electric eyes. A tiara of twisting horns.

The shadow dragon swooped towards Ben, sizzling with imagined sparks.

FOURTEEN

Ben ducked, the illusion scattering over his head, cards raining down all around him.

If the fairy was amused by his trickery, he didn't show it. "There are more of them now. The Lurkers." Von Hart knelt by the catwalk, his chest heaving under star-spangled silk. His impeccable hair hung loose, gold tassels on snow. Sweat glazed his porcelain face. "The presence of sorcery draws them to the earth. They gather like nomads at an oasis. Like flies on shit."

With the charm dispelled, the walls were simply walls again, neon-daubed, seedy and dim. It relieved Ben to see the shades dismissed, sent back to the nether where they belonged. The Lurkers walked between the worlds once more, their ever-brooding threat allayed.

For now.

"Egyptian sorcery. *Puntite* sorcery."

"I think perhaps a mix of both. A chorus of forbidden rites, forgotten prayers. Benedictions to long-dead gods."

"You mean gods that *used* to be dead."

Von Hart nodded. "Empyreal entities like your Queen. The Lurkers hunger for her like urchins at a Christmas banquet. And yet they cannot touch her. Her borrowed flesh is tenuous. She is other-worldly. Other, like them."

"And we're still left sifting through shadows."

Violet flashed in the envoy's eyes, and Ben regretted his blunt tone. The fairy before him, as alien to this world as all his fickle kind, had taken several risks for him, wrenching him away from the CROWS and undertaking an obviously exhausting incantation. No, not only exhausting. Von Hart's slumped shoulders, his forced breaths and enervated flesh – Ben had seen this look before. During his eight hundred and sixty years, he had seen it in Welsh lords over-fond of mead, Jacobite priests puffing tobacco, Victorian ladies willing to bare their breasts for opium . . . And of course, he had seen it when he looked in the mirror on certain mornings, hankering after his old friend Jack.

Magic, the parasite. Magic, the drug. The envoy coughed and wiped his forehead, his fingers playing an allegro of nerves. Von Hart wasn't just exhausted; he was in *withdrawal*.

Ben walked over and helped him to his feet.

"At least now I know whose arse I'll be kicking back into the Long Sleep."

Bold words to cover his unease, that pervading sense of the bottom falling out of the world he knew. That the Sleep as he understood it went deeper, far deeper than what Remnants and humans had chosen to call it, this potentially limitless dimension where gods, dreams and old ghosts spun, discarded, forgotten, but not quite dead. No. Merely waiting for a spark of belief, a shred of faith to rouse them again, bring them crashing back into the *real*—

Von Hart coughed again, this time cynically. He didn't buy it either.

"Poor Ben. You make it sound like that's what you really want."

Ben let go of Von Hart's elbow. The envoy tottered back a step and leant against the catwalk. Ben didn't need to ask him what he meant. It was plain in the envoy's steady gaze. Were his feelings that transparent? Yes, he thought so, because here was another shade clinging to him like Scotch mist. It had clung to him since Insomniac City, since the Big Smoke. Since Mordiford. It haunted the empty rooms of number 9 Barrow Hill Road and lingered in every kiss he'd shared across the years. An ache he had always known was there, brought into focus by firm thighs pressed against his own and hot lips at his ear. Bestial heat that soothed the scar and answered the loneliness in him.

"A Remnant stands between two worlds," the envoy said. Softer now, more cautious. "We are all that is left of the past, exiles in our own land. I mentioned how Man seeks to control the uncontrollable, put nature in a yoke and collar. Well, never forget that we *are* that nature, primal, mystic, elemental. If I've learnt one thing watching the ages turn, it's that no law is strong enough to prevent change."

"What are you getting at, Von Hart?"

"In two days, there will be an eclipse in Cairo. I'm sure you've heard about it. It's all over the news."

Ben knew all right. Bardolfe's holiday. Miss Macha's appointment. He had heard all about the syzygy. He hadn't liked the sound of it then and he didn't like it now.

"The term itself comes from the ancient Greek *ékleipsis*, which means 'abandonment' or 'downfall'. It is a time of change, of *occultation*. Empires rise and empires fall. Kings become paupers and paupers kings. The living and the dead trade places. And some say that laws were made to be broken."

"You're starting to sound a lot like the CROWS." A scowl crawled across Ben's face. "You say that the wheel turns. Well it did turn eight hundred years ago. The Pact was exactly that: a treaty. An agreement. It may not be perfect but it's better than

227

extinction. Better than war. And we *chose* it, you know? Wasn't much of a choice, but we did."

"*Ja.* We chose to be alone." Von Hart slicked his hair into place. "Always, forever alone."

Ben wasn't sure what to say to this. If the envoy believed that they were to blame for their own isolation in the modern age, for their inability to form communities, teach students, mate and breed, then it only stressed the price they'd paid in order to survive. Nevertheless, the doubt was there, nibbling away at him. The ache that would never ease. The bruise that would never fade. The scar that would not heal.

Unless . . .

He pushed the thought away. Von Hart's stare, for all its dispassion, was unmistakably honest. Ben should have expected this, this subtle disdain, this pity underlying their conversation. Was he the only one left who upheld the Lore? Who clung to the hope that the Fay would return, those precious grains falling through his hands? Fine, maybe he wasn't content with the Pact – never that – but when he considered the alternatives – Babe Cathy's threat on the Brooklyn Bridge, Fulk Fitzwarren's vengeful sword, a hundred towns blazing in the past – it struck him as a necessary evil. A dam holding back a flood of chaos.

Now that dam had burst, leaving Ben to wonder whether his code – the decision he had taken and lived by – was due to his personal passion rather than cool objectivity. Centuries ago, a young girl had found and fed him. It was only natural he'd align his heart with her short-lived species, however different from his. But he didn't like Von Hart reminding him of his attachment to humans. Rose was never far from his thoughts. Rose and the invisible worm, flying in the night, ready to devour her. He already knew the weight of his shame.

Like trying to catch the wind.

"I have to save her, Hart. All this *alakazam* aside, I have to save Rose."

And part of him was married to the mystery. He had come too far to turn back now. The events since New York had awakened him, stirring the purpose that had long lain dormant inside him. He wanted to know what Atiya was after, the reason behind her thievery. He wanted to know what the CROWS were plotting, how they intended to spark revolution. He wanted to know what part Sir Bardolfe played and confront him for the set-up at the museum. Above all, he sensed that time was running out. The Cairo eclipse could signal the end of all he held dear. The end of the world he knew.

Von Hart was shaking his head. Openly feeling sorry for him now.

"Then I'm afraid you'll have to do it alone."

"What? This is your fight too."

The envoy held up a hand. "I have seen too much. Camlann. The Hundred Years War. The Inquisition. Waterloo. Flanders Fields. Belsen. Iraq. Oceans of blood. Humans speeding each other towards an early grave. And for what? A fleeting grab at power. A brief superiority. Or maybe just a lust for death." He let out a breath. "Humans are foolish. Humans are frail. Humans will not last."

"You don't know that."

"I can make an educated guess." He offered Ben a wan smile. "Perhaps this change in regime is inevitable. Perhaps it is our turn again."

"You might as well side with the CROWS!"

Von Hart *tsked*. "Don't be naïve. You've seen the Lurkers, haven't you? Encountered magic even you can't resist. To walk

out under that darkened sun, flinging spells and imprecations
. . . What chance do you think we'll have?"

Ben balled his hands into fists, his jaw a bristling line.

"We have to do something!"

"It's your choice, *Liebling*. Go. Fly off and save your damsel.
But know that you fly to your destruction."

The choice was no choice at all. A burning canopy over his
head. A waitress from Vinegar Hill who knew they could never
live a normal life, but who had loved him anyway. Loved him
and paid the price.

"We're wasting time. Consider this goodbye."

The envoy smiled, and some of it even reached his eyes.

"I know," he said, and clapped his hands. "But first, come.
One more thing I will do for you. A small parting gift, so at
least you can face your death with dignity."

Von Hart led Ben to a small door beside the catwalk and down
a narrow corridor into the dressing rooms. Old make-up and
acrid perfume spiced the cloistered space.

The suit hung on a rail in an alcove, surrounded by feather
boas, fishnet stockings and sequinned skirts. Thinking of shed
skins, Ben took in the sight and laughed.

"You've got to be kidding me."

If his scorn wounded the envoy, Von Hart didn't show it.

"You weren't the only thing I retrieved from the car park."
In fact, he was obviously pleased with himself. "I took the liberty
of taking your scales as well. Fulk won't need them now. Why
let them go to waste? Besides, you'll catch your death one of
these days."

Ben recalled the scrubbed feeling when he had woken up
in the room upstairs, the sensation of sandpaper-scoured flesh.

He raised an eyebrow at the envoy, colouring despite himself.

"It took some effort to synthesise the scales into a fabric, weave their substance into this. Nevertheless, I think you'll find it as tough as your flesh. I mean, it *is* your flesh. A second skin. Extra armour, of sorts."

"You . . . synthesised my scales?"

"No mean feat. Your genes are somewhat resistant to meddling. Still, once I realised I only had to work with the magic that was already present, the rest came easy enough. I hope you don't think me intrusive."

Bit late for that.

"It's . . . it's a nice gesture. But surely the moment I spread my wings this will all be rags."

A grin answered him. "That's the beauty of it. The suit will change when you change, melding into your true form. When you take on human guise, the suit will heed and follow." The grin grew wider. "If nothing else, it will protect your modesty and spare you a few shocked looks."

Ben moved in for a closer inspection. The suit hung before him like a reflection, a charred black sheen of tiny heart-shaped interlocking scales, reminiscent of neoprene, a wetsuit padded for war.

An emblem adorned the chest, emblazoned in red and circled by yellow.

"That's *wyrm tongue* for Sola—"

"Yeah. I know what it means."

"All those years," Von Hart said. "Living under the radar, working for crooks. You know, things could have been so different."

Ben reached out and touched the material, rubbing it between his hands.

"Fairy," he growled, but all the same, he was grinning.

Interlude: A Shadow in the Sun

Khan el-Khalili, Cairo

Rose McBriar stood, neck straight, arms held rigid at her sides, in the hustle and bustle of Cairo's most famous bazaar. She could move her eyes a little – the force that held her, uttered from the witch's lips and enveloping her like a steel cocoon, allowed an inch or two of free movement, no more. The rest of the time she was subject to another's will, an invisible yoke around her neck, controlling her motor functions. But like a moth struggling in a chrysalis, her own will appeared to be making some elbow room, bound wings of intention pushing against the unseen walls of her cell. Such things, of course, should be impossible. Witches, magic – *impossible*. By all the laws of the world she knew, her captors should not exist. Rose kept trying to swallow her shock in her bid to survive them.

Straining to look, she could see the jumble of exotic goods stacked all around her. A wall of lamps rose on either side of a yellow Moorish arch, a rainbow of scarves hanging on a stall beyond. Just above her head, a thousand ceramic pharaohs glared down at her from an endless row of shelves. Rugs poured from the shadowed eaves, cascading into pools formed of urns and chests, each one loaded with trinkets to catch the eyes of passing tourists: golden plates, stuffed model camels, vintage cameras, all glimmering cheaply in the shade. Incense and hookah smoke coiled everywhere. The noise and the heat were only rivalled by the smell. Having worn the same shirt and jeans since her unplanned flight from New York, she guessed that some of the smell was hers.

Unable to wipe her face, Rose blinked away a tear. How had she come to be here, in this far-flung dusty place? It all remained a blur, a staccato of memory from when she'd arrived at her sister's in Vermont, pulling into the darkened driveway in the rented car and already hearing Poppy's soft remonstrations in her ears. *You should never have accepted that cheque* and *Why did you let him buy the apartment?* and *What the hell do you see in him anyway? He sounds like a crook!* All of which she'd been prepared to take in the appropriate silence, knowing what she knew and knowing that she could not explain the paradox, even if she'd wanted to. How Ben Bastard Garston made her feel, so safe, and at the same time more aware than ever of her own strength and independence. She couldn't even tell *him* that. She'd taken his advice to lie low against her better judgement, but damn him, he'd scared her badly with his crazy talk of killers on the New York streets who'd apparently mentioned her by name (thanks for that, Ben). Postponing her exams, she had driven up north with her fingers nervously tapping the steering wheel and her guts aflutter. How he expected her to explain all of this to Poppy without her calling the police was beyond her.

As it was, she never got the chance. The minute she'd slammed the car door, the shrunken woman in the purple perm and the tuxedo had stepped out from the bushes and into the driveway, waving some kind of stick. *Hello, Princess.* Then the sensation of drunkenness and flying. Time fleeting past in slurred protests and muffled profanity. *Get yo . . . fucking pawsh off me . . . bish . . .* Later, someone shouting her name. Ben? The shreds of a dream clung to her, an image of her very-ex-boyfriend shouting her name across some paved and gated space. Then darkness again, followed by light. Bright, bright light. The Saharan sun . . . Had she been half awake when she'd stepped off the plane? Had the witch *let* her rise to the surface, let her taste her arid surroundings? And that was the point when Rose had started thinking of her captor as a witch – beyond all logic, a *witch* – though that impression hadn't even seemed that far-fetched, considering the leggy vixen in the bad make-up, torn stockings and pointy hat who sat opposite her during the flight. *A fucking witch!* Rose had moaned and slumped in her seat, wishing for the life of her that the woman was just in fancy dress, but deep in her guts knowing different. The witch may have even spoken to her, but if she had, it would hardly have been reassuring. The words *Sahara* and *Move it* swam through her mental fog. She remembered craning her neck on the runway to look back at the little white craft, what she'd guessed was a private charter jet, even as her terror at her situation came thudding back to her.

Terror swiftly followed by born-Brooklynite spunk. Christ, she was pissed! What the hell kind of shit had Ben landed her in? What the fuck was going on? Witches were *real*? Was she having some kind of mental breakdown? But she could not deny the force that gripped her, and it was only sheer adrenalin, sheer determination to live, that prevented a scream from flying from her throat, a scream that she feared would never end . . .

Anger was easier, a mast to cling to. Anger and blame. None of this – Rose could only think of it as *craziness* – would be happening if Ben had just stayed away, lived up to his lie and left her in peace. *Left you up in your ivory tower.* Or if she'd somehow found a way to *make* him stay away, to blow out her old flame once and for all. *But you waited for him, didn't you? In a tower of your own making . . .* The reason to free herself, though it pained her, was obvious. *Self-preservation.* That was what her sister would've said. Even now, spellbound and dazed in an unfamiliar foreign city in the company of what she could only think of as monsters, Rose experienced the all-too-familiar dilemma, her heart dangling and shifting like the flag in a game of tug-of-war. She'd told herself – *taught* herself – that it hurt less to have Ben out of her life than to have him in it.

You're a survivor, Rose. Remember that. She kept repeating her mantra, an internal chant, in the face of his secrets. And all of his secrets were bullshit! Did he think she was a child? She had known all along that there was something wrong with him. OK, something *more* to him. Normal people couldn't withstand blazing frying pans or smell perfume from five floors down. And then there was the Central Park thing . . . But when he kissed her, she had a nasty habit of forgetting all that, or at least pretending to forget. In a New York subway, she'd walked away and left him to it, surrendering to her inner resolve that she didn't need him in her life. Despite all this, despite standing here like a storefront dummy in the bazaar of her nightmares, Rose was privately enraged by the fact that for all her forgetting, she hadn't managed to convince herself of this decision either.

Men!

Or . . . whatever the fuck he was . . .

Her hands, the palms of which were sweaty yet cold, curled slowly into fists. She blinked, surprised by the pressure of nails biting into her skin. The sensation wrenched her out of resentment and doubt, and back to the scene before her. She stood by a small table set under an awning in a corner of the souk. A man in a tuxedo sat in a chair with his back to her. His collar, bleached white, looked as starched into rigidity as she was. He was talking with a fat, greasy mystic-cum-merchant.

"Please, Abbas," the man in the tux said. "All these things are very fine, but I didn't come here to haggle over mummified cats, cracked jewellery or any other plunder from broken tombs. As one Old Believer to another, I already have the spell I require. And I know the hour of its speaking. Why not save us both some time and give me what I seek?"

He spoke like this, the man in the tux, polite and measured to a fault, as though his words performed topiary on the air, each breath between them laden with pitfalls, hidden dangers. He'd spoken like this from the moment the witch – who, as far as Rose could recall, had somehow been shorter and smaller than the leggy vixen who'd just shared the flight with her – had greeted him as they stepped off the plane. He had leant on the hood of an elegant car, black and soundless on the runway, straightening with a smile as they approached. *Sabah el kheir*, he'd said, the perfect gent. *Please, call me . . .* He'd coughed, perhaps thinking better of giving her his real name. *The shadow.* Then, pleasantries over, the inexplicably shrunken witch had handed Rose over into his care (with another soft utterance, the relinquishing of an invisible yoke), and the man, the shadow, had taken her hand and kissed it as if she was some visiting dignitary, rather than a gagged and bound victim of kidnap. *Welcome to Egypt. I trust Khepri, the scarab, with his bright ball of dung, doesn't trouble you overmuch.*

If he hadn't extended one finger, enclosed in a pristine white glove, directly upward at the sky, Rose wouldn't have realised that he meant the sun.

James Bennett

Those fingers were under his chin now, steepled in a way to suggest great patience, as he bartered with the merchant.

"I have many *shabtis*," Abbas was saying, holding out a small carved figurine. "All working, all sound. Should you need anyone, ah, *replaced* . . ."

Apparently despite himself, the shadow took the figurine from the merchant. He rolled it between finger and thumb, watching the light filtering through the awning play across the worn inscriptions.

"Another relic from the New Kingdom, Abbas? What would the government say?" The shadow let this sink in, watching the man squirm in his kaftan. Then he sighed. "These *shabtis* are hardly rare. They litter the tombs of the ancient dead. Of course our ancestors used to rely on them, believing that the figures served as substitutes for the deceased, in case something happened to the mummy, leaving the soul, the *ba*, lost and wandering. As such, I admit it holds a passing interest . . ."

The merchant started rubbing his palms, but the shadow merely tutted.

"Passing, I said. You're too late for this to be of any use. We made our little switch months ago and we did not use stone." With that, he tossed the figurine back to the merchant, who, after a fumble, managed to catch it, made it vanish back into his robes. "The knife, Abbas." The shadow folded his arms, the gesture looking anything but casual. "I'd hate you to think me rude, but if you weren't protected by so many glyphs, I would have simply strangled you and taken it by now."

The merchant laughed and fanned himself with his palm leaf, visibly amused, clearly terrified. Rose fancied she could see herself, standing pale, stiff, her hair a mess, in the beads of sweat dripping from under his turban. The shift in atmosphere as

238

Abbas brought out the object in question was not imagined, however. A sense of *loosening* shivered over her skin. Her shoes shuffled a little on the sandy floor.

"Ra sails across the sky in his Boat of a Million Years," the merchant said, "and even he never thought to see this day. The knife has been in my family for three thousand years and more, passed down from father to son. The gods will spit on me for such a trade."

"Yes, yes." The shadow swatted a fly away. "We are all cursed in our own way, Abbas."

Abbas frowned at this, the insult noticeably lancing his fear. All the same, he unfolded the bundle of silk on the table and the shadow leant in for a closer inspection.

"You mustn't fear the gods so," he breathed, taking in the curious hook-tipped object before him. "In the old days, the gods were central to everything, overseeing and joined with the world like shorebirds and Nile crocodiles, a symbiotic – and quite mythical – relationship. The ancients worshipped their gods through nature, and in return, the gods promised not to destroy them. But I'm sure you know how easy it is to anger the gods, hence storms, drought, earthquakes and the like . . ." The shadow stuck out his chin, his admiration for this archaic arrangement plain. "Ritual and sacrifice kept the gods happy in the old days, Abbas. But, alas, these are not the old days."

Lightning quick, the knife was in the shadow's hand, slicing through the shafts of sunlight. Abbas gave a yelp and sat back, his wobbling chin only just avoiding the arc of the blade. Rose, startled by the movement, took a step back as well. And then was startled all over again to realise that she had done so.

The shadow hadn't noticed, his attention fixed solely on the blade.

"Nevertheless, the old ways are best." The knife snapped back, the shadow resting one white-gloved finger on its keenly honed edge. "We call this a *des*. The *sem* priests used them in the embalming process, slicing the flesh and removing the organs. Shaped from stone, but sharp as you like." His back remained turned to her, but Rose just knew that smile was back on his face, as thin and cold as the knife. "The ancients held that the crescent moon was also a knife, you know, clutched by a god. Some considered it holy to etch symbols into their skin. Eyes and snakes and flowering reeds. Ankhs and falcons and birds. All rendered in precise wounds. All rendered in blood. Protection matters, I'm sure you'll agree. This knife is an important tool. Sacred. *Necessary.*"

"Then you won't mind paying handsomely for it."

The shadow barked a laugh. Clearly, no merchant in the Khan el-Khalili would let fear get in the way of a good bargain.

"Name your price," he said.

Rose fought the urge to take another step back, suspecting that she could if she tried, as the merchant's eyes strayed over the shadow's shoulder and drank her in, climbing from her thighs and up over her breasts, the filthy, slender shape of her. He met her eyes for half a second before flicking away, back to his pale customer.

Abbas licked his lips. "This woman. Is she . . . *shalakh*? In your possession?"

Rose clenched her jaw. Her nails were biting deep now, tensing at the knowledge that perhaps in the witch's absence, the spell's hold on her was slipping. Or perhaps because the shadow was focusing his attention elsewhere. Under this, she had an inkling that her own determination played a part. Her temper flared, stoking her Irish blood. She was a little tired of being treated as an object, some trinket in other people's hands.

"I'm afraid my companion is not for sale," the shadow said. "Does the scribe trade the tablet for the stylus? There would be no point. Name another price and I'm sure—"

The man in the tuxedo didn't get to finish, because that was the moment Rose lurched to one side and wrenched the shelf nearest to her from the wall. A thousand glaring pharaohs rained down, crashing into the table. Clay shattered, brightly painted chips scattering all around. Rose saw the merchant tumble back on his chair, his palm leaf and turban tilting through the dust, his slippers flying over his head. She didn't take in the shadow's reaction until she'd reached the end of the row of stalls, her pumps skidding on grit as she pushed people out of her way, the alarmed faces and jabbering voices closing in around her like an incoming tide. *Are you hurt? What happened?* She could've begged for help, yelled *Kidnap!* in the middle of the marketplace, but in that moment, with her newly freed muscles flinging blood around her brain, all she wanted to do was get away. Instinct screamed at her to run. Breaking through into an open plaza, she could see over the heads of the crowd to the littered table and the shadow beyond. He still sat there, shoulders straight, visibly unharmed. Calmly, he brushed ceramic chips off one shoulder. His hand closed around the handle of the knife. He opened his bag – leather, bulky, the kind that doctors used – and put the relic inside. Then he climbed slowly to his feet.

Rose ran. She didn't know where she was going. Stupidly, all she could think was *I'm done with waiting tables* as her adrenalin chose a narrow street ahead and yanked her in that direction. Gasping, stumbling, her hair in her face, she turned corner after corner, losing herself in the maze. Twice she tried to speak to strangers, petition them for help, but her tongue lay thick in her mouth and her dishevelled appearance didn't help to bridge the language barrier. Men and women shoved her aside, going about their business. The sky slipped by overhead, a river between the rooftops like an inverted Nile, leading her God knew where.

Twenty minutes later found her crossing Saleh Salem Street, bursting from the labyrinth of buildings in a weary jog. Cars spluttered past, ignoring her waving arms or rewarding them with honks.

"Please," she managed. "Please . . ."

She fought to get herself under control. What did people do in situations like these? She stifled a laugh, reluctant to hear her own panic, high and shrill, a whistle on a derailing steam train. How many people were kidnapped by witches in this day and age? The thought was almost hilarious. Almost as hilarious as how quickly she'd accepted the impossible, these strange creatures with the talents at their disposal . . . But then she had dated Ben Garston. Her nails bit into her palms again, trying to prevent her thoughts from freewheeling into shock. She made her way over a bridge, spanning the unruly lanes of traffic, calling her wits back to herself. *Focus on the practical.* She needed the police, but typically, she could see no police. That she was heading into the outskirts of the city seemed obvious, the houses thinning out, the stretches of desiccated palms and flat yellow land growing wider, and she couldn't decide if that was a good or a bad thing. *I'm just a waitress,* she told herself. *Just . . .* Then the inner voice snapped in, bold and fiercely Brooklynite. *No. You're a survivor. And you must survive this.*

She hugged herself, sheltering arms sliding around her belly and waist, warmth to calm her fluttering nerves. Practicality told her that she should hail a passing taxi and make her way to the US Embassy, beg for sanctuary at the gates. In the dusty road ahead, however, no taxi was apparent. She was heading into some kind of slum, set in the shadow of a low range of hills. A filthy grid of streets and tiny houses opened up before her, but it was only as she began to stumble down the first one that Rose realised that the buildings weren't houses at all. They were *tombs*. The whole area was some kind of graveyard, a dense maze of mausoleums set on the edge of the city. In amongst the graves, the arabesque domes and towers, the narrow gated crypts, more recent hovels rose to the sky, flaked, crumbling and sand-pocked, their walls scrabbling from hallowed ground.

But the place was far from empty. Rose stumbled on, refusing to let the fact slow her. Ragged people, men, women and children, were scurrying everywhere. Most of them appeared to be concerned with the trash littering the place, great heaps stacked against walls or collected in the beds of rusted trucks, engines rumbling as they waited to move on. Women in scarves sat in the shadow of the tombs sorting through the stuff, picking through aluminium, cardboard and plastic like scrawny, busy vultures. Children clambered up and down the stacks, tossing bottles, tyres and cans to one another. Rose found herself witness to a bizarre production line.

What are they doing, here among the bones? Recycling? It looks like recycling . . .

A hand climbed to her throat as she noticed the eyes peeping out from some of the tombs, flat, indifferent, merely marking this strange blonde woman staggering down the street. In turn, Rose took in the washing hanging outside some of the tombs, the crockery waiting to be washed, and she had never felt so far away from her apartment in Vinegar Hill. These people actually *lived* here? She had seen many homeless people on the streets of New York, and worse deprivations among the children cared for by the charity where she sometimes volunteered, but she had never seen poverty like this. The scene before her was like a punch in the guts, and for a moment she forgot about her own predicament. The reeking ghetto, well accustomed to its dereliction, went on about its daily business, rickety donkey-pulled carts loaded down with old newspaper, cardboard boxes, shattered glass, discarded clothes and broken toys creaking around her as if she wasn't there. The men and children collected, and the women sorted, in what Rose imagined must be an ongoing daily scavenger hunt.

"They call them the Zabbaleen, the 'garbage people'." Rose was so shocked, she hadn't heard the footsteps approaching behind her, becoming aware of the shadow's presence only as his hand, cold and firm, settled upon her shoulder. "Thousands of years ago, slaves quarried the stone from the Mokattam Hills for pyramids and temples," he told her, in his usual measured tones. "The poorest still live here, forced into poverty and filth by urbanisation, the 1992 earthquake or other unhappy circumstances. Cairo dumps her trash here and the Zabbaleen scratch out a living from whatever they can find. Wonderful, isn't it? Disease in the area is, of course, rife. Tourists seldom come here. Nor do the police, except on the most pressing business, which makes the slum fitting for my purpose."

Rose, who could see nothing wonderful about it, endured this unasked-for lecture with a stiff spine and empty lungs, a frozen scream that had nothing to do with the witch's spell. The cold crept from the shadow's hand and down toward her heart as he concluded cheerfully, "They call the slum El-Arafa. The City of the Dead."

This was enough for Rose. Adrenalin kicked her into violence, her foot shooting back to connect with his shin. With a grunt of surprise, he released her, and his pain was music to her ears.

Before he could recover himself, she swung out with her fist – her left one, because for all her father's drinking, she *had* picked up a thing or two – and felt a savage kind of joy as it smashed into his jaw. Blood flew and she rejoiced again in the knowledge that her captor was human after all. Talents aside, he was human and therefore fallible. She could escape him. She could.

Her elation shrivelled up in her breast as the shadow straightened, granting her a ruddy smile. She had a second or two as he reached out, his vice-like grip closing once more – this time on air. Nursing her knuckles, watched by the impassive tomb dwellers, Rose went scurrying across the street and dived into a gap between the small buildings. Her elbows scraped on stone and she turned, seeking another path around a shattered statue and scrabbling up a gravelly incline towards another row of tombs, these ones standing dark and empty. Abandoned. Was the shadow behind her? She couldn't tell, her gaze desperately fixed on her hiding place. Hands trembling, breaths coming hard, she pushed back the creaky copper gate, green with age, and crawled into the tomb, a twelve-foot-square musty space that let in none of the sunlight.

In the middle of the room was a raised stone slab, grey, chipped and worn, a grave for some unknown, nameless soul. Someone had recently used it as a dining table, broken crockery and scattered cutlery lying around its base. Her knees crunched through grit and bone as she made it to the far wall, her back against it, eyes wide and set on the open gate.

Instinct urged her to scream for help, but she covered her mouth with both hands, suppressing its danger.

Footsteps on gravel. A shadow passed over the gate. Then it was gone and she let out a long, slow breath of relief. Closing her eyes, she tipped her head back against the stone, letting the coolness of the wall calm her.

When she opened her eyes again, the man in the tuxedo was standing in the doorway. His tall frame blotted out the sun.

"You're so full of life, my dear," he said. "I'm afraid that's why you are here."

"Fuck you," she replied, out of breath and no longer caring.

"That's the spirit." He smiled, all red teeth. "You have no idea what you're going to face come Sunday. I imagine you'll remember my company fondly."

"Just get it over with." Her skin shone in the flickering light, glistening with exertion. She could feel strands of hair sticky on her brow, and her eyes roved around the room, taking in the carvings on the walls, worn prayers to a soul long gone.

The shadow, observing her dismay, said, "I know, I know. Hardly a five-star hotel. Content yourself that you're getting to see the *real* city, none of that Four Seasons fakery, canapés at dusk, excursions in air-conditioned coaches." He affected a shudder. "Cairo is a place of struggle. Always was, always will be, from the siege of Memphis to the Ottoman War to the unrest of today. You see? *Struggle*. Pharaohs, Fatimid and film stars have died here. And, indeed, so will you. A little."

Rose moaned, muttering a weary imprecation. She wasn't going to beg.

"Oh, it's nothing personal. Blame fate if you must." He shrugged. "Now where was I? Oh yes. Protection. Eyes and snakes and flowering reeds. Ankhs and falcons and birds. You won't face this struggle alone, oh no. The dark will surely come for you, but I will be waiting . . ."

The shadow set down his bag. It was heavy, stirring up dust, clouds begriming his jacket. He spoke a word – or a symbol representing one – and Rose felt the air congealing around her again, the noose tightening, the yoke restored.

He retrieved the knife from the bag, the strange hook-ended one he'd recently haggled from Abbas in the bazaar. He held it out before him, the light spilling through the copper gate glinting on the blade.

"I dedicate your sacrifice to Thoth," he said. "Thoth was the god of writing and magic. Topical, I think you'll agree. Think of yourself as papyrus, a scroll for hieratic script. You have no idea how special you are."

Rose said nothing as he took a step towards her.

The shadow paused, tipping his head in an afterthought.

"What do you think, my dear? Do you think he is still coming for you?"

Of course he meant Ben. Who else? Whatever was going on here, whatever trouble she was in, centred on her ex. In the end, after everything, Ben had managed to win the argument. Either by accident or by design, he had put her in the position of needing to be saved.

She hated him a little for that.

You're a survivor, she told herself.

She gritted her teeth as the knife moved in.

Outside, Ra sailed over the City of the Dead, chasing shadows across the land.

FIFTEEN

Wings shredding the morning mist, Red Ben Garston, Sola Ignis, took his bearings from the sun and sped into the south.

Up here, he was almost invisible. Aeroplanes didn't fly so high and winked far below him, criss-crossing the European sky. Below the planes, birds and the occasional hot-air balloon. Through gaps in the clouds, the world peeked in, a green-brown mosaic of cultivated fields and bald hills, ribboned by grey and winding roads. The fields surrendered to the spider web of cities, the roads converging, looping and once again forking, the ever-expanding maze of conurbation. Now and then, Ben looked down and shook ice from his snout, crystals sparkling over his neck, his huge nostrils flaring. After the confines of Club Zauber (not to mention the underground car park), it felt good to spread his wings, but the height was both a blessing and a curse, as liberating as it was depressing. He marvelled at the scale of human progress and mourned the loss of trees. He sighed at the mirror-like Senftenberg Lakes, frowned at the smog rising from Dresden. Civilisation was a double-edged sword, and his hope that it might one day free itself from waste and pollution seemed as thin as the air he breathed. Civilisation came at a price. As one who lived hidden in its heart, he could never forget that.

These heights were perhaps the last true wilderness, a lofty prairie where Ben roamed free. Almost invisible, but not quite, not nearly enough. Where the ancients had descried astrological lines, heliocentric charts and Flammarion wheels, their modern counterparts dissected the sky with time zones and strict meridians, weather systems and airline routes. Degrees of latitude and longitude. Imaginary borders. Where the ancients had sent shrill prayers, woodsmoke and arrows, Ben's contemporaries sent a barrage of satellites, planes, missiles and radiation. The world roared with technology, the noise echoing deep into space. Somewhere, on some radar, in some telescope, Ben knew he was an unexplained presence, a bestial UFO, a winged optical illusion, an impossibly large ghost signal.

Unseen, he slipped above the world, cloaked by distance as much as disbelief. Nevertheless, these transformations were mounting up – both his and the Queen's – and only a fool would think they'd go unnoticed for ever. That blip on the screen, that speck on the lens, when related to others from credible tongues, could well lead to serious trouble. *More* trouble. Trouble that took him from the pages of *Paranormal Magazine* and into the news headlines. Sooner or later, the world would look up and see, and history would repeat itself. And this time not with pitchforks and torches. This time with rockets and guns . . .

No one wanted that. Another good reason to find the Queen, send her packing into the Long Sleep, rescue Rose and resume his covert existence. At a hundred and fifty thousand feet, Europe a shrouded map below and the sun spearing the bitter blue, it almost sounded easy.

As easy as dying, bonehead . . .

Midday found him west of Prague – or what he guessed was Prague – the curve of the Vltava river edged by far-off bridges and buildings. A century had passed since he'd flown this way on some half-remembered journey to the sea, and despite his recent travels, his wings still ached from years of disuse. The hearty breakfast provided by the envoy before his departure – bread, eggs and a fresh pint of milk – was rapidly wearing off with his efforts, and as he sailed over Old Bohemia, he eyed cows grazing on a hillside with a hunger long suppressed. Remembering his vow, he drew deeper on his reserves, flexed his slab-like muscles and descended to ride a brisk thermal toward the Austrian Alps.

The sun arced across the sky, stretching his shadow out under him and into the fiery west. The mountains clawed higher and higher, a bleak, broken horizon, a jagged snow-capped wall. Clouds swelled above them billowing and black, a stacked cumulus fleet like ghostly men-of-war. Faint lightning flashed in their depths, painting the towering ice cliffs, illuminating chasms and crags already filling up with night. Darkness swallowed the sky ahead, stealing the last hour of day. Ben swept in under its cloak, intending to find shelter somewhere and rest for a while under his wings, wait for the storm to pass. Cloud enveloped him, shrouding his descent. Thunder rumbled in the distance like an oncoming train. He navigated peaks and saddles, coasting through an archipelago of rock, across a sea of fog. His prow of horns cut through the soup, his gills cycling the alpine air, propelling and pulling him on. Integral gases warmed his blood against the glacial cold. Steam trailed from him like a robe, ragged plumes puffing outward with every stroke of his wings. His superior senses couldn't help him here, curbed and confounded by cloud as they were. The slough of snow and tumbling stone filtered muffled to his ears, offering no clear direction, and he had lost the compass of the sun. He slowed, veering down a sheer-walled canyon, gliding deeper into the gloom.

The mountains boomed, disgruntled by his presence. Lightning flared, washing the rock. Ben made out shapes in the ebbing shadows, spectres from his troubled dreams. Skulls. Pyramids. Grasping hands. As he soared onward through the clouds, reducing them to swirling *ignis fatuus*, he projected his thoughts on the fulminations, the boiling banks reflecting memories. Here, the strata between two thunderheads became the grin in the Javits Center, taunting him for his ignorance. There, silver inside a bruised belly depicted the pillars of the British Museum, the great gate to knowledge that had led to his torment and pain. Lightning flashed, crystalline, the glint of stolen diamonds. Thunder cackled like Texan witches. Behind the sweeps of cloud, black wings soared and circled, stalking him in shadowy orbit.

Static prickled along Ben's spine, nipping at his nerves. Each salvo against the rock rang like a hammer blow inside his head, the storm closing around him. When one wingtip brushed the cliff face, scattering ice and scree, he pushed himself up to straddle the clouds. A white-hot bolt arrested him, forcing him back and down, fried air shrieking in his ears. The wind blustered, tossing him around like a kite, and he skewed with the gust, changing course. Righting himself, he searched for a break in the clouds, and seeing one above him, rose towards it, seeking escape.

Too late. He realised his mistake, the static tingling in his mind, a sharp, intuitive warning. The gap in the clouds slammed shut like a door, crackling with electrical discharge. Blinded, he rolled, his tail thrashing, a flag ripped free by the wind. He folded his wings, trying to drop out of the trap, the air a cushion beneath him. He looked up, blinking, to see a membranous shadow pass behind the clouds. Scales like glass caught the flash of lightning. A tiara of horns gored the haze. Black claws, glossy, outstretched, came darting toward him.

Queen Atiya dived from the heights, her eyes promising death.

SIXTEEN

His shoulders in her iron grip, Atiya plunged Ben into the storm, trying to drown him under the clouds. Her talons tore through scales and into flesh, onyx knives that drew first blood, scattered gore like wine. Ben thrashed and roared, but her dive had caught him unawares; he was like a fish snatched from a lake. His wings snapped upward with the impact, yanked by the wind over his head. The Queen's wings were *everywhere*. It was hard to differentiate between them and the clouds, black fading to grey as she forced him down into the canyon, into the last light of day. Her eyes, burning blue, impaled him with intention. The storm rumbled and spat around her, and Ben struggled in its folds, an evil heat scorching his flesh, prompting a cry of pain. He lashed out, raking her breast, his claws scoring her scales, as strong, as impenetrable as armour. The friction sprayed sparks, not blood, and Atiya folded her wings in tight, increasing their plummeting speed. Her snout was a blur above him, a grille of determined fangs.

"Let go, bitch . . ."

The words rolled in a growl off his tongue – less eloquent, perhaps, in dragon form, but still approximating rough speech. Nevertheless, the wind whipped the insult away, dashing it against the canyon walls, lost, futile echoes. In reply, the Queen wound her tail around his neck, restricting his movements. His wounds sang as her talons sank deeper, the cliffs throwing his agony back at him. A chill that had nothing to do with the Alps pressed in around him, electricity slicking his throat. Unable to breathe, to draw fire, he strained to focus on the ground. It was approaching fast. Needles jagged from the canyon floor, the rock bottom of one ravine a tier of them, marching hundreds of feet down into the Adriatic hinterland, into Italy, Slovenia and Hungary. Just one ravine, except this one would kill him, and here he'd rot, a snow-covered carcass on a high crag.

He had known this was coming. Shock could not erase the understanding. He'd known it since he'd seen the worm-tongue sigil scratched on his door. A conflict. A fight. *Rampant combatant.* Their coming together was as natural as the confluence of rivers, the outcome of their duel just as certain.

Still . . .

Ben bunched his muscles and clawed upwards, his wingtips brushing the precipice. Snow swirled, maddened by the storm, which pressed into the narrowing chasm like smoky fingers into a glove. Battle-locked, the two beasts dropped into the depths, the speed of their descent lashing the sky.

Looking down, Ben made out individual stalagmites. They looked hungry. *Honed.* He had time to wonder how the Queen had found him and time to remember their psychic link, their minds fused by other-worldly energy, sparks trailing from her brow to his. Was her presence the circuit between them, transmitting thoughts and memories? In the British Museum Atiya had told him that she was a huntress, sniffing out his lair, and as her present tempest engulfed him, Ben revelled in senses beyond his own, in the shared touch of divinity. A final, flash-in-the-pan revelation.

I am going to die.

Needles of rock rushed toward his spine. A crazed soprano wailed in his ears, the air whistling past him, forced aside by their tangled bulk. The world blurred, a grey-white sheet come to smother him, and he closed his eyes, bracing for collision.

It wasn't his life that flashed before him, but his utter failure. *Rose* . . .

Ben gasped. His eyes flew wide. The pressure on his shoulders, bearing a murderous weight, seemed heavier in its absence. The Queen had released him. She shot into the heights, a spear thrown up a smokestack and out of sight, her tail striking scree from the bluff. Ben flung out his plated limbs, his tendons straining as he slowed his fall. Wings scraped the packed snow. Claws gouged granite. A low growl rumbled in his chest. What was her game? She was playing with him! Haunches tensed, he pushed against the boulders on either side of him, his tail sweeping over the jags, sharp teeth deprived of his flesh. He thrust himself up, catching the rising gusts in the crevasse. Pumping hard, he cleared the lip of his would-be grave, letting the wind carry him. In the distance, a darker stain, a slender length of curled horns and sleek scales. Wings of formidable black.

With a roar, Ben went after her. He banked around the shoulders of peaks, slumped pillars that held up the sky. Lightning danced all around him, the crackling wake of the Queen. Blue-white tongues licked at the rock face. Phosphorescence flared under snow. The sweeps boomed with scattering static. He wove with Atiya into the mountains, seeing her appear behind another crag, soar around another summit. The storm pressing down on his back, the clouds torn by outcrops and spurs, Ben followed her, well aware he could be chasing his death. *Why let me live in the museum just to kill me now?* The thought whispered through his adrenalin. *If our link is a two-way street, then she knows that*

I'm on to her. She just wants to throw me off her tail . . . Wings beating a muffled drum, he managed to catch up. Grunting, he reached out to grab the tail in question, pull her out of the sky.

"Don't tell me," he said, through gritted teeth. "I'm not even worth—"

Her body was a whip, cracking at his touch. She moved like silk through greased hands, spinning around to confront him. Her wings fanned up, her rear legs thrusting out, crunching into his snout. Stunned, he flapped backwards, teeth jarring. She gave him no time to recover and leapt towards him, stealing the advantage. Through his stupor, Ben stretched out his forearms, claws spread, grabbing her foot before it connected. Atiya hissed, squirming in his grip, her wings beating snow from the cliffs, shoving blasts down at him. He swivelled, swinging her around, claws twisting as he went. Her hiss became a shriek as he let go, sending her reeling into the darkness. She flailed in mid-air and Ben drew a breath, summoning his inner gases. Jaws wide, he roared flame in her direction.

Heat rippled across her hide. Rippled, but did not burn. The Queen manoeuvred into a dive, dropping out of danger. Fire washed steam from the mountainside. She spiralled down into the folds, fog closing around her.

Ben swore and raced in pursuit. Down here the terrain was a jigsaw of narrow ridges, a Swiss cheese of chasms and caves, all of them thick with vapour. Warmer air rushed through his gills and he gave up the summits with some regret, reluctant to take his chances between the slopes below them. If Atiya wanted to shake him off, she wouldn't find it hard. Instead she stayed directly ahead, her wings spread and level, skimming over the gorge. Losing him wasn't her intention. The Queen had faced him for a reason. If this was a game, she wanted to win.

The clouds boiled above him, sulking on the peaks. The gorge echoed with thunder, lightning flickering as Atiya descended into the mountains, leaving her storm to burn on the heights. The popping in his ears told him that he was sinking lower, his wings puffing snow from buried ledges, flurries floating in the still. Up ahead, the Queen arched her back and dived again, her knife-rack spine vanishing in mist.

Their gradual descent wasn't lost on Ben. The Alps might seem like the ends of the earth, but for all their remoteness they were far from deserted. The world had long since ventured above the snowline. As he lost altitude, the dangers increased, and worry prickled through his annoyance. Having sprung one trap, he was wary of blundering into another. Where was she leading him? There could be climbers, skiers on the lower slopes. Resorts. Chalets. Towns. He told himself that most people would put him and his quarry down to a hallucination, a vision brought on by thin air and cold, but he couldn't count on it. With the Lore broken, all bets were off. And Atiya had no respect for the Lore. Her antics in New York and London proved that she didn't give a shit. She pre-dated the Guild by millennia. What were their edicts to her?

The rising temperature served as a warning. Ben hurried after her, his mind now set on damage limitation, on forcing her back to the heights. He burst from the fog like a depth charge, dropping into a valley. Scarred cliffs rose on either side of him, bordering a broad snowy basin. Outstripping her own shadow, Atiya fleeted across the vale, heading into the sunset. Red and gold lined the horizon, the mountains black against the sky. Land glimmered far below. Rivers cut the hazy green, veins bloody with twilight.

Ben glided in the Queen's wake, another shadow on the

untouched expanse. Panic fluttered in his breast as he made out the structures far below, the squat brown shapes of cabins. A telephone pole beside an ice-black road. Parked coaches with garish logos. The air rushed harder through his gills, pulling him closer to his prey, and he roared at her to stop, to turn back, give up the chase. Atiya paid no attention.

Catch me if you can . . .

Lungs bursting, Ben propelled himself on, leaving behind a miniature blizzard. He shook himself off, his shadow whisking over a plateau. Atiya looked back at him – barking triumph – and speared downwards, heading for the place where the land ran out, frozen fangs overhanging the escarpment.

A large wooden lodge perched on the cliff. Its wide viewing deck, designed to hold a hundred tourists, was thankfully empty – chairs stacked on tables, umbrellas folded. Ben was too far away to see if people stood behind the tall windows. Considering the deepening dusk, he thought not, his suspicions confirmed as he sank lower and saw the cable car – probably the last one of the day – embarking from the little station house a few yards distance from the lodge. The car was a bright yellow square, the colour a precaution against the weather. It was no precaution at all against dragons. Twenty-odd people, dressed in puffy jackets and salopettes, dangled in the carriage over the gulf, a drop of several hundred feet. Skis bristled in their midst like cocktail sticks on an East Village bar. Woollen hats bobbed in time with their chatter and laughter. They were having a real blast. And then came a gurgling scream. Some of the passengers whipped off their sunglasses, blinking as they took in the scene outside the carriage windows. More screams sailed to Ben's ears, and now his eyesight seemed *too* keen as he saw the terror on their faces, the Queen's shadow falling over them. But Atiya was looking back at him, taunting him, his inability to catch her. Too late, her snout snapped around as she sensed the obstruction ahead. The cable car creaked and swayed as the people inside it shuffled backwards, packing the furthest limits of the space. Like a virus, the panic spread. Ben felt the crowd staring out at him, shock and disbelief darting over his wings and foot-long fangs.

"*Atiya, no!*"

His cry was a smoky roar. The passengers answered in a unified howl. Both warnings were useless. The Queen's momentum, swooping down from the peaks, her wings held close to her flanks, prevented any chance of slowing. Nevertheless, she made the attempt, her wings fanning out to lift her bulk upwards, a black comet shooting over the track cable. Ben held his breath as she cleared the car – but then sparks showered off the end of her tail as its bladed length scored across steel. Reverberations travelled from the wheel truck and down the attached metal strut. Some of the passengers in the car lost their footing and fell over. Others cracked heads and there was blood, bright in the jostling crush. Now the screams became warbles and sobs, punctuated by the silence of dread. The land see-sawed far below, a green and white blur.

Sparks snapped and jumped. Atiya spun awkwardly away, her momentum carrying her onwards, her tail leaving a spiral of smoke. The cable car tilted further to one side as the thick strands of wire uncoiled, twirling and twanging apart.

Gravity hurled Ben after Atiya. The Queen, finally slowing, looked up to meet the collision, the impact spinning them out into space, debris showering around them. Ben grabbed her and she squirmed in his grip, her hind legs scrabbling for his belly, for the softer parts of him. Sucking in to avoid evisceration, he made a fist of his claws, clouting her across her elegant snout. He clutched at her horns, determined to saddle her, bring her down. She bucked under him, a wild thing, and veered for the cliff face, snarling. Rubble scattered, their combined weight crashing into rock. Ben wheezed in the churned-up dust. The wind went out of him, forcing him to release the Queen, and she flung herself clear, wings unfolding like a last-minute parachute. Lightning crackled. *Atiya* crackled. She put some distance between them and glided around in a circle, waiting for his next move.

A hollow twang resounded in the gulf, making the decision for him. The track cable split in two, its frayed ends snickering into the dusk. Flailing metal lashed the precipice, the cliff face barking echoes. Broken parts drizzled down, clattering on the roof of the carriage, the wheel truck bouncing off into the gulf. The cable car lurched, hung for a moment on a winding thread, and then followed, a one-way elevator to destruction. Screams trailed through the chill.

Blood pounding in his ears, Ben went after the car, wings tucked in, tail straight, snout aimed earthward. He let gravity claim him, wrenching him down. The ground opened up below, a snowy patchwork of doom.

The cable car fell, spinning in the updraughts, a yellow streak against the towering cliffs. *Death's piss.* Time shrieked between his clenched teeth. If the carriage hit the ground, he would watch, helpless, as it burst into a thousand pieces, spilling glass, wire and metal. Spilling crimson across the snow.

People were already gathering down there, tourists running out of their cabins to stare at the marvels the night blew in. He felt their horror wash over him, a curdled wall that encompassed the cable car and the giant beast behind it. In that moment the foot of the mountain held them all, breathless and frozen, their rational world caving in. Fear – sweaty, rank and all too human – assailed Ben's nostrils. The people below saw him. Through their shock, he felt their belief.

Someone managed to shake off the spell. Pointed and shouted. *To hell with them.*

Ben shot downward, stretching out his claws. Closing the distance, he grabbed loose wires, the mangled mess of the cable car strut. Sharp edges bit into his flesh, hot with spewed electricity. His wings snapped out, catching the air, punched by the sudden pressure. The weight threatened to pull his limbs from their sockets, but he held on tight, his rear legs curling in, his tail winding around the windows to stop the cable car's spin.

The ground lurched, leaping for its prey. Wings fanned snow across the gawping crowd. People wailed and threw up their arms, simultaneously blinded and stung. Just before the carriage hit the ground, its descent gradually slowed. It skimmed inches over a knoll, dislodging sheets of ice and stone, and then came rattling and bumping to earth, skidding down a churned-up furrow of slush, coming to a halt in the drifts, a shipwreck on a bone-white shore.

As the snow settled, sobs and groans rose under the sky. The crowd held its position, no one daring to come any closer, to rush and search for survivors.

Ben unwound his tail from the cable car. He glanced inside it, a great golden eye peering through the tines of shattered glass. He saw injured and comatose people, but no obvious deaths. Shock, not grief, suffused the scene.

Above him on the cliff, a black speck, darker than the settling night, sat watching him. It was impossible to tell what the Queen

James Bennett

was feeling, but he didn't think it was remorse. There was only one way to find out. He bounded across the snow and once more took to the air, zeroing in on the ice-bound heights.

SEVENTEEN

The Queen was waiting for him. She perched on an outcrop, a turret-sized spit of rock that looked like a pebble under her claws. She was a hole punched in the night, a doorway to a deeper darkness, a numinous corridor leading down years. Her flanks rippled and steamed. Tail swishing back and forth, she waited for Ben to rejoin the fight.

They met with a sound that shook the mountain. Velocity threw them into the air, bloodstained confetti swirling around them. Ben's tail skimmed the station house, the roof exploding in glass and wood. The Queen sailed under him through the debris, her body yielding to the collision, letting gravity pull them down. The grappling beasts swept over the summit and crashed down a steep slope, smashing the piste into flurries. Flags splintered, scattering like toothpicks. The drifts melted under their heat, an avalanche of slush taking them down and over and over in a thundering embrace.

Ben laced his claws around the Queen's neck, her weight wrenching him into the torrent. The world spun. Sky, rock, snow. Sky, rock, snow. Atiya snapped at his snout and neck, his roars buried in the landslide. Locking her legs in his, her tail snaked around him in cold, vicious intimacy. Steam shrouded the sky. The scene was a blur diffused with sparks. And Atiya was changing as she rolled, casting off her bestial form like summer clothes shed by a lake, her black mass melting in his clutches. Mind chained to her transformation, Ben felt himself changing too, his flesh a reluctant mirror to her will. His wings crumpled inwards, his haunches and tail shrinking. Their tangled claws gave way to tangled arms and legs, slender and human-shaped. In a violent clinch, they tumbled over another cliff, fell a hundred feet or so on to a flat, icy ledge.

Mud and snow gushed over the precipice, dripping off gigantic icicles and splattering the ledge like dirty tears. Atiya straddled Ben in the slop, her bare breasts pressed against his suit, which, just as Von Hart had promised, had changed fluidly with him, providing a sleek barrier between them.

There was no such barrier between their lips. She sealed her face to his, her tongue working between his teeth, cold and sure and sensual. Electricity shot through his body, tingling in his cheeks, his fingers, his balls. The wind knocked out of him, skull jangling, he found himself responding, drawing on her like a diver for breath, his hands sliding up her muscled thighs, instinct and longing usurping his caution. The Queen was purring deep in her throat, a pleasurable drone vibrating in his bones. Vibrating in the flesh between his legs, summoning blood and betraying him with hardness.

Her purr deepened, becoming staccato, coins falling on glass. It took Ben a moment to realise that she was laughing. Cheeks burning, he pushed her off him. Or she let herself be pushed.

She didn't so much walk as drift across the snow, her feet hovering inches off the ground. He tried to ignore the ache that travelled with her, his flesh mourning the loss of contact even as it recoiled in shame. She turned and looked down at him, a shapely figure cut from the night, her eyes sparkling with amusement.

"Ah yes, your woman," she said. "Your poor mortal *dhillo*."

Ben didn't recognise the word. The meaning, however, was clear, a jibe carried on sepulchral tones.

"Fuck, are you *nuts*?" He climbed to his feet, brushing slop from his chest. "You could have killed those people!"

The storm above them was passing, he saw, the clouds dispersing in dusky rags, giving up the fight. Moonlight painted their shadows on the cliff face, illuminating her sharp-boned face, the way her lips twisted in what Ben guessed was dismissive regret.

"Unfortunate." Her shrug brought home the fact that he was dealing with a creature who was utterly inhuman. "Yet you managed to save them."

"That isn't the point," he shot back. "There are . . . consequences. To everything you do."

"And the fear of them binds you. As does their feeble Lore."

He would have asked how she had found him, how she had come to learn of the Lore, but he already knew. Something about her presence, her *divinity*, had joined them, a delicate thread. Even back in London, before he'd clashed with her at the museum, Atiya had been able to sense him, sniff him out. Hadn't she come waltzing into his lair? Unannounced. Uninvited. It seemed that this unwelcome union worked over great distances too, turning them into a scaled yin and yang. Eyes on the road, fearful for Rose, Ben had acknowledged the bond too late. A thousand feet above the Alps, the hunter had become the hunted.

"As for your love of mortals . . ." The Queen made a soft, but no less harsh, sound between her lips and her teeth.

"That opinion is starting to bore me." But her scorn was getting under his skin. And he responded in kind. "What would you know about love? All I've seen you manage is destruction."

"*Nacas!* You see nothing." The Queen looked away, and Ben believed that his words had stung. He had also noticed that her lips weren't moving in time with her words. She spoke like a foreign actress in a badly dubbed film. It occurred to him that the tongue she used was not the one he heard, the link between them allowing a kind of makeshift communion, his mind deciphering a language long lost. Could things get any weirder? "You see nothing at all."

"Then educate me. You obviously haven't killed me for a reason."

"We are serpents, are we not? I merely honour the accord between our kind," she said. "But you are determined to give me a reason. I have turned back to warn you. Do the same. Do not try to stop me."

"Stop you from what? Stealing half the world's treasures? You know, when it comes to theft, you're not exactly discreet."

A blur and she was before him, her eyes ablaze, a fist shaking in his face.

"You dare to call me a thief? You *dare*?"

She trailed smoke as she moved, her flesh a curtain on to darkness. In the miasma, Ben caught sight of a little girl again. She was skinny, this creature, a bundle of twigs in a filthy T-shirt and football shorts. Cornrows wove neatly across her skull, the face below them sad and gaunt. The image wavered, a wraith clinging to the Queen's body. *In* the Queen's body. He'd seen the same thing up on the stage in the British Museum, a faint visage set behind the other, youth caged by untold age gazing out at him with wasted eyes.

He took a step backwards.

"Tell me. Who is the girl?"

Alarm swam across the Queen's face. Her body was a gate,

banging shut. Ben blinked and the girl was gone, sinking under a lightless sea.

"She is nothing. Something that was and is no more. Innocence, perhaps. Or hope."

"She's a little girl. A . . . foothold, isn't that right?" Von Hart spoke up to remind him. *Once summoned, the Queen anchored herself in human flesh, but she isn't quite . . . corporeal.* Ben was still getting his head around it. "So I guess I do see some things."

She let him have that. She slid away again, over the snow. The stars travelled across her skin, twinkling in her nebulous depths. When she spoke, her voice was low, drifting over her shoulder.

"You know your woman will die, don't you?"

"Not if I can help it." But she had stung him in return. "The syzygy—"

"I am not talking about the witches and their foolish spells." She turned again, frosting him with a look. "I am talking about . . . the rose, yes?"

O Rose thou art sick . . .

Ben scowled. "Don't do that. Stay the fuck out of my head."

Atiya snorted. "Your love of humans. Do you never grow tired of it? You might as well love a sunbeam that flickers through a cloud. This world was not meant to hold them. Time will take them all so quickly. A blink in the life of a god."

"So what do you want? Servitude? A world on its knees?"

"This world is already on its knees. Its golden age not even a memory." The Queen arched her neck, a proud swan. "I have seen your world, little beast. I have drunk of its terror and hope. Humans fear the darkness that gave them birth and harness the light to outshine the stars. They build machines that cough with smoke and poison the very air. They suck up the blood of the earth and pour filth into the seas. They speak boldly of freedom and peace and think they can buy them with war. Money is their temple and greed their god. They stand in defiance of all that is real, turning magic into myth, myth into Remnants, choosing to live in a cold dead dream." She turned, fixing him with her piercing gaze. "What use do I have for dominion? Humans have made their own cage, their own tyranny. And they will bring about their own end."

"Yeah. You get to wondering who the monsters are." There was no point denying it; he had thought the same things himself. "But we live in hope. There is every chance that they'll come through. If we've survived, so can they."

"You call your existence survival? It is exile. It is death. None of your kind will live for ever. Will you breed? No. A handful of centuries from now, and tales alone will remain."

"Call me optimistic." He fended off the bitter truth, clutching at the only straws he had left. "Maybe they'll learn. Maybe with the right guidance, they'll fear less, know more. Maybe one day we'll all live in peace again."

Laughter ricocheted off the rock face.

"That is your dream?" Atiya peered at him, and again Ben had the uncomfortable sensation of her peering *into* him, reading his thoughts. "Yes, I have seen the chains that bind you. The cage in which you stand. The Guild sent most of you into the Sleep, no? The Pact is no truce at all, merely a cell where you wait for extinction." She clicked her tongue, her annoyance sounding harsh in the still. "You might share the humans' blindness, but you will never be like them."

"I said *maybe*."

"That is your dream." The Queen cocked her head, sympathetic. "You long for a normal life. A normal life with the woman you love. The Pact tastes like ash in your mouth, yet you suffer it because you hope. The Guild does not need to hide you. You already hide from yourself."

These words didn't sting. They *burned*. Ben broke the staring contest, looking down at the snowbound slopes. The wind carried sirens to his ears and he pictured the panic down there, police cars and ambulances struggling to cope with the rescued tourists, listening to their tales of monsters on the mountain, winged beasts at war. Beasts that could not, should not be. Only days ago, he would have drawn comfort from the fact that tales like that would fall on deaf ears, dismissed as shock and hysteria. Perhaps in this case as hypothermia and altitude sickness. Sceptical minds didn't need much of an excuse to stay that way. He had seen it a thousand times.

Now he wasn't so sure. This week had shattered the walls of his torpor, awakening him to his uniqueness, his vulnerability and isolation. The truth was all around him. Freezing air that would kill a man. Heights that no human could endure. Since his flight from the Brooklyn Bridge, who knew how many people had seen him? How many strange but similar reports were already zipping around the world, sailing on awestruck radio waves? The Queen was right: he was nothing like them. He was a stranger, an oddity. He would stand out in their mundane midst like a fox in a chicken coop.

And of course, they would treat him as such.

"You are lonely." Atiya was drawing close again; close enough to make his skin prickle, his skull and nipples ache. She reached out a hand and traced the sigil on his chest, the wyrm tongue in red circled by yellow. "Sola Ignis. Lone fire. I can see the words burning in your soul. Is that why you love them so much?" And then, softly, "Is that why you follow me?"

He grabbed her wrist, ignoring how much it hurt him, her heat scalding his palm.

"Don't flatter yourself. I signed the Pact. Might not mean a damn to some folks, but it still means something to me."

"You lie!" Atiya wrenched her arm from his grip. "And your honour makes a feeble shield."

"I believe we were talking about you. If you don't want dominion, what do you want? Why did you steal those relics?"

"I stole nothing! I took what was rightfully mine."

"Why are you here? Who dug you out of your grave?"

"Silence, *addoon*. You will demand nothing of me."

"Then go ahead and kill me. Cut off my head. Leave my carcass to the birds." Ben's anger surprised him. The truth was she had cut him deep, despite his casual pretence. Her insights were an undeniable blade, opening a wound of doubt that bled with vindictive fire. He breathed in, letting ice fill his lungs, then hissed into her face. "If the CROWS kill Rose, then I'd rather be dead."

She stared at him for a moment, blue heat boring into his head. In her steady gaze, Ben caught his own impressions. *A great temple in the desert. A raging storm at sea. Then white light. Light to blind the land.* Whether she didn't want him to see or flinched from his passion, the Queen dropped her eyes and turned away, the night coming between them again.

But Ben wasn't ready to let it go.

"Not so fast." He grabbed her arm again, preventing her retreat, static dancing through his fingers. "I've chased you halfway around the world and you still haven't answered my questions."

He spun her to face him. Whatever the cause of her sorrow, the emotion weakened her, allowing him to pull her close. She sizzled in his grip, glaring.

270

"You are chasing your doom." Their words wrestled for dominance as their claws had on the mountaintop. "And this is my last warning. Let me go. I fly south to reclaim my crown."

"Why did you come here?" He all but shook her. "Why wait for me in the mountains?"

"You think I will risk your interference?" The Queen barked a laugh, another bitter knife. "Once the Pschent is in my hands, I will take my revenge. I will look my traitor in the eyes before I . . ." Fervour or pain prevented her from vocalising her violence. "Turn back. Turn back now. Do not make me destroy you."

"You know, I have a feeling you don't have a choice."

A frown split her forehead, her reluctance plain. "We are serpents. Would you spurn the mercy of a queen?"

"You're nothing like me. You're a ghost. A figment. A dream." He tightened his grip on her arm. "And I won't leave Rose."

"Then you risk all for one mortal life. Your woman means nothing. Your woman will die."

"No!"

"Go back to your slumber, *mas*. Go back to your drink and foolish dreams. I am Atiya, Queen of Punt. Go back. I command you!"

Energy was building between them, crackling from her body to his. Blue streams crawled over her skin and writhed up his arms, climbing his neck and into his hair. The strands stood on end, trembling as her power shot through him, heat sinking into his bones, threatening to tear his body apart, paint the ledge with his mutable flesh.

A burning stench filled his nostrils. Blisters bubbled up on his hands. He refused to release her. The mystery had led him from New York to London, from London to Berlin and up to these heights, chasing a goddess whose age and strength made

271

him feel like a child. Something told him that this was his last chance to get to the truth, and a thought came to him through his pain, tangled up with all the others, Atiya's and his own. Lightning linked them, fusing them as one. And Ben had caught impressions of his own. He clenched his teeth and tightened his grip, pushing his mind towards her, trying to penetrate her secrets.

Atiya struggled, catching his intent. She shouted something, a dazzling roar. Smoke coiled from her, enfolding them in a smothering cloak. Ben pushed forward and embraced her, pressing his heat against her cold. Atiya screamed, jarring the seams in his skull, and then he was falling. Falling into . . .

Darkness. Deeper than death. The deep darkness of time.

A chill enveloped him, dousing his heat. The atmosphere clung to his body, an oily substance slowing his movements, rippling off his flailing arms. No boundaries curbed his surroundings. No ground lay under his feet. His sense of up and down was confused, rendered irrelevant by the gulf. One moment, he was falling, and the next, rising. Drifting. Lost in the endless stuff of her soul.

That was when he realised where he was.

Inside her. The Queen had absorbed him. Just like she'd absorbed the Star of Eebe and the Jackal's Crook. Absorbed him like she had the little girl.

Khadra. The name came to him the second he saw her, a fragile figure in the gloom. She sat with her knees drawn up, her head down on crossed arms. Her prison was a small one, a collection of shadows forming some kind of shack, a vague, shifting vision, blurred skulls hanging on the walls, the sketch of a fire blazing in a hearth. Inklings drenched the atmosphere, like the girl's name, entering his mind like an echo, a shred of alien thought. Fragments of the Queen's consciousness.

But I am the ghost here. A figment. A dream.

He floated towards the girl and she looked up. If he had expected joy at his presence, Khadra surprised him. She didn't greet him like a saviour, didn't seem to care about rescue. Instead, she scowled and scuttled backwards, clutching the objects in her lap. One was a gem, fist-sized, glassy and clear. The other a length of ivory, looped at the top and carved with hieroglyphics.

The Star and the Crook. Stolen goods.

He reached out, and the girl spat something. She raised the Star in one hand. In the other, she waved the Crook, a sharp warning gesture. *Stay back.* It was all Ben needed to know that she was not a prisoner. She *wanted* to be here. She was complicit with the Queen. Fuck, she was a partner in crime.

It was you. You summoned Atiya. You did this to yourself.

In answer, the girl opened her mouth. A river of dust poured out. Dust to cover the world, dust on dust on dust. Dust on hunger. Dust on bones. The relentless dust of death.

And through the dust, the girl's thoughts.

The Queen will bring barwaaqo *to us. The Queen will bring the rains.*

Somewhere, a bird screeched. Ben had come so far to find the truth, but now he didn't want to see: a flood of images in the haze. Images he recognised from TV. Technicolor death that he knew so well. Flat pans of brown earth, yellow plants pushing through the cracks. Dry gullies with stones at the bottom, red trickles winding through the mud. Bony cattle slumped on the rise, seeking the shade under leafless trees. A white sun blazed overhead, merciless through the mirage. The sky rippled like laughter, mocking the corrugated shacks and low stone buildings that huddled below in a restless mosaic. With an awareness not his own, he understood that the buildings lay empty. Their occupants, the few remaining, languished around the village well, a tangled mass of leather and bone, too weak to blink away flies. Eyes watched Ben without seeing. Mouths opened and breathed in dust. He was another ghost in a land of ghosts. Another presence that could not help.

Dhuroob in jilal. The girl's mind met his, her desperation translating into words. *Home.*

A breeze came up, hissing through the withered corn. A baby wailed. Wailed no more.

This is home. This is death.

Ben recoiled from the sight. Disgusted, and appalled by his disgust. No screen stood between him and the vision. He couldn't change the channel, pretend it wasn't there. This was real and now. The hard skin of the Western world could not protect him here. The girl – Khadra – her need was his need. Her grief, his grief. Her hunger . . .

How trivial his fears seemed now.

Grit eddied on the road to the village. An old woman was shuffling down it, where there was only dust a moment before. She was a hunchbacked thing, withered as the crops, her left ear long and drooping. Her claws were strange and inhuman, granting her the look of a fairy-tale hag.

Dhegdheer came. Khadra was opening a door to the past. *Dhegdheer came with promises. Secrets. She came with a map and a shard.*

The hag stood on the step of a filthy shack, speaking to another woman, younger, taller, but no less starved, beads and bones dangling around her neck. The one called Dhegdheer pressed a little bag of stitched grey fur into the woman's hand, her eyes bright with purpose. Ben couldn't hear what they were saying, but he could see the fear in the younger woman's face, the thin, impossible hope.

She told my mother where to find the Queen. She told us how to raise her.

You . . . turned to your past. The cloud of flies buzzed in Ben's skull. *To your myths. To your gods.*

Yes.

You broke the Lore. The . . . Pact . . .

Yes.

He shook off the flies, trying to reject her pain, remember the task at hand. He didn't know how to tell her that the Queen had other ideas.

That wasn't . . . very smart . . .

He had to get out of here. If he could wrench the girl with him from her limbo inside the Queen, surely it would shake Atiya's foothold in the real world, extract the fuel from her spiritual engine. He doubted that the Queen's undoing would cancel out the chaos of the week, restore the Pact, reinstate the Lore – not if the Guild was conspiring with the CROWS – but still, he had to *try*. All that mattered right now was Khadra's infraction, her raising of a goddess, and the dire consequences. Consequences that had almost cost him his life. Consequences that, if the CROWS had their way, would cost them all a whole lot more. *Anarchy. Bloodshed. Revolution.* Atiya's summoning had broken more than a magically binding treaty. It had broken open Pandora's box.

There's a balance to things. He tried to reach the girl with his mind, press his urgency upon her. *If you screw with it, you—*

He didn't get to finish. His assurances meant nothing. She had taken his approach as an attack. With a deft, impulsive motion, she touched the end of the Crook to the Star and the gulf around them exploded in light.

Ben cried out, throwing up his arms. A tide of energy caught him, enfolding him in luminance. The Star of Eebe shrieked in his head, a song that was beyond ancient, beyond earthbound. It was the song of the void, primordial, endless, cold. A song that signalled the end of worlds and perhaps their beginning. White fire claimed him, closing around him like a cage. A brief, blinding fulmination and he was in the heart of the Star.

The Star was falling, falling.

The meteor shook off rock at the edge of space, a flaming Cinderella fleeing a ball. From his crystal prison, Ben watched the stars blink out, fading in the glare of the sun. Compressing air, dense and hot, bore in around his miniature self. He heard the residual rock burn up, searing away from his diamond cell. The meteor punched through the atmosphere and into the blue, shooting towards the earth. Clouds parted, their skirts singed. Continents rose in green-brown slabs, a patchwork grave yawning to meet him. The sea crept in and he thundered over it, leaving a storm in his wake.

Then the sky was full of serpents. They wheeled around him, a winged gyre. The beasts were all the colours of the rainbow, vibrant greens and deep blues. Yellows, browns and reds. Their flanks dazzled him through the molten facets, the glass walls around him. Far below them, a jungle spread, a lush forest carpeting the shore. And in that dark and tangled mass, there rose a temple – or perhaps a palace – thick stone pillars that held up the sky, monoliths with stern, forbidding faces, presiding over the land. He had glimpsed this place before, albeit in miles of endless sand, every surface carved with glyphs, every archway gilded. The temple called to him as if he had walked there himself, not just seen it in the Queen's mind. As if he'd lived there under the reign of the gods, thousands of years ago.

The Star fell and the serpents screamed. Their grappling claws could not catch him, check his breakneck descent. His fire took them, crisping their wings and cracking their scales, changing all their colours to black. Bones sailed across the sun, a pall of ash and trailing smoke washing out over the ocean.

The Star shrieked over the temple, over the knotted branches and vines. A scorching line ran through the undergrowth, the trees bursting into flame. Rivers hissed into steaming plumes. Animals fell charred as they fled. The Star hit the earth with the sound of drums struck all at once by a giant hand. The surrounding jungle took to the air, leafy birds striving for the sky, boughs spread in supplication. Upturned earth swallowed the sun, buried the splintering light.

And with the light, fragments of memory.

Ben clutched his head, resisting the influx – the imploding pressure of remembered time, remembered aeons, flying like bullets into his soul.

A great ship with sails of flax, countless oars in the water. A tall woman standing on the deck, the breeze playing with her white cotton dress. The collar around her neck caught the sunlight, glinting with turquoise, garnet and gold. She wore a tall double crown on her head and Ben knew it was the Pschent. A cobra, ready to strike, coiled from the front of the crown, set next to a sharp-beaked bird, symbols of divine authority. Bracelets encircled the woman's arms and wrists, adorning her sun-kissed skin. Ben gazed at this great pharaoh, this woman king from a distant land, and instantly knew her by name. Hatshepsut.

She alighted from the ship with a man by her side, a bald and barefoot youth robed in leopard skin, his ice-chip eyes belying his innocent face. The youth, a priest, gave his blessing to the land, kneeling to kiss the feet of another woman, one whose beauty and power Ben recognised, having felt the sting of both. Atiya. Queen of Punt. The Queen met the ambassadors with cool grace, her twirling hand a sparrow through the air.

What the hell am I seeing?

But he knew. In Club Zauber, the envoy had shown him the reliefs at Deir el-Bahari, a picture of the past in levitating cards. This was the arrival of Hatshepsut's voyage, her royal ship landing in Punt three and a half thousand years ago. Its importance to Atiya shuddered through him. This was the source of her fury. The seed of all that came after . . .

The scenes accelerated, fuelled by rage.

The three of them were gathered in the temple, the Pharaoh, the Queen and the bald priest. They stood around what could only be the Star, a pulsating sphere in the middle of the chamber, set on a rough pedestal of rock. In the following image, the Pharaoh was presenting Atiya with a gift. The heqa-siin. *The Jackal's Crook. Sparks coiled and snapped off the priest's mask, a silver veil holding wintry eyes. Holding secrets. Hunger. The reflections danced, painting a vague and carnal act. Atiya strewn naked on a bed somewhere, locked in passion with a young man, his back muscles taut with exertion. Then the priest again, standing in the temple and clutching the Crook, a trembling hand reaching for the Star. Its refulgence shimmered in the Pschent atop his head. Atiya entered under an arch, running down the steps towards him, her hands raised, her face drawn. The priest grinned, a dagger in his hand. A dagger that rose and fell, rose and fell, beads of blood staining the flagstones, bejewelling the blanketing darkness . . .*

EIGHTEEN

The darkness of night, cold but earthly, replaced the whirling scenes.

Ben sucked in the frozen air. He was back on the mountain. Back on the ledge. His return to the present squirmed through his guts like a seasick worm, and he fell retching to his hands and knees, the remains of Von Hart's breakfast dribbling on to the snow. He wiped his mouth, tasting eggs, acid and loss. The high crags pressed against his skull, rebuking him for his absence, his departure from the here and now. Looking around, he half expected to see Lurkers shambling out of the rock face, their tentacles reaching to grab him. There was none. Whatever had drawn him into the Queen wasn't magic as Ben understood it. It was raw elemental force. The puissance of gods.

Or perhaps ghosts. Atiya wasn't fully *in* the world, only anchored here by human flesh. Small wonder she wasn't subject to its laws. He turned to look at her and noticed his possession had sickened her too. She leant against a nearby boulder, using the rock to prop herself up. Her shoulders rose and fell with her breaths and her body was faint under the stars, its smoky substance dimmer than before. By now, Ben was familiar with psychic intrusion. He could have told her he knew the feeling.

When she met his gaze, her eyes glimmered, a dusky sheen

of violation. Her voice limped across the space between them. "What . . . what did you see?"

"You tell me. A trailer for the *Discovery Channel*?" he said. Then, because it sounded so childish, "I saw a sky full of serpents. The Star . . . falling."

"Then you have seen the death of my kind."

"Dragons . . ."

She nodded. "The First Breed. The servants of Eebe."

Eebe. God. Or what had once been a god, a higher cosmic entity belonging, perhaps, to a fallen and forgotten pantheon, way back in the day. Her fancy name for the first dragons, the ones who had somehow become extinct, tallied with the name that the Fay liked to call their supposed ancestors. The First-Born. Gods . . . . The connection was clear to him, and not just with his own insight; a residual impression coating his mind. They were a closed circuit sharing a current, a symbiosis of electricity and thought. The Queen drew part of her dialect from him – he understood that too, now – their discourse fuelled by her glimpses of the world. She surfed minds like radio channels, tuning in and out of modern awareness. And what, he wondered, had she learnt from him? The taste of Jack. Submission and loneliness. It hardly made her omniscient.

"The First Breed." Ben felt slightly put out, understanding that he came from a second, and much later, attempt at the creation of his kind. And knowing that this, the warning she had given him – extinction, death – was all too real, a palpable threat rooted in fact. It was hard to keep petulance out of his voice. "But not the last."

Atiya wasn't listening to him. Her gaze was for the past, for the visions he had stirred in her.

"Seventy-three of us took to the sky that day," she said. "In the panic and confusion, there was no time to think about what we were facing, what we might stand to lose. Only two of us remained behind. Parahu, my father, would not let me leave him when the Star fell. He was old and sick, and duty binds, although it kills me to know that it was the death of us . . . We stayed in the palace and watched, the Star, the comet, blazing out of the heavens as we prayed for the best. We watched the seventy-three fly up to the Star, watched as they formed a net with their wings, intending to slow the comet's descent, divert it into the sea. It was folly, of course. Our pride, our isolation, our belief in our power blinded us to disaster. The Star smashed through scale, horn and hide unchecked. We watched our friends and family die."

Ben pulled himself into a crouch. Connections wove through the frosty space, prompting fragments of Von Hart's insights. He would have offered Atiya sympathy, but he didn't want to break the spell. Having come so far, chasing the mystery, he didn't dare disturb her reverie. Perhaps she was tired, weary of secrets. Either way, they both knew what this was. A confession. A surrender. He wouldn't distract her with words.

"Who knows why the Star fell? Was Eebe angered by his servants? Were the old gods dying and shedding their hearts? In those days, we believed that the cosmos hung on the love of the Bull and the Cow. Creation balanced on the horns of the Bull, who gazed forever at the Cow tethered before him. When the Cow turned her eyes away, there was destruction and chaos on earth. This is what came to pass.

"The Star of Eebe. It was ruin. Death. A terrible power lived in the stone. It held the essence of celestial storms. No one could approach the crater where it fell or bear to hear its song. The earth itself shrank from it, the jungle burning, burning . . . For months, we mourned the loss of our kind and lived in growing fear. Fear for the survival of Punt. A wasteland was spreading out from the Star, consuming the rivers, the trees, the birds and beasts, the tribes who worshipped us. But Eebe heard our prayer and a stranger came to us, a sailor from the golden kingdom in the north. Because my father chose to spare him, news of our glory sailed across the sea."

This story was fresh in Ben's mind. The Tale of the Shipwrecked Sailor. He nodded gently, willing her on.

"A year after the Star fell, the Great Pharaoh Hatshepsut arrived, to see the land of Punt for herself, this once-great land of serpents and ruin. Egypt was also touched by the gods, gods both numerous and complex. They were the Neteru, each one joined to an aspect of nature. There was Amun-Ra, the Father of the Sun. Neith, the Cosmic Virgin. And there was Anubis, the jackal-headed Judge of the Dead. The Neteru had placed magic beyond measure in mortal hands. The pharaohs raised temples from the sand and spoke with beings from distant stars. Their magic was the most powerful on earth."

Ben, wrists tingling with the memory of that magic, could easily believe it. In the underground car park in London, hieroglyphs had held his transformation in check, binding him as if he were a man. His natural resistance to spells had meant nothing. Without the envoy's arrival, Fulk would probably still be alive and wearing his hide about town. A shiver ran through him, slipping through the lull of the Queen's contemplation.

"Hatshepsut, hearing of our plight, felt moved to share this magic. Accepting us as the last of a powerful, mythical race, the Pharaoh came to us in peace. She told us she would help. With the Star gnawing at the palace walls, we thought ourselves blessed to receive such guests. Hatshepsut, the Lioness, who ruled as a man and made consorts of kings. Her beauty put the moon to shame. Her kindness, the rain. And in her retinue there came a man, a young and handsome priest, wise beyond his years. Baba Kamenwati. A name that means darkness. A name that means death."

Ben recalled the name. Professor Winlock had mentioned the priest at the British Museum, describing the breaking of his tomb. Kamenwati had been a notorious heretic, the leader of an underground jackal cult. In the tomb, Winlock had found strange and remarkable magic bricks, the little statues depicting demons instead of gods, an unprecedented find. Jaws, claws and fangs, chimerically fused with human physiques. Winlock said that the funerary priests had placed the bricks in the corners of the tomb to prevent the *ba*, the soul, from entering the Duat, the Ancient Egyptian underworld.

The last week had been a crash course in history, and none of it pleasant. The visions lingered, and Ben found that he could picture this man, this bald-headed youth in leopard skin. Baba Kamenwati. He had seen his face, the frost in his eyes. The ice-cold longing . . .

"We were blinded by need." Atiya's voice was a hush in the night, soft as the swirling snow. "Does the mouse turn to the snake in despair? The spider to the scorpion? Eager to please the Pharaoh, Kamenwati promised us deliverance. Only sorcery, he said, could subdue and control the power of the Star, and he prayed to Thoth for an answer. Thoth soon answered and damned us all. Kamenwati and his men sacrificed an elephant. From one tusk, the priest carved the *heqa-siin*, the Jackal's Crook, binding it with spells. From Karnak silver he forged a mirror to the Pharaoh's crown and bid Hatshepsut bless it with a kiss. Then, when the Crook and the Pschent were ready, the Pharaoh furnished me with this sacred regalia, symbols of my bond with Egypt.

"I am no coward, but when I entered the crater, my heart beat like a *batar* drum at a tribal dance. In order to wield the priest's tools, I remained in human shape, forgoing the strength of serpents. In my hand, I clutched the Crook. The Pschent was on my head. I waded through the blackest ash and the earth trembled in time with my prayers, though I found myself unharmed. Thanks to the relics I bore, the Star's ruin could not touch me, but its song was not silenced." The Queen sighed, remembering. "How can I explain the struggle that day? The Star sang to me of other worlds, other times. The past, present and future. It sang a song that no one should hear and the land could not endure. The Pschent protected my mind from madness. The Crook was a . . . *catalyst*, drinking in the stone's power. But the Star did not want taming. The stone crackled and spat, lashing out with *biriq*. Lightning licked the crater and scoured the sky. There, in the heart of the ruin, the Star and I did battle."

In rapt silence, Ben took in the revelation. He hadn't thought of the relics as anything more than a trinity of symbols, dug up by archaeologists and put on display in exhibition halls, on museum shelves or in private collections, as Winlock had done with the Crook. Instead they were magical artefacts, belonging to this revenant Queen. Their potency slumbered, dulled by the passing of time, but he was beginning to grasp why Atiya wanted them back so badly. She wanted to reunite them. Awaken their power. More than this, he was beginning to dread how the CROWS had come to learn of these things.

Star, Crook and Pschent. Star, Crook and Pschent. A new flame will scour the sky, heaven-sent and hell-bent . . .

The witch's prophecy had come true. The grin in the face of the Javits Center was laughing not at Ben's ignorance now but at his fear, making him keenly aware that the Queen's tale could mean the difference between life and death. He edged closer to her, his knees sliding through the slush. Her words were the cliff that Rose stood on. The sword dangling over his head.

"The stone *changed* me." Atiya studied her palms, flexing her fingers. "Changed me for ever. As the sun sank and the Star grew quiet, I discovered its light inside me, married to my flesh. I was still one of the First-Breed, the serpent-born servant of a god, but now I was something else as well." She closed her hands into fists. "The servant had become the equal of the master. I was . . . reborn a goddess. I could draw on the light and summon the storm. I could summon *barwaaqo*. I could summon the rain."

Ben shivered. He remembered Khadra, the girl he had found locked inside the substance of the Queen, her words choking him with need.

The Queen will bring barwaaqo *to us. The Queen will bring the rains.*

"Such power has consequences," Atiya said. "I did not think my union with the stone an event beyond recall. But I was wrong. The storm was in me and I was in the storm. Punt relied on my new-found influence and I drew clouds from the southern seas to wash away the ash. I paid no mind to the natural order. The love of the Bull and the Cow. And I paid no mind to jealous eyes . . .

"Once again, Punt flourished. Hatshepsut returned to her kingdom, and for several years we sent many tributes north, thankful for her boon. We sent unguents. Animals and plants. Ivory, silver and gold.

"Those plentiful years were not without sadness. My father, Parahu, welcomed the Reaper and so I was the last of my kind. The days of the First-Breed, we serpent-born servants of Eebe, were coming to an end. Great empires rose across the sea. The gods slowly withdrew from the earth, and among the mortals there were some who would claim power in their absence. Some who would become kings. And kings who would be gods."

The Queen paused, her sorrow a cloak thrown over her shame. Pride lingered in her eyes, but not without wounds, Ben saw, a dull blue sheen that shied from resting directly upon him.

"One day, Kamenwati returned to us. The priest arrived in a single ship, with only a simple crew. How could I have known that he sailed on ill winds, without the Pharaoh's blessing? How could I have known about the rumours in the north, whispers of cults and heresy, of child sacrifice and dark arts? I greeted him as a *saaxib*, a friend. He came to us in peace, he said, to learn more about my people. For days he resided in my palace with everything that a man could wish for.

"It was not enough. Soon, drunk on wine in the late hours, the priest began to share his ambitions. Kamenwati worshipped death, and appointing himself as death's ambassador he longed to escape his own ending. He dreamt of an immortal kingdom on earth, a kingdom to rival Egypt and Punt, to dwarf and shackle both the great realms and ascend to an authority yet unknown. In the name of Anubis, the jackal-headed god, he intended to betray his Pharaoh and defy the royal dynasty. He craved an Anubian empire, stretching from sea to sea, where life and death would depend on his will and no army would dare challenge him."

Atiya looked up. She held herself in a vice-like grip, her shoulders shaking to the rhythm of her grief.

"He . . . he longed for my allegiance. He longed for the power of the Star. He thought he could break the gates of the Duat and establish his god here on earth." The Queen slumped back against the rock, defeated by the memory. "And when I refused . . ."

"He stole the Star anyway," Ben said. He had seen this part, floundering in the depths of her mind. He had seen the priest's greed, the stone's fire reflected in his eyes. And he had heard Von Hart's divination in Berlin. *Clouds . . . gathered. Treachery . . . stirred. And something went wrong . . .* "He stole your regalia and . . ." *A dagger, rising and falling. Blood spraying the flagstones.* "He murdered you."

But that wasn't all. In New York, the Queen had crashed into the Javits Center, unchecked by steel and glass. In the British Museum, she had torn through the roof of the Great Court like a pterodactyl through a fishing net. Tonight, she had pushed Ben down between the peaks with the ease of a bishop baptising a baby. Her muscles, both bestial and human, rippled with supernatural force. She was the lightning. She was the storm. He could not accept that a mere man, however cruel or learned, could have ended her life with a few savage stabs of a blade. Something else had weakened her, caught her off guard in the palace. Rendered her defenceless, unable or unwilling to resist . . .

"You *loved* him." The truth struck him as soon as he said it. There was no accusation in his voice, but Atiya's face was as good as an answer, betraying the man that Ben had seen in the vision – his body locked with hers on the bed, his bare back beaded with sweat. "You were in love with Baba Kamenwati."

What would you know about love? he'd asked, dismissing the Queen as a heartless ghost, reborn to the world but removed from its cares. She had ridiculed his attachment to Rose, spat on his feelings as futile and weak. He realised now that her scorn stemmed from the very same source as his affection. Atiya was *all* heart, fury bred from spurned love, vengeance from the pain of treachery. Yes, she was a ghost, but she was also haunted. And she did not like his finger in the wounds.

"You followed me and I have given you answers." The Queen threw off the cloak of her sadness. Her substance grew sharper, hardening like clay. "It changes nothing. My purpose stands. The spirit bound within me longs for *barwaaqo*, God's rain. A girl came to the temple, following an old map across an old land. With innocent blood, desperate to save her people, she summoned me forth from my grave. The little fool. Did she think her longing would be enough to control me? Am I not Queen? I have longings of my own. I long to reclaim my crown, restore my former powers. Then I will make the one who brought me to ruin pay . . ."

Atiya made a gesture with her hands, shadow tearing at shadow, leaving Ben in no doubt what form her vengeance would take. Then she moved towards him, floating over the untouched snow. He clambered to his feet and edged in retreat, his back to the looming cliff face. There was nowhere to run. Nowhere to hide. Only this struggle under the stars.

"You need to get with the times, lady," he said. "Baba Kamenwati has been dead for thousands of years. You know, you kind of have that in common."

She wasn't listening to him. "I will bring the rains," she muttered in a small, childlike voice, a voice not her own. Then, in a stronger, echoing one, the voice of a queen, "I will have revenge."

He wrestled with her opposing desires – one to heal, one to harm – and failed to see anything good coming from either. Atiya's tragedy aside, such power did not belong in modern times, untamed, unleashed. Where would her vengeance end? What chaos would come from meddling with the weather? And what of the relics in her possession, the energy they held, the temptation they would offer? Yes, he wished he could believe that the threat only lay at her feet, but he knew well enough that humans, once aware of such power, would do what they always did and reach for it. The Lore would shatter completely. Fingers get burnt. Wars start . . .

He pressed his fears upon her. "What about the consequences?" He hated the whining tone in his voice. He didn't want to beg. "Once you've had your revenge, what then? Somehow I don't think you'll just go back to your grave, take another aeon-spanning nap. You say you don't want dominion, but the people in these times will fear you. And they'll crave your power. A bad mix, if I know anything at all."

"What do you know? You are a wyrm. I am a goddess."

"I know how this story goes, better than anyone," he told her. "The greed grows. The fear doesn't last. Just like in the old days, when my kind were a moving target for any hare-brained peasant who fancied themselves a quick knighthood. Or who wanted gold, wanted to get laid. Suddenly we weren't myths any more. We were *monsters*. And humans always deal with monsters in the same way."

The Queen hadn't slowed her approach, and Ben's plea curdled with his groan.

"What you're planning to do, it isn't right. It isn't natural."

"Half the world lives like kings while the other half suffers and starves. Is that natural? Do not speak to me of humans. I lost my throne, my kingdom and my life to one. Is it natural for such treachery to go unpunished?"

Ben didn't have an answer to that. *Life isn't fair* didn't seem to cover it. Such a callous truth did not ring true. Instead, he clung to his duty, the Pact he had made.

"The Age of Myth is over. You said so yourself. It's a little too late to redress a three-and-a-half-thousand-year-old fuck-up."

The Queen came closer, arms spread and trailing sparks. Her

scintillating aura burnished the ledge, throwing beanstalk shadows up the rock face. Coldness to rival the ice pushed Ben back like a gale, pressing him into jagged stone. In the crux of the radiance, the Queen, a black candle blazing with flame. There was nothing human about her now. Nothing mournful. Nothing weak. She was a goddess on the mountain and she would not bend.

"Gods can return," she said. "Dominion merely lives in human hearts. When I am done, the world will know the power of storms. And the fury of justice."

Ben grimaced. Scales slid over his back, shielding him from the biting rock. As the Queen approached, lightning blistered his lips, nose and cheeks. Static needled his throat. Rubble skittered down, shattering on the ledge.

"I can't . . . I can't let that happen . . ."

His protest was futile. Atiya was changing, her spreading wings eclipsing the night. Stars shone in her massive flanks, splintering off her array of horns. Under her swelling weight, the ledge shook as if a train was approaching. The snow melted under her claws, clouds of steam rising around her. Her tail, a sinuous spear, lashed at the cliff face – once, twice – smashing deep clefts in the mountainside, splinters flying through the rumbling echoes.

Through a cascade of rock, Ben watched the Queen take to the sky. Then rubble crashed down and buried him in darkness.

NINETEEN

Memories, broken islands in space, glimmered in the void. One of them, an important one, bobbed and turned in the comatose tide. The path that Ben walked along was a snow-edged grey stream carrying his delirious feet into the recent past. It cut through the patchy green, winter finally losing its grip on the foliage and fields of Central Park. The late February sunlight, fading too soon, gilded the surface of Turtle Pond. The glass rear of the Metropolitan Museum of Art reflected the shredded clouds, its sloped face a ripple of crystalline trees, hiding the ancient artefacts inside. Ben wore his beaten leather jacket, but he didn't much feel the cold. Warmth travelled through his veins from the hand of the woman at his side, a small, pale hearthstone in his grip. She might as well have held his heart. It beat in his chest like a coal, aglow with contentment.

They walked in silence, for the most part. Now and then she put her head on his shoulder, a mane of tousled gold. They'd been living in the apartment on Gold Street since last July, a couple of weeks after he'd asked and she'd reluctantly agreed, moving from the goldfish bowl of the LIU campus and into his treasure trove. He knew that *treasure trove* was the wrong term, but it was just how he thought of it. Just as he thought of her eyes as moonstones, the colour of gentle rain. Wasn't Rose his most precious jewel?

Yes.

Today wasn't Valentine's Day and it wasn't their first anniversary, but it was pretty close to both. Maybe that was why it had felt so special. Maybe that was why he'd chosen this moment to tell her. Or *almost* tell her. He never quite got the chance.

Together they ambled up to the obelisk, standing tall and grey in the open. The weathered shaft of the ancient monument soared seventy feet into the sky, rising higher than the leafless branches of the trees and overlooking the sparse traffic that grumbled and coughed along East Drive. Crab apple drifted on the breeze. So did the ubiquitous fumes. And faint bergamot, whenever Rose drew near.

"Cleopatra's Needle," she said, her pumps crunching on the snow-covered tarmac as she let go of his hand to cross the broad red hexagon that bordered the towering stone. "One of my favourite places in the city. Cleopatra was some queen, you know. She seduced emperors and generals. Wrapped them around her finger."

She rested her backside against the railings, holding up the finger in question, and he couldn't help but notice which finger it was, the second from last on her left hand, wiggling shyly. Ben, who got that she was teasing him, looked up at the thick, tapering pillar, at the hieroglyphics etched into its side, pitted by pollution and acid rain. Thousands of miles from home, the pointed tip of Cleopatra's Needle snagged at the passing clouds.

He grinned, but awkwardly. "If I remember rightly, that didn't end well."

He wasn't the world's greatest reader, and his knowledge was sketchy at best. He did remember a bit about the obelisk. Hadn't it been a nineteenth-century gift from the then ruler of Egypt? The Khedive? He knew he was distracting himself, so he let the silence flood back in, and he wondered up at that long-lost cryptic language, while Rose McBriar wondered at him – another ancient mystery, had she but known it.

"Ben . . . where do you see all this heading? Us, I mean."

The tone of her voice, hopeful and soft, drew his attention down from the stone and back to her. He would've made a joke, but the way that she bit her lip and kept her eyes averted, looking at the ground, threw seriousness over him like a cloak – a *heavy* cloak, his feet shuffling under its weight, making tiny, ragged snow angels. He knew that look. He'd seen it before, a hundred times. It also didn't tend to end well.

He screwed up his face. Rubbed his neck. "Rose. Maybe there's something I should tell you first."

"Oh?" The glint of suspicion, muscling hope out of the way now.

"Look, it isn't—"

Easy to explain, he was going to say, but circumstance interrupted him, because that was when the youths arrived.

There were five of them. Four guys and a girl, if their grubby state didn't deceive him. Like zombies in a cheap horror movie, they shambled out of the frozen shrubbery surrounding the obelisk, their jeans and jackets muddy and torn. Yesterday's rags. A quick survey presented Ben with a carefully closing circle of washed-out faces and wall-eyed need. He caught the whiff of stale sweat and something else as well, a sweet chemical tang. Desperation, by Crack. Before he could speak, one of them, the girl, slipped her gangly, dreadlocked shape between Ben and Rose, cutting them off from each other. The others hung back as the apparent leader, a stocky, pockmarked youth in a dull green hoodie, slunk toward Ben and introduced himself by way of flicking out a knife.

"Bit late for a stroll, dog," Green Hood said. "Pretty cold, too."

Ben curled his lip. "So you thought you'd bring down some heat, is that right?"

Green Hood looked around, indicating the empty park. *No cops here, dog.* The gang chuckled and the youth made an obligatory swipe, causing Ben to suck in his stomach and dodge backwards.

"Gimme your wallet. And your jacket. Fuckin' do it!"

Something in Ben's face made Green Hood nervous and he lashed out with the blade again. As Ben reached for his back pocket, steel sliced the back of his hand, a quick, vicious sting. He brought his hand up in front of his face, staring in mild surprise at the line of blood welling there. It just wasn't polite.

"Give him it," Dreadlock Girl spat from over by the railings. "Give it or I'll cut your bitch's throat."

To demonstrate, she grabbed Rose's hair and yanked her head back, steel flashing in her own grubby grip.

"*Ben!*"

Ben said, "You don't want to do this."

Now Green Hood was staring at Ben's hand too. He cocked his head a little to one side. He was probably wondering how that thin red line could be vanishing so fast, sealing up like a closed mouth – like someone had zipped the wound from the inside, the gash fading into clean pink flesh. His knife drooped, turned off by disbelief.

The moment didn't last. That was when Rose kicked out backward, her heel connecting with Dreadlock Girl's shin.

"*Hey!*"

Dreadlock Girl staggered back, her knife hand falling to her leg, the other outstretched and flailing for Rose. Rose slipped out of reach and dropped to her hands and knees, her pumps slipping in the snow. Seeing that she was out of danger – at least for the next six seconds or so – Ben moved in to steal the advantage.

The seams of his jacket made a loud popping sound, the leather stretching and tearing at the shoulders. Through the rips, there was an odd, unmistakable rippling of flesh, the glimpse of some harder substance, heart-shaped, interlocking, glossy and red. His annoyance must have shown in his eyes, because Green Hood choked back a cry and stumbled away from him, a sewer rat fleeing a searchlight. He was too late to make good his escape. Ben reached out, grabbed the back of his neck and flung the youth skyward. With a yell, Green Hood sailed twenty feet through the air and smacked into a nearby tree. Groaning, sneakers dangling, he hung insensible from the bare upper branches.

The rest of the gang didn't seem willing to share the view. In a rough huddle, the thugs skedaddled back into the bushes, vanishing as quickly as they'd appeared. Dreadlock Girl limped weakly down the path leading from the obelisk, ducked behind a trash can and was gone.

Ben let them go. He walked over to where Rose coughed and spluttered on the ground. Squatting down, he offered her his hand, but she gasped and cringed, recoiling from the heat of him. Wide-eyed, she stared at the snow around his boots, at the slowly expanding circle of slush.

But it wasn't just the heat, he saw. It wasn't just the shock of the attack, the impossible thing she had seen him do. There was something he had wanted to tell her, but he'd never got the chance. Now her face told him that he never could.

"Ben . . . ?" Her voice trembled in the February wind.

He looked away, cooling and ashamed.

Sometimes silence was worse than lies.

Dawn broke over the Alps. The eastern sky blushed pink, the stars fading behind the moon, scarred and pale above the peaks. Elsewhere, the shadows withdrew, hoarding the last shreds of night. A buzzard keened a lone lament, soaring down the valley where a battered cable car rested in the drifts like a beached yellow ship. The severed wire track draped from the rock face, a ladder that the buzzard climbed, swooping up over the empty ski lodge and descending a shattered cliff face.

The bird landed on a ledge to survey its kingdom – then squawked in alarm, feathers ruffling, as the rocks shifted under it. A claw broke from the shingly ground, sharp red talons clutching at air. The buzzard fluttered away into the pines as the stacked stones skittered aside. A scaly arm thrust out of the scree, dripping dirt and blood. The arm flexed, bones clicking, becoming less askew. A muffled groan, a pained rumble, shuddered over the escarpment.

Ben had sprawled beneath the rubble all night, the constellations creeping by above, a bright, spangled procession. He had lain unseeing under rock, barely breathing, barely alive. Fragile was the thread that held him, an agonising skein. Boulders had flattened him, crushing him into the earth. He could only move his head a little, sucking on pockets of air, his arms, his legs, his back broken. Exposed bone touched the cold stone. The only warmth was his pooling blood, his strewn entrails fetid in the murk. Then blackness without dreams, his unique physiology deciding whether to heal or expire. His brain, intact, chose life. Perhaps disgusted by his bumbling quest, Death did not want him. Or wanted him to suffer more.

The process took hours. Veins met veins like soldered wires. Muscles boiled, slick and wet. Where there was skin, scales formed, ossifying under the burden of earth, tentatively pushing against the rock. Inch by inch, scales covered the visceral mess, sealing lacerations, stitching tissue, smoothing broken bone. Blood flowed and his heart beat, thumping out the rhythm of revival. Once he was whole, his eyes cracked open, and immediately screwed up tight, his nerve endings shrieking in pain. His carapace thickened. His limbs bulged under the debris. The envoy's suit rippled over him, a snug, liquid embrace. With the suit came memory. *Worm tongue. Sola Ignis.* Ben grunted and tasted dirt. Drank snow. Heard the silent dark. For endless minutes, he hauled on awareness like an anchor. Hand over hand he climbed the chain of his scattered thoughts until he remembered Rose.

Remembered cold and scornful laughter.

Your woman will die.

Desperation did the rest. Mammoth proportions spread out in the dark, the human becoming monstrous, man into dragon. The rocks groaned and moved. Ben thrust up a fisted claw, punching his way out. Then, wings folded and tail limp, he rose from the rubble like a volcano, roaring anguished fire.

Exhaled smoke drifted away. He searched the sky, already knowing that the Queen was gone. Her confession, however, was fresh in his mind. He had listened as she unravelled a three-and-a-half-thousand-year-old mystery, and the truth had left him with more than just a painful memory. Her hopes for Punt, her love for the priest, her anger at her betrayal – all of these things were a part of him now. He had shared in her life and her unlife. Staring into the southern sky, a cloudless blue expanse, he sensed the distance between them. He could *feel* her in his bones. In his mind, a hot glowing coal. The lightning that had passed between them had been a kind of copulation, implanting him with communion. It aroused and ashamed him at the same time. He was paradoxically alone and complete. For now, he must push guilt aside and take advantage of the bond.

The Queen was hours ahead of him. She was heading for Cairo and the Pschent. Bardolfe and the CROWS had travelled there too. The web was large and full of secrets. There were threads here, unseen but all around him. Tripwires. Snares. Hints and shadows. All the strands, it seemed, met in Egypt, returning to their ancient source. And was Rose there too, stuck in the middle and guarded by the spider?

Thoughts of the CROWS prompted thoughts of Atiya climbing from her tomb. No, others had *summoned* her. The girl, Khadra, had opened Pandora's box, but she had not turned the lock under her own steam. Someone had given her the key, pushed a map and a shard into desperate hands. *Dhegdheer came with promises. Secrets . . . She told us how to raise her.* It wasn't lost on Ben that the giver of those gifts had been a hunchbacked old woman, a hag with a drooping left ear and long crooked claws. A hag . . . but not a witch. Even in the current crisis, that was highly unlikely. Only the Three were currently awake and active as per the conditions of the Pact, and Ben couldn't see any of the witch's aspects suffering another, a threat to her . . . their . . . its position. Some creature from folklore, then. In other words, a Remnant. Albeit rare, it was true that some Remnants were simply themselves, unique to begin with rather than belonging to any particular tribe. Black Annis, the Wild Hunt and the Wandering Jew, for instance – all had retreated into mystery and myth, but they were out there somewhere. Was it so strange for Africa to have similar oddities? Ben didn't think so. The hag, Dhegdheer, had told Khadra's mother the location of the tomb, and in return Khadra's mother had sent the girl out into the waste, dispatched to raise an old and vengeful power.

Ben was beginning to grasp the breadth of the web and the will of those who had spun it. But why *now*? Why, after centuries of so-called subdual, had the CROWS chosen this moment to strike? He considered the heart of the web, where all the strands met, and his blood ran cold as he thought of Bardolfe, the venerable chairman of the Guild. If Ben's suspicions were correct and Bardolfe *was* conspiring with House Fitzwarren and the Three, then Rose must have fallen into the chairman's clutches, because Ben had seen her, hadn't he? Through that weird sheen in the atmosphere, that bubble between the gates of the British Museum. He had heard the witch's laughter just before they had sprung their spellbound trap, using his former lover as a taunt. Or a lure.

Think of her as a fish on a line. Think of her as bait.

Ben shuddered. It was all connected somehow. He had yet to figure out what role the chairman played, why he had betrayed the Guild and thrown in with the Coven Royal. He could only imagine Rose's terror, finding herself caught up in these tenuous schemes. If he was right, Rose was in the clutches of Remnants, creatures that to her mind would belong in fairy tales, nightmares that had stepped right out of books and into the real world.

Ben spat flecks of blood on the snow. There was nothing more real than his rage. Weariness clung to his body and he had no time to heal fully. It was Sunday morning and the last sands in the hourglass were sifting away, threatening to steal all he believed in and all he held dear. He had no time for hesitation. No time for doubt. No time to hear the envoy whisper in his ears.

Know that you fly to your destruction.

Ben spread his wings and took to the sky.

★   ★   ★

He had a long way to go. He judged the distance at well over a thousand miles. This final push would test his strength to the limit, and he'd still have to deal with whatever was waiting for him in Cairo, a grim and troubling thought. Wings pumping, discrete gills rushing with air, he could not let such thoughts delay him. He flew south, following the Adriatic coast, a blue sweep far below that soothed his reptilian self. He saw a scattering of islands, fleeing the shredded shore like ill-advised ships. He soared on over the Balkans, lands that he knew as Croatia, Albania and Greece, although he saw no dotted lines between them or distinguished any difference in their mountains, forests and fields. A thermal current shot him inland towards Athens, and here, at last, his strength ran out. It was almost midday. Precious minutes trickled through his claws. On this side of Europe, the time zone was uniform. Clocks could not help him, buy him any time. Sheer stamina couldn't help either. His exertions of the night before, his battle with the Queen and subsequent burial had all but finished him. If he pressed on, he would soon find himself drained and falling, a latter-day Icarus tumbling from the sun, hissing into the Mediterranean Sea.

But come hell or high water, he couldn't give up. Giving up wasn't an option.

He was thinking about circling down to rest for a while on the slopes of Mount Parnitha when, for once, Providence smiled. Some distance behind him, he spied an aeroplane, approaching fast. The sleek white dart sprayed fumes over the ocean, a commercial jet that probably bore a load of tourists from Budapest or Rome, some far-off northern clime. He strained to see, calculating risk. Blue stripes on the neck and tail, radiating from a watchful eye, adorned the plane's tubular body. The best part about it was the logo on its flanks. *EgyptAir* in bold italics.

Usually Ben avoided airline routes, climbing several miles higher into the stratosphere, steering clear of potential collision or passengers catching sight of him. In human form, he had enjoyed the luxury of aeroplanes. When not, he had cursed them for invading his erstwhile territory. He had never hitched a ride on one before. As it stood, his options were running out. So, if he could time this right . . . He folded his wings and whistled downwards, surfing the buffeting updraughts. The plane roared in below him, cruising at five hundred miles per hour. Ben shot through layers of pressure, his bulk dwindling to human size as he drew near the jet, a vaguely horned crimson shape with scaled limbs extended. Shrunken wings tensed to steady him and muscles resisting the screaming wind, he settled on top of the plane, alighting near the tail with a gentle clunk. Head down and shoulders braced, he flattened himself as much as possible, a red barnacle melding itself to the aerodynamics. He dug his claws into smooth metal, anchoring himself to the fuselage.

The plane roared on, an oblivious beast with Ben its new-found parasite. He closed his eyes, wishing that he had a god to pray to, someone to petition for Rose's safety. But all the gods were dead or sleeping, and the only one he'd met had almost killed him, dropping half a mountain on his head. *So much for faith.* All he could do was trust to his wits and hope for the best. It wasn't going to be easy.

Ben rode the aeroplane south and gathered his strength for the coming storm.

TWENTY

Flight MS792 slowly lost altitude over the north Egyptian coast. Ben heard the Boeing deploy its flaps, a faint bump in the freezing wind as the plane increased its angle of descent. The wings bounced, bleeding off airspeed. Inside, seat-belt lights would be flashing on, magazines would be folded away and drop-down tables pushed upright. Flight attendants would leave the aisle to strap themselves back in. As the captain buzzed a thank-you over the intercom, first in English and then in Arabic, businessmen would glance at their watches and hope that Customs didn't keep them too long, while tourists gazed out at the afternoon sun, already tasting the cocktails by the hotel pool. Locals returning home would fuss with their kaftans and veils, their attire shaking off any European looseness, tweaked for the stricter observance of home.

It was easy to imagine these everyday scenes. Inside the plane, normality reigned, a world of airsickness pills, taffeta eye masks, inflatable pillows and freeze-dried meals. A world where the monsters belonged to the in-flight movie and the gods were invisible, taken on trust. The mundane reality of Modern Man rumbled on in trivial conversations, plastic earphones, shuffling feet and the background drone of giant turbofans. To Ben, a lizardine lump clamped to the fuselage, the plane was one big metallic metaphor, symbolising the Loreful division, an arrangement he now thought flimsy at best. All it would take was a punch of a scaled fist, a few slashes of his claws, to bring the two worlds crashing together. Nevertheless, he hoped for a less violent collision for the earth's separate realities. If everyone and their mother was right, and a new age *was* to rise from the ashes of the Pact, he hoped that some kind of peace was possible, whether the Fay returned or not. The Queen had plucked out that hope in the Alps, regarding it on the end of her claw like a fly found in a wine glass. *You long for a normal life.* Like the Guild of the Broken Lance, she obviously thought that exposing the Remnants to the world at large could only lead to destruction. Unlike the CROWS, she appeared to care little for dominion, had no wish to subjugate all that was human under a tyranny of myths. Atiya's vengeance centred on the past, a ghost calling to ghosts, and he wondered whether her revenant self, fuelled as it was by mortal flesh, was merely replaying the scenes of her tragedy in modern times, like an after-image of lightning, an echo of thunder, her betrayer long since gone to dust along with the world she had known . . .

Secrets. Dominion. Vengeance. Ben was caught, it seemed, in a trinity of dangerous goals. Was it wrong that he could see another way? In the eight hundred years since he'd signed the Pact, humans had grown and evolved. Wasn't there at least an outside chance that they could come to accept that the world and its weft was not all it seemed? That magic and myth endured? Endured with the same need to survive. Lived and loved with the same fire . . .

As though renouncing the blinkered world, he unhooked his claws from the fuselage and swan-dived into space. Far below, the green diamond of the Nile delta spread its skirts on an ocean of sand. The Sahara surged in umber and gold, dunes sweeping to every horizon like waves crashing on a narrow shore, this verdant vein that spanned countries, defying the arid waste. In all his years, Ben had never flown so far south, and the desert's immensity stunned him, fascination drawing him down into its embrace, sailing on dusty winds. The aeroplane was just a speck above him when his wings spread to their full span, blasting streamers from the dunes. His tail snaked out, a proud red flag. He had reached his destination and there was no time for discretion. Below him flowed the wide brown Nile, the longest river in the world, where the drooping palm trees dipped their roots and the fields drank in their limited green.

The proximity of water no longer soothed him, its inherent comfort cancelled by the sun. Ben didn't trust that sun. Soon the moon would come, sliding across its fiery face. *Syzygy. Eclipse. Abandonment. Downfall.* Occult bodies aligning in the sky, a celestial convergent act, exchanging day for night. Exchanging, perhaps, reality for myth. Light for darkness. Peace for war.

Below him, a city sprawled, a pall of smoke on the sands. Cairo the Conqueror. The City of a Thousand Minarets. Ben had heard the grandiose names over the years. He didn't need the sight of the Pyramids, those three ancient, crumbling wonders, their geometric bellies hoarding secrets, to recognise his location. Atiya's scent threaded through the air, a cerebral fragrance overlaying the confection of fumes – factory belches, shisha pipes, burning rice and camel shit – that led him down and on, swooping over the tombs of the long-dead pharaohs, Khufu, Khafre and Menkaure. The Great Sphinx, a hybrid bulk of lion's body and human head, watched him sweep east and into the city with enigmatic, stone-faced empathy.

Riding the sirocco wind, Ben traced the Dark Queen, his shadow painting the rooftops and the riddle of roads. He sped over a concrete mosaic, the urban heights predominantly flat and open to the elements. Satellite dishes bristled next to clapboard huts, the luxury of TV beside the rooftop dwellings of the poor. He saw roof gardens, billboards, firebombed ruins. Here and there, office buildings and new hotels broke the Escheresque vista, a thousand suns sparkling in glass.

Screams shattered the general hubbub. People looked up, saw the beast overhead.

Ben's wings stirred up dust, rattling washing lines and aerials. The westering sun and warbling *adhan* told him that the hour was roughly three p.m. As much as his sense of preservation urged him to pick out a rooftop and continue to follow the trail on foot, his fear yelled that the day was wasting. If he could catch up with the Queen, surely she could tell him where to find Rose. Fuck her threats. He would face her again, even if it meant his death. In a city of millions, Bardolfe and the CROWS could be just about anywhere. Thus far, they had failed to show their hand. A game of Pin the Tail on the Witch was more than Ben could afford right now.

He swept on, anxious but undeterred. He veered north-east, drawing near the city's heart, his passage leaving a wake of terror in the streets below. He couldn't let their panic stop him. A latticework tower appeared ahead, rising from an island in the Nile. The great river flowed around the island and stretched on through the city, the waters greased by industrial waste. Sailboats bobbed down there, tossed by the beat of his wings. He banked between the tower and a bulbous hotel, diving between two parallel bridges and rejoining the urban sprawl.

The Queen's spiritual scent was stronger now, vibrating in his skull. Following her beacon, he spiralled down to the place where he felt the pull most. The building was a neoclassical hulk of rust-coloured brick, its pillared arch a wide white mouth flanked by granite pharaohs. The palm trees at the front rose almost as high as the domed roof. An Egyptian flag rippled above the courtyard, the red, white and black bands dancing in the gusts of Ben's approach. Sphinxes guarded the plaza below, set before a wide rectangular pool, lilies floating on the ruffled surface. At this time of day, the Museum of Antiquities – Ben recognised the building partly from books, partly from Atiya's insights and partly from a near-crushing sense of inevitability – should have been swarming with tourists.

Instead, it was swarming with soldiers.

Ben had seen the news. Trouble in Cairo was nothing new. Civil unrest, Molotov cocktails and gunfire flashed across his mind's eye just as they had on his TV in London, reports of violent demonstrations, warring sects and capsizing governments as the country strove for democracy. He was far from an expert in world affairs, but his adventures in the criminal underworld had not left him without experience. He would recognise the stench of explosives anywhere. Tanks waited in the road below, their khaki bodies parked in a loose semicircle outside the museum gates, their engines idling like drunken bugs. He didn't think their presence was due to the local riots. In an instant, he noticed three things. One, the building's crowning dome was shattered, a portion of the structure reduced to twisted wreckage on the roof. Two, the tanks' gun turrets had turned on their axes as he descended. Three, all the long barrels now pointed at him.

A welcoming party. Great.

One of the tanks lay on its side, its gun bent, its tracks upended, a police car crushed beneath them. Furrows that could only be claw marks scored the tarmac around the vehicle, charred streaks showing evidence of fire. Or lightning. He sensed the

Queen's scorn and her urgency. She would not let the army stand in her way. He pictured her entrance into the city, a dark cloud crackling from above, spurring panic and men to action. Traffic lined the surrounding streets, cars and trucks stalled and abandoned. Crowds huddled in the lee of buildings, staring up at the sky. Staring up at him. Their shock and fright hit him like a cudgel. Raised mobile phones winked in the sun. A press van wove at speed down the street, tyres screeching as it reached the junction where soldiers guarded a low barrier, no doubt hastily erected, the wooden crosses draped in barbed wire. A soldier tensed and raised his machine gun as reporters spilled babbling out of the van, their microphones waving, film cameras propped on their shoulders. If Ben didn't move, and fast, the local press would make him famous. Worse, the troops would blast him from the sky. Whether Atiya was in the museum or not – her trail was stark, an ache in his skull – she had left him facing a shit storm.

The first shell exploded a few feet above him, narrowly missing his wings. The payload scattered in acrid smoke, tainting the afternoon air. Ben skimmed sideways as another tank took aim, bellowing shot towards him. Again, the shell burst over his head, hot grit peppering his horns. He shook it out of his eyes, growling. *Do they need a bigger target?* The volley pissed him off, but he wasn't about to hurt these people. With no time to explain or allay the shock of his presence, he couldn't blame them for doing their job, even if their job meant killing him. Hell, if they succeeded, his skeleton would probably end up in the museum below. The thought hurled him into a roll, zeroing in on the roof. He noted that the tanks had aimed high. They didn't want to damage the building or the artefacts inside. That gave him his chance. As machine-gun fire riddled the sky, bullets whining off his horns and spine, Ben closed up like a broken umbrella, his tail wrapping around his legs as he dropped through the remaining space and crashed into the ruined dome.

Bricks, rafters and plaster flew. In a cascade of dust, Ben reduced his size to fit his surroundings, the symbiotic suit blooming over his body. Human-shaped with incongruent mass, he landed on flagstones punched by an earlier impact, further cracks riddling through the marble to meet the rotunda walls. The museum boomed as rubble clattered down around him. He stood, the dust clearing, and shook himself off.

"Close, but no cigar."

He saw that he was on the upper floor. A jumble of acquisitions – statues, jewellery, papyrus and coins – lay strewn around him, the antique contents of the display cases, half of them reduced to splinters and shattered glass. Atiya didn't care about these relics. They were trivial to her, Ben sensed, the commonplace items of her age. Two corridors ran off the rotunda, one heading into the east wing and the other into the west. Ahead was a gallery, a broad open space suspended over the ground floor. He started towards the balustrade, but pain brought him up short, embedded bullets needling his buttock and leg. Some of the shooters had hit the mark after all. His flesh was healing under his suit, muscles working to push out the metal. Wincing, he limped onward, his bare feet crunching through debris. Shards and splinters bit into his skin, but he did his best to ignore them. Rose and the syzygy would not wait.

The orbit of damage ran out as he neared the balustrade, indicating where draconic bulk had become smaller and human-shaped like his own, the Queen proceeding into the museum. *Looking for the Pschent*. The atrium yawned below, a grand white space bordered by porticoes. Statues and sarcophagi lined the chamber. At the far end, a monumental pharaoh and his wife presided over all, their faces impassive under carved headdresses. The atrium was empty – but cameras, guidebooks and handbags littered the floor, informing Ben that the day's tourists had recently fled, hurrying for the exits when the Queen had arrived, her talons bursting through the dome.

"Because doors are so last year," he muttered, gruff in the still.

Looking around for sign of her, his eyes fell on an abandoned rucksack resting against the balustrade a few feet away. Through the dust, he could smell food, reminding him how hungry he was, his stomach bubbling and grumbling. He hadn't eaten anything since Club Zauber in Berlin, and that had been yesterday morning. He fell upon the rucksack and tore it open, tossing sun cream, jumper and car keys over his shoulder until he found what he was looking for. He wolfed down the baguette, apple and packet of crisps with a monkey's grace, finishing it off with a can of Coke that he guzzled in one long slug. Then he strained to hear the crunch of boots on glass, the click of a safety catch, but it seemed that the soldiers outside had yet to build up the courage to enter the museum. Distant shouts suggested they wouldn't take long. As he lingered here, he guessed that the troops were manoeuvring into position, creeping with guns loaded along the rust-coloured walls. The thought raised a wry smile. It had been some time since men had hunted him, but this was an old game – one of the oldest – and he'd be damned if he'd let them win.

He tried to focus, calming his mind. His link with the Queen buzzed and thrummed, a harpist using his spine for practice, setting his teeth on edge. He turned and walked back to the rotunda, skirting the rubble and heading into the west wing. *Yes, she went this way.* The ghost of her fervour drew him on, an invisible leash around his neck. Exhibits loomed on either side of him, unearthed arcana and *objets d'art*, fragile scrolls and locked wooden chests, *shabtis*, amulets and beads. Between the cases were larger finds – a crumbling boat, a scarred chariot – both placed behind elastic rope. He didn't stop to inspect them.

On his left, a shadowed archway. The soft glow of lights beyond. Atiya's presence haunted the threshold, a phantom veil of age and desire. Under the arch, the smell of death, but not *new* death, Ben surmised, wrinkling his nose at the faint trace of vinegary odour. Shoulders set, he walked through the archway.

The room beyond was an open tomb. Coffins lined the walls. No, not coffins. *Mummy cases.* The downlights touched their faded faces, their features painted on old chipped wood. Kohl-lined eyes watched Ben blankly as he entered the room, his movements unconsciously slow and respectful. Hieroglyphs adorned the figures, describing the funerary images that ran in panels across their lids. Ben peered at spread wings, indecipherable spells and beast-headed gods. He recognised Anubis, the jackal god, his muzzle poised over a large pair of scales, a feather resting in one of the pans. The sight made Ben recall Winlock's speech at the British Museum and he recognised the feather as a soul awaiting judgement, hoping to pass into the Fields of Yalu. Between the mummies, small statues rested on shelves. The professor had called them *magic bricks*, icons to protect the soul from its enemies, living or otherwise. Ben scanned cat, bird and human forms, and deduced that the statues were the Neteru; gods, not demons like the ones that Winlock had found in Kamenwati's tomb. It came as a relief to him, but the feeling faded as he remembered the priest's crimes, his jealousy, greed and ambition. Kamenwati was more than just a name now. He had a face and a purpose, a purpose strong enough to betray a pharaoh and murder a queen. *No, a bona fide, straight-up serpent-cum-goddess.* Coptic jars stood beside the bricks, and Ben wished he didn't know what was inside them: the shrivelled organs of the ancient dead.

In the middle of the room was a long glass case. Inside the case, a withered corpse. Led by tingling intuition, Ben crossed the room and noticed the faint imprint of hands on the polished surface. Judging by the marks, Atiya had stood here very recently, gazing down at that stark, perpetual grin. The mummy's skin was frayed and brown, preserved for centuries by spices and salt. The wrappings had all but rotted away, revealing stick-like limbs and ribs. There was nothing behind its sealed eyes. The mortuary priests had scooped out the goods long ago, preparing the body for entombment. *Nice.* The intestines, liver, lungs and heart would line the surrounding shelves, pickled in sacred clay. According to Winlock, the priests had intended the embalming process to grant the deceased immortal life, the *ba* living on in the Duat, the Ancient Egyptian underworld. Looking down at the mummy, into its worn, papery rictus, Ben wondered how it would feel if it knew where it was, its tomb plundered and put on display, immortality with a grotesque twist.

"No, not it," he grumbled to himself. "*Her.*"

This was no ordinary corpse, its prominence in the centre of the room betraying its importance. More than that, the miasma of grief that lingered here, a fluttering moth around Ben's heart, revealed the truth of her identity. This was a pharaoh before him, and not just any pharaoh, but the greatest of all Egyptian queens.

Hatshepsut, the Lioness, the Woman Who Was King.

Ben doubted that eternal life had ever looked so unappealing.

This was death. *Final* death. Unlike Atiya, summoned from sleep to bring the rains to a famished land, there would be no such return for Hatshepsut. For all her power, her golden reign of peace and prosperity and her building of temples and tombs, she had still been a human woman. She was born mortal and, like a mortal, she lived out her span of years and then departed this world for whatever lay beyond. The mummy in the case was no Sleeping Beauty. No kiss, however true, would awaken her.

Thoughts of mortality stirred up his dread for Rose. Once again he remembered that day in Central Park when they'd wandered up to Cleopatra's Needle, the memory of the obelisk ironic now, considering everything that had happened after. In that moment of violence, Rose had glimpsed the real him, the monster behind the mask. She must have already had her suspicions and he wondered if they had steeled her for the horror of the CROWS. He feared for her sanity as much as her life. And he could not escape the fact that he had failed her. His attempts at protection had come too late. And what future could the two of them have, even if he did manage to save her? The world was cruel and full of evil, and maybe Von Hart was right: he hadn't learnt a damn thing from his affairs with humans. You'd think that losing Maud would be enough . . .

Ben pulled a face. *When I fuck up, I really fuck up.* He promised himself that if he ever got out of this, things would be different. He'd take more precautions, watch his back.

"First, you better get out of this . . ."

He rubbed his neck, apprehensive. Looking around, he realised that the museum was empty, the echo in his head just that, an echo. Atiya had been and gone, perhaps only minutes before his arrival, her purpose here as dead as the mummies lining the room. As he thought this, he noticed the display case set against one wall, a rectangle of jagged glass with a small placard screwed on the front. The case was empty, its contents snatched, and Ben didn't need to guess at the prize. *The Pschent*. Having grabbed what she had come for, Atiya had stood over the mummy and whispered some kind of final farewell, a parting prayer for the long-dead Pharaoh. *Yes*. Ben could sense the Queen's sorrow, a pall of mourning that chilled the room. She had paid her respects to Hatshepsut and left.

With time slipping through his fingers, Ben swore and did the same.

Interlude: A Shadow on the Sands

This world, the shadow thought, *is an illusion*.

As he followed Mahmud El Azhary, chief marketing officer of the East Katameya Oil Refinery, along the walkway between two feed tanks, he reflected that the ironwork under his feet might as well have been cobwebs. Time would blow it all away. For all the industry going on around him, the trucks in the loading bay fifty feet below, the smoke venting from the distillation towers and the pipework thrumming with crude, the shadow knew that it was all a façade, a shoring-up against the inevitable. Factory workers hurried back and forth wherever he looked, engineers and analysts bustling through the metal maze and tending to the grumbling machines with all the routine urgency of termites. The shadow granted them no more importance than that. The refinery pumped a temporary fuel from a temporary earth for the good of a temporary people. The pipes sucked up chemicals fathoms deep, the fossilised muck of the dead, animals, plankton and algae, converting energy to run cars, ships and planes, harnessing heat and light. Like the workers busying below, the whole operation was chaff in the wind. It was all an illusion of permanence. None of it would last.

Mahmud, the marketing officer, had explained the refining process with thinly veiled pride during the tour, his fez sat atop his bearded face like an eraser on a pencil. He clasped his hands before him, a professional pose that barely concealed their subtle twitch. With an ambivalence he clearly didn't feel, he informed his guests that visitors of note had taken the tour before, of course – executives from US sponsors, Arab tycoons with vested interest – but never a European dignitary. The shadow had allowed his guide to think him so, the sorcerous impression thrown like a hood over Mahmud's head drubbing his rational mind into a deferential pulp. He encouraged the other staff to look away, pay him no mind. A petty parlour trick. It had all been rather last-minute. The shadow had arrived at midday, striding into the main office lobby in his sharp tuxedo and white gloves, his diminutive companion in tow. Setting his leather bag – it looked like the kind that doctors used – on the reception desk, he'd requested to talk to someone in charge. When El Azhary appeared, flustered and frowning, the shadow had spoken a single word – more of a symbol, really, hanging in the air – and then watched as the man's frown melted into a smile. Breathlessly, Mahmud had agreed to show the dignitary and his six-year-old daughter around. Why, naturally he would. It was Sunday, after all, and his duties could wait. Besides, it was an honour.

For an hour or so, Mahmud had led the shadow and his supposed daughter through the refinery, the little girl's plastic doll swinging from her chubby hand. He showed them the huge, bulbous hydrocracking units, the gas plant and the blending pool, their feet ringing on the walkways with all the clangour of a timpani drum. Their route was as crooked and labyrinthine as the surrounding pipework. Pipes wove everywhere, some arm-thin, some thicker than buses, so much so that the place seemed built solely from cylinders and rivets, the tanks in between stout steel prisoners. Navigating the maze, Mahmud told the shadow and the little girl all about the refinery, how his company had completed the plant just three years ago, out here in the desert south of Cairo, a few klicks from the rolling golf courses and luxury houses of Katameya Heights. He regaled his guests with his casual concerns about the environment, rising fuel prices and Middle Eastern competition, typical PR spin. They paused in the canteen for strong lukewarm coffee. The whole time, the shadow and his daughter listened to Mahmud's chatter, murmuring replies through polite smiles. Drinking in the sights, their eyes canny and cold.

"Do you know we process fifty tons of crude every twenty-four hours?"

"Really? That's fascinating."

"We call the conversion method *cracking* because heat and pressure breaks the hydrocarbon molecules down into lighter ones."

"How very . . . scientific."

The tour drawing to an end, the three of them emerged on a mezzanine on the west wing of the plant, a wide latticed area overlooking the car park. Beyond the car park, the sands stretched, a yellow sea, to the skyline of the city. The shadow walked to the railings and looked down, his bag bumping against his leg, the afternoon breeze ruffling the strands of his thin white hair. The little girl sucked her thumb and clutched her plastic doll to the front of her dress, both stained with chocolate or some other sticky substance, dark blotches on the green material. Satisfied with the view, the shadow turned back to Mahmud, who was concluding his spiel with practised aplomb.

"Currently the refinery employs five hundred people, from engineers to corrosion specialists down to the secretaries in reception. EKOR isn't as large as some plants, but our shareholders find it profitable. Egypt is still a key player in the oil game, you know. A recent survey estimated that there were roughly two point nine billion barrels of undiscovered crude left in the country, and our company has its sights set firmly on the future, happy to provide clean and efficient energy for the—"

"Two point nine billion," the shadow interrupted, rubbing his chin. "Some might say that's a limited resource."

"But of course," Mahmud said, knocked off kilter and trying not to show it. "The wells are depleting around the globe, which is why we're investing so much in new technology, seeking out new reserves in our quest for an alternative—"

"And what happens when those reserves run dry? When *all* the reserves run dry? Forgive me, I don't mean to sound rude. Remember you're talking to a layman."

"Well, hopefully by then we'll have—"

"Hopefully?" The shadow arched an eyebrow. "That doesn't sound very promising. When it all runs out, what then? Isn't it fair to say that most of the world depends on this resource? Considering its finite nature, was that dependence wise in the first place? I mean, the ancients existed for thousands of years without the need for all this . . ." he flapped a glove, "siphoned underground shit."

The marketing officer looked blank for a moment. It was clear he had not expected a debate, particularly one along these lines. Confused, he glanced down at the girl. She looked back at him, bored. Green ribbons fluttered on her head. Her pigtails bobbed in the wind, as black as the oil that they were discussing. He smiled, embarrassed, but she didn't smile back.

He cleared his throat and took his chances with the shadow.

"Please, *effendi*, I'm sure one of our pamphlets will allay your concerns. Our company makes every effort to care for the environment. Speculation is not my, ah, department . . ."

"Indeed," the shadow said. "Exactly my point. What you've described is a house of cards, built on shifting sands, and yet no one in these times seems willing to face the consequences. Technology advances on the back of greed and blinds you to your fate. It is a sorry thing to see."

"Fate?" Mahmud El Azhary gave a little laugh, but it didn't quite mask his annoyance. "My apologies. That is also not my field. I leave the future to our scientists and have every faith in the company. Now, if you'll excuse me. As much as I've enjoyed your visit, I have work to do and the hour is getting late."

"Oh, it's later than you think," the shadow told him. "The world would have been better off leaving these reserves well alone. Without divine guidance, without *hierarchy*, Man has slowly but surely engineered his own destruction. He has chosen to pursue the fleeting instead of the eternal. I will show you a better way."

"If you say so," Mahmud said. He obviously thought he was dealing with a madman, or worse, some kind of activist. He presented the shadow with a curt smile and turned towards the mezzanine staircase, his outstretched arm indicating that the tour was over. "Please, follow me."

He drew up short at the girl in his path. She sucked her thumb like a subtle threat. Somehow she had managed to slip behind him.

"You see, Nan?" the shadow said, speaking to Mahmud's back. "These people simply don't care. They talk about *alkylation* and *catalytic reforming* as if these words held the deepest magic. As if they were spells to hold back the dark. They've reduced their history, their *true* history, to the status of myth, and they spit in the faces of gods. It's high time someone took them in hand."

318

"Little girl," Mahmud said, his fez trembling. "Get out of my way."

"A house of cards," the shadow went on, unconcerned. "All it would take is a little push, a nudge, to bring the whole thing crashing down. Nan, why don't you tell our friend here what will happen when it does?"

The little girl grinned. She removed her thumb from her mouth to say:

"Anarchy. Bloodshed. Revolution."

The hunger in her words made El Azhary take a step back. The tour had taken a turn for the worse, and sensing the shadow standing behind him, he spun on his heel, his face a medley of fear. Standing at the railings, the shadow could see that the man no longer took him for some European dignitary, his wide eyes reflecting his peculiar appearance. The sharp tuxedo and white gloves. The fur draped over his shoulder. The pale, enervated skin.

Under the rumble of machinery, Mahmud gibbered something about security. The shadow put down his bag. He stepped towards his quailing guide and flung an arm around his shoulder.

"Come now, let's not bicker. You know I have the right of it. This place is a temple of death. A poisoned chalice. An instrument of doom. You're sucking up the blood of the earth."

"Like leeches," the little girl offered. "Like *vampires*."

"Now, Nan. That isn't polite. Our friend here was kind enough to show us around; the least we can do is mind our manners. This is a business matter, after all. He's shown us the goods and we gladly accept." The shadow gave a sideways glance to the man in his grip. "So tell me, where do I sign?"

Mahmud spluttered. "S . . . sign?"

"Never mind. The paperwork can wait. It's quite exciting,

319

really. I've never owned a refinery before." The shadow's smile vanished, eclipsed by an afterthought. "Although it pains me to tell you, I have some bad news. The new management has no need of your services."

Before Mahmud had a chance to respond, the shadow turned again to the railings, wheeling the man around like a rickety stack of boxes on a trolley. Together they gazed a couple of floors down at the car park, where a Rolls-Royce waited on the tarmac, its sleek body parked between the bays. The westering sun gleamed off the paintwork and windows, rejected by the pitch-black vehicle. The Rolls – a Phantom IV – was a crouched panther, emanating patience. A silver figurehead crested the bonnet, twinkling in the afternoon light. It was too far away to make out the details, but the shadow greeted the sight with a nod. The bare-breasted hag on the broom had brought him south from the City of the Dead, flying through the desert with the speed of his purpose. Here, in this desolate place, that purpose was about to bear fruit. The hour of the syzygy was nigh.

But first things first.

"I think it's time for my friends to join us," the shadow said. "The more the merrier, don't they say?"

As if his words were a signal, the Phantom's rear door swung wide. Beyond, the interior of the cab revealed only darkness, an enclosed abyss that stretched into cold, uncharted depths. The sunlight shrank from it, dispelled by the murk spilling from the car. The shadow felt Mahmud tense at his side, his professional veneer cracking at the sight. A figure climbed out of the cab, clanking heavily on to the tarmac and standing to its tall, ungainly height. Radiant splinters darted through the shadows as the newcomer took a couple of steps and clunked to a standstill, its movements slow and oddly mechanical. Metal creaked. The blade the thing carried scraped across the ground. The figure looked up at the mezzanine blankly, nodded once, and assumed a stiff, statue-like pose.

"Very good," said the shadow, and then addressed the little girl. "Nan, if you'd do the honours. For the sake of privacy, we can't have all these drudges around."

Mahmud El Azhary turned to jelly, his nerve finally failing him. Propped up by the shadow, he watched the little girl, so innocent-looking until she smiled, as unnaturally gleeful as the doll she held. She lifted the plastic baby before her and sang a lilting chant, what might have been a nursery rhyme if not for the taunting tone. Then she turned and showed the doll to the shadow, a child seeking praise.

"Look," she said.

The shadow looked. A persistent buzzing filled the air, humming under the sound of machinery around them. Something small and dark crawled from between the doll's lips, climbing the moulded pink surface to rest upon one cheek.

"Excellent," he said and reached out a hand. The small dark thing hopped on to the end of his finger. He held it up for Mahmud's inspection, the bug distinct against his glove. "Say hello to *Apis mellifera*, or at least a semblance of it. This little creature is a feisty hybrid, a cross-breed of the Western species and their migrating African cousins. Of course, the colloquial term is *killer bee*, but you'll find that's misleading. It is no more potent than any other bee, its sting painful but not deadly." He blew on the insect's wings, and angrily it took to the air, darting around his head. "Having said that, this variety is quick to swarm, as you're about to see."

The buzzing grew louder, competing with the industrious racket. The shadow, the girl and El Azhary watched as the darkness below resolved into a dense black cloud, pouring out of the back of the Rolls as though someone had taken a truckload of match heads and thrown them into the air. The car park thrashed with insectile rage, the cloud swirling around the figure down there, which remained stiff and unmoving, protected as it was from the swarm.

The bees rose as one and spilled into the refinery, a smoky tide rippling under the mezzanine, snaking beneath their feet. Still more bees poured from the Phantom, a dark deluge crashing over the pipework and through the latticed walkways.

The shadow released Mahmud and watched him flee for the stairs, his fez falling off and bouncing on the floor. There was no need to chase him. He didn't matter now. The shadow had pressing business to attend to and his amusement had waned. The afternoon sun would soon wane too, and his destiny was waiting.

He tipped his head to one side, listening. As the first screams echoed to his ears, he smiled at the little girl.

"Come, Nan. Time to prepare. We stand here at Death's door. Let us turn the key."

TWENTY-ONE

Like a large ungainly firework, Ben burst through the dome of the museum, his wings shaking off wreckage. But the pyrotechnics were not down to him. The tanks greeted his reappearance with a swift and deafening salvo, bullets and shells spraying the sky, their clatter and boom reporting off the building's façade. This time, he was ready for them. Holding his breath against the cordite stench, he shot directly upwards, pinions tensed in a powerful thrust. The palm trees in the courtyard bent and fluttered. Soldiers and journalists staggered back, trying to keep hold of their guns and cameras, shielding their eyes from the flailing grit. The tip of Ben's tail wove through the smoke and out of range, a bright red V sign waving goodbye.

Soon, he reckoned, the army would scramble some jets and come screeching after him. Missiles wouldn't be so easy to avoid, not when locked on to his considerable heat signature, and he wasn't about to knock them from the sky, scattering debris and death on the city below. *Not unless I have to.* As it stood, he still had the advantage of surprise, and he arched up into the blue, the museum a spinning red dot under his claws. The tanks couldn't follow him here.

Looking down, he saw that they meant to follow him regardless. More machines were rumbling down the road, and he felt horribly exposed, an easy target for GPS, a flaring blip on a screen. His presence here was desperate and rash, but the consequences would have to wait. He was sure that there were going to be some – and not just from Paladin's Court, if the Guild still even existed. People might put the sight of him down to a hallucination when it only concerned a bridge, a museum or a cable car, but half a capital city? This went well beyond a feature in the weird weeklies . . .

He was in the shit. What else was new? For now, he had unfinished business.

Swooping around in a circle, he tried to get his bearings. His bond with the Queen pulled his snout around like a magnet, and before he questioned the change in her scent, how *determination* now hummed with *distress*, he was speeding off south, leaving the army behind. Minutes later and the city surrendered to desert, the snarled conurbation petering out in dusty roads, derelict shacks and abandoned factories, all half swallowed by the sands. This was a parched and gritty land, far removed from the greenery of home. The only greenery that flourished here did so in rustling clumps, palm trees that stooped over muddy pools like tall and thirsty old men. In England, rivers flowed everywhere, the land rising to misty peaks and sinking into marsh, the rain a constant source of complaint. The natural bond that Ben had with water, an affinity born from his basic morphology, stirred a profound sympathy in him. Khadra's need in the Alps was still with him, a desperate hope he might never shake off, and he marvelled at the fact that life could survive here, clinging to the manna of the Nile like a baby to its mother's teat. He recalled the waste that the girl had shown him, the dry creeks and buzzing flies. The swollen bellies and dull eyes. The reaching, grasping hands . . . The thought of a land without rivers, without rain, horrified him, seeming to him like the lowest Hell. Thirst the cruellest death. His dread for Rose had overshadowed this insight. Now he grasped the depth of Khadra's plight, what had made the girl and her mother ripe for manipulation, driving them to breach the Lore and raise a goddess from the sands. It had been a mistake, a desire that could only bring doom – but one he understood at heart.

Seen from above, Egypt presented a yellow mirror to everything he knew. Irrigation ditches glimmered and flashed like runnels of silver, spindly in the sun, but mostly what flowed here was sand, a jitterbug of dust devils, a scatter of grit, changing direction in the scorching wind. And then he saw people. People running. Their wails threaded through the air as they hurried across the dunes. Their movements confused him. He could see no sense in them, except that the group fled en masse, arms flailing, in a race for the fringes of the city. Mostly he saw men in overalls. A few women in office skirts, their high heels abandoned to the drifts. Eyes narrowed, he made out something else down there. Motes swirled around every head like personal storm clouds, occasionally breaking and swelling out to join a greater cloud trailing above them. The frantic mass was too large for birds, too fluid for smoke, and as the crowd stumbled by below, a berserk pageant across the waste, an angry buzzing filled his ears.

The sound was unmistakable. The cloud was a swarm. A swarm of bees.

What the fuck? Out here in the desert, there was only one place these people could've come from, a hulking grey structure ahead, some kind of gasworks or factory. Smoking turrets and bulbous tanks, all encased in a knot of pipes and intersecting gridwork, lent the place a palatial air, a fairy-tale castle at the end of a quest, walled by a high steel briar. *Yeah, right.*

The Queen's emanations rippled from the place, a rock of torment and rage thrown into the pool of his mind. Why had she come here? Regalia regained, he had expected Atiya to head for home, the Land of Punt that was now Somalia, returning ghost-like to the scene of her murder, hoping to face down a priest who was centuries dead. And Ben had summoned up the strength to follow her, meaning to prevent her by any means possible from her intervention, her futile revenge, her ill-advised summoning of rain, both threatening to shatter the Lore completely. Instead, she'd come here. Why?

He could take a wild guess: Bardolfe and the CROWS. Atiya's presence here must surely have something to do with them. Whatever had thrown the Queen off her intended destination – perhaps some summoning or spell – Ben followed regardless. If there was magic at work in the vicinity, who else could it be but the CROWS? The pieces of the puzzle were falling into place, and of course Atiya played her part. Fulk had even said as much in the underground car park in London. *She's dragon enough for what we have in mind* . . . Ben grasped the fact that the beast he pursued was wrestling with another's will – the will of Khadra, the girl inside her, her beating, earthly heart, who meant to steer the Queen towards salvation and yet found her hope usurped by a stronger resolve, that of a god . . . He shook his horns in the crazy understanding. He thought it unlikely that Khadra, so thirsty for rain, would have steered the Queen to this dry place, even if she could have done. So what then? Had Atiya been lured here? And if she'd been lured, would Ben find the bait dangling at the end of the line?

Lucky me. I'm about to find out . . .

Whichever way you cut it, the Queen was as mixed up in the Three's rebellion as he was. And if Bardolfe and the CROWS had chosen this site for their revolution, then there *was* a chance that Rose was here too, alive or— He snapped off that train of thought and swept down over the fugitives, beating his wings. Sand rippled and bees swirled, the swarm dispersing in tumbling dots. Immediately it regrouped and came at him, but the bees were like seeds thrown against stone, his tough hide resisting their stings. Another beat of his wings and the insects scattered all around him, bouncing off his snout and neck, droning, feeble specks washing into his speeding wake.

Gaining altitude, Ben covered the remaining distance to the refinery. He hadn't needed to play detective. The huge logos stencilled on the tanks announced the fact:

EKOR

And printed smaller underneath it:

THE EAST KATAMEYA OIL REFINERY

He coughed in the stink from the distillation towers, his snout wrinkling at the bitter, sulphurous odour. His enemy had chosen clever ground. There was no way that Ben could risk fire here; the place would go up like Krakatoa. A slow circle around the refinery confirmed his disadvantage. Scanning the labyrinth, he saw that the stench was due to several leaks in the pipework, deep dents and star-shaped holes, no doubt the result of a magical assault. Thick black lines trickled down the sides of the feed tanks, dripping off the tangled tubes and splattering the surfaces under them, pooling in the loading bays and at the edges of the car park. There was a Rolls-Royce down there, a Phantom IV. Ben met the sight with a growl. In the rippling heat, the vehicle mirrored the seeping oil. The CROWS had turned the place into a time bomb.

Gliding back around, he passed over one of the feed tanks, a flat-topped circular turret in the middle of the structure. Four narrow walkways radiated from it, leading into the guts of the refinery. A stairway curved around the bastion, coiling down to the concrete quadrangle that stretched between two glass-fronted office buildings. Sand wove across the area, wind-blown fingers from the Sahara. He took in these details from the corner of his eye, a pilot surveying a target, his attention fixed on the top of the tank and the figures waiting there.

Keeping a cautious distance, he made out the man in the tux and the little girl beside him clutching a plastic doll. Bardolfe, he reckoned, and the last aspect of the triumvirate, The Three Who Are One. Her pigtails and frilly green dress did not fool him. Both were typical of the Coven Royal's sense of humour, innocence masking warped intentions. The girl was surely Nan Nemain, the maiden aspect of the triple facet that the *grande dame* of the coven had years ago adopted, a choice archetype to shroud her fickle flesh. The Remnant had made a joke out of age, just like Babe Cathy on the Brooklyn Bridge and Miss Macha mocking motherhood in the underground car park. The girl below was those creatures combined. Ben knew she would greet him with the same Texan drawl, the same arch contempt. He was surprised she wasn't smoking a cigar.

The man next to her was Sir Maurice, he saw, his thin hair ruffling, ashen in the sun. The last time Ben had seen him, the old knight had been in his striped pyjamas, an antique revolver in hand. He had led Ben through the gallery in Paladin's Court, taking in art, weapons and suits of armour, all the while hiding the truth of his treachery. Now he was dressed for the occasion – whatever that might be – but the tux failed to soften his face, hide his advancing years. Under the cloudless sky, Bardolfe was the spit of venerable refinement, his energetic movements belying his age. He was busy fastening a length of golden chain to the railing that ran around the space. Like elegant script, the chain snaked across the surface of the tank and wound around Queen Atiya, a taut, shining web against polished black scales. She lay, snorting heavily, in the middle of the tank. Ben, recalling similar bonds, shared her sense of helplessness. Sorcery, ancient, potent and strange, must have summoned and bound her, the chains etched with the same gleaming glyphs that had immobilised him back in London. Unlike him, Bardolfe and the CROWS had imprisoned the Queen in bestial form, a divine serpent brought low. Her forearms clawed weakly at the steel surface, her talons leaving silvery scratch marks. The knight and the witch had secured her tail, the chains wound around its bladed length, draping off her ten-ton bulk. Atiya's head rested flat, her ram-like horns rendered harmless.

Ben observed all this in a flash, his dread reserved for the woman behind Bardolfe and Nan. Rose. They had propped her, tied with rope, on top of a pyramid of barrels at the edge of the tank. The reek informed him that the barrels were full, the metal cylinders slick with leakage. Her blonde hair hung in her face and her body slumped, held up by her bonds. It was impossible to tell whether she was alive or dead. To add insult to injury, someone had dressed her – presumably the witch – in a pink medieval gown and a hennin hat, the veil pinned to its conical peak flapping like a mocking tongue.

Bastards!

Smaller objects dotted the tank, but Ben no longer saw them. Nor did he acknowledge the symbols that ran in a precise circumference around Atiya, daubed in some sticky red substance. He might not be able to risk fire, but he was aflame nonetheless, outrage striking the flint of his guilt and igniting into rage. Caution forgotten, he arrowed downward, wings held tight to his flanks. It was a hawk's dive, speed whistling through his horns and saw-toothed spine, his claws reaching out for Rose. He'd send the barrels flying with a lash of his tail, snatch her up like a mouse from a field, blast Bardolfe and Nan from the top of the tank . . .

At three hundred miles per hour, Ben struck an invisible wall. The impact shimmered across the barrier, a dense dome of sorcerous force protecting the scene below. He crumpled like mud thrown against rock, scales rippling from snout to tail, wings buckling. Then he was airborne again, rebounding in a graceless arc over the loading bays and crashing into a factory mezzanine. Metal screamed and broke apart, littering the sky, as he punched through the gridwork, a bull charging a paper cage, and collided with the floor below. A diadem of machinery and tools clattered all around him. The floor sagged under his weight. Wreckage drizzled down, girders and pipes thumping into his flesh. For several long, painful minutes, everything went dark.

Unconsciousness only offered him shame. He was back on the islands, the rocky, broken shards of his guilt, afloat, adrift in the darkness. March pressed its chilly face up against the big glass window of the Legends bar, 7 East 7th Street. The traffic outside was a river of light, fly-specked, filthy and smeared. Ben was sitting at the end of the bar, the unchecked furnace of his hair and red-stubbled cheek resting on one ham-hock hand. The other clutched the neck of a bottle of Jack – his third, as it happened – and he nodded vaguely along in time with the jukebox (Hendrix was playing, "Burning of the Midnight Lamp", if any recollection from that night was clear). His jacket, the leather recently stitched at the shoulders and up the back, looked like it belonged to a man with much less money, but he had grown attached to it and didn't want to buy a new one. The bartender and the waitress did their best to ignore him, occasionally flicking glances his way and all but shaking their heads. The staff had yet to see him fall down drunk, but tonight he was close to it, the drink seeping down to his roots. Still, the gleam of his bottomless green eyes made sure that no one, not the bartender, the waitress or the other few customers, dared to bother him. They poured drinks. Clinked glasses. Chewed peanuts. Spoke to anyone but the broad-shouldered brute who brooded over his tiny half-empty tumbler and all the stuff they couldn't see – the doubt that had crept into his relationship, a slow poison that had left silence in place of questions, silence in place of lies.

The night before he had left New York – months before his sorry return to her rooftop garden in Vinegar Hill and all the chaos that came after – they had made love. He knew back then that it had to be the last time. They had clung to each other like kite string, tangled and tossed by the winds of change. So crazy. So final. So sweet. Then, that night, Friday night, he had gone out alone to get drunk.

Rose had known where to find him. It wasn't hard; he usually drank in the Legends bar on 7th Street. Somewhere in the fog, she'd turned up, bursting into the bar and standing blurred before him. The curls of hair escaping her hat still looked like gold to him, but now he knew that such treasure wasn't for him. His reluctance to tell her the truth, to explain that day in Central Park and all the other strange little incidents, had trapped him between the forbidden and loneliness. He couldn't risk losing her, but was too afraid to keep her. Much like Tantalus, condemned to stand forever in his pool, the fruit on the low-hanging branches was always eluding his grasp and the water receding before he could drink it. And in that moment, he knew he was a blur to her too; he saw the tears streaming down her cheeks. He was a blur to her, an unknown quantity, a wolf in sheep's clothing. Kind of.

"You don't know me, Rose. We're fucking different. Too fucking different."

She asked him what the hell he meant. Why he refused to tell her. Stubborn like her father, she said. *You're just like* . . . but she hadn't been able to speak. Unconsciously, she'd rubbed the scar on her forehead, a gesture that needled his shame, made him even angrier.

"You know. Don't act like you don't." He belched. Snarled to cover it.

She said no, she didn't know.

"You wanna know what I do with my time? You wanna know what I did before, yeah? Well, I'll tell you." He was slurring badly. Spraying spit. He stood up, swaying like a buoy in a storm. "I work for crooks. Dumb dangerous jobs for dumb dangerous crooks, OK?" He was shouting now and he couldn't seem to stop. "And you're fucking dumb to have anything to do with me."

She told him he should come home. She told him, through her pretty tears, that she only wanted a normal life. Marriage. Kids. A future. Was that so fucking wrong?

And he had laughed. Laughed in her face.

"I love you," she said.

Drunk and bitter and mean, he told her she would only fade

away, that there was no hope for them. Then he told his third and worst lie. He told her that he didn't love her.

"Who are you? *What* are you?"

"I can't give you what you want, Rose. Remember the cheque? Well, consider this my greatest act of charity."

Rose had choked and fled.

And in the morning – in the grim, aching, shitty morning – Ben had left New York.

Reverberations brought him round, heavy metallic echoes, approaching him at a halting pace.

Clunk. Clunk. Clunk.

At first he took the noise for machinery. Then, shaking his jangling head and surveying the debris, a bent and twisted blur around him, he saw that none had survived his landing. Steam hissed from broken pipes, obscuring the area. Electricity crackled and spat from dangling wires, and Ben feared for the rank spill trickling down the walls outside. In the haze, smashed dials and snapped levers jutted from the crushed and ruptured units, their former function inscrutable. The floor groaned, warping to the mezzanine walls. Across from him, a platform projected from the side of the factory, a walkway leading off from it and up on to the tank. Up to Bardolfe, Nan and Rose. Limbs aching, he nudged his way out of the chaos, steel joists and a portion of the upper floor sliding off his body. With a clang, his horns skewered the ruined ceiling and, wrenching himself free, Ben transfigured back into the shape of a man to fit his surroundings.

He wiped blood from his mouth, smearing it on the front of his skin-tight suit. Bees were hovering in here. Not many, but enough to fill the place with a soft background hum. The insects no longer swarmed, their fat little bodies zigzagging lazily over the shapes sprawled at intervals across the crooked floor. Through the clouds of steam, Ben made out the blue of overalls and realised that the shapes were bodies, factory workers unconscious or dead, apparently overcome by the bees.

Clunk.

He turned at the sound. It was closer now, on this level. Perhaps only a few yards away. The vapour made it difficult to tell. There was someone out there, halting as they noticed him. He could feel the stranger's attention, hairs rising on the nape of his neck. Squinting, he made out a tall, broad form, bulky and human-shaped. But there was something not quite right about it. Instinct told him what his eyes could not.

Clunk. Clunk.

The figure moved closer, offering no clues. Metal glinted, dull in the gloom. What the hell? Coughing, bruised, Ben took a few steps back and almost tripped over one of the bodies, a workman lying at his feet. One glance and he saw the blood, congealing around the prone form. The long slash across the man's back, glimpsed through the sodden rags of his overalls, looked suspiciously like a sword wound.

Clunk. Clunk. Clunk.

The accelerating echoes, loud and lumbering, lanced through Ben's alarm, a bucket of ice on his addled brain. He dodged sideways as the sword came whistling out of the fog, the blade narrowly missing his neck. Cold steel bit into his shoulder, lodging against his collarbone, fresh blood splattering the floor. Bellowing, he staggered in retreat, the sword slicing out of his flesh, leaving a message of pain. The blade snickered forward again, slicing at the sigil on his chest. Clutching his shoulder, Ben fell back to the mezzanine wall, cornered by mangled machinery and the hulking figure emerging from the steam.

The newcomer towered over him, encased from head to toe in steel. A dented breastplate, polished to a high degree, reflected Ben's shock back at him as he took in his would-be killer. The man was clad in antique armour – a bona fide medieval one-off – each section elegantly wrought, from the curved pauldrons to the trim fauld to the scarred and shapely greaves. The suit would have been a deathly contraption without the bristling array of spikes, designed to take on a very large wyrm that had menaced the lands around Lambton. Spikes adorned every inch, jagging from the gauntlets and hinges, leaving only the smallest gaps in its unique defences. It was a relic of triumph and tragedy, a recent gift to the gallery in Paladin's Court, and now bestowed on a new combatant with his own troublesome wyrm to slay.

The helmet, beaked and vulturine, levelled upon Ben. No heavy breaths filtered through the visor, the bladed grille strangely silent. Peering into the narrow slit above its muzzle, Ben saw pale orbs staring back at him, the pupils rimmed by sickly green, like over-boiled eggs. Around the eyes, the skin was shrivelled, shiny and black, carbonised by flame. Putrescence drifted to Ben's nose, the meaty stench informing him that the occupant of the suit had not escaped his fate in the underground car park.

The man before him was obviously dead. Roast mutton sealed in a tin, revived, he guessed, by aberrant witchcraft.

"Oh Fulk," Ben said, despite himself. "What have they done to you?"

Fulk, being dead, did not reply. Instead, he hefted the sword in his hand – the familiar weapon scorched now, a length of broken, rotten teeth – and cocked his head to one side, a dumb, uncomprehending gesture.

"Don't say I didn't warn you," Ben said, and he had, more than once. He glanced to either side of him, searching for escape.

"When House Fitzwarren threw in with the CROWS, you might as well have dug your own grave. Not that death has stopped you."

Without taking his eyes off Fulk, he slowly edged to his left, sliding along the mezzanine wall. "So what was the deal? Why did the CROWS agree to help you? My head must've come at a price." As he spoke, several cogs were whirring in his mind, recent memories falling into place. The answer lay in the week's events, glaring him in the face all along. When he'd first seen the armour in Paladin's Court, he'd recalled the Tale of the Lambton Wyrm. There had been a witch in that tale, and a witch in the Mordiford tale too, narrated by the brute before him in the underground car park. There was a witch in current events as well. *Always a goddamn witch.* Once again, Ben found the coincidence telling, the threefold appearance of the hag lending weight to his suspicions. "It was the suit, right?" The revelation hit him as he took in the razor-sharp tines, promising a painful end. "Some ancestral link between House Lambton and House Fitzwarren, this old tin can falling into your family's hands. In London, Miss Macha called you a *delivery boy.* That's it, isn't it? The Three called on House Fitzwarren and made their little bargain. But just what did you deliver, Fulk?"

Silence from the helmet. Who knew what subterfuge had taken place? Ben could take a wild guess. Paladin's Court forbade entry to Remnants, so the Three could not have made a direct approach. Cue Fulk and the Lambton armour. The perfect Trojan horse.

"You used the suit to let the CROWS reach into Paladin's Court, infect the Guild with magic. No chairman would deny an audience to one of the noble houses, even one as disinherited as yours. The Fitzwarren patriarchs offered the suit of armour as a gift to the gallery, something that Bardolfe was bound to go for, right? Tell me, were you wearing this junk when you arrived on his doorstep?" Ben pictured Bardolfe laughing on the step at his gift, as other Fitzwarren family members accompanied a tall, clanking Fulk into the hall. But Fulk alone would present no threat, so what hex from the Three had the Black Knight carried? What had House Fitzwarren intended this helmet to hide? What had really been inside the Lambton armour? Inside Fulk, the Trojan horse?

Ben was running out of guesses, his growing horror that he was right reflected in his voice. "Just what did you give the CROWS in return for my head? Your body, Fulk? Your *soul*?"

Whether Fulk heard him or not was impossible to tell. The iron giant just stared at him, dispassionate and dumb. Did memories stir inside his helmet, vague impressions of old scores, years of training, the inculcation of hand-me-down hate? Ben thought it unlikely. The Black Knight was as much a puppet now as he'd ever been, a zombie dispatched by the CROWS to finish off the refinery staff, if the evidence was anything to go by. It would fall to another Fulk – Fulk Fitzwarren CDXIII, if Ben's count was correct – to take up the ancient duty, attempt to win back the deeds to Whittington Castle, that weed-choked, ruined shell, from whatever was left of the Guild.

This was an old fight – the oldest Ben knew – and he was sick of it. Rose was in danger. He wouldn't fail her again.

"You know, I really don't have time for this." He lunged to his right, wrong-footing the slayer. The old family claymore came crashing down, carving the space where Ben had stood a moment before and crunching into crippled machinery. Sparks flew, jolting up the blackened blade and rattling Fulk in his armour. But his goose was already cooked. Soundlessly he wrenched the sword free and clanked around to give chase, a Tin Man in need of oil. Ben backed away as Fulk came at him, the notched claymore swinging. Gone was the dueller's grace, learnt since childhood in some clandestine Shropshire school, his skill checked by atrophied flesh and pounds of medieval steel. Still Fulk came on, silent, murderous, his barbed sabatons thudding on the grid.

The vibrations shuddered through Ben's limbs. Bending down, he watched his arms bulge and harden, a fleshy undulation surging down the sleeves of his suit, forming his own natural armour. Jaw clenched, veins popping, he lifted the fallen girder at his feet. Sweat dripped from his forehead, stinging his blazing eyes. For an agonising moment, he balanced the girder on his knees, then hefted the load up over his head, his legs trembling and swelling. Claws burst from his feet as he braced. With a yell, he pushed his straining muscles to their limits and hurled the girder at Fulk.

A noise like colliding trains rang across the factory. Echoes punched the mezzanine walls. The dead knight fell, swathed in steam.

Panting, Ben stumbled over to where Fulk lay and stood looking down at him. His eyes, bloodless, gazed through his visor without emotion, heedless to his Enemy. For once, Fulk's lunges had not been personal. They were just the blank actions of an automaton, directed by fucked-up voodoo. Still, instinct prevailed. The knight thrashed under the girder like a bear in a trap, his arms and legs pounding the floor, his crushed breastplate rattling. Even if Ben removed the beam, the spiked armour would pin Fulk fast.

Ben picked up the slayer's sword, dropped inches from the man's reach. The hilt was prickly in his grip, slippery with spells, reluctantly held. The blackened blade, fifty-five inches of tempered steel, shone a little brighter, its irritable whine competing with the bees. Well, he wouldn't have to hold it for long. This wasn't the first time he'd had to deal with House Fitzwarren and it wouldn't be the last. The family was a weed, watered by revenge and sprouting perennial. The faces changed, but the task, never. Still, the Black Knight's hunt was at an end.

The sword slashed down. The beaked helmet bounced across the grid.

Ben dropped the blade and shook his head, surprised he had no parting words.

TWENTY-TWO

Ben-between-states reached the end of the walkway and leapt down on to the feed tank. Grim-faced, a red-scaled, flame-eyed man, he strode towards the hub where the Queen slumped in chains. She was a dark mountain rising from the surface of the tank, her horns like outcrops, her scales slopes of volcanic glass. Heavy breaths rumbled under Ben's feet and no storm greeted him, her dormant state seeming faintly irreverent after their previous clashes. Her eyes – hooded sapphire slits – gazed only inwards, blind to his presence.

"Dear me," Sir Maurice said. "You're a tenacious bugger, aren't you? Well, I'm afraid this is a private party and I don't recall inviting you."

The Queen slumbered, but the chairman of the Guild was a different matter. He stood leaning against one claw, an elbow propped on a black talon. Some illusion conjured up by his tux and his smile lent him more of an air of menace than the serpent above him. His pale face, untouched by the sun, radiated triumph, an expression that threw a ball and chain around Ben's ankles and slowed his approach.

"I came for the girl, old man. Give her up. Then we'll put an end to this."

Ben couldn't see Rose from his position, the pyramid of barrels hidden by the Queen.

"Now, what did Aesop say?" Bardolfe stroked his chin, thinking. "'Uninvited guests are most welcome when they leave.' Wise man, Aesop. You should like him. Talking animals and all that. And you should take his advice."

"I'm not going anywhere."

"No? Well, your impudence doesn't surprise me. Do you have any idea of the lengths I've gone to? How difficult it was to arrange your presence at the British Museum? When it comes to guests, Winlock is as fussy as I am. The least you could do was have the manners to die."

"Someone didn't think I was worth it."

"Indeed. Atiya surprised us all. We certainly weren't expecting her to show you mercy." Bardolfe patted the talon and clasped his hands, both clad in spotless white gloves. He was playing the part of the gracious host, exchanging pleasantries over cocktails. "Still, one must always think ahead. My associates wanted you dead, and who was I to deny them? House Fitzwarren had their grudge and the CROWS saw you causing us a problem. A reasonable prediction, it seems, even if you are too late." The chairman shrugged. "Nevertheless, you managed to escape them. One just can't get the staff these days. Isn't that right, Nan?"

Glaring at Bardolfe, Ben hadn't noticed the little girl slipping out from the Queen's shadow. Affecting shyness, she hung back behind the knight, a finger twirling in one of her pigtails. Up close, Ben saw the mess on the front of her dress, the fabric splotched with some brown, crusty substance that he didn't think was chocolate. Whatever she'd been eating, it was sticky-looking, splashes of the stuff on her mouth and cheeks. A doll dangled from her other hand, a pink plastic baby, its lashes fluttering against her leg. The substance smeared both hand and doll, and Ben realised it could only be blood. More bad news.

"I told you. Somebody helped him." The witch, Nan Nemain, whined at Bardolfe's reproach. Her Texan drawl was soft and shrill, ill-fitting to her juvenile throat. She sounded nothing like a child. "A Remnant crony, if I'm not mistaken. Blaise Von Hart. Some jumped-up fairy acting as an envoy."

Ben didn't like this. Von Hart had saved his life, and despite the envoy's reluctance to join him, it troubled him to hear his name. That ridiculous mask, a grinning Punchinello, hadn't helped Von Hart after all.

"Leave Hart out of this. It's got nothing to do with him."

Bardolfe chuckled. "Oh, but it does. This concerns everyone under the sun, Remnants included." He glanced at the witch. "Never mind, Nan. We will get to them all in time. They'll bend the knee or . . ."

He left the thought hanging and spread his hands, a snide apology between them.

Ben took the gesture for a signal. Bunching his shoulders, he leapt forward, intending to knock the knight and the witch flying. If he could buy enough time, he'd grab Rose and take to the air. Once she was safe, he'd return for Atiya, do whatever he could to wipe that smile off Bardolfe's face, even if it meant tearing the feed tank apart.

The shield shimmered as he struck it, a blue sheen pulsing with the impact. The barrier, as seemingly tensile as the strange bubble he had seen outside the British Museum, was in fact diamond hard. He staggered back rubbing his arm, his sword wound reopened halfway through healing. Knives stabbed his shoulder. Blood dribbled down the front of his suit.

"Oh you won't get past my little friends," Bardolfe said. He spread his arms, a pointed finger on the end of each one. "Designed millennia ago to keep things in, and now keeping everything out."

Eyes narrowed, Ben followed the old man's signals. Several yards away on his right, one of Winlock's magic bricks rested on the tank. The statue was knee-high, a crumbling sculpture of a coiled snake, hood flaring, tongue slipping between fangs forever poised to strike. If memory served, this was Apep, the Lizard, one of the funerary demons that Winlock had found in the half-drowned tomb on the shores of Lake Nasser. Looking left, Ben saw Shezmu placed at a similar distance, its leonine head and human body a brooding block. Around both relics, the light held a viscous quality, like cellophane stretched over water, gleaming in the ambience of noon. Beyond the Queen's looming shadow Ben guessed he would see the other two bricks, Ammit and Set, placed equidistantly around the boundary, sealing the hub of the tank in a solid yet invisible dome. He'd hit the damn thing when he'd dived from the sky; his shoulder was still bruised from the impact.

Grasping the reason for his obstruction, his suspicion became a certainty. He levelled his glare upon the knight. What, he now realised, only *looked* like the knight.

"You're not Maurice Bardolfe," he said.

He noticed the patch of fur at the old man's shoulder, some kind of dignitary's stole laced on to the jacket of his tux. Yellow fur, golden in the sun, with dark spots patterned across it. *Leopard skin.* He didn't need to recall his vision in the Alps to place the final piece of the puzzle. The breach in the Lore had alarmed and shocked him, leaving so many niggling questions. Now he had the answers. After centuries upholding the Pact, watching over the hidden Remnants, the Guild would never have betrayed itself and gone against the grain of its purpose. And there had always been a missing player in the game.

"I am a shadow," the imposter said. "The man who cast it a

distant memory. I am the dark side of a Karnak obelisk, escaping the Eye of Ra and stretching across the sands of time."

"Poetic," Ben said. "You know, I'm not as dumb as I look. This location. The magic bricks. You're him, aren't you? Baba Kamenwati. When Winlock broke into your tomb, he must have undone the spells that bound you. Somehow you got out. Wormed your way into the chairman. Atiya isn't the only ghost here. You have also returned."

Returned to finish a three-and-a-half-thousand-year-old story.

"Most astute," the priest said. "I'm impressed."

In his long life, Ben had encountered possession before, some supernatural presence taking control of a corporeal body. During the Black Death he'd seen a small boy walking the Venetian plague pits, his boil-ridden body reanimated by an other-worldly force. In Victorian London he had sat in a darkened parlour, his hands linked to others around a table as some duchess or other made contact with the dead, messages falling from her rouged lips. And only the night before he had found himself adrift in an alien self, spinning through the mystic substance of the Queen, and met Khadra, a living, breathing foothold in the real world. Warm flesh made a handy vessel, willing or not.

He had another, more practical reason to reach his conclusion. Hints and shadows. Fragments of doubt. The pieces clicked together now, confronted by their architect.

"When I came to Paladin's Court, there weren't any guards on duty. You only had those stupid dogs. I thought the lack of security was down to conceit, the assumption that no Remnant would dare to enter the mansion. But that wasn't right. You were waiting for me."

I do know a thing or two about antiques. I'm practically one myself.

The old man had been taunting him all along.

"Oh, I knew you'd come calling, the minute you escaped the CROWS in New York. And come you did, blundering to London and into our little trap."

"Baba Kamenwati." The revelation made horrible sense. Ben could have laughed. "You're a goddamned mummy."

"I *was*." Bardolfe – Kamenwati – wrinkled his nose at the term. Then he looked up, gazing into the deep blue sky, peering down the corridor of time. "Like I said, the man they buried in that tomb is a memory. My early days in the Karnak temple seem almost a dream, all tedious duty and devotion. But my prayers were not for the Neteru, only for one as downtrodden as I. The path of my destiny soon became clear. I established the jackal cult, drawing to me those begrudging of the gods, begrudging of their tyranny. In the darkest recesses of the temple, we, the righteous, performed our rituals, determined to restore Anubis to his throne."

"Righteous." Ben pulled a face. "Infants in the flames. Innocent hearts on altars of stone. That's the way I heard it."

Kamenwati shook his head, but he did not deny it. "One cannot summon the Lord of Death by anointing statues and burning incense. We required the purest essence of life, dispatching souls into the Duat with many incantations. And yet we were ignored." Ben let the priest speak, suppressing his disgust in the hope of finding a chink in his armour, a way through the sorcerous shield. "When I heard about the wondrous land in the south, that Hatshepsut planned to visit Punt herself, I beseeched my master, the First Prophet of Amun, to send me as her spiritual guide. A sailor had spoken of magic and miracles. A great star falling from the sky, powerful enough to lay a kingdom to waste. While all of Egypt marvelled and feared, I dreamt of the distant south, hoping to find the necessary tools to gain the jackal god's attention.

"But how could I have dreamt of this serpent Queen?" Kamenwati looked up at Atiya, her massive snout stretched out before him, her nostrils flaring in slumber. He could not hide his admiration. "A serpent, I thought, who might withstand the power of the gods. Seeing my chance, I drew on all the sorcery I knew and fashioned the Crook and the Pschent. You see how these treasures are truly mine? Even so, I was afraid. My desires had yet to bear fruit and I believed I could advance them through the Queen. Our burgeoning love had softened her heart and promised me a kingdom."

"Yeah. You're a real romantic. You sent Atiya into that crater alone. She faced the Star of Eebe and never came out the same."

"No. She came out *stronger*," Kamenwati said. "Able to command the very skies. To save her land and her people. She did not regret her decision. Has she told you otherwise?"

The stone changed *me*, Atiya had told him on the mountainside. *Changed me for ever.*

"She regretted her blindness. Her trust in you."

"Then she should have shared my ambitions. Her own were troublingly dull." Kamenwati spoke of regret like an alien concept. He certainly seemed to feel none himself. "Duty returned me to Karnak. For several years, Egypt traded with Punt. It was all so material. All so mundane. All so prone to the dust of ages, when the two great realms could have formed the most powerful empire on earth."

"Under the reign of your jackal god. With you in control. It's not exactly original."

Kamenwati conceded this point with a bow of his head. "It's true that my ambition now seems weak. It lacked a certain *completion*. Back then, greed alone returned me over the ocean to Punt. Our rituals in Karnak had not gone unnoticed. Rumours stirred. Suspicions arose. It was time to do or die. In Atiya's palace, I again pledged my loyalty. We drank wine. Made love. And I taught Atiya the game of senet, all the while advancing my pieces over her authority, her banal acts, her trivial boons. The Star had granted her untold power, the Crook and the Pschent the means to control it, and what did this great queen do? Harnessed the clouds to water the crops. Healed the tribes and herds of cattle. With the gift of the heavens in her hands, the Queen was no more than a rustic goddess, a household deity trifling away the chance for dominion. But I was not without purpose."

Ben, who had seen the result of that purpose, curled his lips in a sneer.

"You murdered Atiya. Stole her regalia."

Kamenwati held up a finger, a white exclamation point. "And I paid the price! In the end I was as blind as the Queen, albeit not with love. Across the sea I fled, returning to Egypt with the sole intent of summoning Anubis to commence his reign here on earth. Deep in the Karnak temple, I uttered spells from the *Book of the Dead* and made my offerings. The door to the Duat remained closed. You see, the Star was married to the Queen; the Crook and the Pschent forged only for her. Too late, I realised my error. I could not control their power. Fire lashed out, licking the walls, licking the halls and chambers of Karnak. Burning my mortal flesh. Alerted by my incantations, the Pharaoh sent her guards to the temple. The High Priest bound me in curses and prayers. As the radiance faded from the Star, I found myself in chains. A weak fool, driven half mad. All my efforts undone."

"*Half* mad?"

Like a scorpion burrowing through sand, Kamenwati's face

crinkled and shifted, arrogance giving way to spite. Memory, it seemed, clung to him still, swimming up to hint at his true age. He looked at Ben, and Ben found he couldn't look away, caught in his fathomless eyes.

"Hatshepsut devised such a ceremony for me. She insisted on all the rituals – with several punitive differences. She oversaw the *sem* priests as they washed my body with palm wine and rinsed it with water from the Nile. The priests used no salt. Their purpose was not preservation, nor were their rites benevolent. My undertakers took up their *des* and cut deep into my side, removing my liver, my lungs, my stomach and bowels. These they placed in canopic jars. At the Pharaoh's instruction, the priests plucked out my heart, still wet, still dripping, and burnt it in a brazier. I was never to enter the Duat, so why would I have need of it? The Pharaoh had decreed I would never leave the tomb. To that end, the priests placed the magic bricks, the four little demons, in the corners of the chamber, forbidding my *ba* an exit. A priest took a hook and thrust it up my nose, smashing the stuff of my brain and pulling the strings from my skull. There was no Opening of the Mouth ritual for me. I was never to eat or drink in the afterlife. Never again speak to my god. Never speak to Anubis.

"The Star had changed me too, you see. But where it had graced Atiya with power, it brought me only damnation. Hatshepsut was harsh. The main difference in my entombment was the fact that I still lived. Yes. You're right to wince. Now you understand the mercy of the Lioness, the Woman Who Was King. I felt the blades slip under my skin, scraping against bone. I felt the organs inside me drawn out, like the guts of a fish. I felt the hook slide up my nose and—"

"I get the picture." Ben swallowed, his gorge rising. "The Pharaoh didn't take your betrayal lightly. What did you expect?

A medal?" As much as the details repulsed him, he felt no sympathy, spitting his disdain. "You fucking deserved it."

"Deserved?" Kamenwati moved forward, his gaunt face a challenge. "And who are you to judge me? You, who have turned your back on all of your kind, allowing them to fade from the earth, lulled into enchanted sleep. You, who have plodded through the ages in denial of yourself, sousing dragon fire in whiskey and whoring your talents to crooks."

"I've made mistakes," Ben said. "Unlike you, I'm not a monster."

The irony of this wasn't lost on him.

"We are *all* monsters," Kamenwati said. "Perhaps we don't like to think so, to admit we have the potential. But we are all capable of monstrosity. And all capable of godhood."

Ben said nothing. He was tiring of this game, this sparring of wits. He longed to hurl himself through the shield, make the priest answer in a language he preferred, the language of tooth and claw . . .

"I lay there in the dark, clutching the Crook. Hatshepsut saw fit to bury it with me, a final, biting rebuke. Who knows what she did with the Star and the Pschent. Hid them in a hole as deep as mine? Consigned them to dust and history? The High Priest ordered the tomb sealed and I knew my disciples would never return, my dreams of empire lost. I lay there in the dark, my *ba* trapped, for three and a half thousand years."

Ben was no stranger to longevity, but Kamenwati's age was more than triple his own. Where he had spent his life in adventure – watching people come and go, all those flowers blooming and fading – the priest had spent his in the dark. Bodiless. Undead. Imprisoned in a private hell. And in the dark the shadow would have stayed, if not for Professor Winlock.

"Long enough to learn your lesson." He jabbed a finger at the priest. "Instead, you're making the same old mistake."

Kamenwati opened his mouth to reply, but the wind roared up and smothered his words, grit washing over the feed tank. A couple of jets thundered by overhead, their noses spearing into the south. Their low passage shook the metal surface, leaving the priest's hair crazed in their wake, white weeds weaving in the sun. Ben scanned the rockets under their wings, bulbous fruit ripe with destruction. He doubted that the jets would open fire, sending them all sky-high – the financial loss was surely too great – but he couldn't bank on it. Time wasn't on his side. Neither was luck. The jets arced into the blue, shrieking around to circle the site. Following their flight north-west, a low, billowing cloud in the distance announced the approach of tanks down the road, their heavy tracks churning up sand. Great. The cavalry had arrived.

Kamenwati looked unfazed. As the jets receded, he smoothed his errant hair.

"I have learnt much. Once Winlock had broken into my tomb, I drifted into the modern world, free, lost and alone. A ghost from the sands."

No, there was no mummy. All we found was mud . . . Mud in the bottom of a cracked sarcophagus.

Ben frowned. Winlock would never know how wrong he'd been.

"Fortunately, some had sensed my return. Remnants less oblivious than you."

"The CROWS."

We heard a voice, calling in the dark . . .

Nan Nemain took this opportunity to speak up. "The Coven Royal has an ear for the dead." The words sounded wrong on her lips, a violation of youth. "We were watching the signs. Biding our time. Didn't we tell you that things change? We heard a voice in the darkness, calling, calling . . . A voice that promised us vengeance and power. Anarchy. Bloodshed. Revolution. A return to the authority of myth." The little girl squeezed the doll, her hands around its neck. "The Three Who Are One answered the call. Soon enough, we drew Kamenwati into the glass and communed with the wisdom of ages. When the Cursed One learnt of our bonds, he showed us the road to our freedom."

"You mean the road to Paladin's Court. You used the slayer. Promised him my head."

And now the suspicion in Ben's heart blossomed into a grim certainty, Von Hart whispering in his ear. *Once summoned, the Queen anchored herself in human flesh, but she isn't quite . . . corporeal . . .* Was it possible that the Three had performed a similar possession, securing the Lambton armour and sending it to the chairman of the Guild? And had Fulk been wearing the armour at the time, a living Trojan horse? The coven had delivered more than just a gift. They had delivered a *soul*, a soul squirming for a while inside a human vessel, a parasite, a spectral virus, using Fulk's body as a stepping stone. Ben recalled the dead boy walking the plague pits. He recalled the duchess babbling with the voices of ghosts and he recalled Khadra, locked inside the mystic substance of the Queen. If he knew anything about possession at all, he was fairly sure that the art of transposing souls required some kind of physical contact, a ritualistic invitation, a wide-open door . . . Had the gift of the Lambton armour simply been intended to mask the presence of magic from the Guild, blind the chairman to his danger? Ben thought so. Once inside the mansion, Kamenwati must have leapt from Fulk's body and into Maurice Bardolfe, evicting his soul like a penniless tenant. "You sent this ghoul inside Fulk's body into the heart of the Guild."

"Bardolfe became a living *shabti*. A vessel for the deceased," the priest said. "His knowledge became my knowledge. His authority, my authority. His seat of power *mine*."

And what better place to break the Lore? To undo the bindings of eight hundred years? Birthing chaos at the centre of things, spinning a web and sending out strands like puppet strings, making an African mother and child dance to the tune of rebellion. In her tomb, the Queen had slumbered. Elsewhere, her regalia had slumbered too, the Star, Crook and Pschent locked behind glass, dormant, impotent, dull. Kamenwati had wanted the relics, still craved their untold power. With Paladin's Court secured, seized by the ancient dead, the CROWS had set their plan in motion. Through the hag Dhegdheer the Coven Royal had placed the location of the tomb and the means of summoning in human hands, and then the priest and the CROWS had simply waited, luring Atiya to the source of her rage: the man who had betrayed and killed her, left her realm to crumble into dust . . .

Ben realised then that the Queen had always *intended* to come here, to face down the man she had once loved. A ghost she might be, but Atiya's power had apparently outweighed the desperation of a little girl, absorbed and utilised inside her. Flesh and blood as fuel for the physical, usurped by godly will. Had the Queen known all along that Kamenwati had risen? Ben thought so. Maybe that was what she'd been trying to tell him on the mountain. Maybe her bondage here was simply an echo of her earlier doom, history repeating itself and coming full circle.

Nan smiled. Ben wished she wouldn't.

"Final flourish," she said. "Players bow. Curtain falls."

Ben growled. His fist struck the shield again, a mallet sending sparks across the liquid surface. The barrier pulsed but did not give. The statues snarled stony-faced. The Queen slumbered on.

Kamenwati had lost interest in the conversation. He turned away and plucked a watch from the jacket of his pocket, a fancy one on a golden chain. Flicking the case open, he looked at the dial and then up at the sky. At the darkening sun.

"Well, we had some time to kill," he said, ever the polite host. The wind was rising, scattering sand. "And now we have a world."

TWENTY-THREE

A false dusk stole over the desert. Shadows stretched from the refinery, crawling through the pipework and into the sands. The tanks slowed as they reached the entrance to the plant, halting grumbling and helpless in the road, the long barrels of their guns painting silhouettes on the tarmac. The refinery bled, the air sour with sulphurous fumes. Oil glittered on the pipes and walls, a thick, lethal darkness. Oil pooled in the loading bays and car park, the Rolls-Royce blending with the ever-creeping spill, seemingly afloat on a slick black sea. As the jets circled overhead, birds rose in a cloud from the city skyline, confused by the dwindling afternoon. The wind blustered, a wash of grit and fumes, and a deep hush fell over the land.

Shielding his eyes, Ben craned his neck to follow the priest's unblinking gaze. The air grew chill, the moon dousing the desert heat. Blood streaked the horizon, congealing into an ugly purple, the dam of day broken by the encroaching penumbra, the night flooding in. In minutes, the moon had swallowed half of the sun. It was a black eye bordered by gold, scouring the sands with ominous portent. A minute more and it had obscured the sun completely, the sight a blazing ring in the sky, a flaring golden corona.

The witch, Nan, clapped her hands, a child's delight. This was what the CROWS had been waiting for. *Syzygy. Eclipse.*

Abandonment. Downfall. A moment for magic of the foulest kind, a moment to shatter the peace of centuries and hurl the world into chaos and war . . .

The moment stretched on. The stars described lines, faint silver ribbons arcing through the blue like mercury on glass. The air took on a soupy quality, holding the patterns high in the firmament, the light dripping down to touch the earth. Ben recognised no constellations, no symbols that he knew. The map above him was alien and strange. An equation, perhaps, behind the material. Minutes could have passed, or hours. The moon and the sun did not move, hanging frozen in the sky, an eclipse suspended.

With great effort, he wrenched his gaze from the sight. The priest stood muttering some foreign incantation under his breath. His lips shaped a prayer for silence and time, and the world obliged him. Satisfied with the dark and the still, the halt of the heavenly bodies, he turned and regarded Ben.

"There we go," he said. "A knot in time. A makeshift temple for our rites."

Ben caught his meaning. The world hadn't bent to the priest's command; rather he had removed them all *from* it, displacing the refinery and its surrounds from the everyday continuum. The soupy quality, the pressure of the air, was all too familiar. Ben had felt the same thing in the underground car park and in the confines of Club Zauber. Magic. Intoxicating. Addictive. In its own uncanny lacuna. He stood here on the borderland, the narrow fringe between the earth and the nether. Sweat rimed his skin. Did he imagine the faint rustling in the sky, the slither of tentacles, the clicking of claws? He glanced over his shoulder, seeing only the tanks below, the soldiers milling at the entrance to the car park. The jets had disappeared, flown outside the ambit of the bubble.

"You're crazy. The Lurkers will come. No one will survive."

"Hence the importance of protection," Kamenwati said, an arm sweeping out to indicate the unseen dome that shone a gentle blue in the gloom. "You didn't think I created this shield simply to withstand you? Heavens, no. As I said, you're too late. The hour has come. The revolution is assured. Like a scrap from my plate, you will tempt the appetite of ghosts. Long enough for me to end this world."

"End?" Ben was looking around anxiously, searching for signs of the grey ghosts, the Walkers between the Worlds. This build-up of magic on the edge of their territory must smell like a fucking feast to them. His heart thumped like footsteps towards a gallows. "I thought you said you wanted to rule. You won't make much of a king as a corpse."

"You haven't been listening. I have lived my life and gone to my tomb, only to rise again renewed, reborn. I watched the flesh rot from my bones, the ages pass in the darkness, and yet, I endure. I am Death. Death Incarnate."

"You sure about that? Sure you're not just a piece of maggot-ridden shit?"

Insults. The old play-for-time tactic. Except now there *was* no time and the priest had no heart to hurt.

"Death, Mr Garston. The only certainty. The only true immortality. I will release this world from its physical bounds, its people from their prison of flesh and decay. Their crude, sweaty couplings. Their brief, pointless lives."

Ben faced Kamenwati, his panicked survey of the tank forgotten. The priest's words gripped him like a fist around a snake's neck.

"Think of it," Kamenwati said. "Everything born must die. Flowers, animals and people. Stars. Worlds. Even galaxies. Death is the constant, the power that binds, the force that rules them all. Look around you. Death is *everywhere*. On the TV screen. In the papers. Death is under our feet. Don't tell me you're blind to the age. Don't tell me you can't see it. Corrupt politicians and rising crime rates. Countless wars and drug abuse. Corporations milking the earth, pumping filth into the atmosphere. Glaciers melting. Rainforests burning. Famine and flood sweeping the land . . . This world *wants* death. Its people long for an ending." He raised a hand, offering damnation. "And I am going to give it to them."

Ben wanted to protest, to deny the claim, but he'd thought the same thing himself: humanity was shaping its own destruction. *You get to wondering who the monsters are.* The Queen, chained and comatose, certainly agreed. In death, the priest would unite them all, warp the natural order of things and rule over an undead world, an empire of enslaved souls.

And the tools for his ambition? They lay before him, buried in Atiya's flesh. The Star with its voracious power. The Crook and the Pschent the means to control it. The priest had devised the Queen's awakening for this very purpose, to come to him on vengeful wings at the hour of eclipse, the moment when change was possible. To bring him the rekindled relics.

But . . .

"You can't control her regalia," Ben said, the challenge raw in his throat. "You said so yourself. The Star, Crook and Pschent. They only answer to the Queen."

Kamenwati tapped his lips. Lit by the corona above, he was a candle in the dark, affecting contemplation.

"No," he said, and he did not smile. "But I can control a little girl."

He ignored Ben's expression and turned to the Queen. Atiya

snorted, restless. Perhaps her dreams warned her of the priest's presence. She shifted a little, the chains clanking, and Ben saw the wound in her side, a long, gaping gash where her scales met her smooth underbelly. A skirmish had obviously taken place, a bewitched barrage piercing her flanks and bringing her crashing to the surface of the tank. Blood and smoke issued from the wound, spilling on to steel. Nan Nemain went to it now and stuck her hand into the mess with a relish that turned Ben's stomach, adding further splashes to the front of her dress. She withdrew her fingers and licked them, sighing in pleasure, then plunged in for more. Fist dripping, the witch returned to Kamenwati's side and knelt to paint the ground at his feet, smearing a circle around him.

Dragon blood. A potent ingredient. Some claimed that a serpent's juices granted the user brief invincibility. Others said that the earth itself could not absorb it, but Ben had bled enough in his time to know that that was bullshit. The stuff in his veins was neither poison nor acid. Nevertheless, it held the residue of the long-lost science and spells responsible for his birth. In the wrong hands, it was trouble.

No, it's goddess *blood,* he corrected himself. *The witch has drawn a circle of protection. A circle within a circle . . .*

Nan retreated, pigtails bobbing. Kamenwati raised his arms.

"Grant power to my *ba*," he said, offending the silence. "Grant me power over invocations and blood offerings. Grant me power over the air, the waters and all riverside lands. Grant me power over those who dwell upon the earth and those in the realm of the dead."

The air grew colder. A clicking and slithering stirred at the edges of Ben's hearing, a softly approaching babble. *Lurkers.* But he could not tear his eyes from Kamenwati and the Queen.

"Oh you doorkeepers, you holy guards, who swallow souls in the House of Destruction, open your caverns and halls. I offer Anubis the blood of the dragon. I offer you, Lord, a celestial soul. I offer you this world as a throne."

Breath plumed from Ben's nose. He was so close to the unseen barrier, his claws pressed against it, that the atmosphere crackled and fizzed, sparks bouncing off his scales. The chains strained and groaned as Atiya shifted again, her huge eyelids fluttering. Her talons opened and closed, opened and closed. A low growl rumbled across the tank, shuddering under Ben's feet.

"Hear me! I am Death! By my words and my sacrifice, I demand an audience!"

This got a response. The Queen's eyes snapped open. Caught in their glare, Ben staggered backwards, the hate of millennia scouring his soul. Atiya roared, electricity spewing across the space between them, hitting the shield and refracting into a thousand bolts. None of the discharge touched the priest, merely jagged around the circle in which he stood, trembling with spell-fuelled ecstasy. Ben and the witch looked on as Atiya struggled to rise, forcing her bulk against the chains, her horns goring the air. The railings around the tank squealed and twisted, but did not break. Nor did the chains, golden, glyph-etched and charmed. Further entwined by her efforts to free herself, the Queen snarled and rolled on her side, the feed tank booming. Her scorn hit Ben like a truck.

Mas. Snake.

Nacas. Fool.

And then another mental breath. In their shared understanding, a link forged in lightning and fire, Ben grasped her unmistakable despair.

I am . . . lost . . .

Atiya's anguish thundered through him, but a deeper shock lay beyond it, hurling all else aside. The Queen had rolled on to her side, and with the motion revealed the far side of the tank. Ben saw Rose. Saw what they had done to her.

Tied with rope atop the pyramid of barrels, the perforated cylinders thick with sludge, Rose slumped in the pink medieval gown. Her hair hung lank in her face, dull, dirty gold. The veil of her hennin hat fluttered like a rag. Frantically he searched her body, seeking the rise and fall of her breasts, a twitch of muscle, anything. Long draping sleeves covered her arms, but he could see her face, her neck and an exposed length of leg, the latter peeking through a rip in the silk. Her countless scars, red-raw welts, sent him the bitter truth like a gun blast. Even from a distance, he could see that they were symbols, sigils and whorls carved into her flesh, some maniacal, mutilating spell. Her head lolled on her chest, insensate.

Rose McBriar, who had told him that she hated him, that he was ruining her life. Who had kissed him goodbye in a Brooklyn subway never knowing its finality. Who had given him everything and only asked for one thing in return. Rose, his favourite damsel. Rose McBriar was dead.

The Black Knight sniggered in his mind.

You never had much luck with women, did you?

The Queen whispered.

Your woman will die . . .

No!

Shock forced Ben backwards, away from the shimmering shield. He shook his head, unable to accept what the hole in his breast had already told him was true. Sinking to his knees, he pressed his hands to his skull, trying to contain the eruption inside, a bubbling maelstrom of memories and loss, threatening madness.

Kamenwati said, "Oh you who guard the Doors of the Duat, I know you and I know your names." Fervour drenched his appeal, his voice thick with need. "Come, Anubis! Come! I offer you this world ripe for the reaping. I have bound human flesh in the sacred charms and preserved the seed inside. I offer you the seed of the dragon. I offer you life for unending death!"

Ben looked up.

Seed? Tears streaked his face, hot on his cheeks. *Life?*

The words pierced his stricken mind. In his blurred and smouldering vision, Kamenwati was a black cross, his arms spread wide in his elegant tux, his hair a sketch of snowfall. The priest's attention stayed fixed on Atiya, who grunted and growled, heaving sluggishly against her bonds. The witch, however, was staring at Ben. Nan Nemain, *grande dame* of the Coven Royal, had seen the bullet shot through him, the fact of Rose's demise. He had escaped the Three twice, once in New York and once in London, and yet here she was, drinking in the sight of him. Revelling in her triumph. With a grin to cut steel, she held up her little doll. Its lashes fluttered, the sockets behind them empty and blank.

"Things change," she said.

She tossed the doll over her shoulder. It hit the ground and bounced, its chubby plastic head popping off and rolling, rolling, to rest against the priest's leather bag.

It was a simple act of childish petulance, but the message was plain. Ben grimaced at Rose, forcing himself to look up at her dead, disfigured body. That was all it took to spin him back across the days of the week, back across the desert and the Med and the Alps. Back from Berlin and the British Museum and Paladin's Court and his lair under Barrow Hill Road. Back across the Atlantic Ocean to a penthouse rooftop in Vinegar Hill six weeks ago. He'd told Rose that what she wanted wasn't simple.

He'd told her they were different, denied her, and then, just like he always had, he had hit the road. For eight hundred years, since he'd signed that damn scroll in an Uffington meadow, he had been running away . . .

Know that before God and the King and the knights of this realm, no Remnant spared the Sleep and bestowed the freedom of these Lands shall beget issue of like kind, nor influence, adopt or otherwise endow others into their fold. Since we have granted all these things, for the better order of our kingdom and to allay the discord between us, any Remnant found in breach of this clause shall face swift and lawful execution · · ·

Down through the generations, the Guild had translated the Pact many times, but never revised its codes. The Lore that had bound the exiles from the Old Lands in the early thirteenth century was the same Lore now. Ben had signed the damn scroll in the Manger (and how bitterly ironic that seemed now – irony to choke him like a cherry stone), the deep green dell under White Horse Hill, but even then, he'd been running. He had run from Maud and the burning canopy over his head, the memory of poison on tragic lips. He'd run from countless damsels over the ages – half of whom he could scarcely recall – escaping vows and wedlock and the risk of reproduction. Had he sired another in the past? He did not, could not know. Under the watchful eye of the Guild, it seemed unlikely. These things happened differently for his kind. Precaution was as much a matter of will as it was the use of prophylactics, from pig bladders to linen sheaths and, in these times, rubbers. Conception was quick and gestation long. He had no way of knowing how a woman might bear it or whether she would survive. The matter was unheard of – unnatural, forbidden among dragons, let alone by the Guild. No woman had ever come to him, however, claiming that he was a father, requesting, begging or demanding support, financial, emotional or otherwise. The thought shamed him in his grief; his lack of knowledge or care, his faith in the Pact and loyalty to the Lore blinding him to the possibility of parentage. Blinding him to the hurt of those he had left behind, all of them dead and gone, beyond his amends and explanation. He saw it now, his cowardice. Things changed and things could have been so different. He had run across time and met Rose, the love of his long and spineless life, a treasure he could not own, and here, at the end, he finally understood. The last night they had spent together before he'd gone out and got so drunk, before he'd told her that he didn't love her and then left for Spain. That night. Yes. So crazy. So final. So sweet . . . A spark had leapt from his flesh to hers, igniting inside her womb.

Oh, but why didn't you tell me, Rose?

Then, with ice in his veins, he realised she had, or almost had, when he had returned . . .

And you should've known better. Better than to get involved. Better than to make me . . .

Fall for you. That was what he'd thought she was going to say. In his arrogance, he had failed to miss the obvious truth, the real reason for the dark circles under her eyes and the bottle of wine in her hand . . .

The CROWS had not been so blind. The CROWS had foreseen it. Perhaps the bastard priest had told them. Either way, it was clear to him now why the coven had snatched her and why

Fulk had sneered in the underground car park, reducing her to the level of a useful ingredient.

She was so much more than that. She was his reason to be, to carry on. The ingredient that Fulk had mentioned could only be life. His baby. His seed. Somehow, that seed still lived, if he credited the priest's prayer, sustained by the spells they had etched so cruelly, so precisely on to Rose's body. And Ben thought he knew why. Hadn't Professor Winlock told him? *Infants in the flames. Innocent hearts on altars of stone.* Hadn't Fulk referred to Rose as bait? *Think of her as a fish on a line.* Hadn't Kamenwati laughed in his face only minutes ago, taunting him with the means of his undoing? *One cannot summon the Lord of Death by anointing statues and burning incense. We required the purest essence of life* . . .

Life for death. Living death.

Ben howled. After all his excuses and all his running away, he had failed her, just like he'd failed every woman in the past unlucky enough to cross his path. Rose was dead, and the Three watched him, basking in his pain. The Three watched him and laughed . . .

No flicker of will crossed his mind. Transformation wasn't a thought. It was simply a surge of blind fury. With a roar that shook the sky, he burst into bestial form, a great red wall rising from its crouched and weeping state to rival the unseen dome. His wings flared, pennants of war. Heartsick, crazed, he rammed his bulk against the shield, his tail lashing the top of the tank. The tank shuddered, reverberations travelling through the barrier, but they weren't strong enough to throw the witch from her feet or hinder the chanting priest. Nan Nemain continued to laugh, a child teasing bears at the zoo. With blood in his eyes and fire in his skull, Ben plunged his claws into steel, ripping up sheets and rivets, sculpting metal into jagged waves. He tried again, his shoulder bulling into the wall, his forearms punching into the breach and attempting to dig his way under. The syzygy regarded his efforts with bright disdain. The shield travelled downwards as well as up. The priest's armour was solid and sound, the force from the magic bricks encircling the scene entire. Even if Ben spent the last of his strength reducing the feed tank to scrap, he would only find a transparent sphere, its circumference afloat in the darkness. Furious, he took to the sky, fanning sand and fumes, and tore at the pipework, his fangs locked in exertion. Wrenching a section free, he turned and flung it at the dome, a truck-sized gnarl of metal clanging into the barricade. The wreckage bounced off, clattering in all directions. Bellowing, he pumped his wings and thrust higher, heading for the nearest distillation tower, meaning to tear it from its foundations and bring the structure down on Kamenwati and the witch.

A tank in the road below, keen for an oil-free target, moving or otherwise, took a chance and fired. Ben had dodged the barrage outside the museum, but this time he wasn't so lucky. The shell punched through his right forearm and pierced a wing, shattering muscle, pinions and webbed flesh, fragments of bone spraying the air, blood splashing the complex. Blasted off course, he barrelled into a spin, crashing into the side of the tower. The column buckled, the noise of impact shooting up the funnel in a thick belch of smoke, but the structure held firm. He threw his remaining forearm over his snout, the top of the tank whirling up to meet him. With a grunt, he crash-landed, crushing a section of railings like tin foil and leaving a sixty-foot dent.

The dust cleared. Skull ringing, Ben squinted across the tank at the cruciform priest.

"You cannot deny me!" Kamenwati shrieked. "Come, Anubis. Come! Come and claim your prize!"

Atiya snarled, wrestling with the chains. Her tail lashed out, its bladed length sweeping across the blood-smeared symbols and smashing into the pyramid of barrels. Ben watched in numb dismay as the stack gave way. Knocked from her pedestal, Rose tipped over and fell, her rope-bound form tumbling into the chaos and her hennin hat flying from her head. It hung for a moment, drifting in the gloom, and then fluttered downwards, lost from view.

Kamenwati didn't blink, his eyes glued to Atiya. He spoke a word. More of a symbol, really, hanging in the air. The Queen reared, growling, and then – vanished. Her black mass evanesced, weaving smokily up to the zenith of the dome, fanning out in thick, sooty wings, the unravelled substance of a goddess. The chains wove with her, Ben saw, rising from the tank like iron filings drawn by magnets, the glittering links snaking skyward, holding her essence captive.

A girl sat cross-legged in the middle of the tank, revealed by the lifting darkness. Her bony limbs protruded from her T-shirt and football shorts, now no more than rags. Skin merging with the shadows, she was almost a part of the billowing brume.

Khadra. The girl looked the same as she had in the Alps when Ben had fallen into the Queen, sinking into the spectral depths that were now blowing open before him. Her head was bowed, perhaps by exhaustion, perhaps by hunger. Perhaps by the weight of the Pschent on her head. The tall double crown shone in the gloom, the gleam of burnished silver. The cobra, ready to strike, coiled from the curving brim next to the emblem of the sharp-beaked bird – some lost, vulturine god – the symbols of divinity and rule reduced by the drooping head that bore them. Clutched loosely in one hand, Khadra pressed the Crook to her chest, a pose resembling the pharaohs of old. Inlaid hieroglyphics, sacred seals of command, wound around its ivory length. The Star of Eebe rested in her lap, the fist-sized gem that had started this business glowing with a soft white puissance.

Kamenwati, high as a kite on the stuff of magic, shivered at the sight.

"*Come!*"

And the doors of the Duat opened.

TWENTY-FOUR

In the filthy streets of El-Arafa, the City of the Dead, a tremor shot through the ground. The eclipse had passed some minutes ago and the squalid district went about its business, reeking under the late noon sun. Children on the rubbish heaps, who had paused in their sifting to gaze up at the sky, shrugged and bent again to their task, pulling shabby clothes, broken chairs and dented cans from the collected muck. As the quake struck, the Zabbaleen cried out as one, jumping and sliding down the slopes of trash and heading for the shelter of the nearby streets. Running ahead, a teenage boy in a ragged kaftan ducked into an open tomb, standing under the lintel as his parents had taught him with dust peppering his hair. Tremors in Cairo were nothing new, but like his other slum-fellows – some of whom had ended up here as a direct result of the "powder keg" in 1992 – Hanif was never quite sure how bad they would be. Muttering to Allah, he gaped at the shuddering ground, searching for signs of riddling cracks, the sand shifting like chalk on a drum skin. Seeing nothing, he peered at the sky, and gasped at the growing darkness in the south. At first he thought it was a cloud bank, a storm moving in, but squinting harder, he saw that wasn't right. It was as though some hand had peeled back the day, exposing the night underneath, a torn black triangle rising from behind the Mokattam Hills. None of the stars looked familiar.

A cry distracted him. He glanced up the street, seeing a woman rush from her home – in truth a crooked mausoleum – her hands waving over her head and her lips stretched in a shriek. Hanif frowned. The woman was a fool to flee, especially from shelter, but then he saw the scrawny figure lurching from the doorway after her, rags aflutter in the stirred-up dust. It was too far away to make out the details, and as the tremor passed, rippling under his feet, Hanif staggered back into the tomb, the cool gloom embracing him.

Something cold gripped his shoulder. He turned, startled, and stared into a withered skull. Wormy eyes regarded him. Yellow teeth chattered. In the confusion, he hadn't heard the lid of the tomb sliding open or the thing inside it climbing out. As the dank walls trembled around him, no one heard the boy scream.

Cairo rumbled. Police busied everywhere. Wild reports of a terrorist attack, coupled with the insane babble about giant flying beasts and the awe of the passing eclipse, had turned the day into a circus. *What now?* merchants asked in the Khan el-Khalili, fanning themselves and sucking on tall, ornate hookahs, their assorted wares, carpets, jewellery and spices, starting to dance on the stalls before them. At Tahrir Square, taxi drivers echoed them, complaining to sweaty tourists in the back of their cabs. *As if the riots aren't bad enough*, they said. *What now? What next?* In the hubbub and under the smog, no one mentioned the darkness in the south, the strange narrow fissure in the sky. From the city, the sight could pass for a column of smoke, and in the throbbing confusion, thinking otherwise was perhaps too much, the spectacle put down to a fire or a sandstorm. *What a day*, women said to each other on the shivering streets. *Ah, me. What a day.*

*   *   *

The Museum of Antiquities was closed to the public. The army had cordoned off the Wasim Hasan, the road leading past the grand red building, and traffic on the Nile Corniche moved at a snail's pace, backed up, grumbling and cautious. The museum, recently the scene of gunfire and mayhem, was now an oasis of calm. Soldiers still occupied the building, a skeleton crew with machine guns slung over their shoulders, smoking cigarettes near the ruined displays as they waited for further orders. The rotunda was cool and quiet, sunlight shafting through holes in the dome, sparkling on the antiquated wreckage. Considering the noise on the streets outside, the soldiers breathed a collective sigh of relief. Now that the gas had dispersed, the hallucinations faded (and by God, what a show!), they guessed they were the lucky ones. At least they weren't out there directing traffic, and no one had given them *specific* instructions to clean up the mess. On the benches in the gallery, inspecting the atrium statues or sauntering down the pillared porticoes, the soldiers patrolled the museum with all the languor of a daily coach party.

On the first floor, halfway down the corridor leading into the west wing, Private Farid slouched against the wall by a crumbling boat, the Fourth Dynasty artefact set behind a stretch of elastic rope. He was bored, and his younger comrade, Private Banna, was out of cigarettes. There wasn't much reason to talk, but it was still a preferable state to being outside, marching in the *sefi* heat and dust (Farid knew that the break wouldn't last long; these days, Cairo was as volatile as tear gas). So when he heard the racket coming from further down the corridor, an odd, insistent rattling and banging, his spine was straight and his gun in his hand in a matter of seconds. Banna, his startled mirror, followed suit. Farid frowned, circling his hand. *This way.* A few steps into the wing to investigate and the walls started to shake.

Dislodged bricks clattered down around them, the floor juddering and jumping like a washing machine on spin. A mosaic of cracks spread across the smooth marble, the corridor skewing out of shape. Farid shouted something at Banna. The sense of it was lost in the clamour, but his flapping hand spelt out *earthquake* and his eyes went wide for the nearest shelter, a shadowed archway on their left.

The two men ducked under it as a section of the ceiling came down, plaster dust shrouding the scene. Farid clung to the abutment like a passenger on a runaway train, watching Banna fumble to do the same, the younger man pale and gibbering. When the tremors subsided, passing under his feet and into the city, it took Farid a moment to notice, because the uproar continued behind him, a hollow-sounding din turning the space into an echo chamber. He turned, stiffened, and took a small step backward, then tapped Banna on the shoulder. Banna followed his direction, staring speechless through the archway into the dimly lit room. An acrid odour hit Farid's nostrils, and it wasn't the smell of Banna's piss. The mummy cases lining the walls rumbled and shook, bumping against each other and the walls behind them, a tantrum of ancient wood and paint. Even the cases that had fallen to the floor appeared in an agitated state, a rustling and banging coming from inside them. Farid gawped at Banna. Banna warbled something in reply. A sound like knives dragged down slate drew Farid's attention back to the hubbub and the smashed glass coffin in the middle of the room.

The corpse inside it, brown, desiccated, withered, was struggling to rise, its skeletal hands scrabbling for purchase on the sides of the case. Its rags fell away in a cloud as it stood, exposing a hollow ribcage. Frayed skin, pickled ages ago and holding the sheen of worn leather, drifted in flakes to the ground. With a

371

creak that Farid heard despite the ruckus, the corpse turned its face toward him, its mouth stretched wide in a silent scream.

The tremors spread out, roaring under the city and into the sands.

To the east of Cairo, dust and scree trickled and bounced down the crumbling flanks of the Pyramids of Giza. Camels brayed and bolted, some of the beasts bearing tourists, others struggling to join them. Bedouins fought with the thrashing reins, their robes and *keffiyeh* fluttering in the haze. Tour guides yelled at their panicked parties, and people in sunhats and Bermuda shorts dropped their cameras and phones to the dusty floors of the mortuary temples like bizarre modern-day offerings. The Great Sphinx, with its scarred, eroded face, gazed blankly over the necropolis, watching a babbling mass of people flee from the mastabas and rock-cut tombs, their awe usurped by fear.

And deep, deep under the sands, in glittering vaults yet undiscovered, casket lids budged and shifted, bones clicked for the first time in centuries, and sockets that had once held eyes blindly searched the fathomless dark.

Ben looked up at the fissure in the sky, a smouldering wound revealing slow, smudged stars, tapering to a point above the East Katameya Oil Refinery. Energy cupped the top of the feed tank, shimmering, invisible, and all around him lay a frozen darkness, the area prised from the Cairene afternoon like a bubble in the river of time. On the horizon, the syzygy, a ring of gold around depthless black, seemed pinned to the velvet night.

Khadra sat with the Crook and the Star in her lap, the Pschent atop her head. The essence of the Queen, a tethered nebula, churned and billowed above her. Something moved in the drifts,

Ben saw, a vague, gargantuan form emerging from the egress, the levitating chains parting. Kamenwati had opened up Atiya like a door, a portal into the Duat, and now, with the Guild outfoxed and the Sola Ignis lying wounded, the priest knelt in supplication.

His prayers had found their answer.

I HAVE COME.

The voice was in the air, but also *of* it, drawn from the stolen night. Sepulchral tones ached in Ben's bones, grinding in his skull, words as foreign and forgotten as the Queen's, but which he grasped, nevertheless, his mind touched by the empyreal, the language of the gods. Still, it *hurt*. The voice above him would put birds to flight, send worms wriggling deeper underground. Ben wanted to curl up and hide, huddle under his broken wing and forget the tragedy skewering his heart. To sleep meant death, but there was comfort in the thought, a surrender to the inevitable. He had failed Rose. Death seemed a fitting reward. He was weak. He'd sustained so much damage. He was healing slowly, too slowly. He lay on the doorstep, a bloody lump of scales and horns, reduced to raw meat like his woman and his seed, a meal for the entity summoned by the priest.

Dazed, numb, he peered up at the giant figure emerging from the gulf. He made out a humanoid torso and limbs, mahogany black and smooth as pearl. Arm bracelets and a banded collar glinted in the shadows, clasped around bulging sinews and a vast, bull-like neck. A striped headdress and dangling pendants, both the size of a small boat, adorned the giant's head. A canine snout, long and slender, protruded from the wavering breach, sniffing out the one who called him. His pointed ears curved up to the stars, and Ben suspected they would miss nothing – the sound of an infant's birth cry or a geriatric's last gasp. The visitant's eyes, deep-set, ageless slits, reflected the genuflecting priest like dull ruby mirrors.

There was no mistaking his identity. In the past week, Ben had heard his name on lips both mortal and divine, seen him depicted in statues and paintings more times than he cared to recall. Kamenwati, with his spells, his offerings and choosing of this hour, had succeeded in summoning his master.

Anubis, the jackal god. Anubis, the Judge of the Dead.

MY SERVANT. WHAT DO YOU WANT OF ME?

The question boomed across the tank, resounding from a place far beyond the earth, beyond time, beyond life. A place where the gods slumbered in forgotten deeps. Kamenwati, crouched in his circle of blood, sucked in a steady breath. His shoulders tensed and his hands closed into fists. Ben watched a smile spread across his lips, a slow, humourless rictus, and when the priest looked up, there was nothing submissive in his face.

SPEAK. OR SPEAK NO MORE.

The priest stood. The witch, Nan, drew closer to his side – perhaps in unease, perhaps in expectation, Ben couldn't tell. Above them, the strengthening form of the god, this lord of the Neteru, gazed down in grim impatience, his huge snout jutting from the underworld, the threshold of the Duat. The portal belched a soupy darkness, a cascade of fog carpeting the ground. Still the priest did not speak, his gaunt features an arrogant mask. Ben held his breath, waiting to hear some final appeal, some feverish plea that would damn them all.

Instead, Kamenwati dropped his gaze to the girl in the middle of the tank. He muttered something, a whispered command, the meaning swallowed by the distance. In response, Khadra sat up, her straightening spine showing like a zipper through her threadbare T-shirt. She raised her head, her neck veins popping with the weight of the Pschent, the tall double crown dwarfing her body. Her face remained slack, her eyes unseeing. A thin line of drool trickled from her lips, and her arms jerked, her shoulders twitched, her movements stiff and unnatural.

Ben winced, sensing what was coming next.

"*Imminka*," the priest said. *Now.*

Khadra raised the Crook. She placed its tip, an almost-but-not-quite circle, on the top of the gem in her lap. The diamond burst into life, silvery splinters blasting out, accompanied by a musical scream, the shrill song of the void. Ben's claws went to his ears as the Star bored into his brain, threatening to incinerate thought. Ozone cut through the stench of oil, curdling with the spill from the toppled barrels and the taste of blood in his throat. Clinging to consciousness, he saw the halo of light coalesce into a single bolt, crackling across the tank. He cringed as lightning spewed into the heights, penetrating the portal.

"*Ha!*"

Kamenwati's cry joined with the shriek of the stone. He stood, silhouetted in his tux, his hair wild and his arms weaving. Like a puppet on ghostly strings, Khadra echoed his movements; the bolt from the Star harnessed and steered by his splayed white gloves.

Anubis roared, berating the frozen eclipse. In the collision of shadow and sparks, the god raised a staff that would fell trees, the shaft crowned by a large looped cross – an *ankh*, the Ancient Egyptian symbol of life. He flung out his arms, attempting to stave off the blazing assault, but the Star was not so easily repelled. The diamond burned with the touch of spellbound ivory, its voracious appetite spurred by the Crook. The god's staff shattered in two, glittering fragments spinning in the void, the hulking figure snarling and recoiling. Manifest in fangs of light, the hunger of the Star sank into dark and gleaming flesh, feeding on divinity.

Kamenwati shrieked, drunk on magic. Whatever the Star's life-changing powers, the only transformation that mattered to the priest was as clear and bright as the pummelling lightning. The mechanics of the spell had simply been a ruse. Atiya, the doorway, and Rose, the lure. Smoke and mirrors. *Bait.* All along, the priest had set his sights on a far greater prize than devotion and subservience. His prayers unanswered, his offerings ignored and his *ba* consigned to the dark for millennia, his faith had soured and grown bitter – fermenting into vengeance. This was his final sacrilege, his last act of rebellion. Kamenwati meant to overthrow death.

The consequences would spell disaster. To kill a god was to become one. Even an idiot knew that. With the Star in his grasp, the priest would usurp a throne in the Duat and challenge the ancient and faded power of the Neteru. Ben's original quest seemed trite now, blown into ruinous proportions. If Kamenwati succeeded, it was *sayonara* for all of them. Forget the Guild. Forget the Lore. Forget the Remnants. Forget *life*. Kamenwati had named himself Death and now advanced to seal the deal. Outside the shield, Ben could do nothing to stop him. To shut out the priest and the ambushed god came as a blessed relief, an end to all quests, to stupid dreams. Rose was gone, and with her his strength, his will to resist. The fierce light, the bellowing giant and the gleeful shrieks would all go spinning like grains of sand through the hourglass, falling into a deep and blameless silence . . .

Already Anubis was weakening, his substance devoured by the Star. Black strata tainted the lightning, swirling like ink in water and drawn towards the stone's ravenous core. His canine head, pointed ears and ruby eyes were all just a dusky blur, his outrage a receding din. Fighting was futile, a lost cause, and Ben groaned, his eyelids drooping, barely aware of the fact that his body echoed his sense of defeat. His horns shrank, his tail coiling in, his scales melting into bruised skin. His broken wing folded up to form the stump of his right arm, severed at the elbow and sluggishly bleeding, half-heartedly trying to heal. In a matter of seconds, seven tons of fabulous beast had dwindled to thirteen stone of seemingly human flesh. He curled up in the envoy's suit, sick of the sight of the priest and the witch and their triumph, turning his head from the girl, the god and the flailing essence of the Queen.

Then, from the corner of his eye, he saw her. She climbed to her feet in the smoky shroud that covered the ground, a phantom rising from the grave. Strands of hair stuck to her brow, plastered by sweat and oil. Her gown hung in shreds from her scarred limbs, but Ben's heart leapt at the vision. *Rose! Rose is alive!* Released from her bonds when the barrels collapsed, she must have been jolted out of her comatose state – what he now guessed was some kind of trance easily mistaken for death – and crawled, crawled unnoticed under the fog, reaching the boundary of the dome. He watched her pull herself up, her palms smearing filth on the unseen wall. Groggily she looked around, taking in the wrestling giant in the scintillating web, the floating chains and the reefs of darkness. She took in the figures on the tank, their backs turned to her: Khadra, the pigtailed witch and the jubilant priest.

Her eyes narrowed, slivers of frost. Ben called out, a husky moan escaping his throat. Rose didn't hear him – or if she did, she ignored him – blanking him out in favour of the closest

377

weapon to hand. Hands shaking, she reached down and lifted one of the magic bricks, the knee-high statue of Apep, the Lizard, the sculpture of the coiled snake with hood flared and fangs bared, its tongue forking between them. Grimacing and breathing hard, she balanced the crumbling icon on her shoulder. She swayed a little, a petal in a breeze. Then, managing to right herself, she staggered onward, shuffling up behind the priest. Her muscles strained as she braced her legs, hefting Apep over her head.

"I am not . . . a *prize*."

Eyes glued to the struggling god, Kamenwati and the witch turned too late as Rose brought the statue crashing down on the priest's skull.

Like a needle scratched across a record, his chanting was cut short. As Apep splintered into a hundred pieces, Kamenwati stumbled forward, dropping to his hands and knees, an involuntary act of obeisance. Blood streaked his ash-white hair, dripping down his face and staining the collar of his shirt. Despite the vigour of Kamenwati's soul, Maurice Bardolfe's body remained human. With no warning or chance to defend himself, the priest was as frail as any old man. Stunned, he crumpled, sprawling prostrate across the smeared circle. Nan Nemain leapt back, pigtails bouncing, her young face aged by spite. The witch raised her arms, poised to deliver an answering blow to their reeling assailant, some mumbo-jumbo to blast Rose from the tank.

She never got the chance. With the priest knocked senseless, Khadra slumped, her strings cut. The Crook fell limp at her side, the Star of Eebe rolling from her lap. Lightning lashed out, the single, concentrated bolt scattering into myriad jags. Nan had no choice but to dodge them, a lethal game of skipping rope, forcing her into retreat. Crackling energy swept the area, the swinging boom of a burning ship, and then the gem was quiet, its song silenced, its radiance dispersing like marsh light. The witch was already heading back, recovering the distance she'd lost to the discharge. Her shoulders hunched, her lips pouted. Rose stumbled away from her, heading for the railings edging the tank. Above them, Anubis withdrew, growling and nursing his wounds. His colossal frame rolled and sank like a whale at sea, vanishing into fans of smoke, the vaporous portal left open and empty.

Uncurling from his foetus of grief, Ben raised himself on his one good arm. Fatigue filled his muscles with lead and he half dragged his body forward, wincing with every foot gained. Cuts stung his shoulders and legs, a receding, needling tide. Exposed nerve endings itched and burned, new bone edging from his stump, raw tendons dangling at his side. Sweating, grunting, he hauled himself on, inching to Rose's aid. The air before him no longer gleamed, the cellophane aura giving way to a noxious darkness. When the statue had shattered, it appeared that the circle had broken too, negating the spell upholding the shield. He clenched his teeth, pushing harder against the steel surface, forcing himself to his knees. This was his last and only chance.

A cold pressure slithered over his legs. He glanced, horrified, over his shoulder, glimpsing a squirming mass, the impression of mandibles and compound eyes, and then the questing tentacle clenched around his ankle, wrenching him flat on his face. Steel smacked his jaw, rattling his teeth. His skull chimed an alarm. With one slick, hungry twitch, his stolen ground was sliding under him, cruelly reclaimed by the mob at his back.

Lurkers!

The horde had gathered in the air, their bristling shapes

merging with the night, a thick, packed vanguard floating several feet above the feed tank. Through the wall of carapace and barb, coiling tongues and flickering antennae, Ben could still see the knotted pipework, the outline of the distillation towers. Even here, on the threshold of the nether, the grey ones were not quite real, unable to assume corporeality. Still, that was little comfort. The great ghost-beasts, these mindless guardians, wandered forever at the limits of existence, sniffing out an excess of magic, a careless build-up of eldritch force. Kamenwati, drunk on magic and delirious with joy, must have reeked like an open cesspit, his invocations, his golden glyphs, a banquet of conjuration. The priest's defences were shattered and dispelled, exposing the ritual at the refinery, and so the Lurkers had come, their blind, lumbering forms drawn like flies to shit. And Ben, innately magical and the closest to them, was about to become a tasty entrée.

His remaining hand bulged and hardened, a claw the size of a truck wheel whipping desperately out. Metal screamed as his talons pierced the tank, gouging three long, jagged holes. The tentacle went taut with his resistance, an elastic band stretching to its limits, suckers constricting around his foot. Ben cursed and flipped on to his side, his arm painfully twisted. The ground under him whispered and slowed, scraping against his suit, but now he could see his would-be devourer, the monstrosity looming over him. The blank array of mesmerised eyes. The bulging, cadaverous mantle. The snapping beak about to swallow him.

His legs swelled, the suit melting around his calves, merging with bestial brawn. Bones elongating, flesh fluid, his feet sprouted further talons. His back toes stabbed down like knives, striking sparks from steel. He jerked to a clumsy halt, crying out with the sick sensation of his organs trying to fly through his ribcage.

Thus anchored, he lay panting as the phantom fucker vented a wail. The other Lurkers shuffled closer, drooling over this crumb in their midst. Nothing would stop them from ripping him apart, dragging bits of fabled meat off into the nether. *What a noble end.* The beaked creature shoved its mass against its comrades, seeking to deter them from its meal. Countless eyes returning to Ben, other tentacles slithered out. It was a pallid hydra come to finish him. One yank and he was on the move again, sliding slowly, helplessly towards the Lurker's maw.

"*No! Eat the priest. Eat the fucking priest!*"

The thing didn't seem to understand him. A tentacle coiled around his neck.

At first, Ben thought that loss of oxygen had caused the change in the atmosphere. Spots swarmed across his vision, reminding him of the killer bees. The night grew brighter, the thudding in his ears louder, taking on a resonant quality. A faint sizzling joined the din and there was something wrong with the sky, the seeping stars and frozen corona shifting as though seen through cracked glass. The prismatic vista filled with light, a trailing silver beam shooting out across the desert, a final, glittering hallucination. The train at the end of the tunnel. Death.

No. Clicking and flailing, the Lurkers drew back as the beam sliced across the space between Ben and the ghosts. Mottled limbs, slick with ichor, writhed and recoiled like salted slugs. A brief hiss, and severed tentacles thumped on the tank, instantly vanishing in swirls of mist. Released from the noose, Ben gasped, his head thrown back, sucking in air. Neck smarting, he squinted to follow the length of the beam.

Impossibly, a rider was galloping along it, the hooves of his snow-white steed striking pearly sparks. Like some wingless latter-day Pegasus, the stallion swooped from the night-bound sky. The thudding in Ben's ears resolved into a thunderous charge.

"*Hai! Hai!*"

The Lurkers erupted into chaos at the rider's cry, the mob falling over itself in its haste to retreat. Here was magic that not even the ghosts would taste, a poisoned river winding through oblivion, left behind by a long-departed race. Here was magic that had severed worlds, a power that belonged neither here nor there, and the Lurkers would not come near it. Von Hart had described the Silver Leys in Berlin. They were unmapped roads left behind by the Fay, cutting through the gulfs of the nether and heading God knows where. The envoy had claimed that he could steer these byways within certain earthly limits. That was how he had rescued Ben from the underground car park, snatching him from the clutches of the CROWS.

"Oh dear, *Liebling*," he said, by way of greeting. "Must I do everything?"

Here he was again, at this desperate hour. Blaise Von Hart, envoy extraordinary. His silk kimono, blood red and star-spangled, fluttered and shone as he slowed his horse, his milk-white legs clamped to its flanks, his delicate hands pulling at the reins. The stallion champed and trotted on the spot, its nostrils steaming. Von Hart smoothed his strict blonde parting, making sure that no hair was out of place. Then he leaned from the saddle, peering down at the mess sprawled below him. He pursed his lips, his cheekbones making a bust of his face. When he removed his sunglasses, his sharp violet eyes looked distinctly unimpressed.

Ben groaned. He tried to sit up, then fell back on the tank. Groaned again.

"Like a . . . bad penny . . ."

"Your gratitude is noted. You know, you're running up quite a bill."

"What are you doing here? I thought you said—"

"Get up. Get up, you oaf. You think I came to make chit-chat? You have work to do."

Ben pushed himself to his knees. He regarded his stump and claw. He was between states once more, the main attraction at a freak show.

"*Schnell! Schnell!*"

The envoy galloped off, his horse leaping skyward. The stars his rodeo and the Ley his lasso, Von Hart hurried to round up the Lurkers, chasing them away from the feed tank. Ben watched him go, muttering his thanks. Then he lurched to his feet, assessing the scene.

His first concern was Rose. He found her in the fog, picking her out by her torn gown and messed-up hair. She leant weakly against the railings, searching for the steps that spiralled down to the car park.

Yes, get out. Get away . . .

Nan Nemain hopped up behind her, her eyes set on the escaping sacrifice. Again Ben cried out, and again Rose didn't hear him. Lips quivering, the witch extended a stubby finger. Sensing her presence, Rose turned, shock twisting the wounds on her face. The railings rippled under her hands, the hexed metal sinuous and fluid, snaking up and stretching like jungle vines towards her. Inches from her flesh, the steel tendrils screeched and faltered, curling like thread away from flame. Rose leapt away from the railings, her clenched jaw and wide eyes telling Ben that she moved on adrenalin alone. Nan frowned at her outstretched hand, finger pulling the trigger on an empty spell. The witch tried again, an incantation flying from her throat.

As soon as the words struck the air, the fog around Rose grew sooty and thick, a viscid wave surging over the ground. Muck spilled around Rose's knees, bubbling and sucking at her legs, but before the morass could take hold, it was thinning and dispersing, drifting apart in slimy shreds. Nan swore, the curse unseemly on her young lips, and her expression dissolved into doubt as Rose – finding herself unharmed – shook off the dregs and stumbled towards her.

It took Ben a moment to understand. Rose was human, with no innate defence against magic. The CROWS had had no problem snatching her before. Why couldn't they now? With relief rushing from his lungs, he realised that the sigils and whorls etched on her skin must be stronger than the witch had supposed, protecting her from supernatural influence. Kamenwati had wanted to safeguard his prize, his living (*living!* The thought shone like a neon sign) piece of bait. The priest's precautions now worked against him. More confident with every step, Rose advanced on Nan Nemain, perhaps only seeing a naughty child, one she raised a hand to chastise, her tightly drawn lips far from motherly. The witch glanced over her shoulder, anxiously seeking assistance. Following her gaze, Ben saw the priest rising from the gloom, his face coloured by more than just blood. Kamenwati bared his teeth, but turned away. He had no use for his offering now. He scanned the portal above him. Finding the abyss empty, the god withdrawn, he tore off his jacket, took three strides past the stupefied Khadra and, with a harsh, guttural word, threw it over the dormant Star. Gingerly he picked up the stolen gem, safely swaddled by a silk lining and worsted wool, and all but tiptoed back to the little girl, eager to salvage the means of insurrection.

Not on my watch. Willing strength into his legs, Ben leapt into the air, bounding across the distance. He landed awkwardly, shock jolting into his thighs from the dent that spread under his feet. The priest crumpled under him, his protest slammed from his lungs and his precious bundle rolling away from him. Kamenwati scrabbled at Ben's chest, neck and cheeks. His fingernails broke against scales, his fists beating on tough red flesh with the same impact as thrown cotton-wool balls. Kneeling over his quarry, Ben grabbed the priest's collar, his claw crushing his fancy bow tie. He pulled Kamenwati's face toward his own, his breath scorching enervated skin.

"Should've stayed dead. By the time I'm through with you, you'll wish you had."

Groaning, flecks of spittle on his lips and chin, the priest tried to wriggle away. Lethargy clung to his efforts, his charms disrupted, the sorcerous rush leaking away. Ben had seen the same thing in Club Zauber, the envoy shivering in cold turkey and panting at the end of the catwalk, his forehead dripping, his strength sapped. Kamenwati might as well have wrestled a python. Still he was defiant.

"You idiot! You imbecile! You dumb, blundering brute! Why choose them? *Them!* You're a fucking monster! They'll never accept you in a million years!"

Ben flinched. The priest spoke directly to his fears, just like Atiya had in the Alps, stoking them like hot coals, and the words burned no less than before.

That is your dream. You long for a normal life.

Under him, Kamenwati grew calm, watching him, sensing his doubt. Claw around his throat, Ben could not stop him from reaching up and clamping his hands to the sides of his head. The priest's palms felt like winter, hissing against Ben's heat. Ben tried to pull back, wrench himself free, but Kamenwati held him fast, his voice whispering into his mind.

Does your dream mean so little? Look!

A blink of thought, a page flipping over to the next, and Ben's vision snapped inward, the priest, the portal and the tank gone. He saw himself walking through a museum – the Museum of Antiquities, he thought – a red-haired, ordinary man in boot-cut jeans and a T-shirt. Maybe he didn't look too shabby, either. Josh Homme on his day off. He browsed the displays, the crumbling boat and the painted mummies, just an everyday tourist minding his business.

The scene changed, a wind stirring water, and Ben was sitting in an aisle seat of EgyptAir Flight MS792 – he knew this because it said so on his ticket – roaring over the deep blue Med en route to a holiday in Cairo. The appointments at the office could wait. His secretary would field all calls.

Another ripple and he was dancing in a club in Berlin, some pouting girl pressing up against him in the crush and the sweat and the music. He took a swig from his bottle of beer. Smiled at her. Thought about asking her back to his hotel. He was just a man, after all. Just a man with needs.

The scenes flashed by in his mind's eye, waves overlapping. He sprawled on the couch in number 9 Barrow Hill Road, half watching the evening news, the carousel of war and drought and crime and death that had nothing whatsoever to do with him, removed as they were from his comfortable house, with the nice wine cellar that had nothing whatsoever under it. No sliding walls. No secret stairs. No mounds of treasure. Because he was a man. Just a man.

And then he was in the park in New York, walking hand in hand with Rose McBriar, all their tomorrows laid out before them. Both of them a sped-up flower, bright and brief, fleeting as dust and yet so precious, so endless in the landscape of his heart.

He let the visions wash over him, lulling him with aching desires, the velveteen music of dreams.

Kamenwati whispered.

There will be no bounds in my empire. No gifts I cannot give.

Ben tasted salt, a sea of invitation, hot, unbidden tears. Blinking them away, his mind fumbling toward the present, he found himself staring down at the priest. Kamenwati, who could take his pain away, lay all his loneliness to rest, exorcise the ghost of centuries that haunted his soul . . .

"You call me a monster." Ben let go of Kamenwati's throat, watching him fall back on the tank, the priest's hands slipping from his skull. "You call me a monster and maybe I am . . ."

He struggled to force out his words. The chaos of the week had left its mark, a lesson seeded in his mind, blooming into weary epiphany. The truth was he had lived with his feet in two worlds ever since Maud had found him in the woods, and on and on down the long, long years, half man and half beast, dousing his remorse with bottles of Jack and seeking solace in women's arms. He had clung to the Lore like an anchor, the bedrock of his hope, but in the end, even that couldn't save him.

"But being a monster is an *act*, a choice, not just a physical state . . ."

He had hidden in self-pity and excuses, working for criminals and shunning the light – but change had found him regardless, rising from old and unwatched graves. He had *let* things come to this pass. It was all his fault. If only he had stayed vigilant, forgotten dreams, put his efforts to the greater good . . .

Regret was useless.

He gave his answer. "Same goes for being human. To face the unknown without magic, without gods. That is also a choice."

The priest didn't care for the sermon. He tried to turn and

crawl away, his wild eyes searching for the Star. Ben brought his knee down on Kamenwati's leg, hearing gristle crunch with grim satisfaction, the howl in his ears a pleasant rhapsody.

"*Why them?* I choose them because of the unknown, priest. Tomorrow and tomorrow and the next day. Fuck your cynicism. The humans *know* we're here. On some level, they remember. In storybooks. In films. The Remnants are a part of them, a long-forgotten part. There's hope in that. Hope for unity. For peace. Your gift is nothing. Just illusion and lies. The truth is I chose this shit. To stay awake. To be alone. And they say that the truth always hurts."

Kamenwati lashed out, a clumsy punch. Ben caught the priest's fist in his palm, a golf ball in a baseball mitt. *Crack*. His wrist bone shattered and his fingers bent back, grisly shards sticking through his glove.

"*No!*" The old man squirmed in his grasp, his legs kicking out, rattling on the tank. "I am Baba Kamenwati! Kamenwati the reborn. *I am death! I am death!*"

Ben nodded. "Yeah. You are." He stood, dragging the priest upright, the withered husk of Maurice Bardolfe a scarecrow dangling from his claw. "And you're welcome to it."

Muscles flexing, arm winding back, Ben twisted his hips and released, flinging Kamenwati high in the air. The priest spun over and over, a black-and-white blur across the stars. Screaming, he wheeled like a spent firework into the maw overhead, the churning rift of the portal. As he entered the breach, Ben saw an arm reach out, a mighty limb of black sinew and burnished gold, snatching the priest from his flight. He wailed as fingers closed around him, agony curdling with dread. Ruby eyes, bright and baleful, shone down the length of the god's canine snout, considering his catch. Somewhere in the depths beyond, Ben guessed that a pair of scales would be waiting, one of the pans bearing a feather to weigh against the sins of the heart. For a creature as heartless as Kamenwati, there could only be one outcome. He would pay for his crimes in the Hall of Truth. Anubis would surely summon Ammit – a half-dog, half-crocodile demon, if memory served – and watch as he ate the corrupt *ba*, condemning the priest to eternal suffering.

That suffering had already begun, judging by the screams.

The jackal god sank out of sight, retreating into the depths of the Duat and taking his struggling prize with him.

TWENTY-FIVE

The drifts of darkness above the feed tank thickened like wool around a spindle. With the priest gone, there was nothing to maintain his equations, the nuts and bolts of his spell, and the stalled continuum took up the slack. The portal swirled and slowly sealed, resolving into a thin black funnel, a drape drawn back to reveal the day. The stars faded into the blue, the ashen sands blushing with umber. Birds squawked and wheeled above the city, flustered and returning to roost. The sun blinked a ruddy eye, one moment near the horizon, the next half sunken under it. Like a ball released from a catapult, the moon escaped the temporal glue, then slowed in the heavens, continuing her voyage skyward. The syzygy was over. Time skipped a beat and played on, the stolen minutes reeling back in.

Ben threw his arm over his head as the levitating chains clanked on the tank, spooling in glittering coils. A length fell near him, demolishing the nearby railings, swinging over the car park and then falling still, a pendulum spent. As the echoes receded, he peered cautiously up at the portal. The spindle was shrinking, narrowing to a point above Khadra, who sat cross-legged a few feet away. The girl looked up with clear, grateful eyes, her spread arms embracing the storm. Head thrown back, she drank in the murk, sucking it up like mud from a well. Smoke filtered into her nose and mouth, entwining her torso and limbs with a dense, obscuring cloak. A throb of mist, a tenebrous belch, and glossy scales folded around her. The Crook, the Pschent and the jacket swaddling the Star were swallowed by yards of saurian flesh.

Ben cringed in the shadow of wings. Atiya loomed above him, Dark Queen and last of the First-Breed, friend of Hatshepsut and ruler of a vanished land. The first stars twinkled on her horns. Back and forth her tail swished, slicing the settling dusk. Caught in the fire of her eyes, a mouse between the paws of a lion, Ben also caught her intent. Her silence was a weight on his startled mind.

"*Wait!*"

Atiya did not wait. She did not speak, granting him neither praise nor scorn. He could see she was hurt, the wound in her flank still dripping effervescence, and she seemed less daunting, less *solid* than before. The priest had cut the chain of her anchor with a blade of spells and dislodged her corporal foothold, and the split had apparently taken its toll. Now, with Khadra back in her possession, her regalia absorbed, she wasn't about to waste any time on the worm who'd freed her. Ben had chased her of his own accord, uninvited, unwanted. *Go back to your slumber, mas.* From London to Cairo the Queen had taunted and teased him, fought him and left him for dead. She had never asked for his help, her purpose belonging only to herself. That purpose, he knew, had now been served, one way or another. Kamenwati was done. Reluctantly, Ben accepted her dismissal; they had always been at odds. The Queen spread her wings, tensing against the desert wind. Like a stray patch of night, she took to the sky, leaving him in the stirred-up grit.

Nabad gelyo. Goodbye.

He let her think so. For now.

He climbed to his feet, searching for Rose. She was still by the railings, the warped metal a makeshift crutch, her body slouching like a rag doll. In the last rays of sunset, the sigils and whorls upon her skin shone a sickly red. It squeezed his heart to see her, and there was guilt there too – for leaving her in the first place, for a certain kiss in the Alps and his longing for mythical flesh . . . But Rose was breathing, still alive. *Yeah, you were wrong about that.* He sent his silent reproach after the Queen. Then he pushed his feelings aside in his concern for the lingering threat, and scanned the area with savage eyes.

The witch was nowhere to be seen. He staggered to the edge of the tank, already knowing what he would see. Nan Nemain hadn't hung about. With the priest stunned by the magic brick and finding Rose immune to her spells, the witch had cut her losses and fled. She was running down the staircase that spiralled around the tank, one hand clutching the hem of her dress, her pigtails streaming out behind her. Ben watched her reach the bottom, wondering whether to give chase, the ache in his bones and pain in his stump protesting against the idea. Nan splashed through shallow muck as she hurried across the car park, the pooling oil splattering her shoes. She watched the tanks at the plant entrance, their guns pointing vainly upward and now slowly beginning to turn, but the soldiers weren't about to open fire on a little girl. Or what *passed* for a little girl. As she headed for the Phantom IV, a funeral barge ready to depart, the witch went through fluid transformations, her juvenile form elevating on high stilettos and stockinged legs, her frilly green dress melting into a leather bikini. Holding on to her conical hat, her hair wild, Miss Macha glanced over her shoulder, a flash of smeared mascara and lipstick, making sure she had shaken off pursuit. She shrunk again as she reached the Rolls, fighting to wrench the rear door open, the lightless void inside the cab framing the bulge of her hunched back.

Babe Cathy, *grande dame* of the Coven Royal, paused for a moment to look up at Ben. The tux she wore would have fitted Nan Nemain, the crone's face rendered uglier by the snappy suit. Under her purple perm, her wrinkles converged in a spiteful mosaic. Rings adorned her fingers, emeralds and rubies catching the light as she brought the Cuban cigar to her lips. She sucked in a lungful of smoke, and Ben realised that she was grinning, her petty triumph souring the distance. His knuckles whitened around the railings. *No, no, no* . . . Casually the witch flicked the cigar into the air, the red end spinning, trailing smoke. As it fell, she turned and clambered into the cab, the darkness closing around her, the rear door slamming shut.

The cigar splashed down. A blue wave rushed across the car park, spilling out towards the feed tank. Fire skipped from puddle to puddle, a riddle racing down slick black veins, joining into a rippling deluge. The Phantom swam in the mirage, its polished paintwork and windows reflecting the sweeping flames. Grimy clouds enveloped the scene, shrouding the stalled corral of tanks, a curtain over their impotent guns. Ben watched, paralysed, as the limo's wheels started to roll, the CROWS leaving him stranded on the pyre. Burning fuel stung his nostrils, scratching at his throat. Coughing, he backed away from the railings, heat gusting from the ground below and shoving against his chest and face.

A shadow, thicker than smoke, fell over the car park. The dense cloud dwarfed the Phantom, a brisk downward rush of air fanning the rising flames. Ben looked up, seeking the source of the blast. Through watering eyes he saw the Queen plunging from the sky, wings folded, talons outstretched. With a skull-rattling crunch, Atiya brought her full weight down upon the vehicle. Metal crumpled. Glass shattered. Tyres burst. The silver figurehead, a bare-breasted hag on a broom, took flight from the bonnet and spun into the blaze, a glinting kamikaze dive. Then the Queen snapped out her wings. She swept up over the wreckage, jags of chrome trickling from her claws. She banked, veering south, and with a lash of her tail was gone.

A pancake rested on the tarmac, black and unmoving. Dented doors hung from their hinges like loose and rotten teeth. The buckled cab and fenders resembled a concertina, its music rudely silenced. Smashed headlights winked in the flames, dangling from a mangled grille. A stray hubcap wobbled through the smoke, on its way to nowhere.

Ben had no time to revel in the sight. A moment later and the car park vanished, sinking under the inferno. Hungry tongues crashed over the railings, consuming the scene below. Still between states, Ben's scales instantly thickened, his natural armour resistant to heat, but even he could not survive this for long. And Rose had no such protection. It was only a matter of time until the punctured tank reached boiling point, the liquid inside igniting, hurling the East Katameya Oil Refinery in a fractured compass across the sands.

He turned and ran, his haunches swelling and his stride lengthening as he pounded across the top of the tank. Rose stumbled away from the railings, the fire leaping up there too, travelling from the flooded loading bays. Flames licked the base of the distillation towers and corkscrewed around the pipework, the leaking structure feeding the onslaught. He watched her baulk at his approach, her eyes drinking in his terrible size. He came at her like a behemoth, propelling his bulk on one forearm – the other maimed and curled to his breast. His right wing, a mess of bone and flayed membrane, fluttered like rags in the squall. Overcome,

Rose sank to her knees, her gown ballooning around her. She pressed her hands to her mouth, perhaps protecting herself from the fumes, perhaps stifling a scream. Then her hands dropped into her lap, a vague recognition creeping through her dread.

"Ben . . .?"

Flames surrounded the platform now, washing over the toppled barrels, the spill around them a burning lake. The blaze devoured the scattered debris, the blood-smeared symbols and the grotesque shapes of Ammit, Shezmu and Set, the statues silhouetted by the glare. Ben rushed on, the conflagration scorching his tail. Oil-free patches dotted the tank here and there, islands in a boiling sea, and he bounded from one to the other, vaulting over the spreading furnace. Rose sat in a shrinking oasis, a blustering circle closing around her. The sweltering air tugged at her dress, her hair weaving into strands of molten gold.

An explosion rocked the refinery. The west side of the feed tank ruptured. A crimson tree sprouted in the sky, hot, lethal fruit shaken from its branches. Debris rained down, clunking on the roofs of the office buildings. Windows dissolved in a sparkling mist, shards tinkling into the maelstrom. The factory mezzanines groaned and shuddered. Pipes burst. Walkways collapsed. The blast threw Ben from his feet, the ground careening under him. Roaring, he hauled himself up, a graceless seven-ton phoenix. Ash and smoke closed hands around his throat. His wings thrashed, flattening the flames. Stealing a breath, he bulled his way down the makeshift corridor, burning chunks of metal thudding on his spine.

Reaching Rose, he flung his crimson length around her, his tail sweeping out and reducing the nearby railings to scrap. His horned snout met its arrowhead tip, encompassing Rose in a twelve-foot-high plated barrier. The inferno surged against him, biting at his scales, trying to get in. A minute more and the flames would take him, serve him up like a giant hog roast, Rose the apple in his mouth. Sheltering her with one wing, his claw reached out, gently closing around her body. She sagged in his grip, sapped by the heat, her scarred flesh shimmering. Soon blisters would bubble on her skin, the soaring temperature shrivelling her lungs.

He couldn't let that happen. Tearing his gaze away, he squinted up at the sky. Flames churned and rumbled, the deluge merging above the feed tank, a dazzling canopy over his head. Frost rimed his guts, the chill grip of memory. Once again he had the dizzying sense of time as a circle, history repeating, dooming him to the same old mistakes. Flames roared and he was back in Mordiford, the trees ablaze outside his cave, Maud choking beside him. Afraid to risk the burning boughs, he had crashed through the brush instead, seeking the mercy of the clearing well. That tale had ended in tragedy, with poison dripping from his claws and Maud gasping and spluttering her last.

My egg. My love.

He had been here before. And he had failed.

Rearing, he clutched Rose to his breast, the furnace whirling around him. Steadying himself, he spread his wings, letting the searing wind fill them. Horns piercing the blaze, haunches fired like a bow, Draco Benjurigan, Sola Ignis, leapt into the air.

Another explosion shook the refinery. The feed tank convulsed, spewing debris. Hurled on the updraught, dragon and damsel tumbled in flames, chased by embers across the desert sky.

TWENTY-SIX

Three figures met on the sands. Night had fallen, the stars coming out – the *true* stars – the lion, the bear and a creature that was neither man nor horse twinkling down on the desert. Under the moon, full in the sky, the surrounding dunes were an ocean of milk, sweeping to all horizons.

One of the figures turned from Cairo's glittering skyline toward the empty south, where a pillar of smoke and a ruby glow announced the site of the East Katameya Oil Refinery, burning in the dark. Lights flashed and sirens wailed along the distant road, fire trucks racing to pour water on the howling blaze. Even a mile away, ash and fumes sullied the air, and Blaise Von Hart wrinkled his nose, his distaste returning to the couple before him.

"*Scheisse!*" he said. "*Der Teufel ist los, ja?*"

A creature that was neither man nor dragon looked him in the eye. Ben, who didn't speak German, took the envoy's meaning anyway, wearily bearing his reproach. Covered from head to foot in grime and with smoke staining his suit, all he could manage was a shrug.

"We're alive, aren't we? And that bastard is dead."

If *dead* was the right word for it.

"Very good. I suppose we should throw a party. After all, it's not as if God knows how many people from New York to Cairo

397

are going to remember a pair of dragons. It's not as if vandalised museums, crashed cable cars and exploding factories can't be explained away."

"They'll forget," Ben said. "They always do. They'll put it down to—"

"Gas? Hallucinations? I'm afraid mobile phones and film cameras aren't prone to visions, *Dummkopf.*"

"Give it time. Rumours will spread. The same old Chinese whispers. A month from now, they'll call it a hoax. The latest internet craze."

The envoy didn't look convinced. His frown mirrored the cracked moon above.

"What do you care anyway?" Irritation crept through Ben's fatigue. "It's the Guild's job to—"

"Don't get me started." Von Hart tugged at the sleeve of his silk kimono, a gesture that revealed his feelings on the matter. He was worried, frightened even. The realisation struck Ben as strange, considering the envoy's usual composure. "The Guild has enough problems. As you might guess, Paladin's Court is in uproar. The global divisions will want answers. So will the Remnants. There is going to be a council. Perhaps even a trial."

"Terrific. I stopped the priest from ending the world. Now they're looking for a scapegoat?"

"We all live under the Lore, Ben. This," his hand swept out, taking in the flaming refinery, the unseen chaos of the week, "this changes everything."

Von Hart spoke softly, without blame, but Ben knew it was the truth. After centuries of an uneasy truce, a group of Remnants had staged a daring coup. Aided by Baba Kamenwati, the Coven Royal had brought about a breach in the Lore, manipulating two desperate humans to rouse a goddess from the Sleep. And the conspiracy extended beyond that. House Fitzwarren had played their part, the outlawed family throwing in with witches, a betrayal that continued to shock him. Of course the Guild were not about to take that lightly, once the facts became plain.

And he had committed his own crimes, hadn't he? His transformations the least of them. He didn't want to think about the witnesses left in his wake. The news channels that right this second were probably buzzing with unexplained sightings. The websites that were close to crashing with pictures of curious carnage. The tabloids about to run out of ink with all the preposterous claims. The envoy was right. The Guild would need more than Jenny Hanivers this time. Then there was his obligation to the Pact. He'd had no time to contact the Guild, warn its agents of the crisis, once he was hot on the trail. Whoever took on the role of chairman might forgive him for both these things – after all, he *had* saved their bacon – but he knew they wouldn't forgive him for Rose.

. . . any Remnant found in breach of this clause shall face swift and lawful execution.

The thought turned him to the woman at his side, the frost in his guts returning. She leant weakly against his shoulder, her straggling hair streaked with oil, her tattered gown brushing the sands. The hieroglyphs on her face, her arms, her neck and chest, carved deep enough for the welts to show under all the oil and ash. He didn't catch the scent of bergamot now, only blood and exhaustion. He was not the same person who had sat in the Legends bar in New York, downing Jack and feeling sorry for himself, but his feelings for her had not changed. The ache was deeper now, a combination of shame and fear, curdling with new heights of vigilance. For all the good it would do him. He couldn't kid himself any longer. At the best of times, the worlds of Remnants and humans didn't mix well, and Rose had almost been crushed in between them.

"What they don't know can't hurt them," he said. Unknowingly, he was wincing, clutching the back of his neck. "And they *don't* know, do they? Any more than I did."

Von Hart looked uncomfortable. He shifted a little, crossing his arms.

"*Nein.* But—"

"Then take her away, far from here. Somewhere the Guild won't find her. Somewhere my enemies can't reach. If your stupid council raise the matter, we'll tell them that she died in the fire. The Guild never needs to find out. Take her and put her in an ivory tower. A palace in the clouds. Behind a rainbow. You're Fay, after all. Isn't that what you do?"

The envoy opened his mouth to protest, but the reply came from the woman at his side.

"No." Rose pushed away from Ben and staggered a few steps up the dune, creating some distance between them. Coldness flooded into the gap, her shoulders tensing against pain, the moonlight silvering her scars. "You can take me away," she said to Von Hart. "But only as far as the US Embassy. I'll make my own way from there."

"Rose!"

Her spine stiffened at Ben's dismay. Throwing off the dregs of her trance, the smothering heat of the fire, she turned to face him, her eyes like stones. Smoke and oil masked her expression, but Ben could not mistake her resentment.

"I told you before, you don't own me. You don't."

"Rose, you don't know what you're saying. I—"

It seemed that she did, however.

"You've lied about so much. You said that nothing and no one could hurt us. Christ, you're not even human." Her tongue clicked, a bitter blade. "A Central Park thing? Really? Fuck!"

Rose was no fool. He knew that. That day by Cleopatra's Needle had left her with her fair share of doubts and suspicions. Ordinary men didn't have the strength to throw thugs up into trees. Or swell up like rhinos under the skin. He had hoodwinked her over other things too – flames that somehow failed to burn him and perfume guessed from five floors down – but all his excuses were pointless now. However much she had wanted the truth, it no longer mattered. The struggle on the tank had exposed him. What more was there to say?

"I thought it was for your own good."

"No. No you didn't. I was a trinket to you, and bait to them." Her winter-cloud eyes were full of ice and her voice held the same flat tone, telling him that this wasn't a debate. "I'm neither of those things. And I don't belong here. I don't belong with you. I should never have let you . . ." and here she faltered, "buy all those stupid books." She swallowed, hard. The fists at her sides betrayed her resolve. "I just want to go home."

"Rose, I'm sorry. It isn't that simple. What about . . ." He tried to muster the words. "What about . . ." He couldn't bring himself to say it.

"This burden you've given me?" She raised a hand and cupped her stomach. Gently, though, he thought. "That isn't your decision. You know I've made mine. When the time comes, I'll figure out what to do."

"You said it was what you wanted."

"Was it?"

"You can't just turn your back on me!"

"Yes I can. That bastard, he . . . I felt the knife on my skin . . ." Her wounds held the memory, and she winced, choking it down. "Your friend here is right. This isn't over. And I won't go through it again."

"You need time." Ben hated the whining sound of his voice, the way that the sand sucked at his feet. "Time to heal. Time to think. When I'm done with this shit, I'll come and find you. I'll find you and we'll talk."

But Rose was shaking her head.

"No. Stay away. From me. From us. I don't even know who you are any more." With this, she started up the dune, leaving ragged footprints. There was a horse on the crest, he saw, white in the moonlight, waiting. "I'm a survivor, Ben. And I have survived you."

Ben reached out. Then his hand fell to his side. He watched Rose walk away. Not because he wanted to, not because his heart wasn't breaking, but because he knew she was right. He had flown across half the world to save her, clinging on to a slender hope, two worlds joined as one. *A normal life with the woman you love.* And in the end, she had saved *him.* Saved him and left him with the truth, bitter and beyond doubt. They were different creatures on different paths. Until Remnants and humans learned to coexist, until the Fay returned, the sleepers awoke and the severed world was one, tomorrow could hold no peace for them. As long as he loved her, she would be in danger.

Maud, Rose and a thousand damsels. It had taken him too long to find out.

He barely heard Von Hart approach. Barely felt the hand on his shoulder.

"Say it," Ben said. He blinked away tears. "Like trying to catch the wind, right? Just say I told you so."

Instead, the envoy sighed and squeezed Ben's arm, a brief, cool comfort.

"I'll see that she gets home safe," he said. "Cairo is a mess, but the dead have all returned to their graves. All but one, that is."

"The Queen."

"Atiya is going home. Will you follow her?"

Ben wiped his face. After a breath, he nodded.

"Good. Then this is *auf Wiedersehen*. You know where I am if you need me."

The envoy moved off, heading up the dune. His silk kimono fluttered with stars and he appeared to leave no footprints in the sand. Before he drifted out of earshot, Ben called out after him, his admiration reluctant and gruff.

"You play your cards close to your chest, but you knew all along, didn't you? Ghosts from limbo. The living and the dead trading places. You knew that Kamenwati had risen. You knew what the CROWS were up to and still you let me blunder into this. Why? To wake me up? To teach me a lesson?"

Von Hart paused for a moment, appearing to consider. Then he smiled and replied over his shoulder.

"Never trust the Fay, Ben."

He continued up the dune.

Ben didn't know how long he stood there, counting his losses and waiting for the pain to subside. The numbers seemed endless and the flames, he knew, would only cool with his last breath. He watched the envoy gallop off towards the city, bearing the damsel with him, a plume of dust in their wake. He watched the moon rise a little higher and the stars wheel by overhead, blind or indifferent to his tears.

Then he turned to the south, the only place left open to

change. He spread his wings, embracing the wilderness. Had the Age of Myth truly ended? Lately it didn't feel that way. With a sweep of his tail, Red Ben Garston took to the sky, into nothing that resembled a happy-ever-after.

Noqo

Sanaag Region, Somalia

A girl had crossed the desert and woken a god.

For three days, Khadra had looked through serpent's eyes as Atiya spanned the cloudless sky. Through sunlight and moonshine and with barely a pause to rest, the Queen had beaten her wings for home, the Land of Punt. For Ta Netjer. God's Land. Together, bound spirit to flesh, the dragon and the girl soared high above the earth. Far below, the yellow teeth of the Red Sea shore narrowed to the Bab-el-Mandeb, the Gate of Grief, the rocky and perilous strait that churned between the Horn of Africa and the Arabian peninsula. The Queen's shadow was a dot upon the waters where the two great continents strained to kiss. It flowed across the waves and the tiny traffic, the ships and planes that crossed the Gulf of Aden. South and south they went. South and then veering east, Khadra feeding on spirit and spirit on flesh.

But their bond was weaker, the girl sensed it. At the refinery, the holy man had torn them apart and their severance had taken its toll. The Queen's wound would not heal and bled tendrils of smoke, a vapour trail in the atmosphere. Atiya must bring *barwaaqo* or everything was lost. If the Queen failed, Khadra's quest would have been in vain. Every footstep on hot sand, from the village of Dhuroob to the tomb outside Elaayo, worthless and a waste. She might as well have flung the map sketched in charcoal on cloth to the *jilal* wind. Or simply stayed in Qardho, refusing to fulfil her destiny, offering herself to the toothless old hag. The girl hadn't known that it was Long Ear at the time, waste haunter, demon, eater of children. A nightmare from folklore. A remnant from an older, vanished land. Nor had she believed the hag's claim that she had given Ayan, her mother, the map and the sacred stone. The cylindrical shard of black rock, ringed by arcane symbols, had rested in Khadra's shabby fur bag. At the time it had never occurred to the girl that it was perhaps a fragment, chipped from a talon equally black – the claw of the serpent Queen, no less – many centuries ago. At the time, she hadn't realised how they were deceived.

Later, she had thought so. Later, she had found out.

The girl had crossed the desert and woken a god. It all seemed like years ago, but it had only been days. And now came the time for *noqo*. Now came the time for return.

The Queen swept over the ocean, above the long grey decks of supertankers and the pirates that dogged them, small rusty boats speeding in their wake. She passed above warships and fishing skiffs, UN vessels carrying food and the odd, brave cruise liner. She passed above tuna and sharks. Little escaped the eyes of the Queen and the girl she bore.

Together, Atiya and Khadra returned to Punt. Punt that was now Somalia. And the two of them returned with treasures. A Star. A Crook. A Pschent.

She held them now, this girl that was a beating heart, a heart inside a queen. They were the least of the wonders she'd seen. She had seen towers of light and glass scratching at the sky. She had seen fields as green as jade, lush rolling hills. She had howled into the driving rain high above the mountains and touched the snow carpeting their flanks. She had seen great rivers longer than years and forests wider than dreams. And she had seen the darkness too. The factories and the sleepless smoke. The sprawling cities that growled and screamed, gnawing at the earth. She had seen the people in fancy clothes with sad and empty faces, who jammed the roads with endless cars and tossed food from open windows like jewels from a bottomless bag. She had seen places where the gods still smiled and no one looked up to notice. Bright, dirty, blind places.

Khadra had seen the world.

Had it all been for nothing?

No, she couldn't believe it. The CROWS might have spun a web, but the Queen had managed to break free and Khadra would never give up. There was still a chance for them. Severed or not, a chance. If doubt was leaking into the crack left by their unbinding, the girl did her best to ignore it.

Still the air whispered and sang, rushing past her ears.

You broke the Lore. The . . . Pact . . .

No. She wouldn't listen to *him* either. The red stranger had found her in the Alps, briefly sharing the void where she hid, the soul with which she communed. And the stranger followed them still, a weary speck in their wake.

There's a balance to things.

No, she wouldn't listen. The only balance that mattered was the love between the Bull and the Cow. That and that alone. The Cow had long since turned her eyes away, blighting the land with famine and drought. It was Khadra's destiny to set things right.

And yet . . . And yet . . .

She must not think about it.

I am not the same, Khadra thought. *I am not the same as before.*

Now, on the morning of the third day, the Queen soared over the Gulf and reached the burning shore. Khadra looked down through serpent's eyes and saw that they had returned.

I am not the same, the girl thought. *But the land. The land is the same.*

In the distance, a dark line marked the crests of the Surud mountain range, rising to meet Shimbiris, the country's highest peak. Navigating by the knife-like heights, the Queen glided into the east, passing over the plateaus and plains of the Sanaag hinterland. All Khadra saw was dust. Dust like a dying cough. Dust like the seas of the moon. Dust on dust on dust. Down there, where the rivers trickled through thick mud. Down there, where the cracked wastes scowled at the sun. Down there, where the corn withered and the cattle slumped and the huts huddled in the heat. Down there, where the flies danced on the swollen children and all the wells ran dry. Down there, where Huur, the Reaper, the Old Marabou, stalked and called and pecked.

Down there, people were waiting. Waiting for her.

The *taalo* rose from the sands, a crushed honeycomb of ancient rubble. Crooked pillars supported the sky, the roof caved in long ago, the stacks edging the shattered sanctum like broken yellow tusks. A group of men stood at the top of the steps leading up to the temple floor. With the benefit of bestial vision, Khadra picked out their military uniforms, the glint of their guns, the flash of sunglasses as they looked up, marking the Queen's descent. A loose circle of large peaked tents fanned out from the bottom of the steps, white canvas flapping in the wind. The small encampment left the girl in no doubt that the men had expected their arrival. Beyond the tents, several jeeps and a couple of helicopters, their rotors still and bowed, crouching in

the dust. She didn't recognise the sword-over-shield motif stencilled on the sides of the vehicles, and neither did the Queen,
but both of them could guess what it meant. This wasn't a
welcoming party.

Atiya did not turn back. She circled down over the temple,
thrashing her wings in mid-air. Grit swirled across the space,
forcing the soldiers back, their arms thrown over their faces.
One of the men, blinded and stung, thumped into the side of
a pillar, dislodging a chunk of hieroglyphic brick. Another raised
his machine gun, but a barked command brought him up short,
the barrel lowering as he skittered into the lee of the wall. Bullets
wouldn't help them here, would only bounce off scales. The
edifice suffered a localised quake, the rock trembling and groaning
as, claws stretched, Atiya alighted, a black hole swallowing the
sun. Flagstones popped and splintered. Wingtips brushed pillars,
threatening to topple them, bury the troops under debris. Static
whipped along the colonnades like thin blue mooring lines,
crackling and weaving from stone to scale, a frenzied aura
scorching the temple floor.

In her breast, Khadra felt the brewing storm. The Queen's
horns, a corkscrew crown, reared above the tallest pillar. Her
neck loomed, drawing back, a plated stem ready to bloom and
incinerate the men beneath her. These foolish men and their
flimsy Lore – yes, the Queen marked them now, her extraordinary senses reaching out, placing the agents of the Guild even
as she raged at their gall. She had not invited them here. Where
were their tributes? The insult shuddered through her. Though
her throne was dust and her realm a memory, she was every
inch the Queen of Punt, last of the First-Breed. She had not
slept for three and a half thousand years to let mortals debase
her.

Like a gate into night, her fangs slowly parted. Lightning whirled in her throat.

Then Khadra was reaching out, a spark of urgency in the Queen's mind.

Sheel!

Atiya did not want to stop. She wanted to spew white fire, bring *biriq* to the Guild. She wanted to rend and tear, barge her way down the temple steps, her wings sweeping the tents aside, reducing them to shreds of canvas and rope. She wanted to grab the metal machines, rip the jeeps and the helicopters apart, hurling wheels and blades high in the air. She wanted to scatter their Lore and what she thought of it from the tips of her claws. In a frenzy of violence, she would show these men just how little their authority meant. She would show them what it meant to challenge a queen . . .

But Khadra refused her. Muscle was no defence against the hands that gripped the Queen's will. The girl could feel Atiya's shock at this rebellion, the Queen roaring, her snout bucking, her forearms tensed. All the Queen could do was look down – Khadra could feel Atiya gazing through *her* eyes now – at the reason for her inner resistance.

The men had retreated, clutching their guns. A woman stood atop the temple steps, her skin blending with the Queen's great shadow. A light-green *dirac* billowed around her, the long, sheer dress accentuating her bony chest, her arms like river reeds. Bones and beads clacked around her neck, the tribal gewgaws of *sixir*, the old magic. Her braids pulled her face into a skull, her cheekbones sharp enough to cut glass. Still there was a glint in her eyes. Fear, Khadra thought, but also patience.

Khadra spoke.

"*Hooyo.*" Mother.

It wasn't a question. Khadra peered down at Ayan and tears prickled through the Queen's fire. Atiya was fighting her, the girl could feel it. Her teeth ached and her skin burned. Wasps swarmed around her nipples and between her legs, stinging, stinging, stinging. But Khadra had a foothold now. She was not the same girl who had come to this tomb. Using a chain of will, she pulled herself out of her hiding place. Hand over hand, she climbed, her feet pushing down the Queen's dismay.

No. You cannot. I am Queen of—

"Mother," Khadra said.

Ayan nodded. She took a hesitant step forward, her stiff shoulders contrasting with her trembling lips.

"Must I die?" she said. "I am prepared. If I cannot reach you, daughter, then I have no reason to live."

Khadra caught her mother's resolve in her mind, cradling her willing sacrifice alongside her doubt.

"Khadra," Ayan said, and her eyes were wet. "My lucky one."

Puzzled, the girl answered, her thoughts a flood.

Mother we have returned we are successful we found the Star the Crook the Pschent I have seen such things the world the world but the witches tricked us the dead man cut us but—

"Yes," Ayan said. "We were tricked."

But the Queen has come she has come and we bring barwaaqo *we bring God's rain*—

"No. It cannot happen this way. I should never have sent you. I was wrong."

Wrong? Mother? I don't . . .

Ayan opened her arms, prising the crack of Khadra's doubt a few inches wider.

"Khadra," she said. "Come home."

Darkness gathered around the girl. It sucked at her limbs like tar, shot through with livid sparks. In the nowhere depths the Queen howled, a cudgel beating at Khadra's mind, her soul ringing with rage and loss, shrill with desperation.

We struck a bargain! Blood for a boon!

This was true. Khadra did not deny it. Nevertheless, she had seen more than just the world alone. She had seen the danger of ghosts returned from the grave, how close they had come to losing everything. She had seen darkness and cold white fire. The Queen was great and promised salvation, but her lust for revenge had proved greater. Kamenwati could have destroyed her. The priest had almost usurped a god and plunged the earth into living death. Nor could Khadra shift the blame, much as she wanted to. Tricked or not, desperate or not, she could not ignore the fact that if she had not roused Atiya from her tomb, the risk of catastrophe would not have come about.

The red stranger had found her in the Alps and told her that there was a balance. It struck her now that the love between the Bull and the Cow was no different from the one he meant, that the Pact existed to hold back chaos, preventing disasters like the one she had escaped. Yes, she grasped that the Lore was flawed – perhaps it was a death sentence, as the Queen supposed, the Remnants facing extinction – but she had seen the dangers of breaching the Sleep, the evils that sprang forth. She understood the dilemma. A serpent Queen, a goddess returned to a modern-day country . . . Who could say what would happen? Hope and fear churned within her. The rains would come, and what else? Anarchy? Bloodshed? Revolution? People would view such power and crave it. Atiya would not bend to their will. The Lore would shatter and break. Had need blinded her like the Queen all those centuries ago, a spider turning to the scorpion, paying the price with betrayal and death? Was her ambition as mad as the priest's, at best a selfish desire? In Khadra's quest to bring *barwaaqo*, had she simply become a bringer of war?

She looked down at her mother, standing small and helpless on the stones.

In the end, the sight decided her. In the end, she was only a girl. Weary. Confused. *Homesick*. At that moment, Khadra would have given anything to sit with Ayan in their shack in Dhuroob, just to hold each other and let the dust take them, let the drought devour their bones. At least they would die together. At least they would die where they belonged.

Darkness and light were surging around her, a compound like oil and water, never meant to mix. With her shift of intention, her will reasserted the arcane physics, the division between reality and dream, the mortal and the divine. Like a diver tangled in seaweed, she kicked out for the surface, bubbles of smoke streaming from her mouth. The undertow pulled at her, unwilling to let her go. The Queen's wail was a meaningless mess, the words unintelligible as Khadra wrenched her mind away from their strange symbiosis. The bargain was false. The deal too dangerous. Khadra had seen the light and to the light she returned. Gasping, flailing, she broke the surface, shattered the walls of spectral union and slipped the bonds of shadow.

With a thump, a clatter and a clang, the Star, Crook and Pschent fell to the temple floor.

Then there was a girl running, racing across the flagstones, throwing off the vines of darkness that clung to her arms and legs. Escaping their lingering touch, Khadra flew into Ayan's outstretched arms, the bones and the beads clacking as she buried her face in her mother's breast.

Home.

She was aware of soldiers slipping around them, their boots

413

scuffing the dirt. A mother-and-child reunion clearly held less importance than the discarded relics, which Khadra, perhaps understanding human nature a little more deeply than when she had first come to this place, knew they would hurry to collect. Gently she released Ayan and turned to watch them. Like a bomb disposal unit, three men tentatively approached the Queen's regalia, but without Atiya's kindling presence, she could have told them they had nothing to fear. The Star was simply a diamond again, the uncut, fist-sized heart of a meteor. The Crook was an antique length of ivory, unearthed last year by a recently deceased professor. The Pschent was an artefact of Ancient Egypt, the tall double crown with snake and bird a shimmering, ornate marvel – but no more than that. Not any more. Khadra wondered how much time would pass before the relics gleamed behind glass again, in exhibitions in famous museums, the display cases locked along with their secrets.

Each soldier scooped up a piece of the Queen's regalia and hurried back across the temple floor, passing Khadra and Ayan as if they weren't there, as if they were ghosts from the sands, haunting this abandoned tomb. They loped down the steps, no doubt heading for the small encampment to report the relics' recovery. Khadra looked up at her mother. Before she had a chance to speak, another man was standing before them, the troop captain if the stars on the shoulders of his shirt were anything to go by. The visor of his cap glinted in the sun. His shades reflected Khadra and Ayan, who stood as still as leafless trees, warily awaiting his judgement.

"*Mimsaab*," said the man, greeting them curtly, but not without respect. "You remain in our custody. There are matters that require investigation. You and your daughter have broken the Lore."

Khadra stared at him. Ayan bowed her head. To argue for

mercy on the grounds of destiny seemed pointless now, no real vindication considering the wrongful summoning, the damage done and the near catastrophe. The Guild would surely hold a hearing. Punishment would come. Khadra saw dark days spread out before her with the vestigial insight of serpent wisdom. In many ways, she was changed.

The captain spread his hands, expecting them to speak. When they only offered him silence, he drew himself up and took a step towards them.

"Both of you must come with me."

A shadow arrested him. The captain visibly cringed as another man stepped forth from behind a pillar and, arms folded, stood in his way.

Khadra knew this man. His suit was dark, a sheer layer of small, charred scales, all covered in dust. She recognised the emblem on his chest, emblazoned in red and circled by yellow. The man's right arm ended at his wrist, the flesh there raw and bleeding. *Mending.* For three days the red stranger had followed them, chasing Atiya home. In all the confusion, Khadra hadn't heard him land. The strain of his journey showed in his face, pale under the mess of his hair. His eyes, however, held a fierce green fire, forbidding the captain's approach.

"No," the stranger told him. "They have suffered enough."

The captain didn't argue. He frowned uncertainly up at the broad-shouldered man and gave a curt nod, reluctantly submitting. They spoke briefly, and then the captain was striding off, the man beside him, heading for the tents and the jeeps and whatever judgement lay in store. The red stranger – Ben, his name was Ben – glanced her way before he vanished down the steps, but she thought his smile looked a little sad.

Khadra tugged on her mother's arm, a soft, calm insistence.

415

Ayan's face wrinkled in a question, and then understanding, she nodded. Together, mother and daughter shuffled down the steps and into the waste. No one watched them leave.

Khadra only looked back once. She alone saw the shadow standing by the altar, the heap of ruined stones that had drunk of her innocence. The lingering shadow, a glass vase filled with oil and swirling motes, resembled a woman, bare-breasted, shapely and proud, but she was much more than that. Or she had been once. The woman was only there for a moment, a figment, a memory, a ghost. Then she faded into the sunlight, returning to the past and to dreams and to the depthless place where the old gods sleep.

Khadra and Ayan had walked about a mile, trudging along the rough slabs of the inland road, when they stumbled upon the hooded vulture. The bird, a fat creature of lustrous feathers and scabby claws, rested on a yellow rock, watching them with beady eyes. It screeched as the two of them drew near, a remonstration or perhaps a curse, and ruffled its big black wings in a manner to suggest the greatest displeasure.

Khadra halted and stared at the bird. The vulture screeched again, mockingly, she thought, safe on its perch a few feet away. The girl smiled. She was no longer afraid of fireside tales, of long-eared hags who stalked the wastes, preying on poor lost children. In many ways, she was changed.

She raised an arm, one finger pointing at the bird. Ayan gave a cry as there came a great flash, a brief, blinding crackle of light. The vulture leapt from the rock and flapped into the air, squawking in obvious pain. The echoes followed the bird up and over the desert, its wings leaving a trail of smoke. The girl didn't think Dhegdheer would return.

Khadra took her mother's hand. At first Ayan recoiled from the heat, the tingling feel of her daughter's flesh. Then she sighed and relaxed. She let the girl lead her into the south, away from the outskirts of Elaayo and the endless, roaring laughter of the Gulf.

On the horizon, clouds gathered. Impossibly, they gathered. A billowing black mass was rumbling towards them, welcoming them home. Static danced and flickered in the depths. Tumbleweed rolled through the dust, scrawling a song or a prophecy. The sun glared in the darkening east, fearful of this challenge to his tyranny.

Khadra smiled at the light inside her and walked on into the desert.

And the sands whispered *roob*, rain.

The sands whispered *rajo*.

Hope.

Author's Note

Myths are alive. Stories aren't static. No matter how young or how old, myths are reborn every time a fresh pair of eyes alights on the page to read them.

I have taken several liberties with myths while writing this book. Please don't take my word for it. The stories are out there, waiting for you to read them again.

Among others, *The Romance of Fouke le Fitz Waryn*, *The Legend of the Lambton Worm*, *The Tale of the Mordiford Dragon* and *The Tale of the Shipwrecked Sailor* all went into this novel's bubbling cauldron. Keen-eyed readers will also note that the author has an interesting take on recorded history. Let me stress that this book takes place in the world of myth – a world much like our own – and in any case, who can say for sure which one is which?

Acknowledgements

Dreaming and writing are solitary arts, but the making of a novel is not. This is a good place to mention a handful of people who have helped this story leap from ember to flame.

Firstly, a special mention to Sarah Ann Watts for reading this story when *Embers* was only a short and for reading every chapter thereafter of the novel this became. Her feedback, loyalty and encouragement have proved invaluable and I am for ever indebted.

Thanks to John Jarrold, agent extraordinaire, for his excellent advice, confidence and enthusiasm.

Thanks to Tim Holman for giving me my shot, Anna Jackson for her fantastic editorial skills, insight and support, Joanna Kramer in London and Lindsey Hall in New York for the same and everyone on the Orbit team on both sides of the Pond. Thank you for sharing my vision. Thanks to Tracey Winwood for her patience with the interior symbols and for the fabulous book cover.

Thanks to Aunty Adele and everyone at Fox Spirit Books for bringing my stories to a wider audience. You rock. There are far too many friends, authors and artists to list on one page. All have inspired, encouraged and entertained me over the years, as I tapped away in this spare room or that, drinking tea (and wine) through life's various ups and downs, all across this fair isle of ours. Most notable of whom I'd like to thank are Liz

Smith, Holly Brown, Rhi Firth, Richard Varden, Jan Martin, Mike Watkin, Carolyn Ollson, Jane Hurley-Cosserat, Arron Bailey, Sam Morgan, Abi Harrison, Kelly Jones and Will Williams for boundless positivity, laughs, hugs and encouragement. Also to Julie Hutchins and Julia Knight for unflagging moral support. For fear of leaving anyone out, I will simply say that all of you have my eternal gratitude.

Thanks to Sue for tea and sympathy.

And with love to my family, far and wide, to whom I dedicate this novel.

Thank you.

Look out for the next Ben Garston novel . . .

Ben Garston broke the Lore. It's time to face the music.

Ben Garston – Red Ben to his friends – is about to find out that a resurrected goddess and an undead priest were the least of his worries.

Six months after the events of *Chasing Embers*, the breach in the Lore has shaken the Remnant world to its foundations. Blaise Von Hart, the Fay ambassador, is missing. The Guild has scattered in disarray, making room for the rise of a new human order, the fanatical saint cult named the Whispering Chapter. And the Whispering Chapter has no love of Remnants . . .

Worse, there has been another breach, a strumming of the mysterious mnemonic harp, splintered long ago after sending the Remnants into the Long Sleep. After centuries of slumber, the dragon Mauntgraul, the White Dog, sees the modern world and everything that Ben holds dear as a ready and waiting feast . . .

. . . coming soon!

www.orbitbooks.net

extras

orbit

www.orbitbooks.net

about the author

James Bennett is a British writer born in Loughborough and raised in Sussex, South Africa and Cornwall. His travels have furnished him with an abiding love of different cultures, history and mythology. He's had several short stories published internationally and *Chasing Embers* is his debut fantasy novel. James currently lives in west Wales and draws inspiration from long walks, deep forests and old stones . . . and also the odd bottle of wine.

Find out more about James Bennett and other Orbit authors by registering for the free monthly newsletter at www.orbitbooks.net.

interview

What was the inspiration behind *Chasing Embers*?
A medley of things, really. Fairy-tales and myths. Bond movies. Historical mysteries. Indiana Jones. The occult. When I sat down to write the novel, my main drive was to "make a movie I'd like to see". That was kind of my mantra at the start, but as I got into the research, it became deeper than that. It became "write a book that encompasses your love of Fantasy, old and new". In many ways, *Chasing Embers* is a love letter to the genre, so as you can imagine, a lifetime of inspiration went into writing it. Mostly, I wanted to have fun. I wanted to create a world to play in.

How much research did you carry out to write the book?
A mountain. The images tend to come to me well before the plot. I'll visualise a scene or a conversation, think, "Wouldn't it be cool if a dragon landed in the middle of that…?" and then realise I know next to nothing about the subject. That was certainly the case with the medieval aspect and all these wonderful descriptions of fabulous beasts. To the medieval mind, these creatures really existed and the resonance of that helped the story. Imagine a world

where all of it was true! The historical research is a learning curve and that makes the books interesting to write. I'm educating myself through bunkum, in a way. So far I've learnt about the roof of the British Museum, oil refineries and a bit about Ancient Egypt. I don't worry about getting the odd thing wrong (though I do my best to be accurate) and I'm happy to stretch events for dramatic effect. It's an alternative world, after all. Of course, the overview of history mirrors Ben's long experience, so in terms of his character, that's all to the good. I get to see the times through his eyes. I love it. Nothing is stranger than history.

Which was your favourite character to write?
Ben. I love all my characters, but Ben is always the best fun because he is the least like me. The witches were grimly entertaining and Von Hart always makes me chuckle as I'm writing. Ben remains an exploration. He's part wish fulfilment, part antihero. He's a beautiful mess. And as an author, I get to be mean to him. I love travelling with him the most. He gets to do and say things I never could.

Which type of legendary character or creature do you most identify with?
Fairies. Creatures that are looked upon with suspicion and often blamed for all the ills in the world, but still manage to remain fabulous. Go figure.

What was the most challenging thing about writing this novel?
It was important to me to portray an Africa I might recognise, without denying the strength and beauty of its people. Approaching different cultures to your own is always tricky and you need a willingness to learn, but also a great respect. Africa, as a presence, as an experience, took up a lot of

my childhood, even if I was in the south. Seeing through Khadra's eyes was tough, because I never had that perspective and I know I never will, so you're aware you're writing from a place of privilege. Tremendous privilege. Really, *Chasing Embers* is Khadra's story. Her journey is an overcoming, a dream solution to an impossible situation. That was challenging to write, yes, and I still don't know if I got it right. In the end, I didn't want to write a completely western-centric novel. I wanted to use the elements of the world I've seen and which is every bit as rich as western society.

What can we expect from the next Ben Garston novel?
Trouble. Von Hart wasn't wrong. The events of *Chasing Embers* will have pretty dire consequences for Ben and the Remnant world overall. I wanted to show more of that world, more Remnants and what's become of them in modern times. The establishment has been badly shaken. Things that worked a hundred years ago don't work so well now. We meet some new friends and some new enemies. The follow-up is a darker novel, I think, in terms of its ambition and themes. The stakes are higher, the morality less clear cut, but there is just as much globe-trotting, quips, magic, mythology and horrible things from the nether. Ben isn't in the best emotional state to cope, however – not that he has much choice. *evil author laugh*

What else do you read and watch in your spare time?
I take a break from research by keeping abreast of fiction. I'm a dyed-in-the-wool Fantasy fan (capital F), but I prefer the darker, weirder stuff, so Fantasy is a good place to be right now. Red Weddings and Nazi detectives, yes please! It's a joy to watch these genres evolve and become more

diverse, a shift in the movement that was long overdue. Comics, horror, the odd sci-fi epic. I'm a huge fan of Iain M. Banks and I'm currently enjoying the Radch series by Ann Leckie, which seems to draw influence from the Culture novels, but does its own thing. It feels fresh and progressive. I like gritty noir and dark humour, but I'll also revel in Supergirl. When all is said and done, I have eclectic tastes, devour things obsessively, but I don't sit still for long. That will probably come across in the Ben Garston novels.

if you enjoyed
CHASING EMBERS

look out for

FATED

Alex Verus: Book One

by

Benedict Jacka

1

It was a slow day, so I was reading a book at my desk and seeing into the future.

There were only two customers in the shop. One was a student with scraggly hair and a nervous way of glancing over his shoulder. He was standing by the herb and powder rack and had decided what to buy ten minutes ago but was still working up the nerve to ask me about it. The other customer was a kid wearing a Linkin Park T-shirt who'd picked out a crystal ball but wasn't going to bring it to the counter until the other guy had left.

The kid had come on a bicycle, and in fifteen minutes a traffic warden was going to come by and ticket him for locking his bike to the railings. After that I was going to get a call I didn't want to be disturbed for, so I set my paperback down on my desk and looked at the student.

"Anything I can help you with?"

He started and came over, glancing back at the kid and dropping his voice slightly. "Um, hey. Do you—?"

"No. I don't sell spellbooks."

"Not even—?"

"No."

"Is there, um, any way I could check?"

"The spell you're thinking of isn't going to do any harm. Just try it and then go talk to the girl and see what happens."

The student stared at me. "You knew that just from these?"

I hadn't even been paying attention to the herbs in his hand, but that was as good an explanation as any. "Want a bag?"

He put verbena, myrrh and incense into the bag I gave him and paid for it while still giving me an awestruck look, then left. As soon as the door swung shut, the other kid came over and asked me the price for the second biggest crystal ball, trying to sound casual. I didn't bother checking to see what he was going to use it for – about the only way you can hurt yourself with a crystal ball is by hitting yourself over the head with it, which is more than I can say for some of the things I sell. Once the kid had let himself out, hefting his paper bag, I got up, walked over and flipped the sign on the door from OPEN to CLOSED. Through the window, I saw the kid unlock his bike and ride off. About thirty seconds later a traffic warden walked by.

My shop is in a district in the north centre of London called Camden Town. There's a spot where the canal, three bridges and two railway lines all meet and tangle together in a kind of urban reef-knot, and my street is right in the middle. The bridges and the canal do a good job of fencing the area in, making it into a kind of oasis in the middle of the city. Apart from the trains, it's surprisingly quiet. I like to go up onto the roof sometimes and look around over the canal and the funny-shaped rooftops. Sometimes in the evenings and early mornings, when the traffic's muted and the light's faded, it feels almost like a gateway to another world.

The sign above my door says "Arcana Emporium". Underneath is a smaller sign with some of the things I sell – implements, reagents, focus items, that sort of thing. You'd think it would be easier just to say "magic shop", but I got sick of the endless stream of people asking for breakaway hoops and marked cards. Finally I worked out a deal with a stage magic store half a mile away, and now I keep a box of their business cards on the counter to hand out to anyone who comes in asking for the latest book by David Blaine. The kids go away happy, and I get some peace and quiet.

My name is Alex Verus. It's not the name I was born with, but that's another story. I'm a mage; a diviner. Some people call mages like me oracles, or seers, or probability mages if they want to be really wordy, and that's fine too, just as long as they don't call me a "fortune teller". I'm not the only mage in the country, but as far as I know I'm the only one who runs a shop.

Mages like me aren't common, but we aren't as rare as you might think either. We look the same as anyone else, and if you passed one of us on the street odds are you'd never know it. Only if you were very observant would you notice something a little off, a little strange, and by the time you took another look, we'd be gone. It's another world, hidden within your own, and most of those who live in it don't like visitors.

Those of us who *do* like visitors have to advertise, and it's tricky to find a way of doing it that doesn't make you sound crazy. The majority rely on word of mouth, though younger mages use the internet. I've even heard of one guy in Chicago who advertises in the phone book under "Wizard", though that's probably an urban legend. Me, I have my shop. Wiccans and pagans and New-Agers are common enough nowadays that people accept the idea of a magic shop, or at least they understand that the weirdos have to buy their stuff from somewhere. Of course, they take for granted that it's all a con and that the stuff in my shop is no more magical than an old pair of socks, and for the most part they're right. But the stuff in my shop that isn't magical is good camouflage for the stuff that is, like the thing sitting upstairs in a little blue lacquered cylinder that can grant any five wishes you ask. If *that* ever got out, I'd have much worse problems than the occasional snigger.

The futures had settled and the phone was going to ring in about thirty seconds. I settled down comfortably and, when the phone rang, let it go twice before picking up. "Hey."

"Hi, Alex," Luna's voice said into my ear. "Are you busy?"

"Not even a little. How's it going?"

"Can I ask a favour? I was going through a place in Clapham and found something. Can I bring it over?"

"Right now?"

"That's not a problem, is it?"

"Not really. Is there a rush?"

"No. Well . . ." Luna hesitated. "This thing makes me a bit nervous. I'd feel better if it was with you."

I didn't even have to think about it. Like I said, it was a slow day. "You remember the way to the park?"

"The one near your shop?"

"I'll meet you there. Where are you?"

"Still in Clapham. I'm just about to get on my bike."

"So one and a half hours. You can make it before sunset if you hurry."

"I think I *am* going to hurry. I'm not sure . . ." Luna's voice trailed off, then firmed. "Okay. See you soon."

She broke the connection. I held the phone in my hand, looking at the display. Luna works for me on a part-time basis, finding items for me to sell, though I don't think she does it for the money. Either way, I couldn't remember her being this nervous about one. It made me wonder exactly what she was carrying.

You can think of magical talent as a pyramid. Making up the lowest and biggest layer are the normals. If magic is colours, these are the people born colour-blind: they don't know anything about magic and they don't want to, thank you very much. They've got plenty of things to deal with already, and if they *do* see anything that might shake the way they look at things, they convince themselves they didn't see it double-quick. This is maybe ninety per cent of the adult civilised world.

Next up on the pyramid are the sensitives, the ones who aren't colour-blind. Sensitives are blessed (or cursed, depending how you look at it) with a wider spectrum of vision than normals. They can feel the presence of magic, the distant power in the sun and the earth and the stars, the warmth and stability of an old family home, the lingering wisps of death and horror at a Dark ritual site. Most often they don't have the words to describe what they feel, but two sensitives can recognise each other by a kind of empathy, and it makes a powerful bond. Have you ever felt a connection to someone, as though you shared something even though you didn't know what it was? It's like that.

Above the sensitives on the magical pecking order are the adepts. These guys are only one per cent or so, but unlike sensitives they can actually channel magic in a subtle way. Often it's so subtle they don't even know they're doing it; they might be "lucky" at cards, or very good at "guessing" what's on another person's mind, but it's mild enough that they just think they're born lucky or perceptive. But sometimes they figure out what they're doing and start developing it, and some of these guys can get pretty impressive within their specific field.

And then there are the mages.

Luna's somewhere between sensitive and adept. It's hard

even for me to know which, as she has some . . . unique characteristics that make her difficult to categorise, not to mention dangerous. But she's also one of my very few friends, and I was looking forward to seeing her. Her tone of voice had left me concerned so I looked into the future and was glad to see she was going to arrive in an hour and a half, right on time.

In the process, though, I noticed something that annoyed me: someone else was going to come through the door in a couple of minutes, despite the fact I'd just flipped my sign to say CLOSED. Camden gets a lot of tourists, and there's always the one guy who figures opening hours don't apply to him. I didn't want to walk all the way over and lock the door, so I just sat watching the street grumpily until a figure appeared outside the door and pushed it open. It was a man wearing pressed trousers and a shirt with a tie. The bell above the door rang musically as he stepped inside and raised his eyebrows. "Hello, Alex."

As soon as he spoke I recognised who it was. A rush of adrenaline went through me as I spread my senses out to cover the shop and the street outside. My right hand shifted down a few inches to rest on the shelf under my desk. I couldn't sense any attack but that didn't necessarily mean anything.

Lyle just stood there, looking at me. "Well?" he said. "Aren't you going to invite me in?"

It had been more than four years since I'd seen Lyle but he looked the same as I remembered. He was about as old as me, with a slim build, short black hair and a slight olive tint to his skin that hinted at a Mediterranean ancestor somewhere in his family tree. His clothes were expensive and he wore them with a sort of casual elegance I knew I'd never be able to match. Lyle had always known how to look good.

"Who else is here?" I said.

Lyle sighed. "No one. Good grief, Alex, have you really gotten this paranoid?"

I checked and rechecked and confirmed what he was saying. As far as I could tell, Lyle was the only other mage nearby. Besides, as my heartbeat began to slow, I realised that if the Council was planning an attack, Lyle was the last person they'd send. Suddenly I *did* feel paranoid.

Of course, that didn't mean I was happy to see him or anything. Lyle began walking forward and I spoke sharply. "Stay there."

Lyle stopped and looked quizzically at me. "So?" he said when I didn't react. He was standing in the middle of my shop in between the reagents and the shelves full of candles and bells. "Are we going to stand and stare at each other?"

"How about you tell me why you're here?"

"I was hoping for a more comfortable place to talk." Lyle tilted his head. "What about upstairs?"

"No."

"Were you about to eat?" I pushed my chair back and rose to my feet. "Let's go for a walk."

Once we were outside I breathed a little easier. There's a roped-off section to one side of my shop that contains actual magic items: focuses, residuals, and one-shots. They'd been out of sight from where Lyle had been standing, but a few more steps and he couldn't have missed them. None were powerful enough to make him think twice, but it wouldn't take him long to put two and two together and figure out that if I had that many minor items, then I ought to have some major ones too. And I'd just as soon that particular bit of information didn't get back to the Council.

It was late spring and the London weather was mild enough to make walking a pleasure rather than a chore. Camden's always busy, even when the market's closed, but the buildings and bridges here have a dampening effect on stray sounds. I led Lyle down an alley to the canalside walk, and then stopped, leaning against the balustrade. As I walked I scanned the area thoroughly, both present and future, but came up empty. As far as I could tell, Lyle was on his own.

I've known Lyle for more than ten years. He was an apprentice when we first met, awkward and eager, hurrying along in the footsteps of his Council master. Even then there was never any question but that he'd try for the Council, but we were friends, if not close. At least for a little while. Then I had my falling out with Richard Drakh.

I don't really like to think about what happened in the year after that. There are some things so horrible you never really get over them; they make a kind of burnt-out wasteland in your memory, and all you can do is try to move on. Lyle wasn't directly responsible for the things that happened to me and the others in Richard's mansion, but he had a pretty good idea of what was going on, just like the rest of the Council. At least, they *would* have had a good idea if they'd allowed themselves to think about it. Instead they avoided the subject and waited for me to do the convenient thing and vanish.

Lyle's not my friend any more.

Now he was standing next to me, brushing off the balustrade before leaning on it, making sure none of the dirt got on his jacket. The walkway ran alongside the canal, following the curve of the canal out of sight. The water was dark and broken by choppy waves. It was an overcast day, the sunlight shining only dimly through the grey cloud.

"Well," Lyle said eventually, "if you don't want to chat, shall we get down to business?"

"I don't think we've got much to chat about, do you?"

"The Council would like to employ your services."

I blinked at that. "You're here officially?"

"Not exactly. There was some . . . disagreement on how best to proceed. The Council couldn't come to a full agreement—"

"The Council can't come to a full agreement on when to have dinner."

"—on the best course of action," Lyle finished smoothly. "Consulting a diviner was considered as an interim measure."

"Consulting *a* diviner?" I asked, suddenly suspicious. The Council and I aren't exactly on the best of terms. "Me specifically?"

"As you know, the Council rarely requests—"

"What about Alaundo? I thought he was their go-to guy when they wanted a seer."

"I'm afraid I can't discuss closed Council proceedings."

"Once you start going door to door, it isn't closed proceedings any more, is it? Come on, Lyle. I'm sure as hell not going to agree to anything unless I know why you're here."

Lyle blew out an irritated breath. "Master Alaundo is currently on extended research."

"So he turned you down? What about Helikaon?"

"He's otherwise occupied."

"And that guy from the Netherlands? Dutch Jake or whatever he was called. I'm pretty sure he did divination work for—"

"Alex," Lyle said. "Don't run through every diviner in the British Isles. I know the list as well as you do."

I grinned. "I'm the only one you can find, aren't I?

That's why you're coming here." My eyes narrowed. "And the Council doesn't even know. They wouldn't have agreed to trust me with official business."

"I don't appreciate threats," Lyle said stiffly. "And I'd appreciate it if you didn't use your abilities for these matters."

"You think I needed magic to figure that out?" Annoying Lyle was satisfying, but I knew it was risky to push him too far. "Okay. So what does the Council want so badly you're willing to risk coming to me?"

Lyle took a moment to straighten his tie. "I assume you're aware of the Arrancar ruling?"

I looked at him blankly.

"It's been common knowledge for months."

"Common knowledge to whom?"

Lyle let out an irritated breath. "As a consequence of the Arrancar conclave, mages are required to report all significant archaeological discoveries of arcana to the Council. Recently, a new discovery was reported—"

"Reported?"

"—and subjected to a preliminary investigation. The investigation team have concluded quite definitely that it's a Precursor relic."

I looked up at that. "Functional?"

"Yes."

"What kind?"

"They weren't able to determine."

"It's sealed? I'm surprised they didn't just force it."

Lyle hesitated.

"Oh," I said, catching on. "They *did* try to force it. What happened?"

"I'm afraid that's confidential."

"A ward? Guardian?"

"In any case, a new investigation team is being formed.

It was . . . considered necessary for them to have access to the abilities of a diviner."

"And you want me on the team?"

"Not exactly." Lyle paused. "You'll be an independent agent, reporting to me. I'll pass on your recommendations to the investigators."

I frowned. "What?"

Lyle cleared his throat. "Unfortunately it wouldn't be feasible for you to join the team directly. The Council wouldn't be able to clear you. But if you accept, I can promise I'll tell you everything you need to know."

I turned away from Lyle, looking out over the canal. The rumble of an engine echoed around the brick walls from downstream and a barge came into view, chugging along. It was painted yellow and red. The man at the tiller didn't give us a glance as he passed. Lyle stayed quiet as the barge went by and disappeared around the bend of the canal. A breeze blew along the pathway, ruffling my hair. I still didn't speak. Lyle coughed. A pair of seagulls flew overhead, after the barge, calling with loud, discordant voices: *arrrh, arrrh.*

"Alex?" Lyle asked.

"Sorry," I said. "Not interested."

"If it's a question of money . . ."

"No, I just don't like the deal."

"Why?"

"Because it stinks."

"Look, you have to be realistic. There's no way the Council would give you clearance to—"

"If the Council doesn't want to give me clearance, you shouldn't be coming to me in the first place." I turned to look at Lyle. "What's your idea? They need the information badly enough that they won't care about where you're getting it? I think sooner or later they'd start asking questions, and you'd cut me loose to avoid the flak. I'm not interested in being your fall guy."

Lyle blew out a breath. "Why are you being so irrational about this? I'm giving you a chance to get back into the Council's favour." He glanced around at the concrete and the grey skies. "Given the alternative . . ."

"Well, since you bring it up, it just so happens that I'm not especially interested in getting back into the Council's favour."

"That's ridiculous. The Council represents all of the mages in the country."

"Yeah, all the mages. That's the problem."

"This is about that business with Drakh, isn't it?" Lyle said. He rolled his eyes. "Jesus, Alex, it was ten years ago. Get over it."

"It doesn't matter when it was," I said tightly. "The Council haven't gotten better. They've gotten worse."

"We've had ten years of peace. That's your idea of 'worse'?"

"The reason you've had peace is because you and the Council let the Dark mages do whatever they want." I glared at Lyle. "You know what they do to the people in their power. Why don't you ask *them* how good a deal they think it is?"

"We're not starting another war, Alex. The Council isn't going anywhere, and neither are the mages that are a part of it, Light or Dark. You're just going to have to accept that." I took a breath and looked out over the canal, listening to the distant cries of the seagulls. When I spoke again my voice was steady. "The answer's no. Find someone else."

Lyle made a disgusted noise. "I should have known." He stepped away and gave me a look. "You're living in the past. Grow up."

I watched Lyle walk off. He didn't look back. Once he'd disappeared around the corner I turned back to the canal.

So long as magic has existed, there's been a split between the two paths: the Light mages and the Dark. Sometimes they've existed in uneasy truce; sometimes there have been conflicts. The last and greatest was called the Gate Rune War, and it happened forty years before I was born. It was a faction of the Dark mages against almost all of the Light, and the prize to the winner was total dominion over Earth. The Light side won – sort of. They stopped the Dark mages and killed their leaders, but by the time it was over most of the Light battle mages were dead as well. The Light survivors didn't want to fight any more wars, and the surviving Dark mages were allowed to regroup. Years passed. The old warriors were replaced by a new generation of mages who thought that peace was the natural order of things.

By the time I arrived on the scene, Council policy was "live and let live". Dark mages were tolerated so long as they didn't go after Light mages, and vice versa. There was a set of rules called the Concord that governed how mages could and couldn't act towards each other. The Concord didn't draw any distinction between Light and Dark, and there was a growing feeling that the division between Light and Dark was out-of-date. At the time, I thought it made a lot of sense. My own master, Richard Drakh, was a Dark mage, and I didn't see why Light and Dark mages couldn't get along.

I changed my mind after I had my falling-out with Richard, but by then it was too late. That was when I discovered that while the Concord had all sorts of rules for how mages were allowed to treat each other, it didn't have any rules at all for how they were allowed to treat their *apprentices*. After I escaped, I went to Lyle and the Council. They didn't want to know. I was left alone, with an angry Dark mage after me.

Even now if I close my eyes I can still remember that time, the horrible paralysing fear. It's impossible to understand unless you've experienced it – the terror of being hunted by something crueller and stronger than you. I was barely out of my teens, hardly able to look after myself, much less go face to face with someone like Richard. Now I look back on it I can see the Council was really just waiting for Richard to get rid of me and remove the whole embarrassing mess. Instead I survived.

So you can see why I'm not the Council's favourite person. And why I've no desire to get into their good books, either.

I knew that Lyle was gone and wasn't coming back, but I stayed where I was for another twenty minutes, watching the reflections in the dark water and waiting for the ugly memories to settle. When I was calm again, I put Lyle and everything he stood for out of my mind and went home. I didn't feel like doing any more work that day, so I left for the park, locking the shop behind me.

London is an old city. Even visitors can feel it – the sense of history, the weight of thousands of years. To a sensitive it's even stronger, like a physical presence embedded into the earth and stone. Over the centuries pockets have developed, little enclaves in the jungle of buildings, and the place I was going to is one of them.

The park is about ten minutes' walk from my shop, tucked down a twisting backstreet that nobody ever uses. It's overgrown to the point of being nearly invisible behind the fence and trees. There are construction vehicles parked outside – officially the park's supposed to be closed for redevelopment, but somehow the work never seems to get done. There are buildings all around, but leaves and branches shelter you from watching eyes.

I was sitting on a blanket with my back against a beech tree when I heard the faint rattle of a bicycle on the road outside. A moment later a girl appeared through the trees, ducking under the branches. I waved and she changed direction, walking across the grass towards me.

A glance at Luna would show you a girl in her early twenties, with blue eyes, fair skin and wavy light brown hair worn up in two bunches. She moves very carefully, always looking where she places her hands and feet, and often she seems as though her body's there while her mind's somewhere far away. She hardly ever smiles and I've never seen her laugh, but apart from that you could talk to her without noticing anything strange . . . at least to begin with.

Luna's one of those people who was born into the world of magic without ever really getting a choice. Adepts and even mages can choose to abandon their power if they want to, bury their talents in the sand and walk away, but for Luna it's different. A few hundred years ago in Sicily, one of Luna's ancestors made the mistake of upsetting a powerful *strega*. Back country witches have a reputation for being vicious, but this one was mean even by witch standards. Instead of just killing the man, she put a curse on him that would strike his youngest daughter, and his daughter's daughter, and her daughter after that, following his children down and down through the generations until his descendants died out or the world ended, whichever came first.

I don't know how that long-dead witch managed to bind the curse so tightly to the family line, but she did a hell of a thorough job. She's been dust and bones for centuries but the curse is just as strong as ever, and Luna's the one in this generation who inherited it. Part of the reason the curse is so nasty is that it's almost impossible to tell it's there. Even a mage wouldn't notice it unless he knew exactly what to look for. If I concentrate I can see it around Luna as a kind of silvery-grey mist, but I only have the vaguest idea how it does what it does.

"Hey," Luna said as she reached me, slinging her backpack off her shoulder. Instead of sitting on the blanket she picked a spot on the grass, a few yards away from me. "Are you all right?"

"Sure. Why?"

"You look as if something's bothering you."

I shook my head in annoyance. I'd thought I'd concealed it better than that, but I always have trouble hiding things from Luna. "Unwelcome visitor. How's things?"

Luna hesitated. "Can you . . .?"

"Let's have a look at it."

Luna had been only waiting for me to ask; she unzipped her backpack and took out something wrapped in a cotton scarf. She leant forward to place it onto the edge of the blanket and unwrapped it, staying as far away as possible. The scarf fell away, Luna scooted back, and I leant forward in interest. Sitting in the folds of the scarf was what looked like a cube of red crystal.

The thing was about three inches square and deep crimson, the colour of red stained glass. As I looked more closely, though, I saw it wasn't transparent enough to be glass; I should have been able to see through it, but I couldn't. Instead, if I looked closely, I could see what looked like tiny white sparks held in the cube's depths. "Huh," I said, sitting up. "Where'd you find it?"

"It was in the attic of a house in Clapham West. But . . ." Luna paused. "There's something strange. I went to the same house three weeks ago and didn't find anything. But this time it was sitting on a shelf, right out in the open. And when I went to the owner, he couldn't remember owning it. He let me have it for free." Luna frowned. "I've been wondering if I just missed it, but I don't see how. You can feel it, can't you?"

I nodded. The cube radiated the distinct sense of otherness that all magic items do. This one wasn't flashy, but it was strong; someone sensitive like Luna couldn't have walked by without noticing. "Did you touch it?"

Luna nodded.

"What happened?"

"It glowed," Luna said. "Just for a second, and—" She hesitated. "Well, I put it down, and it stopped. Then I wrapped it up and brought it here."

The cube wasn't glowing now so I focused on it and concentrated. All mages can see into the magical spectrum to some degree, but as a diviner I'm a lot better at it than most. A mage's sight isn't really sight – it's more like a sixth sense – but the easiest way to interpret it is visually. It gives a sense of what the magic is, where it came from, and what it can do. If you're skilled enough you can pick up the thoughts the magic was shaped out of and the kind of personality that created it. On a good day I can read an item's whole history just from looking at it.

Today wasn't one of those days. Not only could I not read the item's aura, I couldn't read any aura on it at all. Which made no sense, because there should have been at least *one* aura, namely Luna's. To my eyes Luna glowed a clear silver, wisps of mist constantly drifting away and being renewed. A residue of it clung to everything she touched: her pack glowed silver, the scarf glowed silver, even the grass she was sitting on glowed silver. But the cube itself radiated nothing at all. The thing was like a black hole.

Left to their own devices magic items give off an aura, and the more powerful the item, the more powerful that aura is. This was why I'd had Luna bring the thing out here; if I'd tried to examine the cube in my shop I'd have had a hundred other auras distracting me. The park is a natural oasis, a kind of grounding circle which keeps other energies out, allowing me to concentrate on just one thing at a time. It's possible to design an item so as to minimise its signature, but no matter how carefully you design a one-shot or a focus, something's going to be visible. The only way to mask a magical aura completely is to do it actively, which left only one thing this could be. I dropped my concentration and looked up at Luna. "You've found something special, all right."

"Do you know what it is?" Luna asked.

I shook my head and thought for a moment. "What happened when you touched it?"

"The sparks inside lit up and it glowed. Just for a second. Then it went dark again." Luna seemed about to say something else, then stopped.

"After that? Did it do anything else?"

"Well . . ." Luna hesitated. "It might be nothing."

"Tell me."

"It felt like it was looking at me. Even after I put it away. I know that sounds weird."

I sat back against the tree, looking down at the cube. I didn't like this at all. "Alex?" Luna asked. "What's wrong?"

"This is going to be trouble."

"Why?"

I hesitated. I'd been teaching Luna about magic for a few months, but so far I'd avoided telling her much about the people who use it. I know Luna wants to be accepted into the magical world, and I also know there's not much chance of it happening. Mage society is based on a hierarchy of power: the stronger your magic, the more status you have. Sensitives like Luna are second-class citizens at best.

"Look, there's a reason not many mages run shops," I said at last. "They've never bought in to the whole idea of yours and mine. A mage sees a magic item, his first reaction is to take it. Now, a minor item you can keep out of sight, but something really *powerful* . . . that's different. Any mage who finds out about this thing is going to be willing to take time off his schedule and track you down to take it, and he might not be gentle about how. Just owning a major item is dangerous."

Luna was quiet. "But you don't do that," she said at last.

I sighed. "No."

Luna looked at me, then turned away. We sat for a little while in silence.

Luna's curse is a spell of chance magic. Chance magic affects luck, bending probability so that something that might happen one time in a thousand, or a million, happens at just the right time – or the wrong one. The spell around Luna does both. It pulls bad luck away from her, and brings it to everyone nearby.

The really twisted thing is that from what I've learned the spell was originally invented by Dark mages as a *protection*, not a curse, because it makes you as safe from accidents as a person can possibly be. You can run across a motorway in rush hour, climb a tree in a lightning storm, walk through a battlefield with bombs going off all around you, all without taking a scratch.

But the accidents don't go away; they just get redirected to everyone nearby, and when the spell is laid permanently, the results are horrible. The closer Luna gets to another person, the more the curse affects them. She can't live in the same house as anyone else, because something terrible would happen within a month. She can't keep pets, or they die. Even having friends is dangerous. The closer other people are to her, and the longer they stay near, the worse the result. Whenever Luna comes to care about any other human being, she knows that the more time she spends with them, the more they're going to be hurt. She told me once that the first boy she kissed ended up in a coma.

I've spent some time researching Luna's curse, trying to find a way to break it, but haven't gotten anywhere. I might be able to get somewhere if I studied her intensively, but Luna's life is hard enough without being treated like some kind of science project. Still . . . "Luna?"

"Hm?"

"There's something I was . . ." Something brushed against my senses, and I stopped. I looked into the future and my stomach suddenly went cold.

Luna was watching in puzzlement. She could tell from my expression that something was going on, but she didn't know what. "Alex?"

I jumped to my feet. "Get away!"

Luna started to rise, confused. "What's going on?"

"There's no time!" I was desperate; we had only seconds. "Behind the tree, hide! *Hurry!*"

Luna hesitated an instant longer, then moved quickly behind the beech. "Stay there," I said, my voice low and urgent. "Don't make a sound." I turned back just as a man stepped from the trees in front of me.

He was powerfully built, with a thick neck and wide hands, and muscles that bulged through the lines of his black coat. He might have looked like a bouncer or a bodyguard, maybe even a friendly one, if you didn't look too closely at his eyes. "Verus, right?" the Dark mage said, regarding me steadily. "Don't think we've met."